FINDING JANE

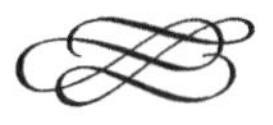

ELIZABETH CONTE

JANE WRITES PRESS

First Edition

First Edition: March 2022

Cover: Original Dress Image from Metropolitan Museum of Art, New York, NY

Cover Art: *Elizabeth Conte, Michelle Morrow, and Shawn Morrow www.chellreads.com*

Editing and Publishing Assistance: *Chell Reads Publishing www.chellreads.com*

Finding Jane is published by: *Jane Writes Press www.JaneWritesPress.com*

CONTENTS

1. Morning Comes 1
2. Death of Fairytales 11
3. Journeys 15
4. Falling 25
5. Finding Jane 35
6. Waking Up 41
7. Dr. Cummings 47
8. Kindred Souls 57
9. Meeting the Family 67
10. First Dinner 79
11. Maggie and the Oak Tree 91
12. Observations 99
13. Awakenings 107
14. Dinner Without Friends 115
15. Mr. Abbet 123
16. Mr. Hodges 131
17. Curiosity 135
18. At the Pond 141
19. Reading at Night 149
20. A Day in the Countryside 155
21. News Day 165
22. Helping Mrs. Baker 173
23. Lightning Strikes Twice 183
24. Honor 191
25. Sent Away 201
26. Taverns 207
27. The Wansey Sisters 215
28. The Manse 221
29. The Levongoods' Hospitality 229
30. Watching 241

31. The Black Raven 257
32. The Dance 263
33. Demons of Man 275
34. Anne's Secret 281
35. Interference 289
36. The Gift 293
37. Guarding Honor 303
38. Stark Reality 309
39. Detectives 317
40. Healing 321
41. Surrender To The Truth 329
42. Shattered 335
43. Legacy 339
44. Comforts of Home 345
45. Commitment 351
46. Lillian's Scolding 359
47. Mrs. Eaton 367
48. London Museum 373
49. Interference 381
50. Surprised 387
51. Forgiveness 395

Acknowledgments 409
About the Author 411

I dedicate this to my mother, Elizabeth, because she inspired me to journey through life, before she left on her next journey.

Her legacy has empowered me to pursue my own dreams.

FINDING JANE

MORNING COMES

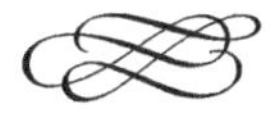

Alone!

Flashing like a billboard, the word screamed across Jane's mind as her brain clicked awake. If she kept her eyes shut, she might ignore her thoughts, but dust-filled beams of light seeped through the bamboo shades and striped across her pillow, forcing her to acknowledge that morning had come.

Five more minutes, she begged the omnipresent god of time.

Jane rolled over and curled into a ball. She squeezed her lids tighter, but sighed, knowing it was no use. She was awake whether she liked it or not. The alarm beeped, confirming the realization. She reached across the empty pillow beside her and shut it off. As if it was their fault she was being forced out, she kicked off her sheets and pushed them to the end of the bed. Fisting her hands, she rubbed at her puffy eyes, still stinging from another tearful night. Her arms reached for the ceiling in a final stretch. The fogginess of sleep now lifted, she tried to suppress her thoughts about Stephen, but it was still too fresh in her memory.

He was gone, and she was… ***Alone!***

After spending seven years with one man, a life so

intertwined, the promises of a lifetime together, it was hard to disconnect him from her. Her from him. But there was no turning back. Stephen packed his belongings four weeks ago, including his surf boards and treadmill–items he couldn't live without, and took his name off the lease of the condo they shared.

Jane was blindsided. One minute her entire world was planned, and next, it was empty.

As the morning light stirred her senses, the emptiness left by Stephen solidified her reality. She was now lying in an empty bed, surrounded by a half-empty bookcase, half-filled drawers in her dresser, and a deserted counter next to her sink that used to be crowded with shaving cream and colognes. His cologne, a mixture of cypress, vetiver, and coastal air, no longer lingered on her pillows. The closet, now barren where his clothes used to hang. Jane knew she should have claimed full ownership of the empty spaces by now, but she found it hard to motivate herself to start each day since his departure.

Her cat jumped off the bed, encouraging her to do the same–*get out of bed!* When her feet hit the floor, he rubbed her ankles with his head, his craggy voice meowing a demand.

"Hello Mr. Bingley. Are you hungry?" she asked, bending to rub his neck.

His response was to rush off in search of food.

Jane followed his furry steps to the kitchen, filled his bowl, pushed the button on the coffeemaker, and pressed the remote on the television to check traffic. A curvaceous brunette, in a tight red dress, and stiletto heels pranced around the set motioning like Vanna White at the various temperatures for the day. Jane wondered when professional women changed from business best to posh porn.

Is that what Stephen wanted?

Jealousy reared its ugly head.

It wasn't as if Jane was unattractive. She was pretty. Not hot.

Not sexy. Not a stiletto-wearing, gorgeous weather girl kind of beauty. Just pretty. Nor did she consider herself a woman who got lost in the mix, but she wasn't one to stand out in a crowd either. Being under thirty allowed her a natural beauty–a youthful glow and no wrinkles. She owed that to her diligence to a strict regimen of sunscreen. She wasn't tall, nor short, at five feet and six inches. Just tall enough to wear reasonably high heels with Stephen without hovering over him. Her eyes weren't jewel-colored, like her assistant's emerald-green beauties, which invariably were a topic of conversation by approaching men at bars. Jane's were brown, as was her hair. Simple, uncomplicated, brown. Not curly, not straight. Just wavy. In fact, there was nothing extraordinary about Jane one could pinpoint as notable, except when she smiled. She had dimples, a charming feature that won over anyone she used it on. Which she didn't because Jane didn't use people.

Jane was a good person. A smart person. A reliable person.

It was, 'her complete package which made her beautiful,' Stephen used to say. It never concerned Jane the value of her attraction. She was with Stephen. They were a couple since college and meant to grow old together. He made her feel beautiful, significant, and loved. She was good enough for him...until she wasn't.

The coffee finished brewing, the bitter and nutty aroma titillating her to pour a cup. She took her first sip, allowing the hot liquid to slush around her mouth before she gulped. "Aww..." she moaned with satisfaction.

Mr. Bingley meowed at the sliding glass door where his litter box lay. After he was done tossing aside the granules from his paws, it was his routine to jump on top of the balcony and peer at the birds who flittered from branch to branch on the tree fronting the condo. It was a little too out of reach for him to capture the object of his desire but it kept him preoccupied while Jane showered and got ready for work. When he would hear the jingle of her keys, he'd jump down and scamper in before she'd shut the sliders and lock him out. He'd find his way to a chair by the window where he wouldn't miss the goings-on without him.

Morning routines grounded Jane. For that, she was grateful. Her job, an exhibit director for The Los Angeles County Museum, kept her days purposeful. She had a major exhibit she was coordinating, and a trip overseas a few days away. It was every bit acceptingly distracting, as was the opportunity to get out of town. She looked forward to something new; an escape from her life, if not for two weeks, to get away and clear the memories lingering at home.

Jane perused her closet, skipping a chic dress with the tags still on. It wasn't red like the weather girl's, but it hugged the few curves she possessed on her lean body. She bought it for Valentine's Day when she thought Stephen was finally going to propose. Instead, Stephen apologized for getting the flu and climbed into bed with a bottle of *NyQuil*, while she coveted a bottle of *Trader Joe's* champagne, re-watching shows on *The History Channel.*

Two months later he left.

Now the dress hung near the back, behind the three bridesmaid dresses she kept for reasons unexplained. Jane grabbed a navy linen suit, a silky, sleeveless top, and pointed-toe pumps. She was still old school–business best. She layered three necklaces in varying lengths over her head and put on a pair of pearl earrings she was told by the Nordstrom's salesperson never went out of style. Walking to her car, a cloud layer rolled in from the ocean. A smirk crossed Jane's face.

The gorgeous weather girl predicted sunny and eighty degrees.

Instead of heading directly to work, Jane decided to stop at The Original Farmers Market on Third and treat herself to her favorite Italian brewed, double-shot espresso with cream. It was something only reserved for the last Friday of every month–her reward for working sixty hours a week, week after week. Allowing one late morning a month seemed like a fair exchange. But with her upcoming trip to London, it was a good day to lift her spirits with her favorite coffee drink, enjoy the outdoor shopping center, and browse the expensive shops' windows. As an exhibit creator, perusing window displays was a favorite, if not productive, pastime, justifying the time spent away from the office. When the barista handed her the cup, it hadn't occurred to her she would be of any importance to the morning crowds buying their pastries, ordering their Kosher meats, or reading the paper at one of the many open tables around the food court. But before she could get her lips around the lid of her addiction, she slammed into a man, spilling her coffee on him. The man jumped back, pulled at his shirt, and cursed the burning liquid. When he looked up, their eyes met.

"Jane!"

"Stephen?"

The two stood before each other, waiting for each to speak first.

"Let me help you with that," Jane finally said, and fumbled for tissues in her purse, cursing herself for not refilling her supply. She plucked a handful from the counter of the coffee bar and glided her hand down the streaks of coffee growing darker on the blue-striped shirt she'd bought him for his last birthday, not missing the abs just below the surface. His six-pack, hard earned conquering waves body and board surfing, still affected her.

He pulled away.

Did her touch have the same effect on him?

It was then the woman beside him came into focus.

The young woman, noticeably blonde, and noticeably beautiful, tucked her arm around his bicep as if to claim ownership. She queued a smile. Out of politeness, Jane feigned one back, but the nicety was soon lost to a snarl tightening her jaw.

"Hi," the beautiful creature spoke, oblivious to the love triangle in which she was now entangled. "I'm Patti, Stephen's fiancée."

Jane glanced at the waif-like hand encasing Stephen's arm. There it was…sparkling.

The moment shattered into fractals.

Was it day? Was it night? Was she standing or did her legs give way?

Jane inhaled, bringing much needed oxygen to her brain.

"You're engaged?" Her voice crackled, serrating the words.

"J-Jane..." Stephen stuttered. "I planned to call you; I swear."

"And tell me what? After seven years, you suddenly got the urge to get married…to someone else?"

Loser! Jerk! Asshole!

The ugly words caught in her throat.

"It's not *that* simple, Jane."

"Well, it doesn't appear all *that* complicated!"

Stephen shifted his stance and pushed back his hair. His habits were too intimate for Jane not to see he was agitated.

"God, Jane!" he shouted. "I was going to tell you. Differently." He paused and stepped closer.

She jerked back.

He retreated.

Beautiful creature fiddled with her ring.

Finally, he spoke. "We're having a baby," he tried to explain.

Jane's thoughts screeched to a halt. Except for one. "Were you cheating on me?"

The question fell out of her mouth before she realized she might not want to know the answer.

Her glance moved to the crowds of shoppers, clueless to her devastation, not wanting Stephen to see she was holding back tears, owing to her sense of pride. Wavering between wanting to punch him or run away, she instead lingered, memories replaying of their breakup.

When Stephen left, there was an understanding the separation was between them, and a shared interest in why the relationship didn't work. Their relationship had grown stagnant. It wasn't a failure by either of them, but between the both of them.

That made sense to her.

His past behaviors now haunted her—the late-night calls promising to be home soon, working weekends, extra trips to the gym, or the spontaneous showers after work started to have more meaning.

Uncontrollable shivers went up her spine with the realization. Her eyes narrowed at Stephen.

"Please don't look at me that way," he pleaded.

Hit him? Slap her?

Thoughts bounced back and forth in Jane's head. She wanted to grab onto Stephen and not let go...to protect the relationship that was her life, her love, the entirety of her being. But the bonds between them, the molecular threads that tied them to each other, ripped apart in that moment, leaving shredded edges. Yet at the same time, an animalistic rage surged through her and she wanted to attack Stephen as if her life depended upon his death. A fierce pounding in Jane's chest reverberated in her ears.

Thump. Thhump. Thhhhump.

Her mouth went dry. The crowded streets of the outdoor mall faded in her periphery. Her body went limp. It drifted, floated among the shoppers. She was now lost in a world that made sense to her a moment before.

The beautiful creature tugged at Stephen. "We should go."

Stephen looked at Jane. She couldn't decipher if it was pity, shame, sorrow, or regret.

"Please..." Jane pleaded, "Go."

Stephen capitulated, and the girl pulled him away.

Without awareness, without thought, her legs moved, walking, then running until she found her car, and slammed the door shut–closing off the world. It was there in the parking lot, amongst the tall pillars of concrete and distant sounds of tires squeaking where she gave into the agony of her broken heart.

Jane didn't remember how long she hunkered in her car. Or calling her assistant to cancel all her appointments. But she cried. And cried. When the tissues ran out, she searched for napkins stored in her console, and moved onto a sweatshirt in the back seat until there was nothing left to dry her eyes. Day eventually turned into evening. Encased in a metal cage entombed in concrete couldn't protect her from her reality–there was no more daydreaming. No more hoping. No more Stephen.

She pressed the ignition and her *Jetta* hummed. Shifting into gear, the car resurfaced into the crowded streets above, cars honking, people walking, lights flashing red to green, green to red. A couple, the young woman's head tucked in the crook of the young man's neck, their arms wrapped around each other, passed in front of her. Her hands gripped the steering wheel and tightened. She looked through her windshield at the night's sky.

Really?

The soon-to-be full moon hovered just above the horizon and stared back at her. It was large and low, an illuminating amulet against the indigo darkness. An energy emanated from its radiance to her consciousness, pulling her. It wanted something. What? She did not know.

Someone honked, and she jolted out of its trance. She made a left and headed home. As she pulled into the driveway, her heart tugged at the darkened condo. The neon sign in her mind flashed again. She didn't fight the narrative. It was her reality.

Alone!

"Time heals all things," her mother's words came back to her. Those were the first words of wisdom her mother had shared with her when she came home to find her hamster lying still in his cage. Harry was her first love and Jane cried for hours at his loss.

Her mother brought her a hot cup of cocoa, scooted next to her on the bed, and caressed her with long, tender strokes across her back. She enlightened Jane about the pitfalls of love, "It was wonderful to have, but horrible to lose." Her mother wasn't trying to destroy the innocence of her youth, but rather inspire her with the hope that love was never destroyed or meaningless, but renewable and full of rebirth.

Her mother took her to the pet store the next weekend to get a puppy.

Jane took her mother's words to heart. Maybe it was because she died long before she could impart more words of wisdom, leaving her to savor the few she had given. She had to believe in something greater than the aching inhabiting her soul. Today wasn't that day. Maybe tomorrow.

Time.

She needed time.

DEATH OF FAIRYTALES

"He's a bloody ass, if you ask me!"

"Yes, he is," Jane agreed.

"A damn fool!" Amy continued.

"I know."

Jane didn't disagree with her friend. There was no defending Stephen anymore. And Amy didn't hold back her condemnation of him the entire drive to the hotel from the airport. They were friends, and Amy supported Jane the best way she knew how-by berating Stephen. But the words held little value to Jane.

Her tears had dried. Her anger gone. She was numb.

But Jane wasn't in London to think about Stephen. Quite the opposite. She was there to work on her exhibit: *Dressing Rituals: Women in the Boudoir Through the Ages.* It was a retrospective of women and dressing rituals, from undergarments to daily clothes, introducing the spectrum of wardrobe changes one must endure for the sake of beauty and culture. It was Jane's largest exhibit yet, in collaboration with The British Museum, scheduled first in Los Angeles and then London for a second appearance. Jane was the Los Angeles exhibit director, and Amy Higgins was her counterpart in London. With luck, or likely by the charm of Amy, they were granted a donation by the Eaton Estate, a prominent land-owning family dynasty from the eighteenth century. The owner of the estate, a direct descendent, was in the middle of a remodel where he discovered trunks of historical clothing when he met Amy and discovered the exhibit's theme. He graciously offered the museum the opportunity to review the items and keep what would be of value. The unexpected donation gave Jane the chance to travel abroad. The gift to the museum was fortuitous, but the opportunity to get away was a blessing. Jane hoped the fresh air of the English countryside, exploring grand estates, and if time allowed, window shopping would distract her from what she left in Los Angeles: a broken heart, shattered dreams, a cynical belief that love was a storyline for feel-good movies; a fairytale for the foolhardy. England was her chance to cope, and maybe move on.

"All right, love. No more talk about Stephen, or may I just refer to him as *the ass?*"

Jane smiled with approval.

The two women only met at the airport that morning, but spent hours upon hours on the phone, first because of the coordination of the exhibit, then about life and love. Late night hours to discuss lighting and staging turned into good old-fashioned girl talk. Amy chatted about the men she slept with–which were many, and Jane sifted through the pains of loving and losing one man. Their virtues of love were as opposite as they come: Amy didn't believe in it while Jane was a hopeless romantic–the cause of her broken heart, or so Amy said.

"I hope you're ready for some fun tonight," Amy said, plopping herself down on the hotel bed to watch Jane unpack.

"No, not really."

"You've got to be kidding, yeh?"

"No," Jane repeated, shaking her head to confirm her answer. "And you won't seduce me with your charming accent!"

The corner of Amy's eyebrow lifted. "You're in the UK, sweetie. I'm not the one with the accent. And besides, what else are you going to do on your first night in London?"

Looking into the mirror, Jane scoffed. She tugged at her skin and pinched at her cheeks. No color emerged. "Look at me. I have bags under my eyes, my skin is dry, my clothes are all wrinkled, and next to you," she gestured to the woman sitting in front of her who looked like she rolled off the pages of the latest *Vogue*, "I look like the nerdy cousin who needs a makeover."

"You look lovely." Amy eyed her friend from head to toe, and added, "More beautiful than I expected."

She winked.

Jane was unmoved by her teasing.

She couldn't compete with a woman who towered four inches over her in animal print stilettos, a short–*very short*–black skirt, a low-cut blouse displaying layers of pearls between her breasts, and a belted leather and knit coat draped over her shoulders. She was an Amazon Queen–statuesque, as if Michelangelo created her out of raw beauty. Her father was English and her mother Jamaican, the combination creating the most eye-catching woman Jane had ever seen. Her hair was chocolate–dark chocolate–and wildly curly, which she wore shoulder-length, not denying its natural beauty. Her magnetic eyes were luminous against her ebony skin, which gave her a mystical quality. Long and lean limbs glided in a synchronized dance when she moved. *Was she a witch, a vamp, or even human?* Jane wondered. Whatever the gods created, she was everything her voice promised. Savvy, sexy, and sassy.

"Come on, Jane," Amy pleaded. "The night is ahead of us. It's time to get your groove back. Who doesn't love drinks, dancing, and, if we are lucky, delightful men?"

Jane froze. Her heart thudded. Her stomach lurched. She

was a single woman now—unattached, no boyfriend, alone. It was her time to explore who she was, what she was capable of, and become the best she could be. *"The opportunity to grow..."* Stephen said when they went their separate ways. But she was unprepared for the visceral reaction to "getting out there" again. That meant letting go, which hurt like hell. Healing, which required stitching up the tattered edges of her heart. And moving on, which she had no idea to where.

Time. She needed time.

"Sweetie, life doesn't stop because of a broken heart. Quite the contrary. There are too many men, and too much good sex to mope around like you're doing. Just last night I met a scrumptious model, with eyes to die for, and an ass I couldn't take my hands away from. He was deee-licious! And he has a mate, equally pleasing, I'm sure. Now how can you turn down a night like that?"

Jane shook her head. If she spoke, her voice would crack.

Amy walked over and threw her arms around her. "I get it. No need to explain. Tonight, get your beauty sleep. Tomorrow...well, we'll leave that to fate." She kissed Jane on the cheek and headed for the door. "Your sensible side is right. We have a long day ahead of us tomorrow. There are some great pubs around the corner. Get something to eat, enjoy the fresh air, and head to bed early. I'll pick you up at eight."

"Thanks." Jane let out a sigh of relief. Had Amy pushed, she'd be walking out the door with her. Amy always got what she wanted.

"Jane?" Amy called from the hotel corridor.

Jane popped her head out the door.

"My granny gave me some advice. I think it's best given to you. Don't lose yourself because of love. Find yourself because of it."

JOURNEYS

Successfully dodging Amy, a much-needed nap ensued after the twelve-hour journey across the pond. Jane woke to a darkened room, discombobulated, and with a growling stomach. She pulled aside the drapes, reminding her she was no longer in Los Angeles. The streets below were aglow with electric converted gas lampposts and lanterns, while people scurried about at the end of their workday. She grabbed a coat, pushed through the heavy doors of the hotel, and released herself into the crowds of young and old enjoying the good weather.

London streets looked like a movie set. Ironic, in that Jane was escaping from the movie capital of the world. But there was no denying the antiquity of the seventeenth-and eighteenth-century stone and brick buildings flanking the streets, reminding her of every Jane Austen movie or regency period drama. It was hard not to get lost in fantasy surrounded by the Crayola-colored stores painted in intense black, golden yellow, fire-engine red, or fern green, each distinctive–no cookie-cutter, corporate buildings like back home. Window paneled shops enticed buyers with international teas, decadent donuts, or hand-knitted socks, while others presented overstuffed flower boxes of begonias, busy Lizzies, and ivy, their store names scripted in gold or black across the windows. Potted topiaries flanked doorways of hotels, and baskets filled with baubles of pink, white, and red petunias cascaded from the ledges above pubs. Each building had a story to tell, distinctive and historical, knowing thousands of years have passed with patrons going in and out of the same doorways. Jane imagined ghosts of dignified men walking the bustling streets of commerce, refined crinoline-clad ladies chatting about the latest scandal, or a gilded carriage with the clacking of hooves against the stone streets turning the heads of the working class. It was a contrast to Los Angeles and its concrete idolization of Mid-century and postmodern architecture, with its busy intersections, black pavement, blinking traffic lights, brand-awareness billboards begging for your attention, and boxed-in cars parked along the sidewalks. London was magical–the change of scenery and escape she was looking for.

Jane followed a couple into a pub with roses arching from the doorway, spilling sprays of pink over the wrought iron lamplights which fronted it. She was told to sit anywhere and browsed for a table near the window. The server suggested the specialty pie and mash, which she ordered along with a glass of wine. She pulled a book from her purse, which she carried for such occasions as this, eating alone, and waited for her meal.

"A little noisy in here to read," interrupted a young man.

Jane popped her head up and looked at the now filled pub, a cacophony of voices echoing off the tile floors and oak-paneled walls. She hadn't noticed the growing patronage but did notice her intruder was an attractive young man with a baby face, blue eyes, and curly blonde hair. It wasn't lost on her that he looked like a younger version of Stephen. *Was the universe playing her the fool?* She smiled out of politeness, but did not reply to the young man, hoping he understood the cue.

He didn't.

"My mates think you might be lonely." He pointed to the bar where a small group of college-aged boys huddled, beers in hand. As if on cue, they waved. Jane appeased them with a queenly wave. The young Stephen continued, "The tall one and the grubby unshaven one are my mates, the skinny one with the wire-framed glasses is my cousin on my mum's side. He got the brains; I got the beauty."

He smiled. An adorable smile Jane knew worked on girls. It would have worked on her had she been less broken.

"Aye, I see you'll be a hard one to crack. I promise we aren't any harm. Ask Louie." He called out to the bartender who nodded.

Did she trust the shaved-head, dragon-tattooed man to vouch for young Stephen?

"We come here regularly, to check out the scene, find pretty girls like you, and maybe get lucky." He winked and tried his smile again.

Jane cringed. *Stephen had a fiancée and a baby on the way, and she was someone's "lucky."*

The server delivered her meal, but the young man didn't budge, ordering a beer while sliding into the bench-seat across from her. He chatted about his work–he was out of university and recently started at a tech firm. He had a dog, a terrier named Duke, and an ex-girlfriend, whom he didn't give a name. Jane nodded when she needed to, answered the few questions asked, and laughed when young Stephen attempted to convince her to spend the rest of her evening with him and his friends.

"You're sweet," Jane said, "But I've got work in the morning, and need to go." She paid her bill, along with young Stephen's beer, and stood to apprise the young man of her intention.

"You don't want to stick around then?" he asked.

No, I don't! The voice in her head screamed, but instead, she curled her lips upward, allowing her smile to say goodbye.

"You can't blame a bloke for trying." He flashed his smile once more.

When the pub door closed behind her, Jane took a deep breath, held it, and pushed it out, cursing Stephen's name. She threw her head back and raised her eyes to the cetacean blue night, noting the pinpricks of white orbs twinkling against the light of the waning crescent moon. How she envied their existence, their purpose exquisitely designed, unaffected by the human experience, and yet so influential in who people were, and what their destinies held. They held all the power while humans were mere pawns being pushed around by their tug of war.

Jane was a true Taurus: stable, practical, honest, but stubborn all the same. Stephen was an Aquarius, the ultimate free spirit.

She should have known better.

A quiet had settled in the night's air. The crowds that busied the streets earlier found their way to their destinations, emptying the alleyways and sidewalk to all but a few stragglers, she being one of them. Laughter mixed with music wafted out of a nearby pub, almost tempting her to join them. Instead, she headed for her hotel browsing the displays of the now closed shops along her path, noting the ones she would revisit in the days ahead. A bell jingled in the distance, where a man left a book shop. The lights still on, Jane darted across the empty corridor, hoping to dash inside.

Jane squeezed the iron-forged handle, pushing the glass door open, and crossed the threshold. The bell at the top of the door alerted the patrons of her entrance. An older woman at the register acknowledged her with a smile before she went back to assisting a customer. A man sitting at a table, one of three cafe-style tables huddled in the corner, a cup of coffee to his right and three books stacked to his left, glimpsed at the jingling bell, grunted, then returned his focus to the open book in front of him. A younger man, college-bound or soon-to-be, the attempt at a sparse goatee a dead giveaway of his incomplete puberty, peeked his head above a bookshelf, eyed Jane, pushed up his tortoise-shell glasses, and ducked back down. Approving of the shop, Jane took off her coat and sashayed to the window display where a collection of century old books caught her attention.

"Lovely, aren't they?" a young woman greeted. "Those books are from the nineteenth century, a few even earlier. An old man popped in one rainy day and plopped them on my counter. He did this for three days without a word. On the fourth day he said, "They need a good home," and he left. Just like that, kismet! Some are tattered, some are missing pages, but it doesn't matter. The leather-bound covers are such a rarity. What's best about them is the smell of the aged paper. There's something about turning pages we'll miss in the modern age of electronic books. Don't you agree?"

Jane nodded.

"You're visiting, yes?" she asked.

Jane looked at what she was wearing. The skinny jeans and blouse seemed universal fashion for a Los Angeles girl in London. She explained, "I'm from California."

"Well, it's nice to get a newcomer to the shop. Find yourself a book and have a cup of coffee. My treat." She pointed to a carved wooden counter with barstools tucked under. A bearded man with a beanie was steaming milk. "I can see Eddy is finishing your double-shot espresso. Italian roast, right?"

Jane knitted her brow. "But how did you…"

"And may I recommend," she interrupted, "Shakespeare's *A Midsummer Night's Dream*. The prose is so meaningful. Reading from a book will be a lost art, and I want as many as possible to enjoy it while they still can."

Jane sought the recommended book, settling herself at the counter where the beanie-clad barista set a cup next to her. She ordered a scone, blueberry with clotted cream, and indulged in the rumblings of the quaint bookstore-the squeaking of sneakers against the wooden floor, the placing of books on and off a shelf, the skid of chair pulled out, the hushed voices of a mother and child choosing a book.

The young woman returned and pointed to the open page in Jane's hand. "Well, what do you think of our lovely friend, the noted Mr. Shakespeare?" She recited, "'The course of true love never did run smooth.'"

Jane smirked.

"Too close to home?" the young women asked.

"Is it obvious?"

"To me. I see more than most."

"Oh?" Jane wasn't sure what she meant.

The young woman explained, "I have a lot of people walk through my doors. You pick up on things after a while."

"So, this is your shop, then?"

"Yes. Part-book shop, part-library, part-coffee house. It's my dream come true. When my gran-mum passed away, I inherited family money and opened this shop. I wanted to create a space for people to escape; to connect with the past. I know many share my same feelings for old books, the art of literature, and the concern the modern world is losing its passion for the beauty of prose."

Jane agreed.

The young woman continued, "Books connect us to those who lived long before us; give us a perspective on individuals and the importance of their existence. They show us heroes, heartaches, lessons to be learned, and love–always love. They can turn an ordinary life into something extraordinary."

Jane had never heard someone capture the essence of reading. The young woman seemed beyond her years. A complete contradiction to her petite frame and birdlike limbs. Even her jet-black hair, cut short, layered around high cheekbones and a pointed jawline, against the backdrop of porcelain skin, made her child-like. Her long lashes were as black as her hair, enhancing her green eyes with gold centers. They were eyes of a cat. But it was the subtle upward curve of her lips, which softened the dramatic image, as well as her girl-like voice, which Jane found hypnotic.

"I'm sorry, I'm rambling, and I never introduced myself. I'm Peyton." She extended her hand.

Jane couldn't help noticing a tulip design just below her thumb.

Peyton rubbed at the distinctive flower. "It's a birthmark," she explained.

"Sorry. I didn't mean to stare. I thought it was a tattoo."

"I wish I was so provocative! It's a family mark, passed along for hundreds of years. Distinctive, yes. But not always considered so harmless."

Jane didn't miss the implication of sorcery.

"I'm Jane. Jane Reynolds."

Peyton's eyes lit up when Jane offered her hand.

No sooner did their palms touch, their clasp froze in suspension.

Time stopped–the background sounds silenced; the commotion halted. No bells jingled. No thrush of the coffee steamer. No shuffle of feet. No hushed conversations. No subtle sounds of pages turning. Stillness. Peyton's head tilted; her eyes moved back and forth, studying Jane–beyond her. Jane found it unusual but did not move for reasons she couldn't explain. Before she could comprehend the dead zone, the bell jingled at the door, followed by a waft of cool air that breezed across her face.

Goose bumps prickled down her back.

Peyton released her. "Will you excuse me for a moment? I

want to talk to you about something personal. Please, will you stay?"

Jane agreed, not sure why. Part of her wanted to get out of there. The other part grounded her butt back on the barstool. Curiosity was her drug. It is what drove her into historical research, down rabbit holes of mystery. It is why she loved her job at the museum...endless hours of archival sleuthing, documentation, and fact-finding which accumulated into something tangible for the world to view and learn from was exhilarating.

Peyton returned, pulled out a chair and sat down.

"Jane," she started, "do you believe in psychics?"

"Well, I guess."

"Please don't think me strange," Peyton pleaded, "I have a gift. Spirits talk to me. And I have a message...from the spirit world to give you."

Run or Stay? Jane quickly calculated the situation. She stayed.

Peyton continued, "You were born during the cycle of a super moon, under the black moon. Rare. Very rare. For that reason, your energy is hyper-sensitive. It's your link. I'm told you are going on a journey. Far away...but not unknown. Be not afraid of the experience, for your soul is always with you. Trust one who is pure in deed; someone familiar to you. The link is written in the stars." Peyton looked at her, demanding her attention, "Listen. Listen carefully. Your love will bring you home if you choose. But if you stay too long, your energy will forever remain, and there is no return."

"What does that mean?" Jane was confused.

"I honestly don't know. What is told to me is never in context. They're just messages I need to give when received. How you use it, or when it becomes significant, is not for me to understand. It's only for you. You must remember, though, the purpose will have meaning when it's needed."

"Who tells you this?"

"Your spirit guide. He travels with you. He tells me he asked to be your light through the darkness–to thank you for your sacrifice. He warns he cannot guide you once you have fallen through. He says, find the seer they call, *The Black Raven*. She will help you, and ultimately, get you home."

Jane rubbed her temples. "I'm not understanding any of this."

"Destiny is guiding you, Jane. Fear not. Your life has a purpose beyond your understanding. I don't know what's in store for you, but you have a special place in this universe. It may scare you, but if you open your heart, you will find its boundaries are far beyond the limitation you have placed upon it."

The instinct to run came back.

Peyton smiled wryly. "I know how difficult it is to accept what I'm saying to you. But I knew the moment you walked through the door I was meant to talk to you. Your energy is ignited. No, it's magnetic! There is something special in store for you, Jane. I can feel it."

Jane looked into her coffee, the foamy cream all but gone. She fell into the black liquid, pondering Peyton's words. She asked, "Do you know *this spirit* you're talking to?"

"No." She shook her head. "He is attached *to you*. He calls himself the summer adventurer, named in honor of you. He reiterates, he's watching over you."

Jane scrunched her forehead; furrowed her brow. "The seer you mentioned…is that you?"

Peyton feigned a smile. "Jane, I come from a long line of seers. My grandmother had the gift and she passed it on to me."

"Yes?" Jane wanted her to get to the point.

"Ramsey is my grandmother's maiden name. I was given her name to carry on the family legacy." Peyton rubbed her birthmark with her thumb. She continued, "Ramsey means *black raven.* It's not I, but someone close to me you will need to seek."

"Well, can't you ask what this all means?" Jane was frustrated, and a little scared.

"It doesn't work that way. It's not a telephone. I get messages in code, not manuscripts," Peyton explained. "I wish I could help more."

"I'm sorry. This all is really strange." Jane shook her head. "I don't understand what it's supposed to mean."

"How do you think I feel? But you took it better than I expected. Most of the time I traumatize people…losing a few customers along the way." Peyton's cat-eyes caught Jane's wide-eyed stare. "You are going to be fine. I know it."

Peyton rubbed Jane's back in slow strokes. She felt like the little girl back on her bed when her hamster died, her mother's touch comforting her. She didn't want to run anymore.

Jane thanked Peyton prompting Peyton to throw her arms around her. She didn't say anything more but slid a smile across her face as if to say, "It'll be okay."

Jane put on her coat and headed out the door, listening to the jingle fade into the night's air as she walked back to the hotel, wondering, *what will be okay?*

FALLING

Airports and tourist shops are cluttered with postcards full of images of brilliantly colored English countrysides. Jane assumed flower fronted cottages and rolling green farms of England were fantasy. Most likely photoshopped to lure the unsuspecting traveler. But as Amy drove out of London, into the surrounding country, fertile green fields undulated over the landscape. Clusters of trees dotted the expanse while sunlight trickled through verdant leaves that shimmered iridescent against the coffee-colored bark. Blooms of Byzantium-purple and lavender-blue poked through the forest floor. Flowers of crimson and magenta, coral and blush, saffron and mustard, intermingled in a dance up stone walls, weaved through fences, and spilled from planters. The postcards *were* deceiving…they didn't capture the true intensity, nor the beauty.

The two women sipped their coffees as they contemplated their plights. Both were exhausted from the previous night, each for a different reason. Amy spent the night with a young model, naked, savagely enjoying his beautiful body. She hadn't made it home to sleep, with only enough time to shower, dress, and grab the two coffees they were now sipping. Jane lay in bed with a man, but in thought only. It was Stephen who preoccupied her mind–penetrated her dreams. Thousands of miles away, and yet, he still haunted her. She wondered how far she would have to go to forget him.

Did Peyton's words hold the key?

"Hmmm," Amy wondered. "You're awful quiet. Did something happen last night?"

Jane contemplated telling Amy about young Stephen, but there was nothing to tell. And the psychic? Still nothing to tell.

"No. What were you expecting?"

Amy raised an eyebrow. "I was hoping you had found a little dalliance."

"No," Jane reiterated, "Absolutely, not!"

"My dear, if you're looking to be swept off your feet, you might as well stop now. Romance has long died along with her friend, chivalry. You're lucky to be asked to dinner, let alone romanced."

Jane sighed with empty resolve.

"Men don't want longevity. Didn't Stephen prove that?" Amy eyed her friend. "Look, I have no illusions of love. I enjoy scorching, sensual, scintillating trysts. When things cool, I scuttle off. As you should."

"Is that how you truly view love?" Jane questioned, familiar with Amy's appetite for a short-term romp with a sexy man. The emphasis on *short-term.*

"I'm sorry, sweetie. It works for me. You're still the romantic, even after the one man you truly loved dumped you. Kudos to you for your confidence in love, commitment, and forever. That's not how I choose to live."

Did Amy have it right all along?

"Jane?" Amy called out. "Did I say something wrong?"

Jane shook her head, but Amy knew better.

"Look…there's someone who believes in love the way you

do. Commitment is hard for some, but not for everyone. Be patient. He'll find his way to you. I'm almost sure of it."

Jane rolled her eyes. "Pray tell, what imaginary lifetime will that be?"

Amy shrugged. She didn't have the answer.

Jane fell silent finding solace in the passing scenery. If she could have her way, she'd tell Amy to stop, jump out of the car, and run through the fields with her arms spread and take flight. Just like when she was a little girl in her uncle's corn fields. With the sun shining upon her face, the blades whipping against her shins, she'd run as fast as she could until her legs buckled and plopped down in the middle of nowhere. Breathless. Unadulterated. Happy. Moments for contemplation, to free her mind from clutter.

From sadness.

There were few opportunities for tranquility in her daily life in LA. If she was lucky, a yoga class or a run on the beach allowed a reprieve from mind-noise. But there were always crowds. Crowds and commotion. Commotion and keeping busy. If anything, the reprieve in England was allowing a door to open to space and time.

The car turned onto a long, tree-lined, single-lane, weathered road. It traveled in isolation for miles until it descended from a hilltop where Jane got her first glimpse of the Eaton Estate.

"There it is," Amy pointed.

Jane couldn't miss it. The brick and stone manor was a beacon among the hills and expansive fields. It wasn't large compared to other estates, nor was it unique in its Georgian style with its hip roof, dormers, and sash windows. But it was how nature seemed to cradle the structure as if it sprouted from the ground. Myrtle green vines climbed along its wall, espaliering high above to the third story. Rose bushes, the old branches showcasing budding blooms, filled planters against the house, backed by sheared hedges of privet under the windows that fronted the house. Purple salvia and catmint bloomed in homage before the queens of thorns, leaving little evidence that dirt laid under their prickly limbs. No barriers blocked the rolling green lawns which trailed from the rose-filled planters to the countryside, like a veil trailing behind its bride. The peaked roofline, boasting seven chimneys, was the only evidence the estate had an abundance of rooms underneath its facade of a quaint country home.

A man opened the front door and scurried along the crushed stone walkway, flailing his arms in excitement at the arriving guests.

"Come, come," he greeted, ushering the two women up the pathway. "Amy, my dear. So good to see you again." He planted a kiss on each cheek. "And you must be Jane? Amy has shared wonderful things about you."

"It's nice to meet you, Mr. Eaton."

"Oh, please, call me Ryan. Only my students call me mister," he ordered, but with little intention of authority.

Ryan Eaton looked nothing like the part of a stuffy, old, university professor. Dressed in a Barbour blue-checked shirt with rolled sleeves revealing his hairy forearms, and expensive jeans cinched by a brown leather belt matching his Ferragamo loafers, he was the epitome of an English gentleman. He was no taller than her, and balding, but had she not been told his age by Amy, Jane would have guessed him a man of forty. It was when he smiled, and creases appeared at the corners of eyes, that his fifty years showed. But the creases were unnoticeable when you saw his eyes. They were blue–ocean blue when the sunlight saturates it. His long black lashes only accentuated the brightness, making it hard for Jane not to fall into them.

"Ryan," Jane corrected, extending her hand.

His hands encased hers, engendering Jane to like him very much.

"Shall we?" Ryan stepped aside, inviting them to make their way through the door.

Crossing the threshold, an overstuffed French Longwy vase filled with lilies, roses, and peonies greeted them, wafting a musky mix of myrrh, honeysuckle, and citrus. Ryan took Jane's coat and placed it on a Charles II winged armchair, next to a marble-topped table which the flower arrangement adorned. Like a child stealing frosting on a cake, Jane couldn't help herself and ran her hand along the oiled wood of the chair, touching the carvings–the purposefully sheared wood–underneath her fingers. If she closed her eyes, she could transcend the moment it was created, knowing the oneness of the craftsman and the wood.

"Isn't it charming?" Ryan said. "I found this in the basement. Shut away as junk."

"I can't imagine!" Jane exclaimed. "It's why I love my job. I get to view, touch, and feel priceless antiques–pieces of art, really."

"Well, my dear, it's rare to find someone who has a similar appreciation."

Amy mused, "Aren't you two kindred souls…"

Ryan laughed. "Indeed!" He winked at Jane. "Come, let me show you more."

Jane, eager to see what lay beyond, had already eyed the artwork and tapestries gracing the wall of the entry. How could she miss the crystal chandelier hanging from the second-story coffered ceiling, bouncing prisms of light against the paneled walls which encased the room? She had eyes! And a hunger to discover the antiquity of the home. But the handcrafted, inlaid floors halted her steps.

"I should take off my shoes," she offered.

"Don't be silly. This house is still standing, isn't it? What harm can you do hundreds of years hasn't?" He took her arm and glided her to the staircase, stopping to point out his ancestry, framed large and small, some relatives more attractive than others.

As Jane glanced up, she caught a woman staring from the balcony. But when she blinked, the woman was gone.

"Who was that?" Jane pointed.

Ryan furrowed his brow. "Who?"

An icy chill swept down Jane's back, unable to conceal her shudder.

"Are you alright?"

"I don't know. I thought I saw a woman looking at us."

"But no one is there," Amy chimed in.

"No doubt." Ryan was unaffected. "You can't escape ghosts in old homes. I inherited the estate after my uncle passed away, and have spent the last ten years restoring it," he reflected. "I have uncovered intrigue, heartache, and scandal alike. No doubt you might be confronted by unsettled lives who once walked these halls."

"Seriously?" Jane lifted her brow.

Ryan patted her hand. "This house is quite endearing. Nothing evil lurks here. Trust me. Just memories."

"Well, while it's still daylight, maybe we should start our project," Jane suggested. "I'm not sure I want to linger after dark."

"Work, work, work! We have the entire week, sweetie. You're in the country, in a lovely estate full of antiques and history, with or without ghosts, and you insist on working?" Amy shook her head and sighed. "One of these days, life is going to make you slow down and take notice of the world around you, and you'll have no other choice but to indulge in it."

"I give you my word, Amy. If the opportunity arises, I will try to enjoy it," Jane replied, with little threat she would have to follow through on her promise. "But we don't want to intrude on Ryan's hospitality for too long."

"I feel no such burden. In fact, it's an honor to have someone who can appreciate what this house has to offer. Most see an old, damp-ridden building filled with outdated junk. Little can they appreciate the lives who made a home here. We have all week. I say, get your work completed today, then allow me to take you and Amy out. I know a fabulous place that serves a divine martini!"

Amy gave Jane a cheeky grin.

"Okay. I'm in." Jane agreed. "Now can we get to work?"

"Follow me, ladies." Ryan took them up the grand staircase, passing four closed doors. "These are my guest rooms. Maybe the next time you come to England you might stay?"

Jane nodded. "I'd like that."

He pointed to the end of the hall. "The master bedroom is over there. The views are spectacular. Unfortunately, the toilet is in remodel, otherwise I would gladly show it to you. The seventies should never have had a say in decor." He rolled his eyes. "The entire room had to be gutted. I'll take you on a tour next visit," he offered with a wink.

Following a back hallway, they reached another staircase. This one, not as grand, led to the top floor. Passing another series of closed doors–the servants' quarters in the olden days and now used as storage–they reached the attic. Ryan opened the door and swatted at dust-laden air, clearing a pathway for the women to follow.

"There they are." Ryan pointed to a stack of old trunks. "There are more in the other rooms, but I thought you could start here. The light is better. I dare say, you have your work cut out for you."

Musty wood penetrated Jane's nostrils, reminding her of what she loved best about her job–getting lost in discovery. She set her bag down on a stack of over-taped boxes and knelt before one of the aged chests held together with pounded nails and tattered leather belts, eager to find out what lay inside.

"You're welcome to open all the trunks and take what you think is of use. If they are not valued now, they may rot away." Walking back to the threshold, he said to Amy, "Coming?"

"You're leaving?" Jane balked.

"Didn't I mention it? Ryan's cousin is allowing us access to the Levongood's country estate."

Jane looked blankly at Amy. She knew little of the who's who in old English society.

"Isabelle Manning was the only daughter of Lord & Lady Levongood. She was a forerunner of the women's movement in the pre-Victorian era, and one of the wealthiest single women of her time," Amy explained.

"If you don't go today, I'm afraid the house will be closed for the season. They are leaving for the summer, and you will miss my cousin's limited generosity." Ryan interjected.

"Okay, leave me here with the haunted. If you don't find me when you come back, you know who to blame," Jane teased.

"We'll be back before it gets dark," Amy promised, and gave her a peck on the cheek.

The slam of the front door echoed through the empty house. Jane walked to the windows and watched Ryan and Amy drive away. She tried to open one, but they were swollen shut. Disappointed, she pulled out her phone, two notebooks, a pen, and got to work.

At first, Jane fretted over the lack of companionship. The thought of a ghost roaming the halls spooked her. But there were no creaking floors, footsteps in the hall, or rattling chains. She laughed at herself, thinking there would be. Instead, the house was quiet, allowing her uninterrupted time. Before she realized, her phone was out of energy, one notebook was half-full, and the attic was losing valuable daylight.

Phone almost dead. Need a break. Going for a walk, Jane texted Amy.

Finding an outlet to charge her phone, Jane headed

downstairs. The house was now shadowed, the halls darkened. It was hard to see anything about the house, or anybody in the house if they were there. She retraced Ryan's steps, the chandelier in the entry lighting the way. She silently thanked Ryan for the gesture and scurried down the stairs. Not knowing why, she glanced at the balcony, expecting the woman–waiting for her. But she wasn't there.

Jane shuddered all the same.

A cool breeze burst through the front door when she opened it. Dark layers of clouds had moved over the early morning blue sky. But she wasn't going to let the gloom deter her. Jane grabbed her coat and headed out.

She walked to the end of the drive and followed a path leading into a cluster of trees. She looked back to mark her way. The Eaton Estate was large, and the architecture loomed in the distance among the green. She was sure getting lost was impossible.

The path got longer, and the forest denser as she trudged forward. Moss covered the aged-gnarled bark, decaying leaves pooled at the base of the trunks, and patches of wildflowers popped up where the sun filtered through the lush canopies, interrupting the brown monochromatic setting with sprays of white. Disney couldn't have created a more magical forest.

Jane continued to meander, following the treaded path up a hill. She was winded after a few miles, but her legs pushed forward, encouraged by the tranquility surrounding her. *Was she exploring or escaping?* She looked behind her, the Eaton Estate long hidden by the forests and fields she had trekked. Just as she pondered turning back, the timbers opened to a valley below, blanketed in tall, swaying grasses.

Jane!

The wind seemed to whisper to her. Or was it the little girl who hungered to let go? Before Jane could decide, her feet took off, running faster and faster down the hillside, the wind at her back pushing further and further, until she collapsed into the myriad of green spikes, her chest heaving from the exertion. Sprawled out, she looked to the sky and laughed out loud. A smile spread across her face.

If Amy could see her now!

Her mind relaxed, and for a moment, she felt free from worry…stress…sadness…Stephen.

She hadn't meant to fall asleep, but when Jane opened her eyes, night had approached. The dark clouds, promising a downpour, hovered directly above. She was doomed to get soaked on her way back. Time was of the essence. She cursed herself for the lapse in judgement and lifted herself out of the grass. But as her body straightened, her head wobbled. A humming wind rang in her ears, causing the vessels in her brain to pulsate. The whirling got louder and louder. She cupped her ears.

"*Please stop!*" she yelled.

She wanted to run. She really did. But her body wouldn't move upon command. Suddenly, she had the oddest sense of falling.

FINDING JANE

The Baker men rose early for their daily duties. Mrs. Baker, who woke ahead of them, stoked the fire to prepare a hearty meal for her husband and two sons. Over eight months into her pregnancy, the weight of the baby on her back and legs hindered her ability to move. But her own chores, and a few stolen moments to rest her swollen legs, would have to wait until the men were fed and out the door.

Darkness lifted by the time the three men headed into moist air, their bellies full of thick slices of bread and cold ham. Edwin Baker and his two sons were never off schedule, and this morning was no exception. As Edwin gathered the tools for the day, his eldest son headed to the barn. Saddling the horse, he gathered the leather reins and pulled the grudging mare from the stable and into the damp and chilly morning. It was always difficult to motivate the beast to move after sleeping in a warm stable. The horse gave attitude, but Edwin's son gave back more.

With the mare in tow, the father and son met with the youngest, Egon, who was dutifully helping his mother with some heavy lifting. His reward? A handful of gooseberries shoved into his coat pocket. With more youth than his brother, Egon raced ahead, passing his father and brother, eager for the head start. From the moment he awoke, Egon had energy to burn. Running through the fields were his moments of exhilaration before he had to expend the rest of his energy on work. Breathing heavily, his legs pounded the ground, while his cheeks reddened from the cold air mixed with the hot blood flowing through his body. Suddenly, he realized the long strands of green corn no longer slapped against his body but crunched under his feet. He stopped and circled around. The corn strands were no longer upright. They lay flattened under his foot. He squinted into the gray distance.

For a young man, Egon had experienced many of life's misfortunes. A man's arm cut off. A cottage burned to the ground with the family inside. A young girl drowned. He was not naïve to the world at large. Robbers and thieves, dirty old men, and slick strangers he was warned. Fearing Satan and God alike, drove his moral compass. He was taught the skills of a farmer by his father, learned what worked through apprenticeship, what didn't work from errors, and was blessed with an intuition of understanding the land's harmony. Nature had a rhythm. And it spoke if you listened. The land was whispering to him now. More like screaming.

Get Help!

He ran. Without sight, and fear driving him. He pumped his arms and pushed his legs with urgency towards his father. But before he reached him, his boots stumbled over a mound, tumbling him to the ground. As he pulled himself up and looked back at the object of his misfortune, he gasped. There before him lay a woman's body, naked and still.

"Papa!" The wind carried the stark cry, slicing through the pre-dawn silence.

Edwin heard the strain in his son's voice. The two men darted toward Egon but halted in lockstep when they arrived at the planted field of corn. The sprouting stalks had disappeared, as if fallen off the edge of a cliff. Edwin dropped his tools where he stood and ambled into the flattened corn. It was miles wide.

"Dear God in heaven," he gasped.

Edwin's son stood beside his father. "What happened?"

"Papa, come hurry!" Egon yelled again, more shrill than the first time.

The two men looked at each other and ran towards the urgent plea from Egon.

"What on earth?" Edwin questioned, his eyes transfixed on a woman in the middle of the flattened field, naked as the day she was born.

"Father!" Edwin's son gasped. "What shall we do?"

"Quick, go get the Master. Tell him it's urgent," ordered Edwin to his eldest.

Edwin bent over the woman. Leaning in close, he saw her chest rise and fall, assuring him she was not dead. He took off his coat and placed it over her naked body.

It was not long before a horse was heard in the distance, the sun breaking the horizon. Henry Eaton, master of the estate, halted at the edge of the field, the corn flattened before him. He blinked, shook his head, and blinked again, trying to see through the grey mist.

"Master Eaton." Edwin waved his hands. "Here!"

The Master caught sight of Edwin Baker's swinging arms and hurried to the two men awaiting his arrival. He found them hovered over an object on the damp, flattened stock.

"It's a woman!" Egon explained.

Master Eaton squatted beside the body and moved aside the hair hiding her face.

"Who is she?" he asked.

"I dunno sir," Edwin replied.

He glanced at the naked legs exposed beyond the tweed coat

covering her torso. They were pale white compared to the dark, wet ground. He lifted the coat from her shoulder, discovering her true vulnerability.

"Is she hurt?"

"We found her and called for you," Edwin answered, to explain he dare not touch the woman.

"I see." Master Eaton nodded, understanding his meaning.

He brushed her cheek with the palm of his hand, hoping for a response. Her skin was warm to the touch, and he could feel her breathing, but she remained still. Concerned, he ordered Edwin's eldest to take his horse, wake Dr. Cummings, and send him to the house. He then ordered Egon to tell Mrs. Bishop, his head caretaker, to prepare a room. The two boys obeyed, leaving swiftly upon his commands.

"Now what, sir?"

Master Eaton removed his cloak and laid it over the woman. He stared off into the distance wondering how she got there. There was no one who lived near, besides the Bakers and himself, and they were off the main road for miles. His jaw tightened with the possibilities. The sun was rising above the trees, the layer of fog thinning, when he realized the fragility of the creature in full view. Brown hair, pale–too pale, and young. *Someone's wife? Daughter?* His own family flashed before him.

"Come. Let's get her home."

"Aye," Edwin agreed.

Master Eaton scooped her into his arms. The woman shifted, placing her arms around his neck, nuzzling her head into his shoulder. Her hair smelled of bergamot and lavender, and her skin like orange blossoms.

"Stephen?" She called out in a sleepy daze. "I don't feel well."

"Hush," he whispered. "I have you." He drew her closer into his chest.

Once they reached the house, Mrs. Bishop was waiting for

them with a room prepared. With the quilts already pulled down, Master Eaton laid the woman on the bed, her arms releasing the embrace around his neck. He glanced at the vulnerable woman, left stripped and stranded, and wished he could do more; her abandonment making him feel impotent. There were better people to handle the situation, and he would have to entrust in their capabilities. He decidedly headed out of the room.

"Master Eaton," Mrs. Bishop called after him. "Your cloak." She handed it to him and lingered for instructions.

Retrieving the garment, he twisted the fabric in his hands. Neroli oil lingered in the woolen fibers.

"I've sent for Dr. Cummings. He'll know what is best."

"Do you know who she is?" Mrs. Bishop asked.

"No." He shook his head. "Please make sure she is well attended to…and comfortable. Anything needed, you have my permission." He turned to leave but abruptly stopped and turned back. "And let's not talk to anyone about this until we know more."

"Don't you worry, Sir, I'll take good care of her."

"I have every faith in you, Mrs. Bishop. Unfortunately, I have a prior engagement and cannot wait for Dr. Cummings to arrive. Invariably, he will know what to do. I shall return in a few days. Notify me of anything urgent."

Mrs. Bishop bid him farewell and reentered the bedroom where her new charge lay. With the skill of a nurse, she tied Jane's hair back, bathed her lifeless body, and dressed her in a nightgown. She wetted a rag and brushed the paled pink lips with moisture. When the woman puckered, Mrs. Bishops tried a few more times until she no longer responded. She tucked a weighty quilt around the lifeless body and closed the drapes, whispering a prayer the young woman would find some comfort in her sleep.

WAKING UP

Crackle. Crackle. Click.

Even with her senses arousing from a deep sleep, Jane was cognizant of logs burning. The sounds of a fire were distinctive. It transported her back to her youth when she watched yellow and orange flames dance against the blackened night sky, snug in her sleeping bag, listening to her uncle play his guitar by the campfire.

Crackle. Crackle. Click.

She lay still, peeking from under the covers. Heavy folds of yellow silk hung from floor to ceiling covering windows, a light sneaking through the opening. Had she the energy, she would've pushed out of bed and pulled them aside to discover what lurked behind, but she was too cozy in the cocoon of covers. Instinctually, she reached for her phone next to the bed, begrudgingly dragging her arm from the warm quilts, but it wasn't there. Only a brass candelabrum housing five candles, burned down to an inch of dripping wax, sat atop a table. Mindlessly, she traced the lines of the damask print which papered the walls, searching for a clock. She only found two small Dutch portraitures and a large painting of a garden, prompting her to sit up and peer around the room.

A draped canopy swagged overhead, in layers of butter-yellow damask fabric trimmed in braided fringe. The four-poster bed surrounding her was an 18th-century George III frame. She recognized the reeding and acanthus decoration on the posts similar to a period piece displayed at last year's furniture exhibit at the museum. Left of the bed was a dresser with a series of drawers of varying sizes decorated with brass swan-neck handles. She placed it circa late seventeen hundred. It was in prime condition, and she wondered how none of the delicate handles had been lost or broken for a dresser its age. An empty vase adorned the top, along with an inlaid-wood box, two books–the titles too far to read, and another brass candlestick holder, which was empty. Just past the door was an oversized armoire–the French walnut closet demanding a presence against the creamy-yellow of the room. A freestanding full-length mirror cornered the room, prompting Jane to brush her fingers through her hair, imaging what would reflect back if she dragged herself before it. As she pulled her hand away from her head, billowing linen fabric brushed against her face. She lifted her arm in awe of the voluminous sleeve, which gathered at her wrist and tied with a bow. Rows of satin pleats folded across the bodice of the nightgown she was wearing, with rounded pearls buttoned to the collar. It reminded her of the flannel nightgowns of her youth, only this one was made of refined linen. It was modest, to say the least, and she laughed at its oddity.

Everything seemed odd!

Overall, the room was both austere and luxurious in its antiquity similar to the kind she'd find at a B&B in Vermont or Upstate New York. But she was in neither of those places. She was in London, ensconced in a room that was not her hotel.

She scratched her head. *Did she meet up with Ryan and Amy?*

She couldn't remember and wondered how many martinis she drank that would cause her to forget.

A door opened, startling her. An older woman entered, heaving a large pitcher and a basin. She placed them on the dresser, along with two small towels, and wiped her hands against her apron that covered a modest, grey dress.

"I see you're awake. Tis a good sign," the woman said, a rich Scottish accent adding a cadence to her words. "And how are ya feeling today?"

"I'm fine," Jane replied, not sure it was the right answer.

"The doctor came early this morning. You were fast asleep. He didn't want to disturb ya, so he said he'd return."

"Doctor?"

"Oh, no worrying there, Miss. You're in good care with Dr. Cummings. He's as skilled as they come," she said. "Are ya warm enough?"

Without an answer, the woman walked to the fire, stoked it, and placed a log on the embers.

"That'll keep you cozy. Cold through the bones when the Master brought you in! It's a wonder you didn't freeze…the way they found ya out in the chilly hours of the morning."

"I…I was found out in the cold?" Jane questioned.

"Oh, yes, Miss. The Master himself brought you back."

Jane remembered feeling cold, chilled through to her toes, then warmth cradling her body. She thought it was a dream.

"Wait," Jane put her hands up. "I'm a little confused. What's happening here?"

"Oh, the doctor warned you might have some trouble remembering things. He was afraid you might have fallen and bumped your head…nothing to worry about, though."

Jane rubbed her head, feeling for a sore spot. She found nothing, except feeling disoriented.

"The doctor gave me strict instruction that I wasn't to push ya. I'm to make you comfortable and see to it you're in good health." She poured some water from the pitcher and handed it to Jane.

Jane took the glass and sipped. The water tasted of minerals–salty, but she drank it anyway, not realizing how thirsty she was. Her mouth was sticky, her throat dry.

"Thank you," Jane said, handing back an empty glass.

"Aye," the woman smiled. "That's what you needed, no doubt," she said, filling the glass once more and placing on the table next to the bed.

Jane eyed the woman carefully, curious about the stranger fussing over her.

Was she friend or foe?

She looked harmless enough–grandmotherly. Grey hair peaked through a white cap, with wiry curls jutting haphazardly around the edges of her face. A natural rosiness on her cheeks and forehead softened the lines of age, muddling Jane's ability to guess how old she really was. She still possessed a robust body, plump around every curve, with solid arms that could entrap anyone into her squishiness. But it was her crooked stature, if not her dragging gait, that hinted at her elderliness. Jane had little reason to feel threatened by the woman…if it wasn't for a nagging instinct that something wasn't right.

"There's no doubt you're better. I can see some spark in those brown eyes of yours. Might ya be wanting a wee bit of food? Cook always has something simmering."

Food was that last thing Jane wanted; her thoughts cluttered. "If I am being rude, I apologize, but I have no idea who you are?"

"Oh dear, Miss, I'm rambling on. Please forgive me. With Miss Maggie on holiday visiting her aunt, the Master coming and going, I forget myself, so eager to talk to people. I'm Mrs. Bishop, the head caretaker here. If I don't know about it, then it doesn't happen." Her eyes thinned; her chubby cheeks puckered. "And if you don't mind me asking, do ya have a name to go along with your pretty face?"

"Oh." Jane hadn't realized she was a stranger, too. "I'm Jane…Jane Reynolds."

"Hmmm." The woman tilted her head and asked, "Are you related to the Reynolds's family in Corset, then?"

"No," Jane laughed at the suggestion. "I'm not from England. I'm visiting from the States."

"Of course. I should've recognized the accent. It's so distinctive, but we don't get many of ya around these parts," she noted.

"Mrs. Bishop," Jane rubbed her face. "It's probably because I'm groggy, but where am I?" The question rattled in her head since she opened her eyes.

"At the Eaton Estate, my dear."

"The Eaton Estate? But of course." The antique surroundings took on meaning.

"Aye. Do you know of it?"

"Sort of. Amy Higgins brought me here. We are doing work for the museum. You might have previously met her?"

Mrs. Bishop shook her head, and a deep furrow buried itself between her brows.

"No?" Jane's eyebrow shot up. Ryan would assuredly have informed his caretaker of their treasure hunt in the halls of the Eaton Estate. "Well, maybe you haven't had the opportunity." She brushed her concerns away. "It's Amy who introduced me to the Eaton Estate."

"Oh? Do you know Master Eaton then?"

"Well, a little. We've only just met." Jane eyed the room. "He invited me to stay at the Eaton Estate, but I hadn't expected it would be so soon."

Jane cringed to think of the drunken night they all must have had that she was given a guest room of the Eaton Estate with no recollection of how. She was sure Amy would catch her up on the wicked evening, seeing she could not recall a single detail, except for the nagging headache pounding between her ears. Jane was not used to hangovers.

Mrs. Bishop's creases doubled, and the color of her cheeks deepened as she narrowed her gaze at the woman lying in the bed.

"Mrs. Bishop, is there something wrong?"

"No, no, Miss. Rest. I'll be back, with some food." Mrs. Bishop scuttled to the door, looked over her shoulder at Jane before making the sign of the cross, and retreated.

What did she know that Jane didn't?

Something just didn't feel right. Jane pressed against her temples to push away the shards of pain piercing in her head. The pain didn't feel like a hangover…it felt more like fear.

DR. CUMMINGS

Knock, knock, knock.

Jane stirred.

Knock, knock, knock.

"Uuuuuuuuggggghhhh," Jane moaned into the empty room.

Earlier, Mrs. Bishop opened the drapes, prompting her to get up, go to the bathroom, brush her teeth, wash her face…feel human again. But when she stood, her head dizzied. She stumbled back into bed, finding refuge under the covers, and closed her eyes instead.

A third rap at the door came.

This time, Jane dragged herself upright. The room was now shadowed with the little light left of the day. She reached for the glass of water by her bedside, swishing the mineral water around her mouth, and swallowed.

"Come in," Jane's scratchy voice called.

"Miss Reynolds?" A man's voice resonated in the quietude. "May I come in?"

Jane nodded, suspect of the lanky stranger, but allowing him to cross the threshold.

"Excuse my informality for entering without proper introduction. I should have waited for Mrs. Bishop, but she was preparing a tray for you. I did not want her to delay getting you needed nourishment," he explained. He bowed his head. "I am Dr. Cummings."

She eyed the man as he set his leather bag on the dresser, opened it, grabbed a few items, and walked to the bedside.

She gestured for him to sit.

He pinched the bridge of his nose and sighed, blinking away his tiredness as he placed himself at her side. When their eyes met, Jane expected a grouchy old man, with his head full of grey hair. Instead, she found fading grey-blue eyes, three-days' growth shadowing his cheeks, and skin heartily colored by the sun, the greying hair merely a badge of age. He pulled his lips into a smile and his weariness fell away.

"May I have your wrist?" he asked.

As if his grey-blue eyes willed it, Jane splayed her arm.

Gently, he wrapped his fingers around it and took her pulse. He asked her to follow his finger from the left, then to the right. He felt the back of her neck, running his fingers up and down to look for signs of swelling, so he informed her.

"You seem to be in good health. Any dizziness since you awoke?"

"A little."

"Hmmm. Nausea?"

Jane shook her head.

"Hmmm," he said again.

He rose, walked to his bag, and put his instruments away. He pulled out a notebook, rubbed at the prickles of his chin before he lifted the pencil cradled in its crease and wrote in it.

Jane watched and waited.

"Miss Reynolds," his eyes lifted to hers, "I am pleased to see you recovering better than expected. I feared the worse when they found you, abandoned, naked, and unconscious."

Jane straightened; her eyes widened. "What?"

In a frenzy, she lifted her sleeves and rubbed her arms, her neck, her chest, her legs–even between her legs in search of damage. There were no bruises or cuts, no pain–anywhere. "I don't understand. Am I alright?"

"That is what I am trying to surmise. I examined you immediately. Thoroughly. I did not find any signs of harm." He cleared his throat. "I am not sure what happened to you or why. But you are safe and in good hands now."

Oddly, she felt safe.

"If you don't mind, I would like to ask some questions."

Jane agreed, curious about what was to come.

"You were found in a field, a few miles from here. Can you tell me how that came to be?"

"I walked there." Jane answered bluntly.

"No one forced you there?"

She shook her head. "I found my way to the field on my own. It was so peaceful, I decided to lay down in the grass, and unwittingly fell asleep. When I awoke, rain clouds hovered overhead. I stood to trek back, not wanting to get caught in the storm, when suddenly a wind rushed in. It whirled all around me. It was so loud…" She covered her ears, as if pulled back in the moment, afraid the sound would return.

The doctor scrawled in his notebook.

"Then what happened?" He pushed for her to continue.

"I don't remember. The next thing I know, I'm in the comforts of this room, my body surrounded by warm blankets and head cradled in pillows." The reality of her situation should have brought her comfort, but she shivered, chilled with the implications being extrapolated from the conversation, the words taking on significance.

Found. Abandoned. Naked.

"Were you with anyone?"

"No."

"Were you going anywhere in particular?"

"No."

"Did you meet anyone?"

"No."

"Could you have been followed?"

"It could be possible." She recalled how isolated she was. "But I don't think so."

"Did you tell anyone where you were going?"

"Yes. I left a message for my friend, Amy…Amy Higgins. She is an exhibition director at the museum."

"And where is Miss Higgins now?"

"Well…" Jane crunched her forehead. "I don't know. She wouldn't leave me at the Eaton Estate, knowing I was hurt."

A hard line appeared between Dr. Cummings' brows. "Does she know the Eaton family? Mr. Eaton?"

"Why, of course. She introduced us. Why else would I be here?"

"Hmmmm." Dr. Cummings began to pace the room.

Mr. Eaton gave Dr. Cummings no indication he knew Miss Reynolds when he left her in the doctor's care. He was an honorable man. Dr. Cummings had no reason to question his friend's integrity. But Miss Reynold's answers were quick, and her ability to communicate was clear. Something was not adding up.

Someone was not telling the truth, or worse, he feared something sinister.

The room grew darker. Dr. Cummings threw logs on and grabbed a stick, lighting one end. He walked to the side of the bed and lit the candles next to Jane, illuminating her face. Likewise, Jane saw his.

"Dr Cummings, what are you not telling me?"

"Miss Reynolds, when Henry Eaton placed you in my care in his home, he assured me you were strangers."

Jane rattled her head wondering if she heard him correctly. "I'm sorry, did you say Henry Eaton?"

"Yes, who else did you assume?"

Jane's stomach lurched. She was being thrust into something where there was no turning back.

"Dr. Cummings, there must be an error. I'm speaking about Mr. Ryan Eaton. He is who I met as the owner, and heir, to the Eaton Estate. Maybe his brother, or relative?"

Instinct was invaluable with doctors, and Dr. Cummings felt a sense of dread come over him. "No. Henry Eaton is the sole proprietor. He has a brother, Patrick, who lives in Scotland with his wife. But Ryan Eaton is of no relation."

Alert! Alert! Alert!

Jane reached out to Dr. Cummings–a lifeline for her panic–grabbing onto his sleeve. Her fingers slid across the woolen fibers and the sensation lingered in her touch. How many times had she fondled the refined threads of woven fabric through her fingers, sorting through wardrobes for exhibits? By touch, she could identify a suit from the eighteenth-century apart from the twentieth century. Naturally dyed threads from synthetics. Machine woven versus hand woven. All have a fingerprint of the era they were created. It was odd to observe such a minute sensation. But it was as if a switch turned on, intensifying her senses.

How had she not noticed?

Jane scrutinized the man before her.

Frocked coat? Cossack trouser? A cravat nicely displayed at his neck?

When she thought about it, Mrs. Bishop's attire was costume of the same century.

Her eyes darted around the room, noting other oddities. There were no lamp fixtures, a television, or a phone; nothing plugged into the walls. The furniture she admired when she first awoke was appropriate in a house of its time, but there was no sense of modernity.

Because of the historical elements of the home, the antiquity seemed natural. Her brain initially absorbed the information and calculated it to be normal. But as her acute sense of detail became heightened, her mind processed the information. The details now stood out like a glaring red light

Jane thrust her linens aside and jumped out of bed, needing to stand on solid ground. It didn't stop her brain from wobbling, or her face turning white.

"Miss Reynolds, is something the matter?"

"Doctor Cummings," she laughed at her maniacal thought, daring to ask the question. "What's today's date?"

"My dear, it is Monday, the tenth of June."

"And the year?"

Instinct told him to step closer. "Why, it's eighteen thirty-three."

Jane reached for him and gasped for air. Her mind splintered.

Did she hear him correctly? Was it true?

She caught her breath. Then calculated the possible, for the impossible was not logical. She wondered if Amy and Ryan were playing a trick on her. Pushing her to lighten up; be more spontaneous. Using the antiques, the setting of the dated house, and friends she didn't know to play parts. That was possible. But when she looked at Dr. Cummings, there was no sense of humor in his expression.

She shook her head, trying to put logic back in its place, like a pinball in a hole.

"Is this a joke?"

"I assure, Miss Reynolds, there is no foolery being presented here."

Jane sat on the bed.

Think, think, think, her brain ticked.

The reprieve didn't help. She inhaled, held it, counted to

ten, and let it out. A trick her uncle taught her when she got scared.

She was scared!

She held her breath again. And…again.

"I can't believe I'm going to say this," she murmured.

"Miss Reynolds?" The doctor touched her shoulder, waiting for her revelations.

"Dr. Cummings, when I left for London three days ago, it was June seventh."

"Yes. you were not conscious when we found you. Days passed, it happens," he explained. "But I assure you, all is well…."

"No, it isn't," she interrupted. "When I left, it was June seventh, two thousand thirteen–not eighteen thirty-three." To clarify, she added, "The twenty-first century, not the nineteenth."

His eyes froze on hers.

Dr. Cummings was well equipped to deal with every kind of unusual and unexplained situation presented to him in a calm, methodical fashion. He was trained to never show his immediate reaction to frightening, horrifying, or unbelievable situations. God knows he had seen many through his years. But he was not prepared to digest the words Jane expelled. His face paled by the information he was now faced with.

"Have I frightened you?"

"No." He rubbed his chin. "Well, yes, a little." He sank onto the bed next to Jane.

They both fell silent.

The bedroom door opened, and both jerked their heads towards the entering Mrs. Bishop.

"Here you go, Miss. Something hot and nourishing for your soul."

Dr. Cummings jumped to his feet, grabbed the tray in Mrs.

Bishop's hands, and placed it on a nearby table. He thanked her for the service and swiftly led her back to the door, with a little nudge at the threshold. Although grateful for the interruption–a reprieve of absurdity–he thought it best she was not privy to Jane's revelation.

To speak, to admit the extraordinary situation, would mean to accept it. Jane brushed her hand against the quilt on the bed, and glanced around the antiquated room, stopping at the candles' flickering light. Her fingers fondled the fabric of her nightgown, letting out a sigh with the realization. There seemed no other choice but to admit it was real.

"Dr. Cummings? What does this mean?"

"I really don't know, Miss Reynolds," he replied. "I am confused myself. Had I not been the one speaking with you, I would be predisposed to conclude this situation as a complete farce and fantastical. But that not being the case, I would like to say I am willing to adjust my current understanding to accommodate that which you are claiming as true. I just need time to contemplate all that has been placed before me."

"So, you believe me? Because I'm not sure I believe myself," Jane confessed. "I mean, I haven't seen what's outside that door. Dare I?"

"I assure you, what I have said is the truth."

Jane threw her arms up. "How is it possible!"

"Possibilities..." He echoed. "I have learned through the years, being a doctor, I am never sure of anything except for the mightiness of God. I have seen the weak live from pure will, and the strong die from pure fear. I am a man of science with the curiosity of a child. All presented to me is a journey of the mind to embrace with passion, openness, and understanding. There is nothing not possible."

Jane covered her face. She wanted to cry. When Stephen left, the feeling of being on her own was scary. This was a thousand times worse. But she didn't want to appear weak in front of the doctor.

"You are pale, and you haven't eaten. Please try to take in the hot broth Mrs. Bishop brought. I will give you something to make you sleep through the night. I promise to come back at first light of the morning and check on you." He rose from his chair, grabbed his bag, and placed medicine on the table with instruction. "I will send for Mrs. Bishop on my way out."

"Thank you, Doctor." Jane extended her hand, noting the weariness returned to his grey-blue eyes. She was sorry for that.

Grabbing her hand, he squeezed it softly. "May our journey be one of fascination, and of friendship. Now, please do not worry. There has to be a logical explanation. I give you my word to help you. But, for the present, do not discuss this with anyone." He looked at the door. "Especially to Mrs. Bishop."

Jane agreed. She wanted to say more, but he turned and left before more could be said.

Her heart tightened. *Did she click her heels three times to return home?*

But upon her request to find the bathroom, Mrs. Bishop showed her the porcelain pot, which was more than enough to awaken her reality that she was no longer in the twenty-first century.

KINDRED SOULS

Mrs. Bishop found Jane wrapped in a blanket, sitting on the window-seat staring into the distance. The drapes were pulled back and the window slightly ajar, allowing the cool morning air to seep into the room.

"Good morning, Miss, you're looking much of health today," Mrs. Bishop greeted, bringing in fresh water and towels. She placed them on the table before adding more logs to the fire. "Why don't you come and warm yourself."

"Thanks, I feel better this morning. The fresh air is helping."

"Aye, it's a lovely day after the rain. But still a wee bit chilly. Dr. Cummings would have none of it if you caught a cold under my watch." She closed the window and shewed Jane into a chair by the fire. "Are you hungry? Cook has warm nut breads coming from the oven."

"I'd love some coffee," Jane said wistfully, daydreaming of a freshly brewed cup from *Starbucks.*

"Coffee, you'll have?" Surprised by the request. "It's an acquired taste, for sure. The Master has it, but none of us have the yearning for it. But you must eat...I'll bring some nut bread, toast and jam as well."

Mrs. Bishop excused herself and promised to return with a tray.

Jane wanted to kick herself. Coffee, especially for women, was uncommon. Next time she would ask for tea.

Strong tea!

Jane hadn't much information on living in the nineteenth-century other than from books she read, or interpretations from movies, the accuracy now in question. She took the usual history courses in college, and her work at the museum was intensely rich in historical studies. But she wasn't sure she was prepared to live within history. Her behavior, vocabulary, and manner would have to be adjusted to fit in. For how long, she didn't know. She hoped Dr. Cummings had more answers. But she had enough knowledge to understand she was a modern woman in a not so modern time. Thus, she'd have to be careful of her words and actions.

A knock came at the door. Jane stood as Dr. Cummings entered.

"Ah," he smiled. "You're up and steady, I see. And your face is quite renewed. Mrs. Bishop said as much."

"Is it?" Jane palmed her hair with both hands, pushing the loose strands behind her ears. The mirror didn't lie. When she awoke, she needed a good washing. According to her calculations, she hadn't showered in four days. A pitcher of hot water was all she had to transform herself. She washed her face, rinsed her mouth as best she could without a toothbrush in her possession, and tried to make sense of her ratty hair. She snooped through the dresser drawers, finding a few handkerchiefs, a caftan she threw over her shoulders, and a hairbrush–which she used to untangle the knotty mess. When she was done, she was not worse-for-the-wear. But in the presence of Dr. Cummings, dressed in finery, freshly shaved, and his hair neatly combed away from his face, now made her doubt her early morning assessment.

A slow smile came across his face. "When a patient is alert, eager, and has a rosiness in her complexion, a doctor can be nothing but pleased." He doubled down on his compliment putting her at ease.

"I feel good," She assured. "But my clear head is only bringing on new concerns."

"Well, one day at a time, I like to say." He sat beside her, "Let's have a look."

She acquiesced to the doctor's instructions, his low and steady voice hypnotizing her into obedience: *Look straight, follow my finger, tell me if this hurts.*

Up close and personal, Dr. Cummings was professional. Jane was very aware he had seen her naked, examined her most intimate parts…but he didn't dwell on the intimacy of their interaction. He was her doctor, she, his patient. But there was something more brewing. A connection to a stranger that felt personal, as if they had known each other long before they met.

Dr. Cummings was a man of importance by his profession. His impeccable demeanor, down to the crisp white shirt with a cravat to match and austere posture, was of a gentleman's breeding. Although his hair was whitening from temple to ends, youth still lingered in the blackened highlights weaving through a full head of hair. His skin was darkened from outdoor exposure, causing creases on his forehead and around his grey-blue eyes, but a lean physique and broad chest were signs of a man still full of life. Jane could not ignore he was handsome underneath the "old" doctor image he seemed hard-pressed to portray.

Jane's uncle had a similar demeanor–the broad stance and resolute manner–he learned while in the war. He was no English gentleman, but a gentle man all the same. His eyes were as blue as a summer sky, and more prominent against his tanned skin, which he earned working outdoors. He was a proud husband, hard-working farmer, and a solid Christian. Dr. Cummings reminded Jane of her uncle, offering her a level of kinship to someone she loved very much. Peyton's words rang in her ears: *Trust one who is pure in deed; someone familiar to you.*

"Doctor, may I ask your age?" Jane asked.

"I am, with the blessing of God, fifty-four years of age. I am but an old man, if not a wise one."

Jane laughed at the prospect he considered himself old, but she was well aware life expectancy was lower in his time. He was correct in calling himself an old man, fortunate to be alive at his age. But with modern technology, medicine, healthy eating, and exercise, a man of his age would be entering his second stage of life. She told him so.

The good doctor shook his head in disbelief.

There were many things she wanted to tell him…about electricity, computers, nano-chips, space exploration, and so much more, but held her tongue. It would all be incredible to him. She could see he was a person who hungered for the unknown; had a voracious appetite for knowledge. But she feared too much information could only destroy his understanding of the world he was born into. It would be unfair to burden him with such knowledge.

"Miss Reynolds, it is of my opinion you are in good health. I recommend getting fresh air and scenery other than these four walls."

"That's wonderful! I keep thinking this is a dream, or a mental breakdown." She smirked. "I need to find out what's going on, how I got here, and how to get back."

Dr. Cummings put his hand up. "Baby steps, my dear. First, get your strength back. Then, understand your surroundings. Find some solitude knowing that you are safe. But be careful beyond that. We know so little right now. We have much work to do." He cleared his throat to continue. "During the night, I ruminated about your situation. I am not unfamiliar with tales of time travel. I browsed through a few books from my shelves to grasp other's understanding about the topic. There are many stories of such journeys. Contemplations of the what if. But none explain the mechanics of how one shows up in the past." His eyes widened. "I never imagined it possible."

"Nor I!" Jane agreed.

"But here we are, in a situation we both cannot *explain.* As a man of science, I never was interested in the occult or tales. Nor do I intend to involve myself now. If there is to be a solution, logic will show us the way."

"And if logic isn't the answer?" Jane explained her encounter with Peyton to Dr. Cummings, retelling the cryptic messages now illuminated by her situation. "I don't believe in magic, either. But Peyton's words seem like a roadmap. A starting point. More importantly, she predicted, 'your love will bring you home.' That has to mean I can get back."

Dr. Cummings laughed to himself. "You are as real as I am. There's no magic in that. I realize your situation is unusual, and I am no fool to think your return will be otherwise. If you got here, you will have a way to return. That is logical!"

"If we follow Peyton's instructions, we need to find someone referred to as *The Black Raven.* Peyton said her name was Ramsey. She is also a psychic or seer. Unfortunately, that's all I have."

"Well, it's a start."

"How so?" With no phones, directories, or internet, Jane could not imagine how to find a complete stranger.

"If you want to know anyone or anything, you seek your entrusted housekeeper. Mrs. Muldoon is whom I will turn to. If she does not know something herself, she will soon find someone who does."

Jane could only hope. Before she fell asleep, she wished to wake to her normal life. Mental billboards flashing in her head, the cat needing to be fed, the misguided weather report…even the heartache about Stephen she wished to have back. Anything would be better than the realization she was in a time warp. But when the light of the morning filtered through the drapes, dread about Stephen was the last thing that crossed her mind. She had to find her way home.

"Where do we begin?"

"First, I have ordered a bath. It will refresh your spirit. Then maybe a walk through the gardens? The Eaton Estate has a notable rose assortment. There is nothing like the aromatic scents of flowers, damp earth, and a summer's breeze to bring some color back to your cheeks and renew your soul. Eh?"

Didn't she wish to escape somewhere to renew her soul?

Jane cringed. She didn't know the universe and quantum physics could take it so literally.

"I'm ready when you are," she said. "But if I might point out, I'm at a disadvantage. I have nothing but the clothes on my back." Jane pulled at her nightgown.

"Ah yes. I took the liberty of solving that problem."

Jane's needs of provisions did not slip Dr. Cummings' mind during his sleepless night. He worried how she was going to fit into the society in which she was being thrust upon. She needed someone to take her in, protect her from talk and scrutiny. People loved to gossip; it gave them something to do with their idle minds.

He continued to explain, "I have sent word to Mr. Eaton about the situation and presented him with…um, er, a plan." His words stumbled out. He was wary about what he was embarking on, and his first apprehension was lying to his good friend, Henry Eaton.

"You told him…everything?"

"No, no," he assured her. "Although a reasonable man himself, Mr. Eaton is not one for fantasy. We will tell him what he needs to know. As it is, what do we know? You are a lost woman who needs help. He can appreciate that."

"I'm not a damsel in distress," Jane insisted. But when she saw Dr. Cummings lift his brow, she needed to defend her feminist ideals. "Women have come a long way, no longer in the background as pretty accessories to a room. I can take care of myself."

Dr. Cummings, not sure if he was horrified or proud of women for empowering themselves, was quick to instruct, "Men are not so enlightened as to the equality of women in this time. I can see you are an intelligent, if not a strong woman. I dare say you would put a few men in their place. But you are also very forthcoming. You must watch your step. Observe. Stay in control. You are an interloper, not a participant. Careful where you go and what you say." It did not slip his mind what could happen to her if she was found out. People did not burn witches at the stake anymore, but they feared the unknown. He continued, "Man is capable of great harm if in fear. I have witnessed the dark side of humanity. My prayer is you will not."

Jane wanted to argue. But she understood the world she was now thrust upon was his world, of which he knew more about than she did. She needed Dr. Cummings's help, if not his camaraderie.

"I understand. I'll be watchful."

"It is best." He nodded. "There is much to do."

Dr. Cummings was a formidable man in height. He stood five inches above Jane, and the size of his hands was twice as big as hers. No matter how many miles she ran, or weights she lifted, she was no match to the man who stood before her. Yet, with the look in his eyes, she feared nothing about him.

"I am out of sorts here. I don't belong." Jane placed her hands on his, "But I believe you're the one Peyton told me about–the person to trust." Her voice quavered. "God, I hope she was right about everything else."

"My dear Miss Reynolds, you are no more, or less, human than I," he said. "From centuries past and centuries to come, you learn people are not all that different. Life is a cycle, and time is merely a measurement. People, their trials and tribulations, are human all the same, no matter what period of time your spirit resides. If the young woman, Peyton, told you it is possible to return, then it will be. You need to have faith. Will you trust me?" His eyes rested upon hers. "I do not know you or the circumstances you are accustomed to. But you are a woman in need, and I was placed here by some strange fate. I am a healer by trade, sworn to protect life. I will not abandon my duty," he pledged. "Fear strengthens us. It drives us to accomplish things unimaginable. We are, no doubt, trying to accomplish something incredible. But God willing, we will do this, together."

Jane's eyes watered, unable to hold back the fear she pushed under the surface. She wanted to believe in him. And the reality was, she had no choice.

He released his hands and pulled a handkerchief from his pocket. "Enough of that."

Grateful, she took the hanky and wiped away the tears.

"Here is the plan. I will present you as my wife's cousin visiting from America. This will give us reason to spend time together and easily talk. You seem like a respectable woman. I would not want to jeopardize that impression."

Jane smiled at the implication.

"I'm grateful for the discretion of my reputation."

"Discretion will be the key," he emphasized.

"Will I stay with you?"

"Oh, dear me, I am an old widower with no accommodations for a lady. It would be improper." He blushed. "My wife, God bless her dear soul, has long been gone. I am afraid I would not offer you the comforts you deserve. For those reasons, I have arranged for you to stay here. Henry has the room, the staff, and the respectability to care for you. He is a good friend. It would not be uncommon for him to offer his hospitality to my cousin."

"That seems like a lot to ask of him," Jane balked.

"You need not worry," he assured. "Henry Eaton is a man of honor. You will be safe with him."

"He has agreed to this?"

"The plans are already in motion. Until then, try to make the best of it."

Jane nodded.

"I have affairs which take me away for a few days. But be assured, I leave you in good hands with Mr. Eaton and his staff."

"You're leaving me? I thought we'd have some time together. There's so much I need to know before I meet other people. Who are they? How do I act? What should I say?"

Taking Jane's hand, he wrapped both of his big hands around hers. "Trust me," he reiterated. "Stick with our plan. I have no doubt they will find you as charming as I have. I will send you news. Until then…"

Jane watched Dr. Cummings depart with a longing that he not go.

MEETING THE FAMILY

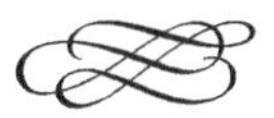

Mrs. Bishop entered with a young girl in tow. She was not more than fifteen, and terribly skinny, Jane thought. A head of dark, wiry curls burst from underneath a tiny cap overpowering her petite face, long cheeks and small, but pointed nose. Although granted youth, she was not blessed with beauty.

"This is young Regina. She'll help you dress. But for now, she'll comb your hair and set it nicely." She pushed the young girl forward.

Jane wanted to decline the help–the idea of servitude seemed archaic. But there was no doubt she needed help with her appearance. She was a modern woman, without modern hygiene or beauty care. If anything, the past few days allowed her natural beauty to be uncovered…no chemical creams, shampoos, or conditioners were at her disposal. She relied on her own health and young age to circumvent the use of over-indulged beauty aids. She had no choice. Every era had their methods to enhance beauty, and if there were women about, she was bound to find forms of lip colors, face powders, and blushes to help improve her *au naturel* predicament. But the lack of modern styling tools–a hair dryer most notably–could not compensate for her hair. Long hair, pulled into a neat bun, a braid, or a twist, was a trademark of beauty in pre–twentieth century. Young Regina would have to work miracles with her 21st century, blunt, shoulder-length hair style. Heeding the advice from Dr. Cummings to fit in, she would have to override her moral convictions and accept the help.

Regina curtsied, her dark eyes meeting Jane's with curiosity. Jane tried to put her at ease with a smile, but it only made her retreat behind Mrs. Bishop, leading to a reprimand.

"Don't frighten, girl. She'll not bite!"

"Yes, Ma'am," the girl replied and moved swiftly to Jane's side.

Mrs. Bishop pulled the drapes aside in a dramatic swoop, letting in a burst of sunlight. But her excitement couldn't be contained when she saw outside.

"Oh, the family has arrived!"

Suddenly, the door swung open, and a young girl ran in, nearly knocking over Mrs. Bishop.

"Hello," the girl greeted. She stood tall, hands behind her back, and smiled.

"Well, hello," Jane replied.

"My name is Maggie, I mean, Margaret Elizabeth," she corrected, rolling her eyes with the mistake.

"Well, Margaret Elizabeth…or do you prefer Maggie?" The girl's head bounced, eyes wide with anticipation. "I'm Jane…"

Mrs. Bishop cleared her throat.

Jane corrected herself. "I'm Miss Reynolds. It's a pleasure to meet you."

Maggie bowed forward and curtsied. She backed up, studied Jane from head to toe, and declared, "You don't look as old as I thought you would be."

"Why, thank you, I think," Jane laughed. "How old do you think I am?"

"Well, my father said you were as old as Aunt Louisa… Uncle Patrick's wife. But you don't look like her at all. You are much prettier and less scary looking."

Mrs. Bishop, having enough, took the young lady by the arm and guided her to the door. "There will be plenty of time for you to insult the guest later."

Maggie groaned at the escort and disappeared as instructed.

Jane walked to the window to see for herself the arriving family. She saw men carrying trunks, while a black-suited man, two heads above the others, managed the commotion. He removed his hat, revealing dark hair with a hint of auburn as the sun danced through the natural waviness.

Mrs. Bishop sidled up to Jane. "That's Master Eaton." She pointed to the black-suited man.

"He looks very dignified," Jane noted

"Aye, yes. He's a proper gentleman at that."

A knock came at the door and Mrs. Bishop pulled herself away from the window to answer it. Moving aside, two servant girls came through with a handful of dresses and accoutrements. She needled through the assortment.

"These will do just fine," she said to the girls, waiting for further instructions. "Notify Mrs. Hampton to come tomorrow. They'll need adjustments."

The two girls snuck a peek at Jane but dared not linger their gaze before they scurried out of the room.

Jane couldn't help herself. The urge to rustle through the stack of gowns hanging from the top of the armoire and stacked on the bed was too tempting. She browsed through the assortment of refined fabric laid before her, running her hands down the details of lace, pleated stitching, and embroidery. It was a costume fairytale come true.

"Are these for me to wear?"

"Aye." Mrs. Bishop eyed Jane from head to toe. "Mrs. Levongood sent them…Master Eaton's sister. You're about the same height, but I am afraid your shape needs filling in. We will find you something suitable with some nips and tucks."

Jane crossed her arms in front of her, all too familiar with her lack of cleavage. A great benefit for wearing tank tops and summer dresses, but not for filling out a nineteenth-century woman's fashion.

"Now, now, no need to be ashamed. Nothing a few babies won't take care of," Mrs. Bishop said, ignoring Jane's scoff. If anyone was familiar with Jane's shape, it was Mrs. Bishop who attended to her every need, naked and vulnerable.

She browsed through the assortment of colorful silks, floral prints, and muslin plaids in search of something particular. When she found what she wanted, she handed them to Regina.

"Help Miss Reynolds into these," she ordered, passing along a lace edged chemise, a waist petticoat, and a corset. "Find a suitable dress among those." She pointed to three dresses she pulled aside. "I'll come and get her when she's presentable."

Mrs. Bishop looked back at Jane. "I'm not going to promise, but I'll try to find some shoes for you. I cannot imagine how a woman with your slight frame should God bless with such long feet." She sighed under her breath and left the room, only to return briefly with a simple black pair of slippers she borrowed from a groomsman's wife. "They are her Sunday best, but they will do." With that, she closed the door and left her in Regina's care.

Timely wasn't a word one could use to describe the dressing rituals for a lady. Jane had researched extensively for her exhibit, but to endure the laborious task herself, 'torment' came to mind. The dress she wore was exquisite, down to the hand-sewn seams. Layers of lightweight floral-printed muslin cascaded to her ankles, gathered at the waist, and belted with a satin ribbon in a contrast color of blue. The bodice, in the same print, was fitted and layered in pleats, with large billowy sleeves from the shoulder to the elbow, narrowing to the wrists. A hint of delicate lace edged the collar, which highlighted the collarbone, creating demurity. It was a simple dress with no adornments besides the pearl buttons along the back and at the wrists, allowing the print to be the star, the figure it graced only spotlighted. Unfortunately, Jane was too overwhelmed with the layering, hooking, and buttoning, to fully appreciate such a fine gown, or how it transformed her into a 19th century lady. She squirmed in the clothes which entombed her, pulling at the heavy sleeves, and tugging the cinched waist, the heaviness precipitating little droplets around her hairline. The servitude of Regina was now more a blessing than a curse.

"You look beautiful, Miss," Regina assured her when she was done.

Jane tried to smile. Instead, she bit her lower lip.

"Now, Miss, don't be like that. Maybe you've forgotten how to be with people, that's all." Regina said, her childlike voice imparting wisdom beyond her years.

"I don't know why I'm so nervous," Jane confessed.

"The Eatons are a kind family. But after all you've been through…"

"That'll be enough, Regina," Mrs. Bishop said when she came through the door.

Regina curtsied and promptly left.

It was apparent Jane's situation wasn't to be discussed. She was a mystery to them all, but no doubt there was gossip about the little they did know. Nothing was ever a secret in a house where servants lingered in the hallways and behind closed doors.

"Ah, as pretty as I expected," Mrs. Bishop said before heading to the door. "Coming?"

Jane followed, in a dash to catch Mrs. Bishop halfway down

the corridor. When she reached the top of the stairs, Jane stopped to glimpse at the house below. She recognized the inlaid floor she admired the first day upon her arrival at the Eaton Estate. The walls along the stairs still exhibited the relatives of the past, only a few less. Before she turned away, she caught a figure looking at her from below, only to disappear in a blink.

Was it her ghost she saw that day she arrived with Amy?

She shuddered.

Mrs. Bishop signaled for her to keep up. Jane brushed off the chill along her spine and descended the stairs. They stopped at a set of paneled doors. Jane inhaled, lifting a sagging sleeve to the shoulder, and smoothing over her skirt with the palm of her hands before nodding to Mrs. Bishop, who rapped softly and entered without further delay.

"Master Eaton." Mrs. Bishop nodded her head. "Lady Levongood, it's nice to have you back. And Young Miss Isabelle, you're a sight of beauty every time I see you." She stepped aside. "May I introduce Miss Jane Reynolds."

Jane took two steps forward and froze. She wanted to greet everyone appropriately but wasn't sure of the proper etiquette. Did she greet the Master first, or the Lady Levongood? Did she shake hands or bow? Her eyes nervously shifted back and forth, wanting the answer to come.

Mr. Eaton made the first move.

"Miss Reynolds, it is good to see you so well," he said. He touched her elbow and guided her into the room, towards the woman sitting near the window. "May I introduce my sister, Lady Levongood."

"Oh please, Henry, do not be so formal with me when I am in your home. My title makes me sound old and stuffy," she chided, immediately rising to greet Jane.

Jane agreed. Lady Levongood was not old, and her title didn't do justice to her youth. She was taller than most women of her time, with soft curves and well-rounded at the bust, explaining Jane's inability to fill her dress. Her face was surrounded by curls of auburn, much lighter than her brother's. Her skin, although fair, was freckled at the nose, offering a childlike quality to an otherwise flawless complexion. Her high cheekbones were notable–modelesque, as were her hazelnut brown eyes. A lady of refinement was easily assessed by the lavender silk dress she wore with an overlay of chiffon hand-embroidered with metallic threads, and the strand of pearls adorning her décolletage. The lavender color only accentuated the golden of her eyes, as did the pink gloss on her lips. Jane thought she was beautiful.

"Please, call me Lillian. My mother would be excited to hear her Scottish heritage honored."

"It's nice to meet you," Jane said, and curtsied.

"And this is my daughter, Margaret." Chastisement interposed in his words. "But I hear you have had the pleasure of her introduction."

"Yes, we've met." Jane smiled at the girl, who sat with her back straight, hands in her lap, and a head hung low.

"The dress is lovely on you," Lillian interjected, deflecting from her niece's indiscretion. "It was lovely on me before my figure changed. Children can take a drastic toll on girlish figures. I hope the others do you justice."

"Yes, I was told you had brought them. I'm humbled." It was only after she captured the reflection of herself in entirety before leaving her room did Jane embrace her bondage. "The gowns are beautiful…and I am humbled by your generosity to allow me to wear them."

"It was the least I could do. It is a terrible shame your trunks got lost. A terrible tragedy indeed." Lillian shook her head. "Unforgivable thievery, if not incompetence on the part of the ship. I hope they get to the bottom of it."

"Yes, indeed." Mr. Eaton gave Jane a quick glance to

confirm their conspiracy. "Dr. Cummings is investigating the circumstances."

Jane's backstory was set in motion.

"Please," Lilian patted the seat next to her, "Come sit next to me and tell me all about your travels. I must say, Henry was so secretive. He has told me almost nothing about you. But men dislike partaking in silly talk of mundane topics such as women." She eyed her brother. "And Dr. Cummings gave us no hint of your arrival. Shame on them both."

"It was rather sudden." Jane said. "Dr. Cummings had no advance knowledge of my arrival, as did your brother."

"Really?" Lillian raised her eyebrow.

To not notify relatives in advance of travel, especially thousands of miles, by sea, and alone, would be highly unusual. Jane searched the annals of her mind for the best lie…a believable truth. She feared Dr. Cummings was overconfident in her ability to pull off her charade.

Mr. Eaton, once again, saved her.

"Lillian, you mustn't be so inquisitive. She has been ill since her journey, and I am sure doesn't choose to reminisce about such unpleasantries so soon."

"Hush, Henry, it is what women do," Lillian scolded. "It is called conversation. Unlike you men, who sit around and mumble to each other, never really discussing anything of importance."

Mr. Eaton was a grown man in his thirties, but it was obvious who was the older and more powerful one in the relationship. Jane could see Lillian held the well-established authority.

"I'm sure Dr. Cummings didn't want to bother you with my unimportant visit." Jane interceded the sibling rivalry. "And your brother was very kind to offer the hospitality on short notice."

"Silliness!" Lillian grimaced. "To arrive with barely the

clothes on your back, after a treacherous journey, and to fall ill. Of course you are important! It is my hope you are finding your accommodations satisfactory?"

Lillian raised another eyebrow, this time her brother the target.

"Very much," Jane confirmed. "Mrs. Bishop has been very attentive."

"You are feeling better, then?" Mr. Eaton asked.

"Yes. The headaches are gone, and after being confined to my room for three days, I'm well rested."

"I pray you didn't lock her away as a prisoner?" Lillian questioned. "You really should have brought her to me right away, Henry."

Mr. Eaton straightened. "It was under Dr. Cummings' instructions that I dare not move her." Turning to Jane, he appealed, "Please Miss Reynolds, forgive me if you felt otherwise other than an honored guest."

"Oh, no!" Jane cringed. "I didn't mean to imply I was unhappy. No. Quite the opposite. It gave me time to properly recover."

Mr. Eaton's lips flatlined; his brow crunched. "If you felt restricted, it was only my concern you were not..." He hesitated. His thoughts shifted to the morning she was found.

The smell of orange blossoms lingered, as did her lifeless body warm against his own. The woman before him was not the same broken creature he carried out of the field.

He cleared his throat. "I was concerned you were not attired to be greeted properly. Hence my delay, and my sister's accompaniment."

Their eyes met and Jane understood. A flush of pink crossed her face, recalling her naked introduction to Mr. Eaton.

He continued, "My house is open for all my guests. You are welcome to come and go as you please. If there is anything you are in need of, or want for, please do not hesitate to ask."

Lillian saw her brother pull at the cuffs of his shirt, adjusting the lengths of equal distance from the sleeve of his coat. A habit he had since he was a boy when he grew anxious. When he added a shoulder roll, she knew he needed to be rescued.

"Henry, why don't you take the poor girls outside for some fresh air. They need to stretch their legs after the morning's journey."

He obliged his sister, grateful to be relieved of his duty as host.

When the three retreated, Lillian languidly rose from the sofa and crossed the room, pouring two cups of tea a servant delivered without notice. Jane noted Lillian's ease and command of the house. It was hard not to miss the feminine touches everywhere, prompting Jane to wonder if they were a reflection of Lillian, or of someone else.

"Do you visit your brother often?" Jane asked, accepting the porcelain cup and saucer.

"Not as frequently as I would prefer. My duties as wife and mother keep me quite occupied. I dare say it is my brother who comes to me more. But he has the opportunity and is less restricted."

"Less restricted?" Jane's curiosity got the best of her.

"He has but Maggie, and she spends most of her time with Isabelle. The two are inseparable."

"Is there a Mrs. Eaton?" Jane asked outright.

"Not anymore," Lillian replied, with no explanation. "And you, Miss Reynolds? Why have you decided to travel all this way–alone?"

Jane dismissed the question by sipping her tea.

"Ah, I see." Lillian eyed Jane. "You are running away, maybe from something or someone? I hope it was not a man who caused you to travel such distances. Men can be beastly creatures and don't warrant that kind of tragedy."

Stephen came to mind. *Had her wish been granted?*

"Maybe one of the reasons." Jane couldn't hide heartache. "But I had other reasons. I always wanted to travel to England. The opportunity presented itself, and here I am."

"England." A careless smile crossed her face. "It is lovely, but the people are rather melancholy and mannered. Always so proper, doing the right thing." She rolled her eyes. "I should have run away to Italy or France to cure a broken heart. And to cure a soul? I would most undoubtedly recommend Scotland, my homeland."

"Aren't you English?" Jane questioned the aristocratic woman in front of her.

"I am Scottish through and through, with my mother's temperament. Or that is what my father used to tell me." She smirked. "My mother was quite the opposite of my noble English father. But they made a beautiful pair; she with her auburn hair and full figure; he with his lean frame and pale skin against his dark jet-black hair. My father was very handsome, as you can see in my brother, Henry."

Jane glanced out the windows and eyed Mr. Eaton. Tall, broad shoulders, well-dressed, slanted against a tree, watching the girls chase butterflies fluttering over a hedge of pink flowers. He moved to capture one of them, but they darted away, laughing at their escape. He laughed, too. A grin lingered on his face as he moved back to the tree, awaiting his next attack.

She agreed. He was handsome.

"All the young ladies were terribly disappointed with my father when he returned married to my mother, with my brother Patrick in her arms and me in tow." Lillian laughed. "He nearly killed my grandmother with the presentation."

"Sounds so modern," Jane quipped.

"It was quite a shock to everyone. But my mother was extremely loved by my father. No one could deny his eternal commitment. Not even grandmother. My mother was not only beautiful but she was also a breath of fresh air in my father's world. After she passed, he immersed us back into English life and it is here we have lived. Mannered and melancholy. Except for Patrick. He was wise to get out."

"You never wanted to leave or go back to Scotland?"

"Oh, please overlook my ridicule of my lot. I may jest, but do not doubt my complete fondness for my English life, my title, or my dear husband, Sir Levongood. He is a good man and has my heart completely…the old fool! It is one piece of wisdom my mother impressed upon me. Marry someone you foolishly love. But, she added, someone who loves you with deep passion and guarded honor. *That* I did."

"You're lucky," Jane sighed.

Lillian looked at Jane, catching the whispered comment. She placed her teacup on the table and walked to the opened doors to the yard. "Come, we will join the girls outside. It is a lovely day. Let us not tarnish it with heartache, perilous travels, or ghosts of the past, but instead live in the moment, shall we?" She patted Jane's hands. "There is plenty of time to learn more about each other."

FIRST DINNER

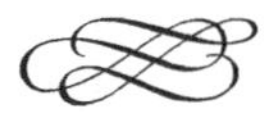

As the sun dipped, the heat of day faded, and the late afternoon turned chilly. It was a cue for everyone to retreat to their rooms and prepare for dinner. This included another dress change–completely unnecessary, as far as Jane was concerned. Regina was waiting, eager to hear about Jane's first encounter with the Eaton family. It turned out Regina was quite friendly when not under the thumb of Mrs. Bishop and chatted about the staff Jane would soon meet.

She confided, *"Never talk around Mary or Sisley–the younger girls on the house staff. They are not to be trusted. Cook doesn't like people in her kitchen. Don't get in her way. Nor does Landry like people in his stable, but he is most* accommodating, if asked. And…I think you are the nicest person I have ever been assigned."

Jane took note. Mostly, she was thrilled the girl found her comfortable to share her thoughts and feelings, especially if they were to spend time together.

Lillian arrived at the door, looking refreshed and more lovely–if that was possible, to retrieve Jane for dinner. But she was late, and not a bit remorseful for her tardiness.

Jane heard Mr. Eaton specifically say to meet in the parlor

at eight. She cringed when Regina informed her it was half past. Jane was never late. Unless she notified someone of her lateness, which meant she wasn't late. The bottom line, she thought it unprofessional, if not inconsiderate. She had no intention to insult her host. She was at his house with the grace of his kindness. Other options for hospitality were non-existent at present. To insult Mr. Eaton upon their first meeting was not Jane's preference in the scheme of things.

When Lillian greeted her with a smile, graciously filling her head with compliments due to Regina's keen skill fitting her in a dress too big and managing a neat bun behind her head, Jane could not reciprocate Lillian's enthusiasm for dinner, unable to conceal her feelings…her face an open book, her purposeful silence a submission of guilt.

Lillian halted at the parlor, turned to her, and gave her some advice.

"Excuse my brother. He is watchful, if not fastidious. A quality he thinks is honorable. I have another opinion." She winked, releasing a mischievous smile. "He's rather a puppy at heart. He just acts like a bulldog. Rather indignant at times, though. Don't let it bother you. Follow me and you will be of no concern to his temperament."

Lillian's words were no relief to Jane when she saw Mr. Eaton seated, a drink in hand, and his lips tight across his face. He stood as the two women entered but made no attempt to move towards them. It was apparent Mr. Eaton agreed with Jane…unpunctuality was rude.

"Good evening, brother." Lillian glided across the room and kissed him on the cheek.

"Lillian." His eyes met hers, before he moved them to Jane. "Miss Reynolds," he greeted.

"Let's retreat to dinner, shall we?" Lillian said, ignoring her brother's admonishment. "Maggie, would you like to escort our guest?"

Maggie jumped to the request, slipped her hand in Jane's, and led her to the dining room. Mr. Eaton set his glass down, not finishing the golden elixir, and followed the female entourage.

"Miss Reynolds," he pulled out the chair next to him, "It would be an honor to have you next to me."

"Thank you," Jane accepted, wondering if it was truly his honor, duty, or punishment. His earnest expression and furrowed brow hinted at the latter.

Lillian sat across from Jane, with Isabelle content to be by her mother's side. Maggie would have no other spot except by Jane, her little face beaming.

Mr. Eaton gestured, and wine was poured; dinner served.

Lillian started the conversation, but as the topic was in reference to the girls' lessons, Mr. Eaton took the opportunity to capture Jane's attention.

He leaned in. "Did you enjoy the afternoon with my family?"

When they retreated outside, Lillian led Jane to the patio, where they could observe the two girls at play. Mr. Eaton didn't join them under the shade of the tree, opting to sit on the lawn, only later to excuse himself from their company all together. Lillian offered pleasant conversation, and was kind enough to keep her questions to a minimal: *How was the voyage over? Did you meet anyone of interest? Have you been to the theatre in London?* She didn't pry into personal information, and Jane kept her answers brief, if not evasive. She felt a fraud but saw no other choice considering her circumstances. Before she knew it, she had made it through the first afternoon, as a stranger out of place and time, without exposing her true circumstances. She hoped Dr. Cummings would be proud.

Now, in proximity, the conversation would become more personal. Mr. Eaton's face was concentrated on Jane's, his furrowed brow gone, but his eyes still intense. They were blue…

ocean blue. Jane had seen those eyes before, just on a different man–Ryan Eaton. But Mr. Eaton's were more intense than Ryan's, stormy, darkened, dimmed–the sunlight unable to penetrate their depths. And she wondered what the cause of such tenebrous eyes was. *Was it her?* He was looking, seeking to know who Jane was–the stranger invading his home and family.

Jane met those eyes–the stormy blue, wanting to tell him everything, to explain she wasn't a dangerous stranger, but just Jane. A girl who is lost, albeit *lost in time*. But she couldn't. Not now. Maybe not ever.

"Your family is sweet." She answered. Short. Precise. Accurate. She would get into less trouble, less web to weave, if she kept her answers simple. "It was nice to get outside," she added.

"I am glad," he said, and took a sip of wine. "It will make up for my previous blunder."

"No, there's no blunder." The thought of him carrying the burden of her care made her uneasy. "Just circumstances to deal with...none of which are your fault."

His furrowed brow returned. There was hidden meaning in her words and Mr. Eaton wanted to know what intrigue lay behind her dark eyes. There was nothing magical about her abandonment in the field. 'Just circumstances?' He sensed something more profound than Dr. Cummings led him to believe. Was he protecting her honor? He did not question his friend's motives, but the woman who sat next to him was a mystery. He was apprehensive of her presence in his home and watched her guardedly in spite of Dr. Cummings's assuredness she was harmless. Harm came in all shapes and forms, and he was not naïve to the kind a woman could unleash.

He continued, treading, in spite of his friend. "Dr. Cummings says you are from the States, but I don't think he mentioned where."

"I'm from Boston. A small town called Quincy." Jane answered. "But I grew up in Illinois."

"Is that where your family originated?" Lillian joined the conversation.

"Actually," Jane jumped at the chance to find a connection between her and the people she was thrust upon. "Although I come from a long line of Americans, my ancestry is English."

"Well, that is redeeming," Lillian remarked. "How is it your family moved so many miles away from their homeland? They must have been true adventurers...maybe it runs in your blood?"

"Unfortunately, nothing so venturesome, or noble, I'm afraid. It was because my great, great grandfather was swindled out of his family inheritance. This caused debt to the King, and he was sent to prison. They shipped him to America to pay off his indenture. He worked himself free and eventually sent for his wife and children to live in America. We Reynolds have been there ever since."

"What intrigue you have," was Lillian's reaction.

Mr. Eaton was more diplomatic. "I am sorry to hear about your family's injustice."

"Well, no need to be ashamed of your familial connections. Families all have their scandals, don't they, Henry?"

Mr. Eaton scowled.

"Don't mind Henry, Miss Reynolds. He thinks if you run from the past, it won't haunt you. We have an uncle, once removed, who made his way to America, and on not such respectable terms, as well." Lillian explained, "If I recall, I think he was drunk and cast from a gambling house for a debt he could not pay, found himself on a ship, and landed on the American shore months later. It seems he established himself once there, but little is discussed about the circumstances of how he got there."

Jane mused, "I guess we all have our family secrets..."

Lillian agreed. Mr. Eaton frowned into his glass.

"Miss Reynolds," Maggie interrupted with a question of her own. "Are you going to marry my father?"

Mr. Eaton cleared his throat–loudly. "Margaret Elizabeth, what is this all about?"

She looked at Jane and then at her father. "Well, father, we were introduced, she's been invited to stay with us, and you pleaded with Aunt Lillian to welcome her into our home..." She met Jane's stare and grinned. "And she's pretty enough to be your wife."

Jane blushed. Mr. Eaton's face went white. Lillian's eyes watered from amusement.

"Silly girl. Always the imagination." Lillian reached across the table and patted Maggie's hand. "It wouldn't be a such a bad plan, your father to marry."

"Lillian," Mr. Eaton interjected. "Do not encourage the girl."

"Oh, Henry!"

Maggie looked confused. "But then, why is she here?"

Jane interceded, "I'm here only for a visit."

"For how long?" The child's voice questioned.

"I really don't know...just for a little while. Until I can get back home."

Jane could feel Mr. Eaton's stare. She dared not meet his gaze.

"To be honest, being here was unexpected, and your father was kind enough to offer your lovely house until I can make arrangements to return."

"Unexpected?" Mr. Eaton echoed.

"My dear, Jane, you seem to hold many mysteries we must uncover," catching her brother's scrutiny. "I must say, I shall enjoy my stay. It is so rare my brother has a guest to indulge in," Lillian lifted an eyebrow and turned to her brother. "Even if not a woman of interest."

Mr. Eaton gave her the pleasure of acknowledging her innuendo, but no words were exchanged.

"How Dr. Cummings kept your arrival so secret is beyond me. But let us not lament over what we cannot change, was my mother's philosophy." Lillian lifted her glass. "To time…may we have plenty to enjoy your company."

"I think my mother would have the same advice."

"The wisdom of women. It is such an understated ability," Lillian quipped.

Jane lifted her glass. "To time, and to women."

Mr. Eaton offered no opinion, nor did he lift his glass.

Lillian, noting the girls shifting in their chairs and her brother fidgeting with his sleeves, suggested they retreat to the sitting room. The girls eagerly led the way and Jane followed, noting Mr. Eaton's tall frame shadowing behind her.

Lillian seated herself on one of the two sofas in the room and grabbed a basket of yarn next to it. Maggie took to drawing at a large table by the window. It was dark outside, the windows only providing a backdrop for the circumstance, but a candle in the middle of the table gave her all the illumination she required. Isabelle strolled around the room, eventually seating herself at the pianoforte. She began to tinker, and the room filled with a concerto Jane did not recognize. Mr. Eaton went to a sidebar, where he poured three glasses of port and passed them out to the women before he settled into a chair in the far corner of the room.

"Do you knit, Miss Reynolds?" Lillian asked as she started to fiddle with her needles.

"No, I never learned."

"Really? Well, I would be happy to teach you. It is quite easy and occupies the many cold winter evenings."

"If you won't be insulted by my lack of ability...I wouldn't mind trying."

A fragile utterance floated across the room. "Excuse me, Miss Reynolds? Do you play music?"

Jane followed the voice to Isabelle, her blue eyes wide in anticipation.

"A little. I took lessons when I was about your age. My uncle thought I would be a child prodigy. I wasn't, but I did enjoy the lessons."

Her lids lowered. Then a smile curled along her face. "Would you like to play with me?"

Jane nodded with enthusiasm and moved to sit on the bench next to Isabelle. "Can you show me the notes you were just playing? I think I can read the music if you're willing to help guide me."

The young girl exhaled, "Oh yes!"

Isabelle place Jane's fingers on the keys and guided her through the notes. Jane laughed when she made mistakes, precipitating giggles from Isabelle. The young girl encouraged Jane to try again and again until she got it right. No one seemed to mind the repetition. Mr. Eaton's head never lifted up from the book he held, and Maggie continued to hum to herself as she drew. It was Lillian, tired of looking down at her needles, who interrupted Jane's music lesson.

"Would you care to play a game of cards, Miss Reynolds?"

Jane shrugged her shoulders. "I'd love to, but I probably don't know any of your card games."

"What do you play?" asked Isabelle, seemingly finding her voice with the stranger.

Jane wanted to answer, poker or blackjack, but worried those games weren't respectable. She answered carefully. "Well," she engaged Isabelle. "When I was a little girl, we would go camping up in the mountains and sit around the campfire and play games called *War* and *Crazy Eights* until we could barely keep our eyes open."

"Camping? Pray tell, my dear, what kind of life were you leading in America?" Lillian scoffed.

"I suppose sleeping under the stars seems odd," Jane confessed. "Every summer, my uncle used to take me camping to discover the raw life of living outdoors, and to teach me to appreciate the luxuries for which I was blessed."

"Sleep outside on purpose?" Maggie's eyes lit up. "Did that not scare you?"

"It all sounds so barbaric," Lillian commented.

Jane laughed to herself. Her present situation, without modern conveniences, wasn't much different from her camping experiences, except she had a nicer place to sleep and prettier clothes.

"It sounds uncomfortable," Isabelle chimed in. "Who chooses to sleep on the ground?"

"Father, do you think we might try camping?" Maggie shouted across the room.

"Do you really want to sleep under the stars?" Mr. Eaton asked, cautious to encourage his daughter.

Jane caught Lillian's glance, both hiding their smirks about Mr. Eaton's inability to commit to something he had no intention of doing.

"Father…" Maggie whined.

Jane warned, "I wouldn't be so eager, Maggie, if I were you. It's extremely uncomfortable to sleep on the hard ground with rocks poking at your back. The nights are cold, days are hot, and you're always dirty." Jane scrunched her nose. "If you didn't watch your plate, wild squirrels stole your food, lizards ran across you while sleeping, and spiders crawled up your nose."

"Ewwww!" both girls screamed.

"If you don't like small creatures, there were larger ones to contend with, like mountain lions or bears."

Maggie's eyes widened. "Have you ever seen a real bear?"

"Thank goodness, we never saw them up close. But there was one trip, when we caught twelve big fish. I personally snagged three all by myself. My uncle tied them up on rope and submerged them in the cold stream to keep before we left for a hike. When we returned, our campsite was torn apart by a bear, who took our fish dinner with it."

"Oh my, that sounds dangerous," Lillian said.

Maggie was more enthralled than horrified. "What did you do?"

"Why, of course, we packed up and went home," Jane laughed.

"It seems you had quite an adventurous childhood, Miss Reynolds." Mr. Eaton commented. "Adventurous indeed," he uttered.

Jane did not miss his utterance. "I agree, Mr. Eaton. At the time it seemed mundane. How I used to begrudge the trips, taking baths in the lake, spending time away from my friends, and living outside in uncomfortable conditions. But thinking about it, my uncle provided me lessons about life, conquering the unknown, and bravery."

"What about your parents?" Lillian asked. "Where were they during these wild adventures?"

Dare she explain a car crash?

"They were in a tragic accident when I was young."

"Oh my," Lillian's hand patted her heart. "I am very sorry."

Maggie yawned, a little too loudly, and her father gave her a look of reprimand. She smiled at him, as only young girls can do to soften a father's temper and ran to give him a hug. To Jane's surprise, his arms swooped around her and he gave her a kiss on the forehead.

"Goodnight, Father," her little voice crackled.

Isabelle reached for the tired girl's hand and started to drag her away, but not before Maggie broke free and swung her arms around Jane.

Isabelle took the opportunity to do the same, only a little more refined–a genteel reach around Jane's neck, pressing her cheek against Jane's. "Good night, Miss Reynolds. I look forward to spending more time with you. And I am sorry to hear about your parents."

"Goodnight, girls," Jane said. "Sweet dreams."

Lillian explained after the two girls left the room, "Isabelle is extremely quiet. They say her beauty is a blessing for she would otherwise be overlooked. She is often ignored because of her shyness. Most people scare her. Maggie is one of the few who will talk to her. It was extremely kind of you to be so attentive."

"I'm glad she found me comfortable." Knowing Isabelle's infamous legacy, she added, "But I don't think you have anything to worry about. She'll grow up to be quite extraordinary."

"In time, I am sure…" Lillian whispered."

Jane couldn't resist a yawn. "I guess I am tired. It's been such an enjoyable day I almost forgot my situation."

"What situation is that?" Lillian questioned.

Jane cursed her slip. Carefully, she answered, "Because I'm so far away from home at the moment, that's all."

"You are an interesting woman," Lillian said, squeezing Jane's hands. "I think we are to become dear friends. No, I know we are."

Jane thought so, too.

Mr. Eaton stood and walked to the door. "Shall I show you to your room, Miss Reynolds?"

She shook her head. "I'll find my way."

MAGGIE AND THE OAK TREE

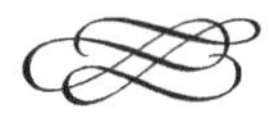

Jane awoke refreshed, encouraging her to get out and start exploring her surroundings in detail. But when she revealed her plans, Mrs. Bishop would have nothing of it. Breakfast was sent to her room, as was the seamstress, Mrs. Hampton. Alterations were on the to-do list and couldn't be put off, Mrs. Bishop said. Jane did not begrudge the order, knowing she needed clothes. But after an hour of poking and prodding–the torment of fitted and formed clothing for women, a knock at the door was welcomed.

"Good morning, Miss Reynolds." Maggie peered her little face through the door. "May I disturb you?"

"Absolutely," Jane replied.

Maggie entered. She did a circle around Jane, admiring her aunt's dress displayed on her before she toured the room. She stopped at the foot of the bed and ran her hands down the fabric of the dresses layered on top of each other awaiting to be altered, and almost sat herself at the window, before choosing to stand behind the seamstress. Mrs. Hampton grunted–a warning to keep her distance, and Maggie stepped back, but not too far, to watch Mrs. Hampton's keen skills transform Jane's shape.

"Father wondered if you slept well. Did you?"

"I did."

"He says you look very different from when he first saw you."

"Really?" Jane could only assume she was the topic of conversation over breakfast.

"Aunt Lillian asked, 'how so?' And Father said you looked 'refreshed.' What does that mean?"

"It means I don't look tired."

"Oh."

She fell silent, her mind churned. "Miss Reynolds?"

"Yes, Maggie?" Jane arched her brow, preparing herself for the girl's unadulterated curiosity.

"Why are not you married?"

Jane coughed a laugh. Another topic she assumed was at the breakfast table. Jane realized she was a spinster to Maggie. Women would be married and have multiple children by Jane's ripe age of twenty-nine. Even in modern times, Jane would be married–should be married–if Stephen hadn't left.

Her heart ached. Not for Stephen's loss, but for the hurt that still resided there.

"Sometimes, it just isn't the right time," she answered, Maggie's wide eye drinking in her explanation.

"Oh," she sighed, not sure what that meant. "Do you want to be married? Because old Miss. Larson, who lives near Aunt Lillian in a big house all by herself, once told me and Isabelle that being married was for foolish girls."

"Well, maybe that's true for some," Jane mused. "But yes, someday I'll marry…if I fall in love."

"Have you ever been in love?"

Jane hesitated. She loved Stephen. But she wondered if she was *in-love* with him. They had been together for so long she never thought to ask the question. When he left, and she found out about his unfaithfulness, she was forced to ask herself truths.

Were Stephen and she meant to be together? Or did he just do what was inevitable?

"Yes, Maggie. I think I was in love, once. But it wasn't forever."

"That seems like an awfully long time–forever and ever. It hurts my head to think about."

"Yes, I guess it is," Jane agreed, wondering if it was even possible to love and be loved that long. Books proclaimed it. Songs were sung about it. But was it real? She wondered.

"I loved someone once. It was Teddy Hamilton, until he pulled my hair and made me cry. That wasn't very nice." She shook her head. "But I'm not *foolish.* I want to marry some day. Father says someone will come along when I am ready. Maybe for you, too."

Jane laughed out loud.

Mrs. Hampton grunted, then asked Jane to turn.

Jane was being fitted into a cream; floral-print dress made of silk challis with an under-layer of muslin. It was a traditional summer style with a piped-seamed bodice, capped sleeves, and a turned-up hem. Jane relished in the intricate details of the fabric covered buttons and satin edged collar. It was pretty, feminine, and although she felt confined in her corset and petticoats underneath, the style was flattering to her silhouette.

"That dress looks nice," Maggie noted. "My mother wore beautiful dresses. Father said one day I may wear them and be a grand lady like my mother."

Jane bent down to Maggie, much to the dismay of Mrs. Hampton. "Was she very beautiful?"

"Oh my, was she!" Maggie's eyes lit up. "She wasn't tall, though–not like you. But she had golden hair and blue, blue eyes. I hope to grow and be just as pretty."

"I think you already are."

Maggie beamed a smile.

"She also had the softest touch. When she rubbed my back,

her hands felt creamy against my skin." Maggie sighed, recalling her mother's touch. "She rubbed her hands with balm to keep them soft. She said the roses were dreadful to them, but they were always soft to me. That's what I remember the most…*miss the most*."

"A mother's touch is always special." Jane sighed for the same reason. She, too, missed her mother's touch.

Mrs. Hampton tugged at the skirt of the dress, prompting Jane to straighten. She obeyed, making a funny face at Maggie.

She laughed.

"Do you like flowers, Miss Reynolds?"

"Who doesn't?"

"Hmmm! One of Father's friends didn't. She said they made her sneeze. Mrs. Bishop had to remove all the vases in the house. I didn't like the flowers gone. They reminded me of my mother."

Jane wondered if that was the reason Mr. Eaton's "friend" had them removed.

Maggie continued, "My mother loved to garden…the blooms, the soil, the worms, the bees. I didn't like the bees. But she would lean into them and tell me, 'Show no fear and they will never sting you.' And they never did! I got to help cut the dead flowers or pick off the old leaves. Then, when we were done, we would sit on the lawn, underneath the big oak tree, and drink lemonade." Maggie paused. "Miss Reynolds?"

Jane cringed in anticipation.

"May I show you my mother's garden?"

A smile widened across Jane's face. "I would like that."

Maggie hopped and squealed.

Mrs. Hampton eyed Jane.

"Not until Mrs. Hampton is done," Jane said, assuring the seamstress she wasn't going anywhere.

"Maybe we can drink some lemonade, too," Maggie

shouted over her shoulder as she ran off to inquire the possibility.

Mrs. Hampton, relieved the intruder was gone, asked Jane to try on another dress. She obliged, promising her complete obedience for the remainder of the task.

"Mrs. Hampton?"

"Yes, Miss," she answered, her lips careful not to move too much or lest she drop the metal pins which delicately balanced on the corner of her mouth.

"About Maggie's mother, when did she pass away?"

She pulled the pins from her mouth, cupping them in her hand. "Oh, she passed a few years ago. She and the baby died of fever. It was a sad day, the loss being so great."

"Maggie had a sibling?"

"Aye, a baby brother. He was a spitting image of his father, with big blue eyes, and yellow curls just like his mother. It nearly killed us all to lose them. May God bless them both."

Jane pondered the significant loss to Maggie and her father. She could understand maybe just a little of the heavy expression that Mr. Eaton held tightly on his face; the protectiveness he commandingly displayed over his family. She realized she was a complete stranger to him, with no one to stand up for her credibility. He had already lost so much in his life.

But in all fairness, he was just as dangerous to her as she to him. She didn't know the people about her and had to rely on her instinct to assess her safety under his care. She wasn't naïve enough to believe men were any less suspect of decency, no matter what year it was. She was still a woman and he a man, and that could always make matters complicated.

They both were on guard.

When Mrs. Hampton finally released her, Jane found Maggie waiting for her at the bottom of the stairs, humming to herself. Maggie slipped her hand into Jane's, as if best friends in a schoolyard, and led her to her mother's sacred rose garden. It was surrounded by an expanse of boxwoods, entered through two large arbors covered in golden yellow roses interweaving the wooden design. They followed a crushed stone pathway that meandered through the varying bushes. The fragrance was overwhelming as they neared the assortment of silken flowers. Maggie pointed out the most fragrant ones, insisting that Jane bend over and take in the tantalizing aromas. Jane had never seen a small child so enthralled in a garden. She watched the animated creature cupping the bowl of a rose, bring it gently to her nose, and succumb to the fragrance. It gave Jane a whole new appreciation for the much-coveted flower.

When they finished their garden exploration, Maggie guided Jane across the lawn to share her favorite space. Jane found herself underneath a giant oak–years in the making–that would have stories to tell if it could speak. Its thick trunk carried long expanses of limbs hovering high above. The round, dark-green leaves filled around the branches, allowing little light or heat to seep through, giving them a reprieve from the sun. It sat high on a small hill and hovered over the great yard of the Eaton estate. Someone had planned the location just so, with a short walk from the main house, but ample distance to get away and ponder the happenings from afar. It was a contemplation point. As they sat underneath the shaded refuge, Maggie chatted endlessly, describing vivid details of her mother, sharing all that she could remember.

Jane realized it was a sacred place for Maggie and her mother. A place they were together forever.

"Isn't this fun?" Maggie asked, wanting Jane to share in her joy.

"Terribly special." She winked in acknowledgment.

Jane leaned against the oak tree, allowing Maggie to place her head in Jane's lap. She stroked the young girl's dark curls, listening to the sounds of the afternoon. Ducks honked in the distance, birds fluttered by, and the sounds of the daily happenings around the house sauntered through the air as the two enjoyed the stillness of the afternoon.

"Do you believe in Heaven?" Maggie asked in a hushed voice.

"I think I do. I hope my parents are there watching over me," Jane replied honestly.

"What do you think it's like?"

Jane's first thought was it must be something just like that moment: peaceful and surrounded by a bounty of trees and flowers. It couldn't be much different. She expressed this to Maggie, who lifted her head, looked around, agreed, and laid her head down again.

"I miss my mother," she sighed.

"I know," Jane whispered.

Maggie sighed deeper, and her eyes drooped, finally shutting. Jane let the girl slumber in her arms, her little body rising and falling in rhythm as she napped. Jane cherished the moment, as if she were sharing it with Maggie's mother, whose arms no longer could cradle her daughter.

From the distance, Mr. Eaton saw the shadow of the figures against the grandeur of the tree. How many times had he looked out to see his wife and daughter so entangled? Maggie rarely visited the spot anymore since the death of her mother. There were times, right after the funeral, when he would find her there, curled up asleep with tear-stained cheeks. But as time moved forward, he found her less and less, until she stopped visiting the once beloved spot altogether. Watching the woman's arms around his daughter, he wondered what Maggie found in Miss Reynolds to share the sacred place with her.

OBSERVATIONS

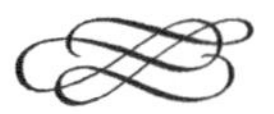

Jane didn't venture off without Lillian and the girls' companionship, nor did they leave her to herself. She wasn't sure if this was Mr. Eaton's way of caring for her or watching her. Either way, it was purposeful. But if she admitted it to herself, she appreciated the personal attention. Exploration of an era gone by, the newness of her surroundings, grasping the unbelievable probability of a time-slip fascinated her, like a little kid exploring Disneyland. Wide-eyed and captivated, fantasy intermixed with reality, excitement, and anxiety on the same side of the coin, her fears hid underneath the surface, only pushed deeper with every turn of a corner. It was not forgotten Peyton warned of limited time. And in the last moments of consciousness, eyelids slammed shut, excitement transformed to exhaustion, Jane's disquietude resurfaced, causing her to worry her stay may be too long. But no sooner had the sun lifted from the horizon, and a new day began, her hunger to see what it brought superseded her fear.

Breakfast started in the Morning Room, or on the terrace, if the weather allowed. A walk in the gardens ensued, and afterwards, the girls went to lessons taught by Mr. Tanenbaum, a local man of strict belief in a well-educated populace. He was a small stature man–almost birdlike, of forty-five, with thinning hair and glasses which magnified his black, beady eyes, grateful for the opportunity after the university fired him because of his inability to discipline young, adolescent boys. More precisely, he was tormented by their constant trickery, causing a breakdown, and eventually his dismissal. Mr. Eaton employed the man, seeing the potential of his education and genteel disposition as a benefit to his daughter. He walked five miles every day to the house, insisting it was good for his digestion, if not good for his character. He would only have to command, "Coming?" and the two girls followed, leaving Jane and Lillian to the household duties.

Contrary to Jane's belief, an estate commanded management. It was similar to running a small hotel with employees, duties, and decisions. Lillian showed Jane the operation of a house its size, its history, and demonstrated the command of it. Although not the mistress of the house, Lillian oversaw its administration while she visited. Jane surmised this was for Maggie's benefit and not a slight of power from her brother.

It was not misconstrued that Mr. Eaton mastered the estate. His presence commanded it. He joined the family in the mornings for breakfast, his steadfast demeanor on display at the head of the table. He was well-mannered, cordial, but did not engage in conversation unless demanded upon, which the girls were careful not to do, gauging his brow, furrowed or straight, and his jaw, clenched or relaxed. A greeting for the morning, or wishes for a pleasant day, was the extent of his sentiments. He read his daily mail as the ladies chatted, his eyes peering from the noted words only to extend thoughts of interests. When his plate was empty and his tea drank, he'd excuse himself for the day where they wouldn't see him again until the evening.

He'd dressed for dinner in a fresh suit and waited with a

drink in hand, immersed in the newspaper, as Lillian was almost never punctual. She would make her excuses, which he accepted with cordiality, but Jane saw his jaw harden at her dismissiveness for his need of punctuality. During dinner, conversations entailed activities the girls took part, for which each had to report to him as a means of their continued lesson plan. Lillian corrected grammatical errors, of which there were hardly any, or asked for more details, if too few were given. Mr. Eaton reciprocated with reports involving the neighbors and their affairs, surprising Jane that he shared business matters with Lillian, and for which she was well versed.

After dessert, which always followed dinner to Jane's delight, they retreated to the parlor where the usual routine proceeded: Maggie drew, Isabelle played the pianoforte, Lillian busied herself with needlework, and Mr. Eaton read. Jane learned the skills of knitting, which Lillian eagerly instructed. The household, with its inhabitants, had a harmony, and Jane somehow found a place in it.

Mr. Eaton did not actively engage in conversation with Jane, easing her fear she would have to lie to him. If they passed each other throughout the day, he would catch her eyes, nod, and pass. Occasionally, Jane looked back, but never caught him doing the same. She was never more grateful he was aloof, if not indifferent to her presence. He kept his distance, leaving Jane's care to others. There was interest in her by other means–gossip, inquisitions to staff, and feigned interest via questions to his sister. But in his company, she was just another female in the room. So, it came as a surprise, the night before Lillian and the girls were to depart, he moved from his corner chair and purposely planted himself within conversational distance.

"Miss Reynolds," he leaned forward, "I hope my sister properly engaged you these last few days. It was my desire to make you feel at ease in our presence."

Jane offered him a smile, which he did not reciprocate, and

nodded. "Lillian has been great…and the girls. I've enjoyed our time together. There's so much to learn, especially about your heritage. You have quite a regal legacy."

"Legacy? Yes. Regal, no," he mused. "I have no doubt Lillian did not skip the not-so-regal relatives." His eyebrow reared upward towards his sister.

"Oh, Henry, what is the fun of family if you can't indulge in the scandals?" Lillian smirked.

"Father used to say, with great honor comes scandal, the two forever linked. It is God's way of balancing life."

His eyes met Jane's, curious if honor tied to the other side of her scandal.

Jane wanted to satisfy his curiosity and searched the annals of her meager wisdom to match his sagacity. "Yin and yang," she said. "Weakness encourages strength. Fear develops courage. Happiness arises from sadness."

"Exactly," he said, her thoughts mirroring his own. "Tell us, Miss Reynolds, there must be more to you than the fascination of the mundane lives of the Eaton legacy."

Jane worked a lot. And when she wasn't working, she window shopped–for work. Visited museums–for work. Browsed antique stores–for work. Read historical books–for work. The Eaton Estate was a theme park of interest for her. But he wasn't asking about her work, or her interests. He sought more personal information. Who is Jane Reynolds? After Stephen, the question became elusive. How did she let him into her world without knowing herself?

She deflected. "There is nothing special about me."

Lillian scoffed. "I have found you anything but boring, my dear. But that is because you are such a good listener. My brother knows I adore an audience." She grinned, arresting her brother's ridicule.

To Jane's surprise, amusement crossed Mr. Eaton's face. "It is one of your many qualities, dear sister."

Lillian tipped her head to her brother. "Actually, it has been quite enjoyable to share our family history. I have forgotten all the memories here…" Lillian looked around the room. "It seems so long ago when we were all together. Mother and father. The parties and holidays. The happiness…" She paused. "Maybe it takes a newcomer to remind us how fortunate we are to have so much to remember, which makes life full."

Mr. Eaton knitted his brow. "I suppose it does."

The two siblings looked at each other with an understanding.

Jane felt the fraud. "You give me too much credit."

"Nonsense. You have given us a renewal. I don't recall the household so alive. Mrs. Bishop has rediscovered her purpose. I heard her humming in the halls. She hasn't done that since…" Lillian paused, in remembrance of whom Jane did not know. "And Cook! Grumpy, old Cook. When you expressed interests in the kitchen, I nearly froze. The woman permits no one in her space. But she stopped her baking to give you a tour. The last time I disturbed Cook, she threw me out."

"That is because you have no interest in what goes on there," Mr. Eaton said. "But I assure you, the fascination will soon be exhausted as the novelty fades, and Miss Reynolds becomes bored with the house and us."

"Oh Henry, you are such a man of practicality," Lillian scoffed.

Objecting to his sister's criticism, he countered, "Practicality is always a wise perspective, Lillian. It keeps things orderly and without surprise."

"Would it surprise you someone discovers this household and its inhabitants to be of interest?" She questioned, with innuendo. "Order and calm. Is that how you plan to live out your days? That sounds dreadfully lonely."

A flush of color surfaced in Mr. Eaton's face. His jaw clenched, and his shoulders stiffened.

Lillian did not let up on her brother. "You need an education about the passion of life, Henry. Where would we all be if we lived life so carefully? You and I would not exist if Father did not let his guard down and throw caution to the wind."

"The key word is caution, dear sister. Caution has its purpose. Frivolity is only enjoyed in the essence of a careful and planned existence," he debated, with a demeanor of propriety. "Otherwise, chaos ensues, and where does one find happiness in that?"

"Sometimes, happiness is just in the moments, adrift in the chaos, to remind us to have faith, and discover more exists; that the impossible is possible if one reaches for it."

A silence fell between them. Jane shifted in her seat. She looked around for the girls, who were gone. They snuck out long before the two siblings began to argue.

Abruptly, Mr. Eaton rose from his chair. "I have things I must attend to before I retire."

"We are set to leave late morning, Henry," Lillian called after him. "You better not head out too early. You will bid us farewell?"

"Of course. I will see you off." He bowed and departed.

Jane listened to the rhythmic thunk-tap of his shoes climb the stairs. A door creaked and shut. Silence.

Lillian shook her head. "What hubris! So much like my father," she uttered.

"Do you really have to go?" Jane already mourned her friend's departure the next day.

"I am afraid duty calls. Mr. Levongood is a dear husband, but if I leave him to the duties of greeting a house full of guests we expect in a few days, his patience will not hold. You will have to convince Dr. Cummings to join us. It would be my honor to have you both."

Dr. Cummings's plan did not include for Jane to leave the

Eaton Estate. And the only place she really wanted to go was home.

"Wouldn't that be nice." It was all Jane could offer.

"I don't want you lonely after we depart. There is much to keep you preoccupied here until Dr. Cummings returns. Henry will see to it."

Jane attempted a smile but worry halted the completion.

Lillian squeezed Jane's hand. "Don't worry about my brother. He has demons to bear. Be yourself, Jane. You are a lovely woman, and he would be a fool not to notice."

AWAKENINGS

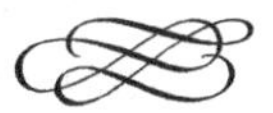

Commotion cluttered the halls as the household staff prepared for the departure of Lillian and the girls. All of London expected Lillian to entertain for the summer, or until it got too hot, whereby everyone would leave for a seaside excursion or foreign travels. She hadn't planned the trip with her brother, but when he requested that she return with him to the Eaton Estate, she perceived an urgency. She obliged; with the understanding it would be a brief interlude. But after meeting Jane, she postponed her obligations in London. The request by her brother became an opportunity to develop a new friendship. Unfortunately, her social duties called her back and she could not prolong the inevitable.

She and the girls left early afternoon with as much ceremony as they arrived: a hustle of the staff carrying luggage, loading the carriage, and storing food baskets under the seats. Maggie, along with encouraging Isabelle, ran around with the gardener's dog while Mrs. Bishop directed where things should be properly placed. Mr. Eaton only entered the scene when all was settled, and the girls stood by the door to say their goodbyes.

Isabelle put her arms around Jane and hugged her with urgency, then swiftly disappeared as to not display unnecessary emotion. Maggie fell into Jane's arms and squeezed her so tight she almost knocked the wind out of her. Jane's tears finally came when Lillian didn't hold back her own, and the two women hugged twice before Lillian let go.

Once the carriage pulled away, the staff immediately dispersed, eager to return to their regular daily duties. Guest were a blessing only because they broke the monotony but allowed for little spare time in their schedules. Their goodbyes were for duty only.

Jane lingered. She waved her last goodbye when she no longer saw the carriage in the distance, with the probability she may never see Lillian and the girls again. A swell of emptiness unexpectedly pulled at her heart. She had spent only a short time with them, but it felt like a lifetime. As she turned back toward the house, she became acutely aware of how time was a precarious element of her reality. Time passed neither quickly nor slowly. A week and a half had gone by, yet it seemed like a lifetime. She wondered what it meant for her return.

The clouds never lifted from the morning, settling a haze in the air. It was as if Mother Nature sensed the mood of the events and responded to Jane's emotions. She sauntered to the parlor to find solace in the lingering energy of her departed companions. Eyeing Mr. Eaton's empty chair, she plopped herself on the seat and curled her legs underneath the layers of her dress. She felt naughty for inhabiting his prized possession, but as her body sank into the softness the cushion offered, she did not regret it.

It is where she discovered his little secret.

Thinking him uninterested when he sat in the shadowed corner most evenings, he watched Isabelle's hand glide smoothly across the piano keys, viewed the concentration on Maggie's face as she drew the pictures from her imagination, and studied his sister's quiet contemplation about her day while she knitted. Jane saw from his chair, perfectly situated, he was involved in their lives, watching over them. She mentally scolded herself for the misconception of his aloofness.

Jane preoccupied the rest of her afternoon practicing her newly learned knitting skills. She was proud of her accomplishments, but worried without Lillian to peer over her shoulder, mistakes were inevitable. She noticed the quiet of the house. Eerily empty. The only sound was the clink of her needles as she looped and pulled the yarn from one side to the next.

Heavy steps came down the hall and stopped at the parlor. Jane waited for whomever lingered to enter. But minutes went by and still the door stayed closed. The steps retreated.

Whoever it was, they decided to return, and the door swung open.

"It is cold in here. You need more wood on the fire." Mr. Eaton's voice echoed from the door, his stature filling the frame.

Jane startled, the deep resonance shattering the quietude. "Yes, it is. Surprisingly chilly for June."

"I'm afraid an English summer will disappoint you. The warmer weather will not arrive for a few more weeks. These walls keep it downright cold in here." He walked to the fireplace and added a few logs. He rested his elbow on the mantle and leaned forward. "I see you have taken to Lillian's pastime."

Jane lifted the needles with the yarn dangling from her lap. "From the lack of skill, I don't think the shawl I'm knitting will be any use to me, or anyone. I insisted on starting small, like a scarf, but Lillian had higher aspirations for me."

"Lillian is very gifted."

"Yes," Jane sighed, "Unfortunately, she left me to fend for myself."

"Lillian–always the optimist. Your enthusiasm only inspired

her more, never releasing you from her instruction. You delighted her."

Jane hadn't thought about how she might have affected Lillian. Instead, it was she who brought her so much happiness…and distraction. With Mr. Eaton, his stature hovering over her, she worried about her replacement.

Jane grimaced. "I may curse her name with every loop, but she gave me something to do while alone."

"Hmm," he sighed, picking up the poker and pushed around the burning logs. With a house full of staff, and himself as host, she was far from *alone.* He wondered if it was more a commentary of her situation–the circumstances for which he was uninformed. He had not heard from his friend, Dr. Cummings, and thus he was still in the dark about the guest who remained in his home. He had to admit, there was nothing she had done to concern him. Her presence was unfamiliar, but she was intriguing all the same. That he could not deny. It was obvious she was well educated, not lacking the ability to converse on many topics. Her manner was polite and mood congenial. But there was a strength she exuded at odds with her femininity. It's not as if she was rude, offensive, or even brazen, and therefore he could not find fault with her peculiarity. But the positive effects she had on his family were commendable.

Lightning flashed across the darkening sky.

"It seems the weather is worsening. I'm afraid you will not have the opportunity to explore more of the grounds today."

Jane pulled herself away from knitting and looked out the window. "I don't mind rain. I actually enjoy walking in it, smelling the cleansing. But the mist is thick. Almost ominous."

"Yes. We get them in the summer. The pull of the moon drags out the demons sometimes. We have wild winds, and then the rains come, even after a lovely day of sunshine. Be careful of the black clouds in the distant. I wouldn't want you to get caught in a downpour."

"No. Neither would I." Jane shivered, all too familiar with roaming the Eaton Estate and getting caught in a storm.

Mr. Eaton walked to the windows overlooking the lawns and peered at the darkened skies above. Another light streaked across the sky. Thunder roared, and the rain began. Pellets of water pounded the rooftop. Eventually, it softened to a pitter patter, creating a meditative rainfall. He lingered at the window, a shadowed figure against the wet and dreary background. When he turned, his eyes fell upon Jane, her eyes intent, her lips mouthing the movement of her hands, *insert, loop under, pull through.* He found it peculiar she chose his chair to find reprieve. He never claimed it as his, but no one else dared climb into it. She seemed at ease in his surroundings. He did not know if this was her own assuredness or his hospitality. Either way, he found it notable.

Jane felt his eyes on her but dare not lift her head for fear he wanted to talk. She didn't.

"I am bothering you," he said. "You were intent on knitting."

"Yes…I mean, no." Her brow crunched. "I mean, you don't need to leave on my account."

"You dishonor my intentions. I am happy to oblige if you wish for privacy." He tugged at his sleeves, pulled at his collar. With Lillian's departure, he was uncertain how to fill the role as host. His staff could tend to the needs of guests, but he was unsure about his own abilities to entertain a woman properly. *Again.* He thought it was prudent to invite his sister to care for her, make her feel comfortable in his home. He hadn't needed Dr. Cummings to suggest it! But he could see he was failing at his duty. "This is a big house, plenty of room for me and my guests. You are certainly welcome anywhere. I have many other rooms to occupy myself without disturbing you." He tipped his head. "I apologize for the intrusion."

"I'm the last person to ask anything of you, Mr. Eaton. This is your house..." Jane abruptly rose from his prized possession. "This is your chair. I didn't mean to intrude."

To her surprise, the corner of his lips curled up, and his eyes crinkled at the ends. He had the same long lashes as Maggie. Dark and curled. But she did not inherit the same dark blue eyes. A log dropped, causing him to turn. The firelight danced across his face, shadowing his chiseled jawline, highlighting the cleft of his chin. He was *tall, dark, and handsome* to Stephen's blonde hair, sun-tanned skin, and lean surfer physique. The two men couldn't be more different, yet she was attracted all the same.

"Quite the contrary. You are a guest of mine, and I have made you feel otherwise. My attempt at being a suitable host has been strewn with blunders. My sister would be ashamed, indeed. Please." He reached out and touched Jane's arm. "You dishonor me if you do not stay."

As if his touch willed it, Jane fell back into the chair.

"Good day, Miss Reynolds."

She insulted him, scared him away, or both. Whatever the reason, he was leaving, and she felt confused by what was transpiring. She called after him.

"Mr. Eaton!"

He turned and his eyes met hers. His seemed bluer, softer–less stormy. Hers were dark, wide–blustery.

"If I could tell you..." She bit her lip. So much wanted to come out of her, but she was forbidden. "You didn't ask for this–for me. I hate to think I am causing you to feel uncomfortable in your home. I'm sorry for that."

He wasn't sorry. He felt the loss of his sister's company, and the exuberance of the girls. Days were long; nights even longer by himself. He had forgotten what it was like to surround himself with loved ones. With their departure, he had a consolation–Jane's continuing presence.

"Have dinner with me."

Jane scrunched her brow. "Huh?"

"Although not as entertaining as my sister, my daughter, or niece, I hope you will join me for dinner. We can talk more, and you can have your afternoon, alone."

Jane smiled. "I would like that."

"Very good. I will notify Mrs. Bishop to send tea. Please enjoy your afternoon, rain and all." He bowed his head and retreated.

Had she turned, Jane would have seen him looking back at her.

Jane wasn't sure when she fell asleep, but when Mrs. Bishop nudged her, she realized the day transpired into evening. The fire embers smoldered, emitting a golden haze throughout the darkened room. The heavy mist thickened outside, and rain continued. Dampness crept into Jane's bones, her fingers and toes turning into icicles. Mrs. Bishop sent her upstairs with orders to the staff to draw her a bath.

Jane sunk into the sultry hot fluid and indulged in the luxury. Regina placed lavender flowers on the top, filling her nostrils with sweet floral and herb scents. It reminded her of the daily lotion she slathered all over her body after a shower, a mixture of lavender, citrus and orange blossoms, taking her back home, if only for a few moments granted in the bath. When the last remnants of the warmth dissipated, she braved the chilly air and wrapped herself up in a robe. She tried to dry her hair by the fire, but the attempt only created a droopy mess. She prayed Regina was capable of a miracle.

"Oh Miss, you look beautiful." Regina handed Jane a mirror.

"How did you do that?" Jane praised the girl for the upswept hairstyle.

"Mr. Eaton will be very impressed."

"I'm not trying to impress Mr. Eaton," Jane insisted, unsure of her motivation. "I just don't want to offend my host looking like a wet dog. That's all."

Regina giggled. "It must be a sickness in the house, then."

"What is?"

"Mr. Eaton requested a bath as well."

DINNER WITHOUT FRIENDS

Mr. Eaton glanced at his watch when Jane entered the dining room. Seeing her, he quickly stuffed it into his pocket.

She was on time.

"Good evening, Miss Reynolds." He pulled out a chair and gestured for her to sit.

Jane smelled of lavender with a dash of rose oil behind her ear, which Regina suggested, while wool, sage, and leather blended with his pheromones. With her olfactory prompted, she breathed him in, indulging in the intrinsic smell of a man. Heat flashed through her, and she pressed her cold palms against her cheeks, praying the candlelight hid the effect it had on her.

There was no change in Mr. Eaton's expression to indicate he noticed the flush on her face. Likely, even if he had, his disposition, which Jane categorized as *calm, cool, and collected,* prohibited him from showing any rouse of emotion.

Freshly shaved–no stubbles dared show themselves, Mr. Eaton changed into a navy woolen suit with a crisp white shirt and cravat tied in a bow. His waistcoat, hidden but for the collar, had a fanciful pattern of latticed feathers, the hue of plum. An ornate upgrade from the tan cotton waistcoat he wore earlier, underneath a brown coat and tan pants to match. With his back pressed straight against his chair, bathed, shaved, hair combed, clothes pressed, and if Jane peered under the table, shoes shined, he modeled the epitome of a gentleman. He oozed refinement, and Jane worried she lacked the gentility or polish needed in his company.

While Lillian hosted, Jane called upon the etiquette skills taught by her mother, only to be interrupted upon her death. Her uncle continued the education of manners for a lady, of what he could impart, along with the help of the ladies from the small farm community she was raised. But she discovered modern etiquette did not mirror English refinement. She shadowed Lillian's behavior to the best of her abilities to learn what she lacked. Now alone, no longer in the shadow of an English gentlewoman, she was put to the test. She only hoped she could pass Mr. Eaton's standards for a lady.

Jane placed the napkin on her lap and heightened her stature against the chair.

"Thank you for asking me to eat with you tonight. I wasn't sure if we'd still formally dine together with Lillian and the girls gone."

"But as usual..." he replied, assuring his etiquette was commonplace.

Mr. Eaton offered her a glass of wine. She nodded and raised her glass, her fingers strangulating the stem as he poured the red liquid. She would have preferred a shot of Tequila...or something that would mollify her nerves faster, reneging her earlier anticipation, but wine would suffice.

Mr. Eaton gave the signal and dinner was served.

"I beg your pardon if I fumbled earlier today. I relied on my wife to be the charming hostess of guests." He cleared his throat. "My sister is quite the conversationalist, begging me to admit I allow her to compensate for my weaknesses. I hope you do not find me disappointing."

"I'm not good at this, either," she admitted. "And it would be a lie to say Lillian didn't ease our situation." When he raised his brow, she added, "You're doing just fine."

Color flushed his face and the corner of his lips moved upward; a spark of light surfaced from the depth of his eyes before it was gone. He pulled his fingers through his hair, pushing back a curl which fell loose upon his forehead, regaining his slip of composure.

"My sister is charming," he confessed, "but can be exhausting."

"Not to me." Jane felt an urge to defend her newfound friend.

"No, of course not," he tried to take back his sentiment. "She is an excellent woman. I would be lost without her, for many reasons. She has taken on the responsibility of my daughter as if Maggie were her own. I could not be more grateful for her guidance and nurturing. Lillian does her best with her."

"Oh, you have no reason to worry about Maggie. She's bright, imaginative, and extremely loving…everything you could want in a child."

"That is not my doing. I am merely a man with little ability to tend to a child," he commiserated. "Let alone a daughter."

"You give yourself little credit, Mr. Eaton. A father's influence is vital to a daughter. There are great things you can teach her. Although I didn't have my father for long, my uncle equally filled the roll and was extremely influential in the person I've become. That kind of love is not easily replaced."

"It was only your uncle who raised you?"

"Yes. Unfortunately, his wife, my aunt, died leaving him alone. When I was orphaned, after my parents died, I moved in with him, and both our lives were forever entwined. He was good for me…"

"And you were good for him."

Jane nodded. "Yes, we completed the circle for both of us."

"Is he no longer alive?"

Jane shook her head.

"I am sorry to hear that."

"Me, too. So, you see, a father's influence and love are cherished, even if you can't see it now. And Maggie has the blessing of her aunt to balance out what you cannot provide–a woman's influence."

"A blessing and a curse." He smirked. "I admit, Lillian's modeling benefits my daughter, but she gives Maggie allowances I would not afford. And gives Maggie confidence to be…"

"Independent?" Jane interjected.

"Yes. I was going to say, unbridled. My sister is much like my mother: eager, passionate, strong-willed, and independent. Lillian is passing on those traits."

"You know, where I come from, women are encouraged to become free thinkers and doers."

His eyes narrowed. Although he found it quite attractive in the woman he was sitting next to, he wondered if this was a quality he wanted for his own daughter.

Jane added, "Life in America isn't as civilized as you are accustomed. Men and women must develop equally if they want to survive the rat race. It's not a bad thing."

"Hmm." He sipped his wine. "I see my daughter for the unique individual she is. Maggie has a heart of my wife, the spirit of my mother, and the will of Lillian. My sister is developing what is only inherently in our bloodline. But in a more civilized world, her freedom to entertain those qualities may not suit her in matrimonial pursuits." He hastened to add,

"I am confident my sister is preparing her for what is her proper place."

Jane crossed her arms. She wanted to argue his exceedingly barbaric idea to marry his daughter as the end of all ends, but Dr. Cummings's words rang in her ears.

Watch your step. Observe. Blend.

"And you, Mr. Eaton? Whom do you take after, your father or mother?"

"My sister would eagerly reply, my old, stuffy grandfather," he mused.

Jane couldn't disagree. Mr. Eaton was not old, with no more than a few years separating them. But his heavy brow, along with his guarded manner, were halting. He was careful in his expression; determined in his actions. His thoughts were controlled, his words careful. He walked strong, allowing little room for fault, if no time for frivolities. His youthful exterior was but a cover of the aged soul that resided inside.

He noted her silence. "You agree with my sister, then?"

"No," she lied. "Who am I to judge. I don't know anything about you."

"Nor I."

His eyes met hers.

"I know there's much you want to know about me." She encouraged him, not knowing how far he would push for answers. "Ask me. I will answer whatever I can."

His eyes widened at the dare. "Who's Stephen?"

"What?" she squeaked. "I mean, you want to know about Stephen?"

"I am too bold."

"No, of course not. It's a fair question."

"You called his name when I found you, and I wondered..."

"Stephen was my fiancé." Her voice softened to a whisper. "Not anymore."

“I did not mean to pry. I promised Dr. Cummings I wouldn’t invade your private affairs and now I see why.”

"You’re not intruding. Your question surprised me, that’s all. If you must know, he called off the engagement months ago, and I only recently discovered why.”

“I’m sorry he did not honor his commitment. You seem like a respectable woman. He should not have been so careless of that.”

He leaned forward, and she saw his own sadness staring back at her, inviting her to trust him with her truth.

“It wasn’t I with whom he had to be honorable.” Her eyes narrowed. “He is marrying the woman pregnant with his child.”

He cleared his throat. “Oh, I see.”

“I’m still trying to understand; to give purpose to it.”

Jane paused in thought–lots of thoughts. The seven years she spent with Stephen flashed before her in milliseconds, images of their past imbedded in her brain. As the memories slowed and the last picture of Stephen was him turning the corner with another woman, she returned to the man in front of her.

“Is it too scandalous?”

“Maybe he is doing what he thinks most honorable. After all, there is a child involved.”

“You can’t be serious!” Jane bellowed. “Honorable to him. But what about me?”

“My mother used to tell me, in all tragedy lies a hidden blessing. We are not always granted happiness, but as long as we breathe, we are promised more to come. What we seek is up to us. For through the harshness of winter, does the beauty of spring find its way.”

“Is that your poetic way of saying I am the maker of my own destiny? Because I didn’t ask for Stephen to leave me.”

"It seems you have little faith in destiny," he said, unsure if he was a victim of the same belief.

"It's not faith I'm lacking. It's a man's ability to love." Jane lowered her eyes; her lips flatlined.

Mr. Eaton looked at the woman next to him, her dark eyes shadowed by the long lashes hugging the curve of her lids, wanting to understand how the softness of her face could hide the hardness in her heart.

"Have faith, Miss Reynolds. Better things await you. There are many fine men who will not judge you for your circumstances."

"My circumstances?" Jane balked. "Mr. Eaton, if you are insinuating I should be ashamed by what happened…"

"I meant nothing of the sorts," he quickly defended.

A silence fell between them.

Jane wanted to flee. She rubbed her temples, feigning a headache.

"If you wouldn't mind, I think it's best if I turn in for the evening."

Mr. Eaton stood. "I've insulted you. I apologize."

Jane held her tongue. "Thank you for the invitation. Good evening, Mr. Eaton."

He walked Jane to the door, allowing her to escape. He'd hope she'd look back…a second chance to apologize. She didn't.

He retreated to the study, poured himself a drink, and found his usual spot–a red velvet Fauteuil chair, with a table next to it to hold his drink. He reached for his book, but the words blurred in front of him. The silence was deafening. The last week had reminded him how nice it was to have women in the house again. More to the point, it was Jane who was most pleasant, and yet all she wanted to do was escape him. He shook his head, cursing his foolishness, and swallowed the last of his whiskey before he withdrew to his bedroom for the night.

MR. ABBET

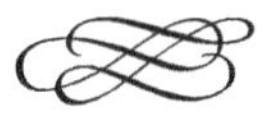

Regina found Jane sitting on the bed, her arms wrapped around her knees, tucked under her night clothes. She pulled the drapes aside and opened the window.

"Lovely day, isn't it?"

Jane didn't answer.

"Did you have a pleasant time with Master Eaton?"

"Don't ask," Jane barked, still harboring anger about the antiquated conversation with Mr. Eaton the night before.

"Aye."

"I'm sorry, Regina. That wasn't meant for you."

"Aye," Regina repeated.

Jane wanted to say more. *Men! Arrogant, self-centered, righteous, men!* But she didn't. She wasn't sure her anger was towards Mr. Eaton or Stephen. Maybe both. Maybe neither. She couldn't tell. Sleep didn't help clarify. The anxiety returned. Thoughts of doom and dread spiraled into a sleepless night.

Someone knocked, and Regina raced to the door to answer it, then stepped aside.

"Mr. Eaton!" Jane stood and clasped at her robe. He was

the last person she expected to see. The last person she wanted to see at her door.

"Miss Reynolds, excuse the interruption." He did not miss her hair down, falling along her shoulders, one side tucked behind her ear, still in her bed clothes. "I believed the news too urgent to wait. Dr. Cummings sends his regards and enquires if you are being properly tended to." He did not wait for confirmation or denial. "He wanted to inform you Mrs. Muldoon has come through. He is on his way to London to investigate further. He will fill you in on the details when he returns."

Overjoyed with the news, Jane rushed towards Mr. Eaton and spontaneously threw her arms around him. "That's terrific news. Maybe I'm not lost here after all!"

His body stiffened, prompting Jane to step back, all too aware of her faux pas, allowing for his retreat.

He didn't.

"I am afraid my hospitality duties, once again, fall short. I have some business to attend. As it is a lovely morning, I encourage you to explore where you like." He added, "I would hate for the day to go wasted."

Jane nodded. "Thank you, I will."

"Good day, Miss, Reynolds." He turned to leave but looked back. "It is nice to see you so happy, even it means you soon will leave here."

Regina didn't miss his implication, nor Jane's tilted head and open mouth.

"Maybe your evening went well after all," she giggled.

Jane shook her head. Not in disagreement, but to clear the confusion of feelings running through her mind.

She put up her hand. "Don't say another word!"

"Aye."

~

The news from Dr. Cummings put a spring in Jane's step, or that's whom she gave credit. She needed a sign to keep her going–to believe home was possible. After stuffing down warm rolls and fresh preserves, Jane took Mr. Eaton's suggestion. Two steps out the door, she shielded her eyes from the glare of the light bouncing off the watered landscape; colors illuminated. Puffy clouds floated in the blue canvas above, and birds sang to one another across the trees. The rain bath from the day before brought an earthy aroma which permeated from the soil. She inhaled with rapture. They were signs of a good omen, or at least, she hoped.

A short-haired Beagle bound up to greet Jane. His name was Oscar, the gardener's dog. They met the day she toured the gardens with Maggie and became instant friends. She bent and patted his head. In return, he licked her hand. He waddled away, but half-way across the lawn, looked back at Jane to follow. Out of curiosity, she did. He led her to a weathered grey structure with a slatted shingled roof and black, peeling-painted shutters. The dog barked at the door, alerting Jane of his wish. She dragged the crooked, dry-rotted panel across stones, inching it open. The dog crept inside, settling himself up against the wall. He walked in a circle three times before he plopped himself down.

The shed structure housed an assortment of garden paraphernalia. It was dark and cool inside, decorated in cobwebs along the roofline and across the shelves. The sun filtered through the slats of the shutters, filling the cavernous space with dusty rays of light. As Jane ventured deeper, she tripped over a stone, grabbing onto a shelf to catch her fall. But not before a thick sliver of wood slid its way into her finger. She yelped. The dog lifted his head, but sensing no great threat, tucked his nose back into position next to his feet.

"Miss, you alright?"

Jane startled at the thick Yorkshire accent.

A silhouette stood in the doorway, blocking the light. He stood as tall as Jane's shoulders, a boy-like stature contradicting his wrinkled face. She splayed her hand with the protruding wood now throbbing in pain. He walked further into the shed and placed tools on a shelf, freeing his hands. He wiped them against his apron and gestured for Jane to move forward into the light.

"May I look at that for you?" the man asked. With her approval, he cradled her hand and quickly tugged at the piece of wood. A pillow of blood bubbled, and Jane brought her finger to her mouth.

He took a handkerchief from his back pocket and carefully wrapped it around her bleeding finger.

"Be careful roaming by yourself. Dangers lurk when you least expect them."

"Thank you," Jane said, grateful for the aid. "I apologize for intruding. The dog led me here. I was curious about what lay inside. I hope you don't mind, Mr…"

"Abbet, Nicholas Abbet. I'm the head man here."

She squinted at the vastness before her. "You take care of all of this property?"

"Well, I'd not take all the credit. There is only so much these old hands can do any longer. I have men about. I give them the heavy things and save my time for the details," he confessed.

"God is in the details," Jane murmured.

He smiled, a missing front tooth for all to see. "That He is! But it's not I alone who strives for such beauty. It's the master's attention to his land, and his father before him, that makes these grounds magical."

"Magical?"

"Aye. There is a special energy that lies about. Old Master Eaton talked of it the moment he stepped on the land. A vast wasteland of death and decay back then. He said to me, 'If not for the grace of God, I would not be one with the earth as I am here.' He felt purpose here, as I do, to bring forth the beauty you see. It was he who showed me how to caress the branches of the fresh growth, and cup the softness of a new petal. Nature speaks if you listen. Old Master Eaton taught me that long ago. I was a young lad then. Can't say I would've wanted anything more of life."

"Mr. Eaton owes you much appreciation."

"Aye, he's a good man. Knows the labor of the soil. It is he who contours much of the garden you see close to the house, none too proud to indulge in hard work."

"I'm sure he's extremely proud, endowed with such property," Jane said, a little circumspect at Mr. Eaton's egalitarian leanings. He was a man of wealth, land, and power. The people who worked for him, who tended to the surrounding farms, were under his control, as well as his political preference. Jane didn't mistake his ulterior motives were for his own gains.

"It's more than that, Miss. His lovely wife, God bless her soul, loved this land. Tended her flowers until her hands were raw. It was a gift she had–creating beauty. A destiny of her own, I suppose. After her passing, Master Eaton took over in homage to her. I've seen him spend hours trimming those hydrangeas she adored." He pointed towards the house. "There, on the other side of the wall. The way they bloom, arising in front of the outside court, is no mistake. It's personal to him."

"Yes, they're breathtaking," Jane knew exactly what he was referring to. She had noted the emerging pink flowers growing through the balustrades, early blooms clustering on top of the bushes. It was at breakfast her first morning with Lillian, where they sat under the branches of an old elm offering them shade from the morning sun, she noted how well the plants grew underneath the shadowy leaves.

Jane knew with certainty his accomplishments would live

well after his own life, having experienced the awe of seeing it for the first time when she came over the hill and laid her eyes on the estate the day she arrived with Amy.

"Mr. Abbet," she reached forward and touched his hand, "your hard work, the love for this land, will forever be honored. I guarantee it."

He did not pull away but put his hand on top of hers. "Thank you, Miss. You are more than kind, indeed. You've made an old man feel worthy." He grabbed his tools from the shelf, nudged the dog to move from the shed, and closed the door behind him. "Have a good day, Miss."

He headed down the lawn, the dog sauntering behind him.

"Mr. Abbet!" Jane waved his handkerchief in the air. "You forgot…"

It was too late. He was gone, as was the dog, leaving Jane to herself.

When Jane returned to her room, she found Mrs. Bishop placing a bouquet of flowers by her bedside.

"Those are beautiful! Are they from Mr. Abbet?"

"No, Miss. Mr. Eaton sent them up."

Jane's eyes widened. "For me?"

"Aye. Picked them himself. Along with flowers for the whole house!" She griped. "I've been arranging flowers all day…He ordered a bowl in the drawing room, parlor, library…even in his gentlemen's room. Haven't seen the likes of this since…well, never mind." She wiped her hands down her apron. "It's just nice to see life back in the house. Oh, I can't forget, Mr. Eaton's asked if you'd join him, with his neighbor, for tea. Said something about making up for his blunder."

A smile spread across Jane's face. "Yes!" She said a little too quickly; a little too enthusiastically. She tried again, more restrained. "I mean, tell Mr. Eaton I would be happy to join him."

Mrs. Bishop didn't need an answer. She was already at the armoire, pulling a dress to change into.

MR. HODGES

Jane heard voices come from the study. She cautiously peered through the open door, not wanting to intrude on the debate inside.

"Miss Reynolds, please come in." Mr. Eaton motioned to her. "May I introduce Mr. Hodges."

A gawky, pasty man stepped forward to greet Jane. He took her hand she offered and bowed. "Miss Reynolds. I heard the rumblings of a stranger in our parts. Some as elaborate as proclaiming you fell from the sky. But I can see for myself, you are no more than a mere woman."

Jane feigned a smile before rescinding her hand from his grasp as quickly as was polite. His clasp was clammy, and he held hers like she was a frail china figurine. She stepped back, but his droopy eyes didn't leave her. Instead, he languidly ogled her, stripping her clothes piece by piece. He lifted his head and fluttered his lids twice before he gave her a smile.

Jane wanted to punch him, or vomit. Both would have given her satisfaction. Instead, she turned her back, getting as much distance from him as the room would allow.

"We were discussing some issues about the current strife

among some landowners," Mr. Eaton said. "Mr. Hodges and I seem to be at odds."

"Now Henry, I am sure this lovely woman would not want to fill her head with such mischief."

Jane turned. "Quite the contrary, Mr. Hodges. But don't let my presence interfere with your business. Please continue."

Mr. Eaton cleared his throat. "Well, yes." He turned to Mr. Hodges. "Tobias, you cannot stop men from wanting a voice in their livelihood. A man must have a means to better himself. He needs control of his destiny and the power to make a good life for his family. It's a natural course to want to be more involved in how you are governed."

"But my dear man, if they gain control, who knows where we will end up. They are not educated. Few men have the moral fortitude, let alone the understanding of what is best for them," Mr. Hodges countered.

"Times are changing. The way we have managed our properties will have to be reassessed, no doubt. These people want some say in how they are represented. That does not sound unreasonable."

"I think I know what is fair and best for all concerned about my land and the people on it," Mr. Hodges argued.

"They are not children." Jane interjected, unable to hold her tongue.

Mr. Hodges cocked his head and pursed his lips. His lids fluttered twice again before he released his pucker to speak. "Excuse me, my dear?"

"The men you are referring to…they may not be formally educated, but they have a vested interest in how they are governed. Everyone deserves that. They pay taxes just like the rest of you and should have a say on the rules and regulation that will benefit or take away from their livelihood."

"Hmph!" Mr. Hodges turned his nose up. "You have much to say for a woman."

"And why shouldn't I, as a woman?" Jane's eyes narrowed.

"These are concerns for men to worry about. You have much more to preoccupy yourself than the ramblings of a misguided group of men who are not thinking about the general good of society but are out to wreak havoc. I fear you hold the common man up to a higher standard than he holds himself. The reality is that few men have the capability of understanding what is best for them," Mr. Hodges stated, letting his chest rise and fall in heavy succession.

"I see you're fond of aristocracy," Jane smirked. "But just as your own government is changing to more democratic leanings, you fail to realize the common man, and the common woman for that matter, have the capabilities to rule with logic and understanding if given the opportunity."

Mr. Eaton stepped forward, planting himself between Mr. Hodges and Jane. "I see you are well acquainted with our political turmoil, Miss Reynolds."

"Not well acquainted. But enough to know your government will transform in the years to come."

"Am I to assume you can read the future?" Mr. Hodges' left brow darted up; his chin jutted out.

Jane laughed. "I'm not predicting anything you can't infer yourself, Mr. Hodges."

"Please enlighten us, Miss Reynolds, why a woman like yourself would have interests in such lofty affairs?"

"I think all the more because I am a woman. For if there is no man to take care of my concerns, I would be at a disadvantage. Most people want the opportunity to be self-reliant. The inability to be equally involved in matters that will affect one's life can be unsettling." She lived and breathed those words. "But to not have the power to even try is defeat."

Both men fell silent. Mr. Eaton rubbed his chin. Mr. Hodges fluttered his eyes.

"I probably said too much. I fear my American thinking

doesn't always adhere to your English sensibilities." She extended her hand to Mr. Hodges. "Please don't hold your host accountable if I have offended you. I will leave you two men to discuss your affairs."

"Will you not join us for tea?" Mr. Eaton called after her. "Or dinner, tonight?"

She shook her head. "Not tonight, Mr. Eaton. I fear I'm the one who blundered this evening. Maybe it's best if I dine in privacy." She turned back and added, "Good evening, Mr. Hodges, and good luck with your pursuits."

Mr. Hodges bowed, and Mr. Eaton nodded, allowing for her retreat.

CURIOSITY

A note arrived early the next morning from Mr. Eaton.

Jane unfolded the paper, breath halted, fearing a reprimand in order. She hadn't intended to be argumentative to Mr. Hodges, but the man's haughtiness was unpalatable. Declining dinner was the most she could do to conceal her twenty-first century beliefs from Mr. Eaton's decidedly elitist neighbor. She was safer in the confines of her room, where her tongue was not so easily tempted. She only hoped she hadn't offended her host.

Dear Miss Reynolds,

My regrets. I have been called to some private affairs. My sister will have the best of me! I hope you enjoy another lovely, albeit rather warm, day. Mrs. Bishop is at your disposal. I would be honored to have you join me for dinner upon my return this evening.

With regard,

Henry Eaton

Jane folded the letter and tucked it under her pillow for safe keeping. It was a sign–she didn't offend him. For that, she was grateful. Or it is what she told herself when she took the handwritten note to read it again–three times over.

Not sure of what to do with her day, or more so not sure what to do with herself until dinner, Jane decided to embrace the opportunity and browse the museum-like house. There were treasures in every room, around every corner, passed up when Lillian gave her a tour. How she wanted to stop, touch, feel the furniture and decor for their antiquity. Didn't Amy suggest she slow down and take notice of the world around her? With surprise, she found the Charles II chair, first seen in Ryan's entry, tucked in a corner of the drawing room. It became her favorite chair when Lillian and she gathered in the afternoon. Maybe because it reminded her of home. She was sure to tell Ryan upon her return. And since the news from Dr. Cummings,' she knew she had to seize the moments.

When she passed Maggie's room, a tug pulled at her heart. The fireplace was empty, acknowledging the lack of residency. Ruffled red fabric decorated the bed; a red toile to match the papered walls. A porcelain doll lay alone atop pillows, awaiting the next time her child friend would hold her. Jane picked it up and placed it at a table with two chairs, in preparation for the little girl's return to have pretend tea and crumpets. The child-sized table sat in front of windows where the curtains were pulled and a view of Maggie's oak tree lay just beyond. Her heart tugged again.

A maid walked by and bid Jane good morning, pushing her to move on. But she didn't get far. Mr. Eaton's door was ajar and curiosity got the best of her. Lillian allowed Jane access to the entire house, but one room never made the tour, probably out of respect for her brother's privacy. But curiosity was one of Jane's foibles. It drove her to do things which weren't always copacetic. Like snooping in Mr. Eaton's room.

It didn't surprise her the room was meticulously tidy. It was assuredly his decision to live in such precise order. The walls were bosky green, the ceiling coffered in dark oak. Large windows encased one wall, while an Elizabethan four-poster bed centered on another. A fireplace, equally ornate in carvings, decorated a third wall, two filled bookcases flanking each side. A mirror, encased in a sculpted gold frame, hung above the mantle, bouncing light from the windows into the entire room, bringing much needed brightness to the solemn space. A tight backed sofa held two velvet pillows scrunched to one end and Jane pictured Mr. Eaton's head resting on them, the light of the embers illuminating his face. A stack of books sat atop a table next to it, one splayed open and turned over. She noted the title, *An Essay of Concerning Human Understanding,* by John Locke and wondered what interests Mr. Eaton pursued with such liberal ideas of his time.

But nothing stood out more than the view. Green velvet drapes pooled aside from expansive windows, framing the hills and forests surrounding the property. From afar, cottages dotted the hillsides, large clearings, rolling hills, and planted farms abound. The enchantment of nature–the verdant landscapes and the woods of the trees, intermingled with the decor of the room, merging the two spaces as if swallowed by nature. Where the room ended and outside began was parted only by a framed glass wall. From Mr. Eaton's vantage point, he must feel like a king.

Only when Jane turned did she see the small portrait. It hung near the door, no bigger than the size of a book. It was all too obvious the resemblance to Maggie. It was her mother–golden hair, porcelain skin, and pinked cheeks, her ice-blue eyes portraying sadness. Her lips were demure and pointed, her nose high-bridged, betraying her good breeding. All her features were small, which only added to her delicateness. Against a darkened background, she was ethereal...like Vermeer's *Girl with a Pearl Earring.* Jane had seen no portraits of her in the halls and wondered why she was missing among the relatives. Now she saw Mr. Eaton kept her near to him...in his personal space.

There was no woman's touch to the room. The bed had no

ruffles or lace, but simply topped with linens and a satin quilt. Jane spread her hands over the satin. It was cool–luxurious to the touch, almost a sensual pleasure. Jane wondered if it was the last remnant of his wife.

She walked into his sitting room. It, too, had a fireplace, smaller and less austere, a dressing table, and two chairs with a table between them. The same breathtaking view encapsulating the room. Wet soap laid on his toiletry table, along with a shaving tool, and an unfolded towel. She lifted the soap and brought it to her nose. Spices and herbs, along with a waft of wool from the wardrobe, and oiled wood from the paneled walls, filled her senses. It was the essence of Mr. Eaton.

"Can I help, Miss?" A young girl walked in and set her things down.

Jane startled. "I…I saw the door open." She placed the soap back on its dish and made her way to the windows. "And caught sight of the beautiful view. I couldn't resist."

"Well, it's not for me to object. Miss." The young girl joined her at the window. "The site is grand, though. I don't blame one wanting to take a look. It's the grandest view of all the rooms…except for the mistress.' But no one uses those rooms anymore." She pointed to something. "I used to live over there. Through those trees. See the cottage just beyond?"

Jane nodded.

"There's a small pond if you follow the stream, hidden there. It's a private place my mum would take my brother and me to swim as little ones. She'd collect meadowsweet as we'd play in the cool water, naked as the day we were born. The way the light comes through the trees, it's like God smiling down on you." She looked back at Jane. "So, when I come to do my work, it's like I'm with my family again."

"It doesn't look far from here. Do you ever go home?"

"I've got a family now–a husband, two scoundrels, and one

on the way." She rubbed her belly. "I've no time for playing anymore."

Jane's mouth went agape. The girl–for that is exactly what she was, a girl–was too young to be married with children. She was no more than twenty. Yet, the burdens of hard work already wore away at the young girl's face, creating dark circles under her eyes and heavy crevices across her forehead. Her brittle hair and colorless skin were sure signs of poor nutrition. She was still pretty, which youth allowed, but she would lose that luxury if her hard life continued...which it invariably would.

Jane turned to leave. "I'm sorry for intruding. Tell Mr. Eaton I meant no harm."

"Oh Miss, as long as you don't let him know about my secret, I'll not tell him yours."

Jane smiled, solidifying their deal.

Jane didn't bother with the rest of the house, her curiosity redirected. She found Mrs. Baker and asked her to put together supplies for an afternoon adventure. Inspired by the young maid, she was on her way to the pond.

AT THE POND

Dr. Cummings contemplated taking Jane to the fields where she was found. He roamed the area to assess the power it held but discovered little evidence of what she claimed. There was no wind tunnel or pull he could surmise. If more was learned, he promised to take her back, and hopefully, send her home. Until then, he warned her to be careful and not roam too far until he could guarantee her safety.

A part of Jane wanted to run back to the field. But she heeded Dr. Cummings' warning. First out of fear. Then, out of curiosity about her surroundings. *Dare she indulge?* She didn't belong in the past. Each day she awoke, the moment before she lifted her lids, she'd pray it was all a dream. But the experience captivated her at the same time. Days passed seamlessly, as if it was the most natural occurrence to be thrown into an alternate universe. And with each passing day, she grew more comfortable. *Was it destiny or a mishap?* Whatever the reason, she was there, waiting. Waiting for Dr. Cummings to find the Black Raven. Waiting for answers. Waiting for something she didn't quite know yet. It would be gone soon enough, and merely a blip in her memory.

"It's no concern of mine what you do with your time, Miss, but be careful not to wander too far." Mrs. Bishop warned Jane after she told her about the maid's sanctuary. "I know of the spot, but it's deep in the trees. Where the fairies play, and the mind can be coaxed."

"I promise, Mrs. Bishop. It isn't terribly far, and I could use a little adventure," Jane insisted.

"It ain't right for a young woman to be traipsing about unaccompanied." But she wouldn't have Jane going hungry either and handed her a small basket of bread and cheese. "I see you're antsy. It might do you good. You don't seem like a woman who idles."

Jane smiled at the old woman.

"Go on then..." She shewed her out.

Jane hiked with determination through the tall grasses and footed pathways until she finally made her way into the forest of trees. Trainers would have made the trek easier, as would less cumbersome clothes, but the sound of trickling water encouraged her to keep going. The further she delved, the thicker the trees. She followed the stream, wetting her face along the way, until she found the source of the gurgling water—a dark, oval pond. The ripples glistened as rays of light rained down through a clearing in the treetops. Meadowsweet surrounded it like a cradled baby in a warm blanket, just as the maid described. Velvet grass unfurled to the pond's edge, and Jane settled herself near the slapping water. Taking off her shoes and stockings, she dipped her feet into the watering hole, testing its temperature. *Chilly!* But she liked it. She laid on the grass and spread her arms, the velvet strands tickled her neck. Gathering the layers of fabric, she hiked the skirt of her dress over her thighs, before plunging her legs into the water, causing goosebumps to cover her body. The sun-drenched her skin, dissipating the chill, when she closed her eyes and allowed the sanctity of the site to overcome her. Quiet surrounded her, except for the popping of a fish surfacing for a fly. The silkiness of the water encircled her legs, softly slapping against her thighs. Her thoughts drifted into mindlessness. Strangely, Mr. Eaton and his satin quilt came to mind when she floated off to sleep.

"Miss Reynolds!" Mr. Eaton ran to her, dropped his coat, and fell to his knees. "Jane…" he called, his voice barely a whisper.

Jane stirred. Dark blue eyes stared into her own, panicked. She reached out and brushed her fingertips along the man's jawline, feeling the prickly sensation poking through.

"Henry…" she wooed.

Mr. Eaton jerked back and rose to his feet.

The dreamy blue eyes pulled away. Panic turned to shock.

"Mr. Eaton!" Jane stumbled to get up. "I…I'm so sorry."

"I thought you were hurt," he explained.

Jane ran her hands down the fabric of her dress and tugged at the sleeves before she looked up.

"I didn't mean to alarm you."

He cleared his throat. "I was overly presumptuous and misread the situation. By your stillness and your display of..." he paused, moving his eyes down to Jane's skirt that now covered her legs. He could not control the physical reaction of seeing the bareness of her ankle to the top of her thighs, the desire to feel the silkiness in between those legs spontaneous. Nor could he control the anger he now possessed.

She followed his gaze, realizing the scandal. "I'm so embarrassed. How would I know anyone would find me *here?*"

"But I did," he pointed out, his eyes dark; targeted. "I thought harm had come to you–once again."

"I meant no harm, Mr. Eaton, truly," Jane pleaded, meeting his stare.

He turned from her and reached for his coat. A momentary reprieved to gain his composure.

"When you are ready, I will escort you back to the house." His chin lifted, but his eyes didn't. They only narrowed.

Jane would have complied, out of respect, and embarrassment. But she found him rude, his haughtiness in overdrive.

Her ego stepped forward. "Thank you, but I think I can find my own way back."

"Miss Reynolds." His jaw clenched. He crossed his arms and dug his right boot into the grass, leaving a divot. Until that moment, her spiritedness was charming. But he was finding the mixture of his anger and passion getting the best of him. His next few words were fervid. "I have a duty and obligation to escort you. I must insist."

Dare she yell at him?

She clenched her fists instead. Her next few words seethed. "My apologies, Mr. Eaton. You, nor anyone, have the right to *insist* on what is best for me."

He cleared his throat with a growl. He had never felt so helpless in dealing with a woman. It was all he could do but leave her with her intentions. "I will speak to you further when you return." He abruptly turned, leaving Jane to grasp the seriousness of the situation.

Jane watched him until he disappeared through the branches. She could hear the echoing of each heavy-footed stride crunching branches under his feet, revealing how much he was offended.

~

When she walked through the door, skin flushed from exertion, her own anger had not receded.

Mrs. Bishop waited to greet her. "Oh Miss, you're to see Master Eaton as soon as you enter the house." She pushed her towards the closed doors, where he waited.

Jane resisted, choosing her words purposely. "Tell Mr. Eaton I will see him shortly, when I'm presentable."

Mrs. Bishop shook her head. "No, Miss. He insisted."

With Mrs. Bishop's plea, Jane complied. She knocked at Mr. Eaton's door but didn't wait for his invitation to enter.

"You wanted to see me?"

Mr. Eaton didn't look up, but kept his eyes focused on a ledger in front of him. His hand moved about on the open page.

Jane cleared her throat.

He looked up; his eyes stormy. "Please Miss Reynolds, have a seat" He gestured to a chair across from his desk.

Jane refused, opting to stand. "Is there something you wanted to say to me?"

"I do not mean to be indelicate, Miss Reynolds…may I be direct with you?"

She nodded, crossing her arms.

He stood, dropping the pen from his finger's grasp. "I realize when you were found, it was because of unfortunate circumstances. I do not know of the cause and have been rather obedient, not intruding on how you were in such a predicament. As you do not know me, I am one to be practical and do not over dramatize situations. It is with regret, I now question those circumstances, especially after finding you indecently exposed. Anyone could have happened upon you. You might have put yourself in another misfortunate predicament with such behavior."

"As I explained, I believed the area to be private." Jane threw up her hands. "My dear God! I was in the middle of nowhere. But that really isn't the point. My intentions were not to be indecent, but just to seek some solitude. If you found my behavior inappropriate, maybe it's your intentions you should question."

Mr. Eaton's eyes widened. He moved towards her, narrowing his stare. His voice came out low and steady. "Miss Reynolds, I assure you I have no indecorous intentions. It is common decency to behave accordingly as a lady. I hold significant risk taking in a stranger, and a woman at that. You must appreciate my reputation, as well as yours."

If he was waiting for a reaction, Jane gave him none.

He continued, "You are not from here and may be unfamiliar with the expectations of behavior. It is not without curiosity I have allowed you some liberty with little objection. My fascination, you accuse me of, is only my duty to accept you as my guest. But I cannot ignore behaviors that will violate the standards of decency. I have a duty to show my daughter, along with my household, a sense of honor to behave by. I am not asking of you for which I would not expect of myself. I am requesting, while you are a guest in my house, you respect the standards I have established."

Jane's heart pumped. Blood sprinted through her veins. "I would defend my honor, but I have nothing to be ashamed of. I wasn't intentional in my behavior. But now I see that I might have to be."

She turned and headed to the door.

"I have not finished," he called after her.

"But I am! Good evening, Mr. Eaton."

She opened the door to find Mrs. Bishop, listening, of course, but also to help her get away.

Jane retreated to the privacy of her room, hoping for a reprieve from her rage…and from *him.* But as the night darkened the room, and silence settled in the house, her thoughts cleared. Remorse replaced her wrath. Her modern sensibilities had gotten in the way. Mr. Eaton's generosity was far more than what he was asking in return.

Shame replaced her remorse.

She waited for an invitation to dinner, hoping for the opportunity to redeem herself. But it never came. A soft rap at the door only presented a tray by Mrs. Bishop—with no note attached. She tried to ignore the implications of the gesture, but Jane cringed at the meaning. The household was certainly abuzz with gossip, as she was sure a tray sent to the room was the highest insult. Her only consolation was she did not have to face Mr. Eaton. But more alarming, he did not want to face her, either.

READING AT NIGHT

After confronting Jane, Mr. Eaton retreated into his private quarters. He checked his watch every hour, on the hour, waiting. Waiting for the staff to finish, the house to quiet. At half past midnight, he finally descended the stairs. He made his usual rounds before bed, checking the fires and the doors. Although he had a staff, he closed the house for the evening. His father instilled in him the role of caretaker and master. He did not take his roles for granted, even when he was left alone.

Except…except for Miss Reynolds, to whom he was caretaker–for now.

He heard the crackling of a fire in the library. He nudged the door ajar, seeing the firelight glowing upon Jane's face. Her brow was tense, struggling to read by the limited light. She snuggled in the sofa's corner with her left hand holding a book, and the fingers of her right hand rubbing the fabric of her skirt in a slow, rhythmic tempo. She appeared harmless. Peaceful. Nothing like the demon he accused her of being that afternoon. Guilt flooded him. His anger was misconceived. It was not Jane he was angered with, but more at the implications of her accusations. Shame rushed through him, pushing thoughts to retreat. But he entered the room instead.

"You could not sleep?"

Jane jolted by the unexpected voice.

"I didn't mean to frighten you." He presented himself from the doorway and pointed to the flickering flames. "I saw the fire."

"I asked one of the servants to add new logs. I couldn't sleep." She cast her eyes away from his stare, ashamed he was the reason for her restlessness.

Mr. Eaton moved closer and caught the title clutched in her grip. "Ah, the fine sonnets of Shakespeare. Not light reading to indulge, so late at night?" he remarked.

"No, I suppose not. But a young woman encouraged me to read his works. I found the book on your shelf. I hope you don't mind."

"Of course. It is what I want." He looked at the fire. "For you to be comfortable here."

Jane closed the book and laid it on her lap, her focus turned to the flickering flames.

Silence fell between them.

"Please join me," Jane said, patting the sofa cushion next to her.

He hesitated, but overruled his carefulness, sitting himself at the other end of the sofa.

"Mr. Eaton, may I ask a direct question?"

His brow went up, and he nodded his permission.

"Why did you take me in? I'm a stranger to you. We both are aware, Dr. Cummings knows nothing about me, either. Yet, you are going out of your way. That's unusual. I can't help wonder why someone would be so generous without getting something in return."

How much was too much to ask from a stranger, from a man? The afternoon revealed Mr. Eaton was growing more cautious of her. *Rightly so*, she concluded after hours alone in her room, realizing how dreadful she had behaved. But she wanted to know what was driving him, to continue her intrusion into his life.

Would she, could she, get home before it all came to a head?

"It is what a man does for one in need," he simply replied.

"But you have gone above and beyond duty, taking me into your family with no reservations…until today. For that I'm sorry."

"Miss Reynolds, you are a woman who has been involved in a tragedy. It would be dishonorable to do less than I have the power to do. I have not doubted your sincerity, nor your honor, and I apologize if today I made you think I have."

"You weren't out of line, Mr. Eaton." Her eyes lowered. "I know Dr. Cummings has asked a lot from you. Probably more than he should."

"Dr. Cummings is a great friend of mine. And it is he who asked me to shelter you as my guest. He deserves your gratitude, not I. So, you see, I am not as honorable as you surmise."

"So, my earlier accusation was justified?"

"Well," he answered, but her smile caught him off guard, and he smiled, too. He felt warmth spread all over his body and silently cursed himself for the damning effects of a woman. "I am forever in Dr. Cummings's debt. He was here every day during my son's illness. He came in the middle of the night on many occasions. After my wife took ill, he sat with me evenings, keeping me preoccupied. She was never without care because of the kindness of that man. I was never without the support of a friend. I would do anything for him."

Something changed in his eyes. Pain. Loss. Love. Feelings all too personal, making Jane blush at his vulnerability exposed. The austere man of today was not the same man before her. He was, when not aware, a gentle man in spirit. His demanding exterior was more façade of the man he wanted to present, but maybe not the man who truly lived inside. She had the urge to reach out, connect, share. But the afternoon's incident was a warning. Prudence was expected.

"I was sorry to hear about your wife's illness after losing your son, only to lose her soon afterwards. It seems everyone had great esteem for her."

"My wife, Olivia…." Mr. Eaton's voice faded. "She was a noble woman. Most certainly beautiful. But it was her generous heart most admired. She was conventional, but that is not to say she didn't bring liveliness to this house. She was not nearly as spirited as my sister, nor you, for that matter." He dashed a smile at Jane. "But she was a breath of fresh air. With little prompting, Maggie's sweetness is a direct reflection of her."

Mr. Eaton couldn't recall when he spoke so freely, or so personally, with a woman. With another woman who wasn't his wife. His conversations concerned business or family affairs. Since Jane's arrival, a closed chapter of his life reopened: sharing himself, his thoughts, his feelings with someone. He was trying hard to not convolute his need for closeness with his guest. But he couldn't help noticing how powerfully demanding her dark eyes were when she looked at him; the way her smile pulled at a part of his heart, scarred and off limits. He was overwhelmed at the familiarity she brought, reminding him of the man he used to be.

Her hair was carelessly pulled up, with wisps falling around her face. It reminded him of how his wife used to hurriedly pull her hair up after they made love. It was uninhibited, and it had an effect on him that did not go without sentiment. He indulged his gaze, following the length of her neck where the glow of her skin glistened in the room's light. Although he was quite aware of her sensuality that afternoon, it was here that he noticed what a beautiful woman she truly was.

"Yes, Maggie told me all about her mother under the oak

tree. I felt like I knew her from all she shared with me. Those are nice memories for a young girl."

"Yes, I saw the two of you sitting under the tree," he noted. "It was their special place. I am sorry Maggie does not have her mother to share it with anymore."

"She has you," Jane reminded.

"I would not want to change her memory."

"It won't erase her mother. It would create a new experience, to share with you," she refuted.

The light of the room dimmed as the fire burned low, shadowing Mr. Eaton's face. He rose and poked at the logs. The newfound light revealed something she had not expected–a man looking at her with desire.

Jane stood. "I probably should go."

"Please do not feel like you have to run off on my account." He reached for her arm.

Jane had forgotten how a touch could create a thousand ripples of excitement. She held her breath, only exhaling as he let go.

"It's late, and I am invading your space, again…if not your life."

He stepped closer, blocking her retreat. His body shadowed over her. When Jane dared to look up, she found his eyes looking into hers. They were the same eyes she gazed into as she awoke that afternoon by the pond. The pools of darkness were now inviting her to dive in.

His voice softened to a whisper. "You are not invading my life. Your arrival has been an unexpected pleasure. I have only benefitted from your arrival."

Jane's insides melted. She wanted more. Of what, she wasn't sure. Her uncle's words rang in her ears when she was a teenager, "*Nothing good happens past midnight.*"

Jane stepped back. "I really should go."

"Yes, if you like." He moved aside. "Shall I walk you to your room?"

"That isn't necessary," she replied.

"Then let me get you a light." He lit a candle from the mantle and handed it to her. The light flickered, illuminating her face, revealing the flush across her cheeks. He walked her to the door, allowing her to leave. Had he been more brave, he wouldn't have let her go.

A DAY IN THE COUNTRYSIDE

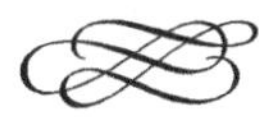

After the experience under the oak tree, Maggie would awaken Jane with a soft knock at the door, tip toe to the side of the bed, and whisper in her ear, "May I come in?"

Jane would throw open her quilt and the sinewy girl would crawl under Jane's arm and slide her cold feet against her warmed body, stealing away her heat. Jane would tell her stories about carriages that could fly in the air to travel the world, or about fairies who had magical boxes they could hold in their hand and talk to little girls from far, far away. It was Jane's playful way of staying connected to *her* world. Not sharing all she knew was hard. So, she made it a fantasy world for Maggie. They would lie together until Mrs. Bishop came and ordered the young girl to go and get dressed.

But she did not have Maggie to awaken her anymore. It was Mrs. Bishop who came to her room and got her up in the mornings.

Jane reminisced as she entered, "I miss Maggie."

"That little wee one always waking you up?" Mrs. Bishop questioned.

Jane smirked and chose not to answer. She stretched her arms and leaned back against the pillows.

"No hurry, I see. I don't blame you after your day yesterday. Master Eaton was in quite a mood after you left."

Jane smiled to herself.

Mrs. Bishop raised an eyebrow.

"I guess you can say we made amends," she explained.

"Hmph?" Mrs. Bishop remarked half-heartedly under her breath. "I thought he had sworn off the company of women all together."

Jane pushed out of bed and grabbed her robe. "What do you mean Mr. Eaton has sworn off women?"

"Oh, tis has nothing to do with you." She flicked her hand through the air to scatter away the notion. "He seems to enjoy your company, and that's more to be said about most," Mrs. Bishop replied.

"Most?"

Mrs. Bishop ignored the question, scurrying to get Jane's clothes ready for the day. "Will you be wanting breakfast in your room?" She asked before leaving.

"No. Not today. Tell Mr. Eaton I will be down promptly."

But promptly was not soon enough, because he was not at the table when Jane arrived. In fact, he had already left, so the servant informed when she delivered tea. Cook sent out breakfast, whereby Jane ate alone. The open windows allowed the morning breeze in, teasing pleasant weather. The roses just outside filled the room with sweet aromas. Birds chirped, and in the distance, a dog barked. Jane shrugged. No matter how enticing the day was presenting itself, she was already disappointed.

"It's lovely out. Why don't you join me?"

She twisted around to find Mr. Eaton in the doorway, his hat in one hand, and his coat in the other. She tried to be nonchalant, but her lips parted, and a full smile spread across her face. It took all she had to not jump out of her chair.

"I was just about to leave when I thought you might enjoy a ride in the country. Would you?"

"Are you sure? I mean, is it proper for me to join you?"

"I have made you cautious about me. I hoped our truce was solidified last night."

"It was." A flush of warmth spread through her remembering him holding the candle, his face illuminated before her–the look of her own desire reflecting in his eyes. "I just don't want to intrude while you work."

"Before our children, my wife was a constant companion to me on my rides. She was a great asset and brought me much comfort. It would be my honor to introduce you to the people who live and work on my lands."

"I would love to. But if you recall, my last introduction to your neighbor wasn't quite beneficial," she reminded him.

"Miss Reynolds, there is no offense," he replied. "Mr. Hodges and I are not the same men. We have our differences. It is obvious you are a well-educated woman with much to say. And if I were to admit, it was rather amusing to watch him fluster."

Jane smiled. "Well, I was happy to provide you with some entertainment."

"Ah, yes. Well," he fumbled with his hat in his hand. "If you are going to ride, you may want to change. That dress is much too pretty for the dusty roads ahead."

Jane brushed her hands against the cotton fabric of her dress. She couldn't miss the compliment. But before she could reply, he excused himself and headed out to the stables. Wasting no time, Jane jumped from her chair and ran down the corridor.

"Mrs. Bishop! Mrs. Bishop!"

"Aye, I'm right here," Mrs. Bishop appeared at top of the stairs. "What is the emergency?"

Jane looked up. "I'm going riding…with Mr. Eaton."

"Are you now," An eyebrow shot up. "Come along then, Regina will find you something to wear."

The boots were a little small, the coat too big, but the top hat with a fluttering veil fit perfectly, turning her into the epitome of a lady ready to ride. But when the stable boy brought a dark chocolate mare, Jane froze, doubling guessing her enthusiasm to ride. She had absolutely no experience riding side saddle and was sure she would fall flat on her face if she tried. She rubbed the mare's head and whispered for her to be a good girl, kissing her for good luck. It was Landry who came to her side and boosted her on the saddle. But Jane started to slip. She grabbed the reins and threw her leg over the pommel to straddle the horse. She smoothed her skirt, hoping to conceal the unorthodoxy.

But Landry looked at her curiously, as did Mr. Eaton.

"My uncle raised me…and taught me to ride," she explained. "I'm afraid I don't know how to ride any other way."

Mr. Eaton quickly rectified the situation, ordering Landry to replace the saddle, which better suited her, concluding, "I am sure your uncle was an interesting man, as you bear witness."

"Is that a compliment, Mr. Eaton, or are you making fun of me?"

"Maybe a little of both," he admitted.

"It's nice to see your sister didn't get all the personality," she poked back.

"Ah," he said, and kicked at his mare. "We shall see."

Jane groped the reins and gave her horse a kick, matching Mr. Eaton in stride.

"It's been a while since I've been on a horse," Jane admitted, finding her balance. "My uncle put me in lessons when I was nine. And I only rode in the summer. I stopped riding when I went away to school. I hope I won't slow you down."

"My business with the farmers is not urgent. It won't be necessary to push ourselves. We can take our time. There is only one obligation. I promised Mr. Baker I would introduce you, so he can see with his own eyes you are doing well. He will be our last stop."

"Mr. Baker?"

"He and his sons found you. They have been concerned about your wellbeing."

"Then I'm honored you've asked me to spend the day with you so I can thank them myself."

"I believe it is my honor you decided to join me," he corrected. He pulled his horse forward, indicating for her to follow.

As promised, he did not push the ride as they made their way to various farms. Mr. Eaton greeted the men in charge, assessed the stock and fields, looked at the horses, or lent a hand where needed. Wherever they went, Jane was introduced as the cousin of Dr. Cummings, visiting from America, no one questioning her status. Everyone seemed to know of her–but no one knew about her–and was excited to meet the elusive cousin of the doctor. Jane was sure there would be gossip by evening's end. For that reason, she was pleasant and mostly quiet. She shook her head, smiled a lot, and was sure not to give any opinion other than how much she enjoyed the hospitality.

By late afternoon, they headed to the Bakers' farm. But not before Mr. Eaton veered off course through a field instead. He led the way through aisles of corn stocks, soldiers of green saluting the sun, until they came to a flattened area. He stopped and turned around.

"Does this look familiar to you?"

Jane looked around, surprised at the question. "No."

"You were found somewhere over there," he explained as he pointed. He turned his horse around and rode directly towards her, stopping close enough to see her eyes.

"Do you really have no recollection of how you got here or why?"

She turned her eyes away. "Are you doubting me, Mr. Eaton?"

"I just want to uncover the truth, Miss Reynolds. It was only out of concern which enticed me to bring you here. I thought it might help you."

Jane scanned the field surrounding her. When she left the Eaton Estate on her fateful walk, she traipsed through a forest of trees and ran through a valley of grass. The trees at the top of the hill were familiar…unchanged. Tall and stoic, pillars of nature unbound by time and space. But the valley below was transformed into a corn crop. What lay before her was still expansive, miles upon miles of green, as before…only different. She sensed *it*…a cauldron of energy surrounding her. She walked the horse around the space, wondering if the lightheadedness would return, but nothing other than a light breeze brushed against her skin. *Was it teasing her?* She was aware of the need to get home, but how and when loomed. She shivered with a sense of what was to come. Turning towards Mr. Eaton, she wondered what possibilities lay ahead?

"Shall we go?" He asked.

Jane turned the mare and followed Mr. Eaton's lead, who looked back every few minutes to make sure she wasn't far behind.

He didn't want to lose her.

The Baker house wasn't far from the corn fields, a quaint one-story structure covered with stone. A weathered brown thatch covered the roof, with a single stone chimney atop, grey smoke escaping from above. Mrs. Baker greeted them at the door, insisting they stay for tea. Jane was apprehensive about burdening Mrs. Baker, who was about to give birth at a pin's drop. However, with an approving glance from Mr. Eaton, she recognized it was only polite to accept her invitation.

Mr. Baker took her hand in his and praised God for her good health. The two boys bowed as they met Jane and would not take their eyes away from her. Mrs. Baker slapped them, demanding they be polite. But they paid little attention to her reprimand. Both were heads above their mother, and men in every aspect of their duties. They just took her swatting in stride.

Mr. Baker was not a big man, rather small compared to his wife, but large in importance to his family. His sons were never far from his attention or guidance, and when they sat at the table beside him, they acknowledged his place. They were quiet when he spoke and only spoke when spoken to.

Mr. Eaton joined the men at the table, while Jane helped Mrs. Baker with tea. She tried to shew Jane away, but Jane insisted, leaving the woman no choice.

"Aye, I heard of things like that, but had never seen such a display," Mr. Baker recalled as Jane placed a cup and plate in front of him. He tipped his head in gratitude and continued to explain the flattened crops where Jane was found. "The storms about these parts have roared, and the effects produced, in some instances, are mighty curious."

"The sight was incredible, if not unusual," Mr. Eaton chimed in. "I heard about other places with similar experiences, but I never thought they had credibility. Upon closer examination, what did you find?"

"My sons and I looked at the flattened areas. It's easy enough to lift. Strangely, the stocks are not as damaged as we first thought."

Jane listened intently, not interrupting their conversation.

She had seen many pictures in her lifetime of the beautiful designs of crop circles all over the world. *Was this the same thing?* She wished she could describe the curiously artistic displays, strange phenomenons of flattened fields, but did not want to have to explain how she knew about them.

Mr. Baker continued, "I dunno how to account for the peculiar forms of patches in the field, not knowing if it be wind or rain to cause it." He looked at Jane. "And I dunno know how your pretty self got mixed up in it. It was a terrible injustice."

"Well, you look like you're no harm from it, Miss," Mrs. Baker interjected, steering her husband away from the elephant in the room–Jane found naked, left for dead, and no one knows why. Not that it was hers, or anyone's business. And she was going to keep it that way.

Jane touched Mrs. Baker's arm. "I am good…no harm came to me," she assured. Who knows what harm may have befallen her if found by not-so-reputable passersby? "I am honored to be able to personally thank you. I owe you so much."

"You owe us nothing more than your gratitude. God has blessed us. Knowing you are thriving is all we really need," Mr. Baker said.

"It doesn't seem like enough…"

"Ah, my dear Miss Reynolds. Never undervalue the simple blessing of gratitude. Things can be taken; money spent. But gratitude," he pounded his chest, "fills your heart forever."

"I agree. But we should go. We have taken too much of your time and hospitality." Mr. Eaton stood.

"Nonsense, Master Eaton," Mrs. Baker insisted. "You've given me time to spend with my husband and boys, and there's no waste in that."

Mr. Baker showed them to the door. "Good day, Sir. God speed to you, Miss Reynolds."

As they mounted their horses and followed the road, taking

them further away from the Bakers' cottage, Jane grew melancholy. She like the Bakers very much, and leaving meant saying goodbye forever, reminding her how transient she was in their lives. Would they remember her? Because she will always remember them.

She turned to Mr. Eaton, rocking back and forth in his saddle, as they meandered through the rolling green hills together, the evening soon upon them, and she wondered, would she be remembered by him?

"We are almost home. Would you like to walk for a while?"

Jane agreed, not wanting the day to end.

Mr. Eaton dismounted first, then helped Jane. He reached around her waist and pulled her towards him. She almost fell into his arms if it weren't for the horse pulling away. Jane quickly grabbed the reins of the beast, a little resentful he interrupted the moment.

"What a beautiful life you have here," she said wistfully.

"I have never complained," Mr. Eaton replied.

"Nor should you," she admonished. "It truly is spectacular. I never imagined a life so pure as this. It is magic unto itself."

He looked at his surroundings through the eyes of his companion. "Yes, I suppose it is."

"I never realized how much your job entailed." She chuckled. "Well, in truth, I imagined it mundane and tiresome. I pictured wealthy landowners sitting around, snubbing the poor, praising themselves, and dancing with ladies."

Henry laughed out loud. He never saw his life so fanciful.

"You should do that more." Jane pointed to his lips.

His brow crinkled. "What?"

"Laugh. Be happy. You have dimples when you smile," she explained. "Just like Maggie. You don't show them very often. It's a shame."

"I smile when it is appropriate."

"Appropriate? Ha! Always so controlled. Just like your sister claimed," she teased.

"Well, Miss Reynolds, it may be because I am rarely in the presence of someone who makes me want to smile."

Jane halted in her tracks. She met his eyes. Ocean blue, calm and inviting. She wanted to kiss him. Kiss him hard and long. *Did he even know?* Instead, she pushed forward, her horse in her hand, hoping the evening breeze would cool the surging heat spreading through her, limb to limb, fingertips to toes.

They cleared a hill and the Eaton Estate presented itself.

"We made it home," Mr. Eaton said, grabbing her reins.

Mrs. Bishop rushed towards them as Landry took away the tired mares.

"Dr. Cummings arrived, Sir. Says he has important news for Miss Reynolds."

"For me?" Jane's face lit up. "Where is he?"

"In the Library, for now. But you might want to freshen up." Mrs. Bishop pointed to her dusty hems. "I have Regina waiting for you."

"Oh," Jane sighed, lifting her skirt from the ground. "Yes, I suppose I should. But please tell him I will meet with him soon." She dashed towards the house. But before she reached the door, she turned. "Oh, Mr. Eaton?" She took a few steps towards him. "Thank you…for allowing me to share your day. I had a wonderful time with you." She released a broad smile across her face.

"I enjoyed it as well," he replied, not concealing his dimples.

Mrs. Bishop looked at Master Eaton, then at Jane.

When he caught her scrutiny, he coughed and straightened, trying to erase the remnants of the uncharacteristically exhilarated expression on his face.

NEWS DAY

The men were talking when Jane arrived at the half-open door to the drawing room at the west end of the house. It was one room Jane spent little time in because of its larger size, used for small parties or holiday gatherings, so Lillian said. The two men, dressed in dark suits, contrasted with the cheery golden yellow fabrics with fir green accents. The damask wallpaper, heavily draped windows, silk woven rugs decidedly were a woman's influence, and they both looked out of place in the feminine space. As if planned, Jane's pale-yellow dress with white piping and lace collar harmoniously blended with the room's environment. It was only the swoosh of her skirt which gave rise to the men of her entrance, halting their conversation.

Dr. Cummings rushed to greet her. "My dear, Miss Reynolds."

Jane wanted to embrace him, but with his prompt, she took his hand instead, the smile across her face assuredly expressing her own excitement about his return.

He eyed the woman in front of him with pleased curiosity. "You look quite improved. I hoped to find you doing well in the care of Mr. Eaton. From the glow in your cheeks and the smile on your face, you are in good hands."

"Miss Reynolds joined me riding today," Mr. Eaton interjected with an affected gaze towards her. "I thought the fresh country air would do her some good,"

Dr. Cummings, well acquainted with Henry's temperament, noted surreptitiously, "I see it did you good as well."

Mr. Eaton registered the comment with a lift of his chin but heeded it with little debate.

Jane was equally aware of Dr. Cummings' implication. A warmth spread through her shoulders, climbed her neck, and she was sure, colored the apples of her cheeks. When she first entered the room, she looked towards Mr. Eaton, hoping their eyes would connect with a singular understanding of their mutual attraction. But he gave no indication of shared feelings. She now felt foolish about reading more into their day together. Turning from the gentlemen, she swished her skirts across the room to stand by the window and hide her misconstrued sentiments.

Dr. Cummings followed her.

"You are retreating from us?"

"No," she lied. "I am just admiring the darkening sky."

She couldn't tell him of the thoughts flooding her mind. The comfort she experienced in her surroundings, the sense of belonging in a place she didn't belong, and the attraction towards a man responsible for it all.

"Come." Dr. Cummings took her hand. "Let us stroll through the rose garden while the moon is rising. It would be remiss if you left and did not capture the fragrances of early evening. The cooling breeze lifts the sumptuous aromas and fills the air. It is an experience everyone should take the time to enjoy." He turned to his friend, "Henry, you won't mind if I steal this fine young woman? I would like to discuss plans for her return home."

Henry cleared his throat, "No, of course, but… then you have plans to leave soon?"

"I…" Jane hesitated. She didn't have the answer. "I cannot take advantage of your hospitality forever."

Dr. Cummings explained, "You have been kind enough to host this young lady, Henry. She has a home, and I am sure people are eager for her return."

Henry's eyes darted downward, out of his friend's purview. "Yes, I understand."

But he didn't understand. He had more questions for his friend, for Jane. *What people? Where is home? And what really happened in the field?* He wanted to demand more of them. But before he had the chance, Dr. Cummings placed his arm around Jane and escorted her away.

Henry scowled to no one but himself, throwing back the last of his drink before walking to the sideboard and refilling his glass. He trusted his dear friend to behave honorably, but the intimate proximity as they parted left an impression.

Dr. Cummings guided Jane to a bench in direct view of the waning moon. It was just rising, but the clear sky gave way to the bright bulb with the ability to entrance anyone who looked.

Jane dared not, for fear of where it would take her. With the doctor's arrival, it was a reminder the goal was to return home, and all connections to the people and places would be mere memories.

"It's such a pretty garden," Jane said, admiring the rose garden's transformation under the illumination of the moon. The magenta and fuchsia pink flowers glowed fluorescent inside the forested green bushes, the white buds illuminated like floating lightbulbs balanced atop wooden wands, and the purple petals darkened into black velvet, melting into the purpling night sky. In the daylight, the garden was a colorful explosion of nature's bounty. By night, it was a mysterious maze of optical illusions.

Dr. Cummings sighed. "Aw, yes." Memories flooded his thoughts. "God's infinite wisdom of interconnectivity–nature and man."

"Maggie shared it with me the other day. She understands so much for so young, instinctually understanding the connection of the earth, its ability to breathe life, and foster love into one's soul. I used to when I was her age. Maybe I forgot; got too busy. Too many distractions in life, work…love. But life here isn't needlessly *busy,* is it?"

"Busy? There never seems to be enough time to do all that needs to be done. But needless? No. Everything has meaning and purpose. Everything. Don't lose sight of that."

A momentary silence fell between them. Each for their own reasons, but with the same underlying question: What was Jane doing there?

"Maggie took me to her sacred place," Jane pointed toward the prominent tree, now a looming shadow in the distance. "She shared memories about her mother, and we drank lemonade. She misses her very much."

"Yes. What a sad turn of events for them all." Dr. Cummings explained, "I could not stop the powers at will. The fever turned for the worse, infecting her lungs. The weather got terribly cold that year, and too many got sick. When young Ian fell ill, his mother was never more than two feet away from him. But he quickly succumbed to the fever, and I fear Olivia grieved too much to fight for herself. Maggie was nearly six, then. A critical time for a mother's love. But then again. All time is precious, isn't it?"

"Maggie still has her father."

"Hmmm." Dr. Cummings' eyes shadowed. "Sometimes too much sadness changes a man."

Jane didn't know if the answer was more about him, or Mr. Eaton. The doctor saw too much death in his life. Not only his wife, to whom he expressed much devotion, but the losing of friends, patients, and communities he served.

Jane slipped her hand through his arm. "Shall we walk?"

"Ah, yes," he accepted. "Let's not delay the good news I have."

"I was hoping."

"Don't get too excited, for there is still work to do. But I may have found the seer you mentioned. There is a woman they speak of. She has a reputation for healing, but also predicting things." He spoke matter of fact, as if discussing supernatural abilities was a common topic of conversation.

"What makes you believe this is the woman we are looking for?"

"It's only rumored, but the locals talk of her ability. I cannot know until I speak with her personally."

Jane squeezed his arm. "When can we go?"

"We? No. *I* will go," Dr. Cummings emphasized. "If she is of value, I will take you to her. My priority is to keep you safe," he cautioned. "The mysterious scares people. That is why it has been difficult to find the woman we seek. No one dares talk about her for lest they might be cursed. You must be careful as well," he warned.

"But if she is the right person, according to her great granddaughter, she will expect me."

"My dear, trust me. I think it is best to stay here at the Eaton Estate. It's not that I want to keep you from her, but for the safety of all involved, especially Mr. Eaton and his reputation, I need to keep you tucked away. I fear rumors have already spread."

"Mr. Hodges mentioned it."

"That old pompous ass?"

Jane chuckled. "I'm afraid so, on both accounts."

"He has that effect on people," he mused. "But I must insist. Your place is here, with Henry."

Was it? Jane wondered if her presence wasn't getting complicated. Over the last two weeks, she kept distracted. There were too many pleasantries preoccupying her time. Mr. Eaton being one of them. Without intention, and maybe one's coping device to suppress danger, her fears had subsided.

Until…

Dr. Cummings' words reminded her she wasn't on a vacation or in a dream. She was light years from her reality. They were relying on a psychic, who had no validity other than wishful thinking. And there was a real possibility she may never return home.

"Peyton warned if I stayed too long, I may not return. How long is too late? What about those I left behind? Is anyone looking for me? What if I've fallen through a hole in the sky and lost forever? Thousands of people go missing every year with no sign of them." Her voice wavered. "What if I'm stuck here forever?"

Worry gripped her; tears fell.

Dr. Cummings wrapped his arms around Jane, and she fell into him. It surprised him she had not done this earlier. He was so wrapped up in the adventure he had overlooked the perspective she and her way of life were in jeopardy, and the lives she intervened were equally affected. The worse, or the better, was yet to be discovered.

"Now, don't get discouraged." His fingers slid across her cheeks, swiping away at the droplets cascading down. "Jane, my dear, I am fully devoted to your cause. You have me. I won't abandon you."

Jane sniffled, and Dr. Cummings handed her his handkerchief.

"Thank you," she said, taking the monogrammed linen from his hand. She wiped away the last of her tears and blew her nose, curling the handkerchief into the palm of her hand. "I'm a grown woman, Dr. Cummings. I was raised to handle almost everything thrown my way. But honestly, I'm afraid. This…this is so much bigger than I could ever imagine."

"It's understandable."

Jane pulled away from the comfort of the doctor's shoulder. "Are you sure I can't go with you to London?"

He shook his head. "I think it best you remain here. I can make the trip faster and return with news before you miss me."

She already felt a tug at her heart.

As if he read her mind, his hand covered hers, giving it a tight squeeze.

She met his eyes. "Why are you so good to me?"

His brow furrowed. "Because you deserve to be cared for."

Jane freed her hands from the comfort of his touch to tuck the loose hairs which had fallen from her bun while in his embrace. "I must look horrendous. I can't let Mr. Eaton see me this way. What he will think of me, crying like a baby?"

The doctor thought quite the contrary. He found her vulnerability a charming balance to the strong persona she presented. "Why don't you settle in for the evening. I will make your excuses to Henry."

Jane pressed her cheek to his, leaving the soft brush of her lips at the base of his ear. "Thank you and good night."

Dr. Cummings watched as Jane dashed away but didn't miss his friend Henry coming from the other direction, not missing Jane's embrace or her tear-stained face.

HELPING MRS. BAKER

Freshly baked bread aromas wafted through the halls of the Eaton Estate. Jane inhaled the cooked wheat reminding her of her childhood. Her mother cooked fresh bread at the end of every week and the sweet aroma filled the house. After school she would run through the door, slice the crusty end, and smother it with butter, the creamy richness filling the pockets of the cooked dough. It was long ago, and yet the simple aroma aroused the memories of comfort and happiness. Her mouth watered.

"Mmmmmmm. It smells heavenly," Jane remarked to Mrs. Bishop at the foot of the stairs.

"Oh, Cook is baking batches of bread for the Bakers. Edith has gone and had her a baby girl. I'm not sure of the value of that. But she wanted one dearly, and Mr. Baker is happy with another wee one under his roof. What's that man thinking?" She shook her head. "Cook has been busy preparing enough to keep those men fed so the poor woman can tend to her little one without interruption."

"Well, I think it's a wonderful blessing," Jane countered.

"Hmph! After birthing a couple of babies, you might

change your mind," Mrs. Bishop commented wistfully as she walked away.

Jane found her way to the drifting scents. She wasn't always accepted in the kitchen but when she found Jane alone, Cook invited her in to observe, even allowed questions, always adamant she stay out of her way. But baking since sunrise, Cook readily accepted Jane's offer to help that morning. She allowed Jane to take loaves of bread from the hearth and replace them with meat pies, cut vegetables for the stew, wrap biscuits in cloth, and label jars of jam. After her hard work, she rewarded Jane with a plate for her own of baked goods fresh out of the hearth, a jar of preserves, and a bowl of butter.

"You must have cooked all night," Jane said, noting the abundance of stuffed baskets on the table, as she indulged in the gifted food set before her.

"I have. Edith is my cousin, on my husband's side. She is a good woman. Always taking good care of me when I had my little ones. She's got those grown boys and a man to feed. Can't imagine those big lugs giving her a break. I cook. That is what I can do to make her life a bit easier."

"Then tell me, what more can I do to help?"

"Eh, I just got to deliver this batch of food." She waved her hand in the direction of an overstuffed basket sitting atop a stool next to the door.

"Cook?" Jane waited for her to look up. "Let me deliver it for you?"

Cook shook her head. "Oh no. That is not for a lady like you to do."

"You look exhausted–no offense."

"None taken."

Jane continued, "I have no plans for today. I would be honored to help."

"The Master would have my hide if he found out I was making you work, do chores, and such."

"You didn't *make me.* It's the least I can do after all the family has done for me. Mrs. Baker was so kind to me yesterday. I would love to feel useful again. Please? I promise I will be there and back before Mr. Eaton even discovers I've gone."

"Oh then, be it as it may, you can make yourself useful."

Jane threw her arms around Cook, who shewed her off, but not before her cheeks rosied and her lips curled upward. Jane was sure to tell Lillian, if she ever saw her again, she got Cook to smile.

The cool of the morning turned into a hot day as Jane prepared to leave. Landry had prepped a horse for her with 'the saddle she preferred.' But Jane insisted on walking, wanting the exercise. With a satchel across her body, the basket in hand, and a hat to keep the sun off her face, she took instructions by Cook to follow a flattened path to the Bakers. It was a little longer by foot, but it was sure to keep her safe. Jane halted when she came upon the alternate path, through the forested trees where the sacred pond hid, if she veered left. A flashback of waking to Mr. Eaton looking over her, remembering the blue of his eyes and feel of his stubbly face, made her flush. "They were thoughts…just sleepy, sophomoric notions," she said out loud, releasing her unclean feelings into the abyss, and continued on the path Cook suggested.

The Baker house was quiet, shutters closed, with a single line of smoke rising from the chimney. Straggling sheep and a half dozen chickens moved out of her way as Jane made her way to the door. She waited, after knocking several times, when she finally heard footsteps shuffle across the floor.

"My, Miss Reynolds, it's nice to see you," Mrs. Baker said, wiping her hands down her apron.

"Good afternoon, Mrs. Baker. I come bearing gifts from your cousin," Jane swung a basket of pies and breads in front of her, the aromas of baked goods seeping through the crevices.

"Oh, my cousin Agatha! She is such a dear. Please, please, come in," she insisted, moving aside for Jane to enter.

It was stuffy and there were dirty dishes still on the table. Jane placed the basket down and opened the windows to let in some light and air.

"Why are you not resting? Where's your husband? The boys, at least?"

"Oh well, Miss, I've given birth two times before...three if you include the one that didn't make it to the fourth month. No need to be making a fuss over me."

Jane took her by the arm and seated her in the nearest chair.

"You should not be up and about caring for your family when you have a baby to tend to..." Jane surveyed the room. "And where's the baby?"

Mrs. Baker tilted her head to a crib by the fire. Jane walked over and peered at the tiniest human she had ever seen. The little girl had slatted eyes, pink skin, and dark brown hair lying flat against her scalp.

"She's precious," Jane whispered.

"Well, as the proud mother, I'd not be one to deny it. My little darling, she'll be. All mine and just for me."

"I will not take any excuses. While she's sleeping, I want you to lie down." She pointed her finger and shook it. "No! Don't you even refuse and give me a million reasons why it isn't right. I insist! Once the baby awakens, I will bring her directly to you. Now get, before I carry you to bed."

Pure exhaustion won, and Mrs. Baker was soon resting.

Thankful for the temperament of a newborn, Jane had plenty of time before the cries of hunger got her attention. She cleaned the dishes, unpacked the food, swept the floors, and was amid boiling water to wash the dirtied sheets when the baby squealed. She wiped her hands and eagerly picked up the infant. Jane cooed at the little face and her tiny dark eyes slightly opened to investigate the stranger who held her. As promised, she carried the squirming ball to Mrs. Baker, who already woke to the distant cries.

"What are you doing up?" Jane chastised when she saw Mrs. Baker waddle towards her. With the baby in one hand, she led Mrs. Baker with the other to a chair near the window to enjoy the bright day. After placing a pillow behind her and pulling her feet onto a facing chair, Jane handed her the precious bundle, cleaned and ready to suckle on her mommy's breast.

"Now what do you think, making a fuss over me like I was the queen. You're more than kind, Miss Reynolds, you are a saint." She grabbed Jane's arm to pull her closer. "You don't know how much this means to me."

"There's no need to thank me. I'm sure you have done this a thousand times for others."

Mrs. Bishop tipped her head. "Aye."

Jane made some tea and placed a few biscuits on a plate next to Mrs. Baker before moving onto the laundry. Throwing her arms around a basket of wash, Jane headed outside. But no sooner she opened the door, she was accosted.

"Miss Reynolds!" Mr. Baker exclaimed. Seeing beads of sweat coming from her hairline, and her sleeves rolled up, with his wife's large apron covering up her pretty dress, he grabbed the basket swiftly from her hands. "A lady in your own right shouldn't be toting the work of laundry."

Jane wiped her brow, pushed her sleeves even higher, and pulled the basket back to her chest. "I'm perfectly capable of handling a load or two of laundry," she huffed. Determined to complete her task, she headed out the door only to bump right into the chest of Mr. Eaton coming through with the two Baker boys following him in step.

It was her time to shriek. "Mr. Eaton!"

A collision at the door ensued, and Jane moved aside to

allow the dirty, tired, and hungry men to enter. The two boys nodded as they passed, and Mr. Eaton closed the door behind him.

"Miss Reynolds," he said, taking the basket from her arms. He leaned in and whispered in her ear, "What are you doing here?"

"I can explain," she blurted, not wanting Cook to pay for her strong will. She wondered if he was angry. But his jaw did not clench, nor did his brow furrow.

"It is a nice surprise to see you," he said instead.

She narrowed her eyes to his to confirm he meant what he said.

A smirk crossed his faced indicating he did.

She swiped away at the sweat trickling down her neck, and brushed back the loose hairs around her face, tucking the longer strands into her once-coiffed hair. There was no glamour in the work she was doing, and she cringed to think about what the mirror would reveal. But when she looked over at Mr. Eaton, she couldn't have been in better company.

Usually presented as a gentleman, Mr. Eaton was every bit a working man standing in front of her. His billowy white shirt hung loosely from his waist, unbuttoned at the collar, and sleeves unevenly rolled up his forearms. Dark stains encircled his armpits. Mud coated the hems of his pants, as well as splattered on the sides of his face. His hair was tousled, pieces sticking against his head. Grassy mud dried against his neck, and his face was reddened by the heat of the day. He was in no better predicament than she.

"You're a mess!" Jane declared.

He looked down at himself. "It seems I am."

"Aye! Mr. Eaton had a hard time with old Mueller, the most stubborn of the mules," Mr. Baker explained.

"Who won?" Jane questioned, not really needing the answer.

"It was a toss-up," Mr. Baker goaded.

Mr. Baker explained the tug of war that ensued between the old mule and Mr. Eaton, explaining how he ended up in the mud, face first. The room roared in unison at the retelling of the story, though Mr. Eaton only found humor in the aftermath.

Jane admiringly watched as the room fill with laughter, including Mr. Eaton. His whole demeanor changed as his body succumbed to the humor, even if at his expense. He looked at Jane, and to her surprise, he smiled at her. It was more of the man she saw yesterday, and a part of her yearned for more.

When Jane didn't join the room in laughter, he saddled up to her and asked, "You don't find my mishap humorous?"

"I was just observing. It's nice to see you all happy. You are so…" she paused. "Real."

He tilted his head and waited for her to explain. But she didn't, choosing to ignore his curiosity.

"Do you come here often?" She glazed over his attire. "Disguised as a common man?"

He straightened, tucked in his shirt, as he proceeded to explain, "Often enough. Mr. Baker and my father were good friends. He has been a part of my life since I was a boy. I come to help when he needs an extra hand."

"Don't you have men to help?"

"Yes." He scrunched his brow. "But I am happy to help. These are my lands and I am grateful for the men and women who choose to work on them. I am not above that. Especially Mr. Baker and his family. They are good people."

Jane glanced over her shoulder at the family congregated around the baby. "Yes, they are." She looked back at Mr. Eaton. "You are different here. Comfortable. Content."

"Do you think I am an unhappy man otherwise?"

"I am just making an observation," she replied, as she jetted from the kitchen to the table, carrying food.

"And what is it you see?" he questioned.

Jane hesitated. *Dare she be honest?*

"That you hide the real you."

He stepped in front of her, demanding her attention. "And who are you, Jane Reynolds?"

Jane halted. But before she could answer, or lie, Mrs. Baker rose from her chair, taking Jane's attention away from the man in front of her, demanding an answer to his question.

"Don't you dare lift a finger!" Jane admonished. "Sit down and take care of your sweet baby." She pointed at the men in the room. "I'll tend to these big babies."

Mrs. Baker obeyed and slipped back into her chair, curling the newborn to her chest.

"And the rest of you..." Jane barked, "...wash up decently. I will not have filthy men at the table." She eyed Mr. Eaton in particular.

The boys immediately jumped and were out the door.

Mr. Baker kissed the head of his wife and followed his sons. But before stepping outside, he called, "Are you coming, Sir?"

"Yes, I am right behind you." Mr. Eaton replied, following the trio of dirty men.

"He's enamored with you," Mrs. Baker said after the door closed.

Jane looked up. "Huh?"

Mrs. Baker smirked, knowing Jane heard her.

Grateful for the food Cook sent, Jane created a spread for everyone to eat.

When the men returned, shirts tucked, faces scrubbed, and hands cleaned, they gathered at the wooden table–the center of the home–and the harmony of a family ensued. Mrs. Baker, at one end of the table, cradled the newborn in her arms, while Mr. Baker sat beside his wife, fussing with his daughter, his face unable to conceal his contentment. The boys, who sat across from one another, jeered, and jabbed for possession of the food. Mrs. Baker begged them to stop, but it had little effect. Mr.

Eaton sat at the head of the table but did nothing to claim his importance. He was merely a friend at their table participating in the day of a life of the Baker family.

After they filled their bellies, all the food nearly eaten, the men rose, stretched off the aches their bodies registered after a short reprieve, and headed back to work. The boys thanked Jane as they left, but not before they kissed their mother on the head.

Mr. Baker reached for Jane's hand and shook it with vigor. "God sent us an angel when he dropped you in our field," he said. "Thank you for caring for the love of my life. You are a special woman, Miss Reynolds. May God bless you, my dear."

Jane couldn't help herself and threw her arms around him. He squirmed from the gesture, but she didn't let go until she properly showed her gratitude. He blushed profusely and rushed out the door.

Mr. Eaton nodded to Jane to indicate his own gratitude, but before he closed the door, he stopped. "We are all indebted to you, Miss Reynolds. Thank you."

He bid Mrs. Baker a good rest of the day and closed the door behind him.

Mrs. Baker lifted an eyebrow at Jane. "That man cares about you..."

Jane looked at her. "Huh?"

Mrs. Baker smirked. She knew Jane heard her.

LIGHTNING STRIKES TWICE

As Jane closed the gate of the cottage, leaving Mrs. Baker napping with her newborn, hot air smacked her across the face. The heat from the late afternoon sun was bearing down. Exhausted from an average day's labor of a farmer's wife, she dared to consider a plunge in the pond. She knew the risk, but it was by chance Mr. Eaton found her for the first time. The enticement of cool water, and to bathe the sweaty grime from her body, far outweighed the threat of him finding her again.

Lightning didn't strike twice.

She headed for the trees, winding her way under the dense canopies, offering reprieve from the sun. When she reached the pond, it glistened as if it was a cauldron of diamonds concealed in water, the sunlight penetrating its depths, catching the facets. Jane had to shield her eyes from the glare. The tricking water allured her to the pond's edge where she cupped handfuls of water and splashed it against her face letting its cooling affects trickle down her neck and chest, tempting her to strip herself of the confines of her clothes and submerge her whole body into its blackened depths. Reaching behind her back, she undid her hooks, untied the laces of her corset, and slipped out of her sweat-soaked layers, except for her chemise, relieving herself of the weighty clothes now in a pile on the grass next to her. With one foot in, assessing the water temperature as neither freezing nor warm, she dove in, submerging herself into the dark depths of the pond. As she emerged, the crisp water wiped away the grime from the day. Weariness gave way to relaxation. She turned onto her back, flapped her arms in rhythmic strokes, and floated above the surface, watching the clouds drift pass the treetops. All the surrounding sounds were muffled in her water-filled ears, and she faded into a state of tranquility. Nothing mattered, not space or time.

Peyton's words returned, "*Your soul will be with you.*"

Her daydreaming also returned.

Mr. Eaton floated across her mind. The thoughts of him made her fantasize about things too embarrassing to admit. She could not deny when he entered the Baker's cottage the heat of his body radiated towards her, tingling her skin as he neared her. Pangs of desire ignited.

But there was more. Something familiar. Something that tugged at her heart.

Not only did her insides tickle when in his presence, but she yearned for more. More time with him, more discovery, more closeness. She physically ached with desire, not only in her body, but in her soul. She had no right to indulge in such fantasies, knowing the impossibility of the situation. Her emotions were free falling, if not irrational. But she had to admit, if only to herself in the quietude of the forest, this man, outwardly austere, antiquated, arrogant–which should make any modern woman cringe, if it weren't for the genuineness residing in his soul, tapped into her heart in ways she hadn't experienced since Stephen, and it frightened her. It didn't make sense…nor did she want it to. Not in that moment. Not today. Not there in the sanctity of parallel time.

She plunged under the water to cleanse her thoughts, hoping to cool the desires pulsating inside. When her fingers pruned, her thoughts no longer consumed about a man neither reasonable nor feasible, she dragged herself out of the pond. Like a wetted dog, she shimmied the water from her body and unpinned her hair to let the water-soaked, moppy mess fall to her shoulders, picking out the twigs and bits of plant matter that found a home in the wet strands. The late afternoon air was warm against her skin, but the chemise was wet and cold, the combination causing goosebumps to rise and fall against her skin. She closed her eyes, tilted her face towards the sun, and allowed the warmth to penetrate her, and prayed to the sky above.

"You got me here, now tell me why?"

When she opened her eyes, she stood face to face with her answer.

Lightning struck twice!

"Mr. Eaton!" Jane gasped. "I…I…" the words seemed to fail her. Her body trembled.

He didn't speak. Instead, he took off his coat and wrapped it around her. He touched her face gently, where he wiped away the water falling from her brow before bringing her lips to his and pressing against them. They lifted and fell, slowly, pressing harder each time they came down upon hers. He hungered for her as he immersed himself, pulling her lips open a little each time until his tongue intertwined with hers, tasting the heated sensation inside.

Jane's legs weakened.

He plunged her lips again, and again…and again.

Jane pressed her hand on his chest to steady herself. His heart pounded against the palm of her hand.

He gazed into her eyes, searching her face for what her lips expressed–her body demanding of him. Jane drew herself closer, urging him for more. His hand slid down the small of her back as he pulled her into him, chest upon chest. Heart against heart. He winced at her hardened nipples pressed against him, and returned his kisses in full fury, plunging his tongue deeper inside the warmth of her mouth.

"Henry," she moaned.

"Say that again," he asked.

"Henry," she exhaled, wanting the air to lift it, swirl it, and wrap him in a blanket of her feelings.

"You whispered it once to me, and I knew I wanted no one else to say my name with such sweetness," he explained, placing another kiss on her lips. He took her hands into his, opened her palms, and kissed them softly in the center. "I am not apologizing or condoning my behavior, only declaring you have beguiled me through to my soul. But how can one explain his behavior when it comes to the heart?"

Jane sank into his embrace. His breath hot against her cheek, his strong body wrapped around her, she quivered. He pulled her tighter, harder, into his embrace. His lips came down again and brushed her satiny texture against his, demanding more. She capitulated, not having the strength to resist him. Not wanting him to stop.

Alert! Alert! Alert!

The neon sign flashed in the bowels of her brain.

Jane pushed out of his arms. She wasn't an innocent maiden, and had he persisted, she would have given into him completely. But as the warmth against her lips cooled, she recalled the line of decency he himself preached…and crossed over. She was well aware of the time and place she resided. A gentleman would never be so physically amorous if he respected her as a lady. His kisses were demanding more of her. Much, much more!

"Mr. Eaton!" she shouted.

Henry stepped back in confusion.

"I dare say Mr. Darcy would never have boldly kissed Elizabeth that way!" She reproached. "What kind of woman do you take me for?" She tore his coat from her shoulders and threw it at him.

Henry's eyes dropped to the ball of fabric crumpled at his feet.

"Jane," he entreated, "I meant no offense."

Jane narrowed her eyes and gritted her teeth. "If you please," she snarled, lifting her hand in a circled frenzy, signally him to turn around.

When his back faced her, she grabbed the pile of clothes left at the water's edge and found a haven behind some bushes to dress. She grunted, struggling with the antiquated clothing, damning hooks, ties, and strings, cursing the absurdity of women's fashion and subjugation of the nineteenth-century. Damning men! Damning herself for almost succumbing to her desires.

And maybe, damning the realization that she, too, had fallen in love with him.

With determination–and the need to flee Henry immediately, she put herself back in the remnants of a properly dressed lady. Albeit a little less tidy without Regina's help.

Mr. Eaton waited, as any proper gentleman would, until he heard footsteps pound the pathway. When he turned, he found Jane fleeing from him.

"Please, don't storm away so angrily," he begged, wanting to explain; plead his case of love. But she was beyond reproach, ignoring his words.

"How dare he think I would be that kind of woman," she murmured, each word giving her more strength to push farther away from him, realizing no matter what year it was, men were still fiends.

They walked the long way home, Henry in tow, both in silence.

Clearing the hill, the Eaton estate in viewing distance, Jane suddenly stopped when she saw a man at the house waving frantically at them.

"Henry," she called to him. "Is something wrong?"

Henry caught up to her, panting, happy to have her by his side again. But it was short-lived. His body stiffened, and his heart sank when he realized what lay ahead.

"Henry?" Jane questioned as he pushed past her and forged ahead.

"Jane…" Henry's voice fell off. "Please forgive me," he whispered, the words floating past her in the breeze.

Not explaining, nor looking back at her, Jane watched as he hurriedly put on his coat, pulling the cuffs of his shirt through the sleeves. He swiped at the remnants of mud that still lingered on his pants, failing miserably at his attempt to erase the signs of battle with Old Mueller. He buttoned his shirt and fussed with his collar, pulling a cravat from his pocket, and tying it, taking great effort to make himself look presentable by the time he reached the house.

Jane realized her own predicament. The back of her dress was hooked unevenly causing it to fall off her shoulders, the corset underneath sloppily tied revealing more of her chest than would be considered appropriate. Her hair, still wet and wild, lay loosely upon her shoulders, and her cheeks were flushed with adrenaline from passion and anger. She tugged at her bodice, lifted the sleeves in place, smoothed out her skirt, and quickly twisted her hair into a bun, using the sole hairpin she found stuck in the wetted mess to hold it in place. Without stripping herself completely and starting all over, she had no other way to rectify her appearance, nor did she understand the importance of doing so. All she knew, Henry was in a hurry and made a great effort to erase any implications of what had occurred that day.

As Jane neared the house, she saw why Henry was so frantic. Besides a well-dressed man, a notably young and lovely woman awaited his arrival.

HONOR

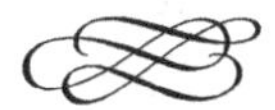

Anne stood by her uncle, twisting her hands around each other, anticipating Henry's return. Her nerves quivered; not certain she could maintain the calm charade if she waited one more minute. Her uncle offered his handkerchief, and she wiped the perspiration along her hairline as the late afternoon sun beat down on the terrace.

Mrs. Bishop advised the guests of Master Eaton's prior obligations, and he was expected to return by late afternoon. The two were agitated by the lack of prepared hospitality after traveling for two days but accepted Mrs. Bishop's kindness of light refreshments as they waited.

Anne now regretted the decision as the perspiration trickled down her back and her coiffed hair crushed under her bonnet. After all, she wanted to impress Henry, not frighten him away.

"Sit down, my dearest niece," the older gentleman requested.

"I cannot, Uncle, for I fear I will not endure what I'm about to ask of Henry if I do not keep my stance," the young woman replied, politely refusing.

"As I have assured your mother, I will be of every use in case

Mr. Eaton does not agree to your conditions. He will have no other choice but to follow through accordingly."

Her hands circled again. "Uncle, I do not wish to be demanding of Henry. I beg of you, let me have a word with him as I choose. He has never been unreasonable or unkind."

"As you wish." The man plucked at his cuffs and sat, bored with the long wait. Looking into the far reaches of the gardens, he spotted the two figures coming over the hill.

"I see his return now. You will not have long to wait."

The young woman scurried to the windowed door of the terrace and glanced at her reflection. After smoothing back flyaway hair uprooted when she removed her hat, she pinched her cheeks and wiped away the last of the moisture surrounding her hairline. To her surprise, when she turned, Henry stood within arm's reach.

"Henry!" She presented her hand to him, but immediately retreated when he did not return her gesture.

"Did you not get the correspondence? Mother assured me she sent a note to inform you of our arrival. I do hope we have not intruded on you," the young woman fretted.

"No," Henry replied, turning to look behind him.

Jane was on his tailcoats, breathless. When she arrived on the terrace, she became fully aware of her disheveled appearance compared to the beautifully coiffed woman standing across from her.

The woman cast her eyes upon Jane, not missing the familiarity of her place besides Henry. She had heard about Miss Reynolds but expected a more presentable woman from Lady Levongood's description. The woman before her was far less affecting than previously suggested to her. With greater confidence, Anne turned her attention to Henry, surmising Jane insignificant.

"You remember my uncle, Samuel Milton?" She gestured to the man beside her.

"Yes, it is good to see you again, sir," Henry shook the man's hand.

Jane shifted, reminding Henry of her presence.

"Excuse me." Henry stepped aside but made no eye contact. "This is Miss Jane Reynolds, a guest of Dr. Cummings, visiting from America."

"It is a pleasure to meet you, Miss Jane Reynolds," Mr. Milton took Jane's hand she offered.

"Thank you, Mr. Milton, it's my pleasure as well."

He nudged his niece forward. "May I be so kind as to introduce my niece, Miss Anne Benning."

The young beauty curtsied, followed with a smile. She did not extend her hand, but Jane met her eyes and bowed her head in recognition. With a slight squeeze of her arm by her uncle, Miss Benning continued the conversation.

"It is quite a pleasure to meet you as well, Miss Reynolds. I have heard so much about you from Margaret Elizabeth. She describes you as a magical being. The young girl could not stop telling us all about you. It is nice to put a face with a name."

"Yes," Uncle Samuel explained. "We saw them on their way to London. Your sister extended an invitation for us to join her summer festivities. We are headed there tomorrow."

"It seems Margaret Elizabeth will accompany your sister for the summer." Miss Benning added. She stepped closer to Henry and placed her gloved hand on his arm. He looked down at the motion before he caught her sapphire eyes looking at him. "What an opportunity for both of you."

He did not react to the beautiful woman's touch, nor did he move to stop her. She left her hand resting on his arm.

Pleased with his niece's ability to maneuver her position, Uncle Samuel moved closer to Henry, but his eyes targeted Jane.

"Miss Reynolds, I am certain it is nice to finally put a face with a name of Mr. Eaton's fiancée?"

Jane feared her face went white. Her limbs went limp.

Uncle Samuel snickered, pleased with the effect.

Henry's shoulders stiffened, his jaw tightened, and his eyes darkened as he stared at Uncle Samuel. He pulled away from Miss Benning's touch, letting her hand fall.

"My dearest Anne, with all due respect to your uncle, you relieved yourself of that commitment."

"Oh, Henry," Anne laughed, with the instruction by her mother to nullify any negative reactions with a carefree chortle. "You should know the temperaments of a woman by now. You are not going to dishonor me over a childish display of moods, are you?"

Henry scowled.

Anne feared too much time had passed allowing Henry's feeling for her to soften. His face was impassive. His blue eyes, she once abashedly succumbed to, were now iced over. She tilted her head and tried a more kittenish approach, using her femininity for all it was worth.

She encircled his arm with hers and leaned into him, her pink, glossy lips nearly touching his ear when she suggested, "Do we really need to revisit our last argument? Let us discuss this in private, shall we?"

Allowing himself a moment of weakness, Henry looked at Jane. Her once flushed cheeks were now depleted of color. Her eyes glared at him with bewilderment, her spirit crushed under the weight of the revelations. Wanting to reach out to her, he could only suffer in silence, knowing she fully comprehended the situation. He could not move, for he feared, if he did, he would pull her into his arms and never let go.

Uncle Samuel intervened.

"Miss Reynolds, let us allow these two to settle their affairs without the company of bystanders, shall we?" He offered his arm to Jane, which she accepted, and guided her toward the house, leaving.

Henry untangled himself from Anne's grasp. At one time, he coveted her touch. Now his body cringed at her advancement. He turned his back to her, preferring not to look at the woman who had caused him so much shame in the last year. He thought he was over the effect she had on him, but a magnitude of emotions overcame him. His feelings were raw about Jane, only to be thwarted by the arrival of Anne. His emotions quickly changed from bliss to aggravation to stark anger.

"Henry, you're not still angry with me?"

"Anne, you cannot return and claim your innocence to this situation?" He looked at her. "Four months ago, you dishonored me by ending our engagement. Our friends and family witnessed my humiliation. Now you ask me such a question?"

"Henry, I am sorry for the indelicate way in which I handled the situation. My behavior was thoughtless, if not obsessively inconsiderate. I should have spoken to you with more forthrightness. Given you the chance to fight for me. I wrote to you, on several occasions, to explain but did not hear a response. Hence why Uncle and I have come to see you."

Anne clutched her chest, her eyes watered.

Henry did not wish her harm or unhappiness. He was not a vindictive man. Nor immune to Anne's fragile femininity. Moved by her tears, he took her into his arms and her head fell to his shoulder.

"If you are asking for my forgiveness, I granted it long ago."

Anne peered up with a childlike naivety and proclaimed, "Henry, I am not just asking for forgiveness, I am asking for you to honor your proposal."

Henry's fiancée. Henry's fiancée. Henry's fiancée!

Jane's mind filled with a thousand questions. Her ego sank to a new low.

"What was I thinking...having romantic fantasies?" She mumbled.

Uncle Samuel, pouring himself something more suitable for a man, looked up. "Did you say something, my dear?"

Jane shook her head. She was in no mood for conversation, or to play the part of Henry's guest with Uncle Samuel. She desperately wanted to escape. Scream. Cry. Hide.

"Oh," he remarked, distracted with his own thoughts. He walked to the window unashamedly to watch the quarrel outside. He wanted to evaluate Henry's reaction to determine the success of his niece's influence. With Henry's guarded expression, it was hard for him to confirm if his plan was working. He was more than confident of his niece's beguiling manner, but not confident in Henry's attachment towards her. He relied more on Henry's honor for a successful outcome. In the end, Uncle Samuel would win, one way or another.

Or another was why Uncle Samuel was there.

As if he knew she was ready to bolt, Uncle Samuel left his observation, found a chair closest to Jane and sat down. He did not speak right away. He sipped his drink and viewed her. Assessed her. She was a curious figure he hadn't counted on.

He was no novice when it came to lovers. Nothing went unnoticed by him: the untidiness of Jane's hair, the flushed cheeks when she first came into his view, the mismatched buttoning of Henry's collar. He never missed the hidden subtleties of a forbidden tryst. He had many of those and planned to exit life with many more before the good Lord took him. But he didn't expect to find a situation like this. He honestly did not think Henry had it in him to be so dishonorable. It gave him a new appreciation for the man. Unfortunately, with the introduction of Miss Reynolds, he would have to quickly recalculate his plans.

"My dear, you are a long way from home. What is the honor of your visit?"

"I'm visiting my cousin, Dr. Cummings."

"You are a relative, then?"

"Yes, on his wife's side."

Jane was getting comfortable lying.

"A rather young, and might I add, beautiful relative." His eyes followed down Jane's body to fully appreciate his observation. She was not young in chronological years. He could see by the maturity of expressions on her face, although her clear skin did not reveal any flaws of age. Her slim body, long, lean arms, and perky breasts were all signs that she was unchartered in the ways of children and men. He added, "Dr. Cummings is a fortunate man."

Jane was trying, really trying, to be polite. It was hard when faced with lasciviousness. She eyed the door, hoping someone, anyone, would walk through and free her from this man.

Uncle Samuel eyed the door as well, hoping they would not be disturbed. He swallowed his drink and contemplated filling it but leaned into Jane instead.

"You are traveling alone?"

Jane smelled the whisky as his breath blew across her shoulder. She shivered, unable to conceal the chill up her spine. The cold room and damp chemise only contributed to the havoc on her nipples. Uncle Samuel's eyes lit up when he noted the effects.

Jane pulled away, hoping he would retreat.

He did.

He leaned back and twirled the empty glass in his hand.

"The States are rather far...it seems like a long way to travel. You must be very fond of the doctor." He wanted to know her purpose. More importantly, her purpose with Henry. "Are you planning a long stay?"

"The doctor and I only just met. But it's hard not to like him very much. As far as travel, my plans are tentative."

"Hmmm. Your trip here may be more than visiting the good doctor?" He winked, insinuating a hidden agenda for

Jane's stay at the Eaton Estate. "A prospect of marriage, maybe?"

Jane stood. "No. Of course not!"

He rose as well. "My apologies."

He walked to the side bar to fill his drink. He needed the distraction. The more he observed Jane, the more desirous he became. He needed to keep his wits about him to deal with the situation with his niece. He came here as Anne's chaperone–not for his own pleasures. Her reputation was on the line, and he was here to emphasize to Henry what was best for all involved, hoping he would comply with his niece's request. After all, she once received a proper proposal from the widower. She was beautiful, charming, and a lady in her own right; any man would be lucky to have her admiration.

It was difficult to understand Henry's choice to marry a second time. Cherishing his own bachelorhood, Uncle Samuel questioned the necessity. He knew Henry's daughter was well attended to by his sister, and he was not in want for companionship. He saw that for himself with the woman before him. No one would think less of him to live out his days in the company of friends. Maybe he was lonely. Uncle Samuel greatly empathized that a man had needs. He himself never needed those traditional ways to keep the companionship of a lady. But he was a man of means, which allowed him to choose any lifestyle he wanted. It was good to be him. Henry was different. He needed the comfort of a woman...and that woman was going to be his niece.

Jane followed Uncle Samuel's movements around the room. He was not a tall man, nor a man of handsomeness. His athletic physique and well-dressed manner made up for his lack of physical attraction. He had a full head of hair with long sideburns which only further accentuated his high cheekbones. His eyes were dark, the color of chocolate. Eyes that hid secrets. Jane watched as he pursed his lips, which only confirmed his haughty manner. Although trying to be pleasant with conversation, he seemed to have an ulterior motive behind the charming I.

With his glass filled, he walked up to her, reached forward, and grabbed something out of her hair. A small twig twisted between his long fingers. A sneer moved to his lips.

He said rather bluntly, "With all due respect, my niece is but a child. But she will learn the ways of a woman with Mr. Eaton's guidance. A prudent choice for all concerned." His lips twisted. "Margaret is a dear child, but a son will carry on the family name. And with so much at stake, I do hope those two can resolve their issues. Don't you agree?"

Jane got another chill, but this time it was a sense of warning.

"I'm sorry, Mr. Milton, would you find me dreadful if I excused myself?"

He bowed slightly, but before she ran off, he grabbed her wrist and pulled her into him. "Don't fret, my dear, these things have a way of working themselves out. We can always find you someone who is more available."

Jane lost her balance under his grip, and her body fell into his. She felt him move with pleasure. Shocked, she jerked, pushing him away. Their eyes locked, each assessing what to expect. Jane didn't trust him. Uncle Samuel saw a conquest in more ways than one.

Sounds of feet against the hardwood floor jolted them from their stand-off. Uncle Samuel moved aside for Jane to retreat. When the door opened, she ran out of the room, brushing past Anne and Henry without saying a word.

"Oh my, Uncle, what did you say to our dear Miss Reynolds?" Anne asked, clueless to her uncle's intrigue.

"I merely inquired about her afternoon." He walked up to Henry to face him. His eyes narrowed. "She had quite an exhausting afternoon. More than she expected. I suggested she not concern herself with any obligations to Mr. Eaton and his guests. I assured her we would all understand her departure."

Henry stood within steps of the threshold of the door. He had a choice to run after Jane or stay. But duty and honor came first. Neither warranted spontaneity in his course of action. He promised his hand to Anne and would honor his commitment.

Pleased with Henry's and Anne's news, Uncle Samuel offered to pour Henry a drink. He knew Henry needed one.

SENT AWAY

Mrs. Bishop knocked gently at the door, not wanting to wake Jane too abruptly. But there was much to do. She could not afford for her to wake at her leisure. She needed to get Jane out of bed.

"Come in, Mrs. Bishop, I'm up."

Jane's eyes were swollen and red. She had been crying into the late hours, finally falling asleep before dawn, only to be awakened by a commotion in the hallway. Apparently, Mr. Eaton's guests were early risers. She lay in bed with her legs curled to her chest, as if her tummy ached. But it was her heart that anguished, and there was no medicine for that kind of pain.

She made her excuses from dinner the prior evening, claiming fatigue. A tray was sent up with a note from Anne wishing her a speedy recovery. But she was not in the mood to eat, no matter how kind the gesture. She stripped down to nakedness, wrapped herself up in a large quilt, encircling herself in a cocoon of pity, and crawled into bed. Nothing could stop the shards of agony piercing through her heart. She felt like a fool for allowing herself to be swept up in Henry's arms. Her attraction to him was irrational, and now she was disgusted with herself for allowing him to take advantage of those feelings.

It was just a kiss! She tried to convince herself, but the words circled around and around until she was dizzy.

But she knew those words weren't true. It wasn't *just* a kiss. It was more. More than she bargained for. Whether right or wrong, she had never been kissed so passionately, held so intimately, or experienced the love a man so deeply with just a kiss.

She didn't want to be the other woman. And yet, she stood shamefully in front of Henry's fiancée, with his kisses still lingering on her lips. She was disgusted with herself. There was no way she could face Anne again. Nor did she want to see Henry. She feared she might hit him, or worse, buckle under her desire.

"You're a sight!" Mrs. Bishop declared when she entered, Regina in tow.

"I couldn't sleep."

"Aye, I see." She was no novice to love herself. She witnessed the mutual fondest between Master Eaton and Jane. It grew ever more evident each day. With Anne's arrival, she only surmised the cause of Jane's malaise. "Let's give Regina a chance to make you presentable."

Regina waited by the mirror, comb in hand.

Jane obediently crawled out of bed, tucking the quilt tightly around her nakedness.

"I am a wreck!" She slumped in the chair.

Mrs. Bishop shook her head in shame. "Well, I can't say you don't look a fine mess." She dampened a towel with water and tea, instructing Jane to place it over her eyes. "I have some coffee being sent up. We will get you going in no time."

"Going?"

"Mr. Milton and Miss Benning are leaving for London…the

poor girl. She ate something that didn't agree with her delicate system, almost postponing the trip. But she assured me she has recovered and is eager to get into the city. I've got to have you packed and ready to go with them in the hour."

Jane twisted her head around. "I'm going to London?"

"Yes. Master Eaton instructed me to pack your things."

"He is sending me away?"

"Yes, Miss," Mrs. Bishop answered.

A tidal wave of anger welled up inside Jane. She didn't know whether to scream or throw something. But she resigned: neither was a good option when she saw Regina's eyes widen at the rash of red blotches creeping up her neck and into her cheeks.

Jane stood abruptly, tightened the quilt around her body, swooping the excess in her arm, and stormed out of the room. The servants didn't miss the half-naked woman stomping down the stairs. No one dare question the fury, allowing the drama to descend without interruption. Reaching Henry's study, she didn't wait for an invitation.

He rose as the doors exploded open. Jane stood before him, her reddened, puffy eyes glaring at him, betraying her sleepless night, for which he knew he caused. He stood upright, shoulders back, chest out, ready for the attack.

"How dare you!" She pointed at him. "Who do you think you are? I'm not a whore you can just arbitrarily throw your sexual desires on and then cast off with little regard. You have no right to send me away without asking, nor do you have the right to disregard me. I am not so fragile to understand your expression of love was merely desire. I will not be a ruined woman for the momentary indiscretion!"

"Good morning, Miss Reynolds," a man's greeting interrupted her.

Jane froze. She closed her eyes tightly before turning to the voice which came from the corner of the room. Prying her lids open, it was with great despair she found Uncle Samuel sitting against the wall, legs stretched, hands gripped against the arms of his chair, seemingly enjoying the spectacle from the sidelines.

Jane gulped; a knot twisted in her throat. She squeaked out a barely audible salutation. "Good morning, Mr. Milton."

"It is nice to see you," he replied, taking pleasure with the whole connotation of it. "It seems you have recovered from your illness…which unfortunately denied us of your company last night."

She clenched her teeth before she answered. "I am much better, thank you."

He stood and moved closer to her. "Please do not berate your host, for it is all my doing you that are leaving with us today. You see, I thought some excitement would do you good. It seems you have limited companionship here." He gave a glance towards Henry. "It is not suitable for a woman, such as yourself," his eyes scanned her half nakedness, "to hide away in such isolation. I have convinced Henry it might be best if you join the festivities at his sisters. He almost guaranteed Lady Levongood would be happy to see you again."

Jane tasted the bile of nausea. She wondered if Anne's sickness affected her as well.

"You look worried, my dear." He leaned in, his breath brushing her shoulders. "I promised Henry I would personally take care of you, as if my own relative."

Jane straightened. "I'm not worried, I assure you."

"Well then, it's settled. I promise to have you back in a few weeks as a proper guest of Mr. and Mrs. Eaton."

Jane dropped her jaw and looked at Henry.

His blue eyes turned dense and dark, exposing nothing—nothing he didn't want her to see. Although he stood solidly behind his desk, his legs weakened under him. It took everything to not carry her away from this situation.

"So, you're to be married?" Jane braced for his answer.

"Yes, they are to wed in a few weeks, as originally planned," Uncle Samuel interjected, releasing a broad smile across his face. "No need to prolong the inevitable, would you not agree, Miss Reynolds?"

"A few weeks?" Jane's voice went up a few octaves. She cleared her throat. "I guess congratulations are in order." She turned to Uncle Samuel, "I will be ready within the hour."

"Splendid, my dear!" Uncle Samuel exclaimed.

Jane turned away from both of the men and grabbing the length of her quilt walked out as graceful as a queen leaving her court.

TAVERNS

Not long ago, Jane experienced the trip from London to Wiltshire. The return journey to London promised a much more arduous and lengthy adventure in nineteenth-century transportation. The bumpy and dusty roads extended the trip to a three-day ride, with stops in the evening at various established taverns. Normally, friends along the way would welcome them into their homes, lengthening the trip, promising a more pleasurable journey. But the exodus to the city for the early summer festivities left most homes vacant. More pressing, in less than a week, the Levongood's gala commenced, making the travelers eager to arrive in London sooner than later.

The first night, Anne and Jane shared a meal with Uncle Samuel before they retreated to dingy accommodations upstairs. Jane was not eager to be in proximity to her nemesis all day *and* all night, forced into companionship, but she had no other alternative. Lucky for her, Anne feigned tiredness and wanted to bed immediately. But Jane noticed her face had grown paler throughout the ride Her plate went untouched at dinner. Concerned, Jane assessed Anne's condition, the best she had knowledge of. She listened to her breathing. It was not heavy or labored. This ruled out a series of illness. Most likely, Anne suffered from the flu, a killer in her time. But with early remediation, she could recover in three to five-days. She tried to remember the homeopathic methods she often read in magazines. *Was it feed a cold, starve a fever, or the other way around?* Fevers helped the body fight infection, but only if they lasted for a few days. Coughing cleared breathing passages. Rest, as well as drinking plenty of fluids, was essential. Dehydration and diarrhea needed to be watched. They killed many, even in modern times. With that being the extent of her medical knowledge, Jane elevated Anne's head with an extra pillow, instructed her to drink two cups of hot tea before she went to sleep, and prayed her symptoms didn't get worse.

Anne awoke in better spirits, even requesting a small breakfast. Jane hoped it was a sign she had turned the corner of her illness. But she did not keep it down for long. Once on the road, she remained listless, leaning her head on Jane's shoulder, sleeping through the bumpy ride. Uncle Samuel read the paper from cover to end with prying eyes on Jane, watching her breasts as the carriage moved them about in rhythm. He was not discreet and smiled when she caught him eyeing her. Falling in and out of sleep, Jane made a mental note to stay away from him as much as circumstances allowed.

The carriage pushed on until night fell when they finally arrived at their second tavern. It was much cleaner than the first night, and it had plenty of windows to aerate the sweaty smells of the traveling inhabitants. Anne headed directly to the room, making no excuses. Although Jane wanted to linger in the dining room, to stretch her legs and enjoy the cool breeze filling the space, she had no desire to dine with her lecherous chaperone. He had offered his company, trying with great persuasion to convince her to stay with him. But Jane declined his invitation in lieu of taking care of Anne, requesting a plate of food to be brought up instead. Anne could not keep much down and did little more than drink hot apple cider, Jane insisted she drink. She soon fell asleep, allowing Jane reprieve from nurse duty to read until her candle gave out.

Had they pushed, they would have arrived in London on the second day. But Uncle Samuel insisted they stop in the next town. He had business to attend, so he said. Jane was happy to accommodate him for Anne's sake. She was a good sport, never once complaining, but Jane knew the travel was difficult for her. So, it surprised her when Anne could exert energy enough to sit up by herself. She swung her legs to the side of the bed and yielded her listless body forward.

Jane escorted the weakened girl to the table and put a quilt over her shoulders. Anne requested a bowl of water whereupon she splashed her face and wiped away two days of dried perspiration. Gathering her golden mass of curls between her hands, she pulled her hair from her face and tied it into a neat bun. A swift action to go from invalid to a proper lady. She inhaled, filling her lungs with air, and exhaled, releasing whatever had taken hold of her health, rejuvenating a small amount of dignity. For only with guided assistance did Anne relieve herself, Jane carrying the basin to and from her bedside. A constant nursemaid and caretaker, she helped bathe and dress Anne, feed her, and put her to bed.

Anne put her hand on Jane's arm. "Thank you. I am humbled by your devotion to me. I don't think I could have survived this journey without you by my side."

"Well, don't overdo it. You have a long way to go until you're fully recovered," Jane warned. Anne was still pale, and Jane worried her renewed sense of health would be short-lived. "Would you like me to get you something to eat; bread or some broth?"

Anne nodded, and Jane scurried off to the kitchen below.

The tavern owner was a hard woman. Her hands were

large, her waistline thick, her wrinkles deeply embedded in her face. It was difficult for Jane to see any feminine quality about her except for the large, fatty breasts bulging from her neckline. But despite her looks, a motherly concern presented itself upon Jane's request for food. The tavern owner did not miss the sick traveler upon their arrival, and instantly suggested a soup of beef broth with vegetables and a loaf of bread, along with a pot of tea. As she walked away, Jane saw her limping heavily to one side. She pondered the life of the woman who endured such physical harshness. The average life was difficult, if not short, only reminding Jane her circumstance was a blessing–not a curse.

Tray in hand, Jane made her way upstairs, passing two women on the staircase. Not terribly overt in their adornment, they had an electrical charge of sexuality in the way they puffed their chests and swung their hips when they walked past her. She could only surmise the kind of women they were. Grabbing the handle of her own door, down the hall, another door opened and a woman emerged, straightening her skirt. She called out for the other two women to wait for her. Jane glimpsed at the gentleman as he shut the door behind her. It was Uncle Samuel. Not surprised, but equally shocking, she pushed open her door, only to shut it as quickly and lock it.

"Jane? Is there something wrong?"

Jane shuddered, not able to rid herself of the disgust, as if it was actually crawling on her. "Nothing to concern yourself." She averted Anne's stare and placed the tray in front of her.

Anne lifted the spoon and pushed around the chunks of parsnips swirling around the bowl.

"Please eat, Anne. You're a mere twig of a woman." It was not unnoticed her cheeks had sunken in the past few days.

"I will. I promise to finish what you have placed in front of me." She took three slurps, only to put the spoon down, uninterested in another bite. Her eyes forlorn, and on the verge of tears.

Jane sat next to her. "Are you feeling ill again? What is it?"

"Oh," she moaned, covering her face with her hands. "It seems foolish, but I don't have another to confide. You've been so kind to me, and you're a woman who might understand..."

Jane didn't want to be her confidant. It seemed wrong. But because of Anne's fragility, she felt she had no choice.

"Please, go on."

"I hope you do not think me a child." She twisted her birdlike hands together. "It is about a man."

Was Anne going to expose her crime of passion with Henry? Jane braced herself.

"Have you ever been in love with a man who wasn't right for you?"

"Well..." Jane should have thought about Stephen, but it was Henry who came to mind. "If I were to admit–yes."

"Did you..." She paused and lowered her eyes. Her thoughts took her back to feelings of love, which transformed into urges of passion she couldn't control. She had desires she didn't know were possible in a woman. They made her blush in remembrance, and guilt surfaced, shaming the pleasure that once consumed her. "Did you have uncontrollable feelings? Thoughts you never dreamed possible? Things you might be ashamed of?"

"I think it only natural, when you're in love."

Anne looked up. "Do men have the same feelings?"

Jane recalled Henry's heated passion. How he parted her lips, hungry to taste her, his body against hers begging for more.

Jane's body flushed with heat. From passion? Guilt? Both?

"Yes," she answered, wanting to be truthful, but not scare her. "They feel as strongly, if not more."

Anne blushed, and Jane wondered what innocence was lost. She knew the power of Henry. She could only imagine his effects on someone as young and naïve as Anne. She felt sick to her stomach at the possibilities.

Anne stayed silent, waiting for more.

"If you love a man and he feels the same, you should not be ashamed about your feelings toward each other. Love is a beautiful thing. But be careful not to be fooled or misguided. Men can, and will, take advantage."

Anne glanced out the window, but it was black outside. Only her reflection stared back. "Love *is* a wonderful thing," she whispered. "But what becomes of you when it is no longer in your grasp? Is it possible for a woman to give herself to someone when love is not present?"

Jane's muscles tightened. Her guilt overwhelmed her. She thanked the heavens for the darkened room where her crime was not visible on her face, exposing her deception. Jane intruded on Anne's happiness. And Anne was now questioning Henry's feelings about her.

"Miss Reynolds?" She caught Jane's eyes. "May I ask you something more?"

Jane wasn't sure how much more she could take but nodded.

"Can one die of a broken heart?"

Jane wondered what agonies lay underneath the surface of such a young life thus far. She seemed lost in the complexities of love. Jane wanted to hold Anne in her arms…give her a puppy! Tell her *time heals all things.* But in truth, she was just as confused about love as Anne. She had no right to extol wisdom. But she tried to give her hope–to tell her that not all was lost because of her intervention.

"It's in our nature to love. It's no less important than breathing. But do not despair of love. It has a way of finding you when you least expect it." She lifted Anne's chin and looked her in the eye. "You're a person worthy of love. Never forget that. The man who finds his way to you will adore you. Give him time."

Jane meant what she said. Anne was beautiful, indeed, and found no fault to dislike her. She was polite, sincere in her manner, and tenderhearted. Fragile and demure. She, herself, wanted to take care of her; keep her safe from the big, bad world. Jane understood how a man would find her pleasing–why Henry would choose to marry her.

Anne stood. "Thank you…" Her voice faltered, and she turned away.

"Anne?" Jane reached out to her, wanting to tell her more; explain if she could. But she slipped out of her grasp.

"If you don't mind, I would like to get some rest," Anne said and climbed into bed, bringing the covers to her chin. "Goodnight."

Jane blew the candle out, climbed into her own bed, and stared into the darkness, listening to the voices penetrating through the walls. Only before she drifted to sleep did she hear muffled crying coming from the bed next to hers. Had she been alone, it would have been her own crying she would have fallen asleep to.

THE WANSEY SISTERS

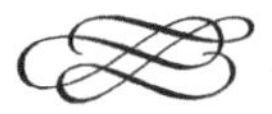

Jane awoke to the sounds of someone moving about the room. She sat up to find Anne bathed, dressed, and pinning her hair in front of the mirror.

"Feeling better?"

With her mouth holding pins for her hair, Anne nodded in response instead. When she finished the updo, she poured Jane tea.

"Do you take sugar?"

"You went downstairs for tea?" Jane questioned.

"I can be quite helpful to myself," she smirked. "I did not want to disturb your slumber, so I retreated quietly downstairs and asked for a tray of tea. The innkeeper was kind enough to carry it for me. I am famished. Shall we go downstairs to dine?"

Jane, excited with Anne's recovery, didn't waste time dressing. Anne helped with her hair, offering powder for her face, and a tinted lip salve. The transformation was inspiring. They headed downstairs where they ordered biscuits, jam, and, to Jane's pleasure, coffee. Anne eyed the black liquid as Jane brought it to her lips. With one sip, Jane almost coughed it out, but drank it anyway.

Even bad coffee was better than none.

Uncle Samuel was nowhere to be found, so they dined without him, both silently grateful for the reprieve from his company. Afterwards, when Anne had her fill–two biscuits and a half a pot of tea, and with no sign of a recurring nausea, she suggested they browse the shops before they were again cooped up for hours in the carriage.

The fresh air resuscitated Anne as they strolled the tinkers' and tailors' wares. Her cheeks filled with color, and life returned to her eyes–the sapphire blue sparkling once again. She was on the mend, easing Jane's worries.

As Anne was a lady of importance, reputation, and of money, shop owners recognized her status the moment she came through their doors. Every shop they entered the shops help was immediately directed to her, if not the owner himself, who gave his undivided attention towards her. She purchased a few toiletries for her stay in London, as well as browsed fabrics, purchasing yardage for gowns to be made at a later date. Her spending was unconditional for her wants.

Upon leaving the perfumery, Anne excitedly handed Jane a gift in sentiment. She purchased a small bottle of perfume Jane admired earlier. It wasn't the scent that captivated her, a light floral of jasmine, but the beauty of what the fragrance was encased, a shaped bottle made of molten green glass with an ornate silver cap. It had no price and Jane dare not ask. She was sure it was expensive, even for Anne. Knowing it would never make it home with her, Jane begged Anne keep it for herself. But Anne would hear nothing of it, insisting Jane accept her gratitude.

"You've been so kind to me..." She threw her arms around Jane and nestled her head next to Jane's, with tears in the corner of her eyes. "It is but a small thank you."

"Stop it!" Jane ordered but squeezed her all the same, equaling Anne's tears.

There was no turning back, Jane officially liked Anne. It was hard not to, and she silently damned Henry, who was never far from her thoughts. She knew she had to rid herself of the silliness, but her heart wouldn't obey her head. His kisses still lingered on her lips.

She damned herself instead.

The two women walked side by side, taking in the day at a leisurely pace. Uncle Samuel seemed in no hurry to find them, so they took advantage of the time. Many people were passing through, like Anne and Jane, headed to London for theatre, arts, parties, and of course, to be seen. Beautiful dresses paraded in front of them, with elaborate bonnets and darling parasols to match, along with men in their finery, far exceeding the small town's day-to-day clientele. It was a glimpse of Jane's expectations of what lay ahead in London, only on a much smaller scale. She had no intension to leave the Eaton Estate, nor disobey Dr. Cummings's orders, but since her forced departure, butterflies fluttered inside her stomach, experiencing the nineteenth century world on a larger scale. Jane was in her element of observation, taking it all in and storing the sights and sounds, the people, and places, in the recesses of her mind.

"Look at that beautiful hat!" Anne nudged Jane with her shoulder. "Shall we go in?" But before she stepped through the threshold, she froze with the call of her name.

"Miss Anne," a petite and superbly dressed woman called. A second one, a little younger, equal in stature, and equally dressed, squealed with delight upon the confirmation it was her.

Anne paled. Her eyes lost their brightness.

She grabbed Jane's arm. "Please stay with me."

"Are you alright?" Jane whispered.

But before she could answer, the two refined young women descended upon Anne with hugs, seemingly and genuinely happy to see her. Jane questioned the mixed reactions.

"Miss Celia, it's a surprise to see you," Anne said, her voice transformed to light and cheerful. She gestured to Jane. "May I introduce, Miss Reynolds."

The elder of the two young women nodded. "I am Miss Celia Wansey." She moved aside for her sister to step forward. "And may I present my sister, Miss Carina Wansey."

"How nice to meet you," the younger sister greeted.

Jane nodded in recognition but did not extend her hand. Not out of rudeness, but because her hand was held tightly within Anne's grasp.

"We are on our way to London. Father has been terribly busy and sent us away to keep us preoccupied," Celia explained.

"Or more likely to find us husbands," Carina giggled, excited about the prospects.

"I am sure you will be better entertained in the city," Anne offered.

"Well, if all goes well, Mr. Taylor and his cousin, Mr. Perkins, will join us at the Levongood's party next week, as well as at the Harding's event," Cecilia said.

But the younger sister couldn't contain her excitement. "They both have requested to call upon mother while in town. Can you imagine two gentlemen callers?"

Her sister gave her a look of authority, suppressing the younger girl's enthusiasm. Her eyes lowered with the reprimand, but she did not give up her childish grin.

"And your mother," Anne intervened the sisterly drama, "How is she?"

"Well, just heartbroken since Patrick left for America. It's as if she has no other children." Celia rolled her eyes. "Carina and I have tried to keep her preoccupied, until she adjusts to his departure, but with little affect."

"I am sorry to hear that," Anne said. "Has your brother written to inform you of his venture?"

"We finally received a letter a few days ago. He has settled and found himself a small shop. He happily reports business came through his doors as soon his sign went up. Father is thrilled. Mother only cries. She hoped he would fail and come back home."

"We may never see our dear brother again," Cecilia bemoaned. "But that certainly won't do if one, or both of us, gets married. Shame on him for leaving!"

Anne gripped Jane's arm tighter.

"Mother is visiting a sick friend at present, but it would delight her if you called, Anne." The younger said. "We would love to spend time with you, like in the old days."

Anne's legs weakened, and her body leaned into Jane. "I…I…"

Jane cleared her throat, giving Anne an askewed glance. "Unfortunately, Anne's uncle expects us," she interjected. "I fear we are late already. Maybe Anne can set a time in London to call on you and your mother?"

"Oh, of course. It would please mother very much," Carina said.

The older sister added, "You, of course, are welcomed, Miss Reynolds."

Jane offered them a demure smile, accepting the kind offer.

The two women bid their farewells with more hugs for Anne before they walked away in the opposite direction.

Anne relaxed, releasing Jane from her grip. They walked to a nearby bench and sat. Jane waited for Anne to explain the nervous reaction to the young women, but she did not offer any clarification, and Jane didn't pry. There was obviously more to Anne than she was willing to share.

They all had their secrets.

When they headed back to the tavern, Uncle Samuel was waiting, his hat and gloves on the table next to him, and an empty glass in his hand. He waved when he saw them enter, seemingly in good spirits, with no concern as to their whereabouts. Jane shuddered to think how his time was preoccupied. She prayed they would make good time to London. She was not eager to spend one more night in his care.

THE MANSE

Nineteenth-century London equally competed with any modern city with its commotion and mayhem: the clanging of bells, the thumping of heavy-footed horses against the paved streets, carriage wheels in constant motion, advertisements and signs begging for patronage, the mixture of the vastly wealthy and the extremely poor, seamen and merchants roaming the streets, all in a frenzy of togetherness. The fine ladies lifted their heads, snubbing the working class around them. The military men paraded around with importance, taking long side-glances at the pretty ladies who strolled by. Thick air saturated with grime lingered on everything. Pungent smell of coal, smoke, rotting food, stale water, sweaty clothes, and dirty people forced Jane to cover her nose to prevent her from gagging. Although a beautiful city in architecture and design, the reality was it was dirty, crowded, and stinky. Elements Jane never conjured when she read the likes of Austen, Bronte, or Wharton.

As they distanced themselves from the hum of the city, they emerged in a quieted region portioned by grand mansions. To Jane's understanding, Lillian had a dwelling in the city, her husband used for work, she for the theater and shopping. Their "city" home was miles outside. Outside of the filth and sour elements, but close enough for culture and entertainment. Tree-lined streets and green parks greeted them as they neared their destination. Jane released her handkerchief from her face to breathe in the cleaner air. Uncle Samuel fidgeted in his seat, eager to exit the tight quarters. Anne, however, cowered in her seat, her health taking a turn for the worse.

The carriage drove to the top of a hill, where it finally stopped in front of a small castle guarded by scrolled iron gates. The horses pounded their hooves against a pebbled entry to the front of the grand entrance. Jane gasped. It was a Georgian manor mostly comprised of tan stone, bragging many buildings, oversized windows, and too many chimneys to count. Hedges lined the front, but most of the property was surrounded by trees and rolling lawn, offering privacy for miles. Later, Jane would discover, after a guided tour, the back of the house showcased the more pristine landscape of manicured lawns, topiary trees, and formal, boxwood-hedged gardens. She would also discover the grand expanse of the house.

The full manor accommodated sixteen bedrooms, two reception rooms, a library, a ballroom, an orangery, a morning room, a formal dining room, a personal salon where Lillian would gather her most intimate of friends, a study for Sir Levongood to entertain equally, a large parlor for mutual entertaining, and a small conservatory where Isabelle could retreat to indulge in her musical talents, a separate bungalow for staff, and labyrinths of cellars. This did not include the stables or the rooms above, nor the cottages on the property. There was nothing intimate about the house. It was a large, elaborate behemoth, obviously meant to reflect the wealth and importance of its inhabitance.

There was no shortage of servants who hovered to assist the newly arrived guests, but it was Lillian who greeted them as they exited the carriage. With a slight nod to Uncle Samuel, she allowed him to take her hand. He did not linger with the honor and stepped aside for the women. Lillian eyed the pale and thin Anne and gave her a cheek-to-cheek hug, welcoming her into the family before instructing a servant to show her to her room immediately.

"A hot bath…and tea, lots of tea," she shouted after the servant who followed Anne into the house.

"Jane!" Lillian beamed. She took Jane's hands into hers and swung them outward to inspect her reunited acquaintance. "My dear, you look quite well, even after a long ride through the summer heat. How do you maintain such a healthy disposition? Oh, come here…" She pulled Jane into her arms.

Uncle Samuel eyed their embrace. He cleared his throat, separating the two. "Mrs. Levongood, how good of you to extend your hospitality. My niece, soon to be your sister-in-law, and I are more than honored by the invitation."

Lillian eyed Jane with the interruption but gave her complete attention to her soon-to-be family relation.

"Sir Levongood and I are honored you and your niece are joining us, especially with the big news. Unfortunately, many of the guests have not yet arrived and we are at a disadvantage to offer suitable conversation at present. Would it be too much to ask you to spare Mr. Davenport the tedious conversation of us women and join him in the study for companionship? He has arrived without his wife and must be dreadfully tired of my company."

"I would be delighted." He bowed.

"Ah, you are a dear man," Lillian feigned, instructing one of the man servants to show Uncle Samuel the way.

Lillian linked her arm in Jane's and walked towards the house. "It is most unkind of me to send him away, but *that* gentleman is a trifle more than one can handle on such a warm day."

Jane couldn't agree more.

When they crossed the threshold of the ten-foot doors, a servant swiftly took Jane's bonnet and gloves, disappearing as quickly as she came. A sweeping, hand-carved staircase greeted her as she stepped into the mosaic-laden entry. Painted ceilings highlighted with gold and carved moulding surrounded the room, with sixteenth century tapestries adorning the walls; flowers and their fragrance filled the entry. Paneled doors opened to the parlor where arriving guests would gather, but Lillian whisked her away before she got to peek inside, further down the hall to Lillian's private parlor. She confided that she wanted a space where they wouldn't be disturbed.

But before the two women opened their mouths, the door burst open and without care or proper etiquette, Maggie ran in ignoring her aunt. "Miss Jane, you're here!" she squealed.

Jane swooped the girl in her arms. "The house has been so empty without," she said, and squeezed her tight. "Let me look at you…" She brushed aside her curls behind her ears to reveal her beaming face. The resemblance to her father was uncanny. His refined angular nose and his serious brow. And just like that, her heart ached.

Maggie touched her face. "Is anything wrong, Miss Jane?"

Jane shook her head. "I miss you, that's all." She gave her another squeeze before releasing her.

"As we all did," Lillian added. "Upon my return from my brother's, I couldn't help to tell Sir Levongood all about you, hoping for your introduction. Then my brother wrote me of Dr. Cummings' plans for your return. We thought we would never see you again."

"Well, here I am. You can't get rid of me that easy."

"Nor do we want to!" She feigned a pout. "I am more determined than ever to give you a reason to stay and keep you with us forever."

Jane knew the impossibility of her staying forever but said nothing.

"Maggie, darling," Lillian eyed her niece seeking a chair to sit. "Miss Anne was not feeling well upon her arrival. Please be a dear and check on her, then report back to me."

Maggie didn't want to leave, but her training did not allow for young girls to pout, especially in front of their aunt. With a nod, she obeyed and left the room.

"Now that we have some privacy, may we talk?" Lillian didn't wait for an answer. "It is not without happiness I find my brother's betrothal to Anne a joyous event. I do not know the circumstances for which this happened so quickly, but I find my brother's lack of intimacy in transpiring the good news a tad negligent. A note came only yesterday about your imminent arrival, where he concluded his state of affair that his future wife would be landing in my care. I have never been so ill prepared!"

Jane agreed but dare not fuel the flames. "I'm sure your brother meant no disrespect. It happened rather quickly."

"Dear Jane, I do not mean to put you in the middle of this, but living under the same roof, you must have knowledge of what transpired?"

Jane was all too privy about what occurred, but she was not so inclined to answer Lillian. It was too shameful: Henry's loving embrace, Anne's arrival, casting her aside and erasing all that transpired between them. Jane wanted to crawl into a hole.

"Jane?" Lillian pulled her back.

"I only learned about your brother marrying Miss Benning on the day of my departure. Her uncle pulled me away shortly after introductions, and it was then they discussed their plans, in private." Jane turned away. She did not want Lillian to see the emotions surfacing. Anger, shame…longing.

"I don't understand. It is unlike Henry to act so impromptu. It was all discussed and settled in so little time." Lillian struggled with the pieces, trying to understand her brother's motives. "I have no problem with meeting his demands, but I find his actions out of character."

"It was my understanding your brother and Miss Benning were previously engaged?"

"Yes, and unfortunately, my intervention started the whole affair." Lillian grimaced at the recollection. "I only wanted to see my brother happy. He is still a young man, and very handsome at that. Any woman would be honored to have him as her husband." She recalled the many women seeking his companionship at gatherings. "He declared he was perfectly content to live out his days as a bachelor. But I could not imagine him alone, settling for that lifestyle." Lillian twisted her sleeve nervously. "It was after Christmas; they announced their engagement. I offered my home for the event, hoping for a spring wedding. There seemed no need to postpone the happy occasion. But her mother insisted she wait, to have a July wedding, and so it was planned accordingly." She rose and walked to the window. There she lingered, reflecting upon the past events.

Jane waited.

"One cannot deny winters are long and cold in the country. Anne found other company to keep. It was rather shameful. I, in earnest, tried not to judge. She is young and the prospect of marrying an older man may have been objectionable. Of course, with Sir Levongood fifteen years my senior, I was not apprehensive to see such a match."

Jane was at the end of her seat. She never imagined such a tale of intrigue about Henry. She now understood Mrs. Bishop's protectiveness and a little more of Henry's guarded manner.

"Henry is truly a kind man but has his pride. He did not want to dishonor Miss Anne, so he stood with strength and scoffed at the gossip. He had asked for her hand in good faith and would never disregard his commitment. But it was Anne herself who confronted him and told him she loved someone else."

Jane's jaw dropped with shock. She never imagined Anne could cause such a scandal.

"She and Henry were not mismatched. There was an attraction for both parties. Who could deny Anne's beauty? Having a new mother for his daughter was certainly a pleasing prospect. Although not the deepest of sentiments, it was a good beginning for a relationship. I think it was her respect for him, as a gentleman, she was so direct. But it was not without some embarrassment when Henry took the news."

Wow! Wow! Wow!

Jane had to pick up her jaw.

"I know my brother is not forthcoming, but is there anything in his actions or words you might conclude is hurriedness to reinstate the wedding?"

Jane shook her head.

"It is difficult for me to comprehend his motives. I want Henry to be happy. But I fear his actions are for honor rather than for love." She sighed. "My brother is a sensible man. And I must trust his decisions are in good faith." She looked at Jane for reassurance.

But Jane didn't know what to say. When Maggie's sweet voice interrupted them, she sighed with relief.

"Aunt Lillian? I checked on Miss Anne as you asked. She is feeling better but asks we do not disturb her. She wants to rest before dinner."

"Thank you, my child. Now come and show Miss Jane to her room. I fear I have exhausted this poor woman with too much conversation. Please show her where she will be staying."

Maggie ran over to Jane and took her hand.

Lillian put her cheek against Jane's. "I am so happy to see you again," she whispered in her ear. "You are so dear. Had I met you only months earlier, maybe I would have chosen differently for my brother." She pulled away and looked directly at her, making sure Jane understood her intention.

Jane tried to smile in acknowledgment but turned away to conceal the torment her words had caused.

Was it her watering eyes? The way her lips fell? The drop of her shoulders, or the heave of her chest? Whatever it was, her reactions did not go unnoticed by Lillian.

"Jane, are you sure nothing else occurred that would hasten his decision?"

Wishing she could confide in her, Jane shook her head and let Maggie drag her out of the room.

THE LEVONGOODS' HOSPITALITY

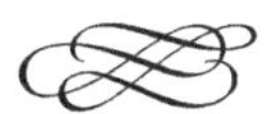

Jane followed the cacophony of voices to the parlor, not expecting the small gathering huddled in conversation. She heard no commotion of carriages, luggage dragged down the corridor, or voices floating in the halls from arriving guests since her own arrival. In fact, her room, if you want to call a small suite a room, which overlooked a tiered lawn with a forest of trees in the distance, offered complete privacy. The house lay so peaceful the quietude lulled her to sleep, more exhausted from her trip than she led on. Only when a knock came to her door, by a young girl sent to help her dress, did she learn of other guests' arrival and the invitation to gather in the parlor prior to dinner.

No one noticed when Jane sauntered up to Lillian, all eyes and ears focused on a balding, portly gentleman who engaged the party in a comedic story about his recent experience with a skunk. She entered the small crowd just as the stout man declared he was not harmed by the experience, except maybe for his notable reputation, which was now in ruins when spotted running across the lawns, flailing his arms….and even screeching, he admitted, in cowardly escape.

Together, they burst into laughter.

It was then, Lillian greeted Jane with a soft kiss on her cheek. "You look lovely," she whispered.

"I'm sorry for running late. I took a nap," Jane confessed with an apologetic smile. She brushed the ribbon-laced bodice of her dress, silently admiring the layers of chiffon and satin. "And thank you for the dress I found in my room."

"It becomes you." Lillian eyed the dress, pleased with the effects of the coral color against Jane's skin and dark hair. "Come, let me introduce you."

Lillian introduced Jane to the robust man telling the story, her husband, the esteemed Sir Levongood. He stood well beyond his wife, his thick legs supporting his broad frame. But he characterized the same polished refinement as she, despite his portliness. He was well-dressed, well-mannered, and, well…aristocratic.

He took Jane's hand and bowed before her. "I am honored to meet the woman who has brought such delight to my wife and daughter." He smiled and his blue eyes disappeared into fatty cheeks. "I can see why Lillian used the word *lovely* when she described you."

Jane blushed at his candidness.

He leaned in closer. "More importantly, she said you are her match. And that, my dear, is the greatest compliment." He winked, and a lush set of lashes flapped down over one eye, the other sparkling blue, hinting at mischievousness.

And then Jane understood–what Lillian found charming about her husband. Sir Levongood stood before her, old, bald, and fat. But he was jolly, kind, and sincere. Not afraid of the world, of other men, of strong women, or of himself. His persona more than made up for his lack of handsomeness.

Jane liked him instantly.

The prominent banker and his wife were the next introductions. Mr. Cornwall, a man in his fifties, was a reputable member of society, and his refined clothes and manner, reflected his status. His wife, Henrietta, had no redeemable qualities of beauty. Her height, two inches taller than her husband, not proportionate to her extraordinarily long arms, contributed to her gawkiness. Nor did she resemble her husband's finery, except for the rubies dangling from her neck and adorning her wrist. She chose diamonds for her ears. The importance Mr. Cromwell tried to impress upon Jane, Lillian later informed her, was bestowed by Mrs. Cromwell who contributed the wealth of the relationship; Mr. Cornwall had married up. They talked pleasantries with Jane but were careful of the stranger. They neither said too much, nor too little; enough to be congenial. They heard about Jane's familial connection to Dr. Cummings, whom they held in the highest regard, but she was a stranger, with no history, no known privilege, or money in the bank. Jane's saving attribute was her friendship to Mrs. Levongood, a value worth high honor, but not enough to expose themselves in temperament or information.

The Parsons, a short couple of ample size, were introduced as relations. Mrs. Parsons was Sir Levongood's second cousin. The resemblance was uncanny, only pint size. Mrs. Parsons was cherubic–a young, sweet face and chubby body. But her grey hair gave away her true age, too old to adorn the pink, ruffled dress she stuffed herself into. Each was personable towards Jane and favorably welcomed her, more so than the previous introduction.

"You must come and dine with us," Mrs. Parsons insisted. "Of course, if your schedule allows. We certainly would not want to take you away from our dear Lillian."

"It would be our honor," Mr. Parsons added, prudent to welcome a friend of the Levongoods.

Mr. Edmond Quinby, an esteemed lawyer, patiently waited for his introduction. Jane didn't miss his sideway glances at her.

He stood the tallest in the room of men, and athletically fit in comparison. Probably considered attractive, he had a full head of blonde curls–the other men did not possess, broad shoulders, and a *Cary Grant* cleft adorning his chin. But he was acutely pale, and his drooping eyes gave him a puppy-like expression, downgrading his handsomeness to Jane. But no one could deny his impeccable style. He was a Peacock among the other dark-suited men. A multi-layered cravat filled his collar underneath an embroidered vest of birds threaded in turquoise, blue, and saffron yellow; his shoes were impeccably shined. A curl was not out of place on his head, his eyebrows notably trimmed, and his hands were well-groomed. No labor for this gentleman. Jane found him almost too pretty–overt and ostentatious, as was his personality, equally pretentious, monopolizing her attention to sing his own praises. Jane feigned interest, if only to be polite, but was thankful when Lillian finally dragged her away to the next and final introduction.

Lastly, Jane met Mr. Davenport. He was a sinewy man with a pointed nose, an equally angular chin, who stood eye to eye with her. He greeted Jane with a grin which extended from ear to ear, his crooked teeth on full display. He tittered when he spoke with an effervescence to his cadence. His cheerfulness was contagious, and Jane found him the most authentic of the group.

"My dear," he greeted, "I have only heard many, many lovely things about you. Yes, yes, just lovely. I am terribly excited to finally meet the woman who has captivated so many."

"I know so few people, but glad I haven't offended too many," she recalled her failed attempt with Mr. Hodges, "...yet."

He laughed, pleased with her sense of humor.

"Witty as well as lovely. What a charming, terribly charming quality." He gave her a sly smile. "I apologize, with the deepest regret, that my dear wife was unable to make the trip. She has such pain, oh my, such pain in her knees and feet. Her mobility is less than she desires." He scowled. "Poor dear. Poor, poor dear, indeed."

Jane wanted to continue with Mr. Davenport, but Anne entered the room, on the arm of her uncle, and all eyes turned, her presence sparkling like a precious emerald hitting the light, ceasing everyone's conversation.

Jane saw Anne the way every man saw her...the way Henry saw her.

Only a fool would deny she was stunning. Classic, naturally gifted with elegance and a diaphanous beauty. Petite, with a long nape which gracefully held up the delicate frame of her face, her body curved in well-balanced proportion. Her skin was milky, her cheeks rosy, and her eyes as blue and sparkly as the finest stone. The golden strands of her hair curled around her face, creating an aura of light. She truly was an angel in a room of misfits. Well rested, bathed, pampered, and prepped, no one would have known the girl was sick for days. Mr. Davenport's jaw fell open. A smile spread across Mr. Parson's face. Mr. Quinby darted across the room to present himself.

She did not linger long with anyone, eventually finding her way to Jane. Three days together, an illness, and secrets created a sisterly bond.

A friendship, Jane admitted.

It was only then Jane did see, up close, the remnants of her illness lingering in her paled complexion, hidden by powder and rouge.

"How are you feeling?"

"Much better," she feigned. "Lillian sent remedies to ease my illness, as well as a hot bath. She is too kind. I am blessed to soon call her sister."

But before Jane could question her more, a servant announced dinner. Everyone paired in couples, the men acknowledging the closest female in proximity. Mr. Davenport quickly extended himself to Anne, honored for the opportunity to have the young beauty at his disposal, he proclaimed. He beamed when she accepted and led the way into the dining hall.

Uncle Samuel walked from behind and extended his arm in request. "My dear Miss Reynolds, would you do me the honor?"

Jane's insides recoiled, wanting to run to anyone, even Mr. Quimby, to escape him, but took his arm out of politeness. When his heated body finally pulled away, leaving her seated next to Sir Levongood, she sighed relief when she saw him seated at the other end of the table. Jane flashed a smile at her hostess, thankful for his placement far, far away from her.

Lillian didn't miss Jane's gratitude and bowed her head with acknowledgement.

Sitting next to the host had its benefits: Sir Levongood's ability for conversation was captivating and his generosity pouring wine throughout dinner appreciated, the numbing effect proving helpful when the conversation turned to the upcoming nuptials.

"May I present a toast to the lovely young lady in the room," Mr. Davenport bellowed across the room and lifted his glass to Anne. "Miss Benning, may marriage be the haven of comfort, much comfort, as it has been for me and my lovely wife, Mary."

Everyone cheered.

"My dear, we could not be more excited for you. You have chosen wisely. Mr. Eaton is quite an honorable man," Mr. Cromwell added.

Honorable! Jane scowled. She grabbed her wine glass, whereupon Sir Levongood dutifully filled it when he noticed it neared empty.

Mrs. Cromwell leaned into Lillian. "You must be delighted to have such a sweet young lady joining your family?"

Lillian patted Anne's hands. "We are so pleased with

Henry's choice. Quite blessed with Anne, and for the future prospects of our family growing."

"Here, here!" The room consented.

Anne blushed with the intimation.

Uncle Samuel raised his glass to the table once more. "To my precious niece. Beauty becomes you, but love makes you irresistible. Henry is held captive."

Jane could not bring the wine glass to her lips. Uncle Samuel's cryptic words held more innuendo for her than for Anne. When she looked his way, his black eyes narrowed to hers. He tilted his glass to her and gulped the garnet liquid in one swoop.

Jane darted her eyes away, but they landed on Anne.

Her hand swept the side of her face, brushing away strands of hair from her eyes–like a bird taking flight, graceful and undemanding, directing everyone's attention to her fluttering lashes. Being loved and admired seemed commonplace for her. She had her place in the group that encircled her, all excited about her life ahead. She knowingly, and politely, redeemed her place among them, as a queen takes her seat next to the King.

"Does he truly love her?" The words slipped from Jane's head to her breath, her tongue loose from too much wine, in earshot of her host.

"Does it matter?" Sir Levongood whispered back. His eyes glazed over the beauty at the center of attention. "I have a feeling she will convince him otherwise."

"I'm sorry, I didn't mean to insinuate…"

If Sir Levongood was flabbergasted, he did not indicate. His blue eyes met hers. "I see you are cynical about love."

Hypnotized by his eyes, kind and direct, she could not lie. "I have my reasons," she admitted.

"Ah, the trials and tribulations of the heart. But I count my blessings." He smiled towards his wife. "I have had little reason to be so doubtful of the power of love. It has been good to me thus far."

"You are blessed. You and Lillian seem to have caught the moon and the stars. That's hard to do."

"It is not as difficult as you think. You just have to keep your eyes open, pray for a miracle, and grab onto it as soon as you see it. Otherwise, the opportunity might slip through time." He winked. He moved his hand over Jane's, giving it a squeeze. "Don't give up. I didn't, and see what fate brought me? Now if you will excuse me, I must invite the men to the study. Lillian will want her time with you and the ladies."

As if they could read each other's thoughts, Lillian rose on cue, inviting the women to the salon for more entertainment.

The men went through one door, and the women through another, a spirit of lightness transcending upon them. The men were free of the women, and the women free of the men. Free from scrutiny. Free to be themselves.

"Lillian, there must be excitement stirring in the household with the coming nuptials. You, dear cousin, will have your hands full with preparations," Mrs. Parsons said as the doors opened to the salon and she found her way to the sofa. "And how kind of you to host the event. Your gardens will make a lovely backdrop for the event."

"I am honored Anne would have it nowhere else," Lillian said, with diplomacy. But Jane knew about her inner frustrations.

"Oh my if the weather does not interfere. It is only a few weeks away, and the heat is uncharacteristically bearing down on us this season. I do hope you are honeymooning near the shore. But I fear the dreadful weather is everywhere," exclaimed Mrs. Cromwell.

"I am sure a pretty girl like Anne will have no reason to be out in the weather once married, and on her honeymoon," Mrs. Parsons teased.

The room filled with giggles. Except for Mrs. Cromwell. She pursed her lips, fervently fanning herself.

Anne said nothing. She allowed the ladies to stir about her private affairs.

"Now ladies, we cannot be so bold in front of our new guest." Lillian scolded the group of women, watching Jane out of the corner of her eye who had retreated to the corner of the room. "What will she think of us?"

Jane wanted to get away from Anne; away from everyone. The wine's effects faded, only adding to her darkened mood. Talk of the wedding and thoughts of Henry with Anne on their honeymoon made it hard to assuage her guilt.

It was just a kiss! Her gut tightened. *Just. A. Kiss!*

"Jane?" Lillian waited for acknowledgment, but when it didn't come, she called out again, "Jane?"

Jane blinked. "Huh?"

"The ladies can be quite indecorous," Mrs. Cromwell eyed the other ladies. "You really must forgive them."

"Oh, Miss Reynolds, please excuse our playfulness. With the good food and perhaps too much wine, maybe we have lost our sense of sensibility," Mrs. Parsons added.

"I'm not offended, ladies," Jane assured, bringing her attention back to the room, and to the multiple sets of eyes now on her.

"My dear, we have been remiss not to engage you more," Mrs. Cromwell said. "Lillian alerted us to your arrival and told us of your appalling circumstances."

Jane eyed Lillian.

"My oh my," Mrs. Parson interrupted. "Many have warned the waters are terribly dangerous to travel. Mr. Parsons would never dare involve me in such an excursion. I can only imagine the conditions." Mrs. Parsons couldn't imagine anyone traveling so far from home. She has never been anywhere but England, nor did she find a reason to leave.

Lillian rose, sauntered across the room, and purposely sat herself beside Jane, the women's eyes following her. She took Jane's hand. "Oh, the distressed girl was taken ill for days. My dear brother, Henry, was nearly beside himself when he called upon me for help. It was a miracle we didn't lose the poor thing."

They all gasped at the thought, grateful they were not in the same predicament.

Lillian smirked, satisfied with the dramatics.

Jane rolled her eyes at Lillian. "It really wasn't as bad as Lillian says." Jane assured them. "And as you see, I am in very good health."

"I have no doubt," Mrs. Parson's said. "But what a terrible experience!"

They all agreed in unison.

"Dr. Cummings must be thrilled about your visit. The poor man, losing his lovely wife so early, and being alone for so long. Are you two close?" Mrs. Cromwell questioned, hinting at the meaning of Jane's visit.

Jane nodded, offering little more. The rumor mill about a future marriage prospect was far more harmless than discovering she fell through time and landed in the past.

Lillian suggested a card game, interrupting the opportunity for more speculation of Dr. Cummings' love life. The ladies cheered with consent rising from their chairs and gathered themselves around the game table, previously set by an attentive servant, awaiting their arrival. Jane sighed relief from the questioning and observed the ladies take their usual places. It was like watching a well-rehearsed dance, each moving in rhythm to the other. Mrs. Cromwell sat to the left of Lillian, Mrs. Parson on the right. Anne, the newcomer, but certainly a future conspirator, sat in the empty seat across from Lillian. They playfully spoke to one another, a tease here, a jest there, admitting their sorrows and struggles wrapped up in half-truths, and some in lies. But they all seemed to understand–the language of women sharing the same experience in a world where they couldn't expose anything with real intimacy. So, they did it in the salon, away from the men, drinking sherry, chit-chatting as they played cards. And for a moment in time, released from the cages of their lives.

Jane was not a part of their camaraderie, nor had the right to intrude.

The men eventually joined them, bringing the wafting scent of liquor and cigars. Sir Levongood, not wanting to interrupt his wife, still holding a glass of whisky, found his way to a large chair. Mr. Quinby and Mr. Cromwell lingered at the door, immersed in a conversation they didn't leave in the other room. Mr. Davenport, lonely for companionship, sought the company of Anne, who excused herself from the table after a few games to find reprieve in a book. Mr. Parsons and Uncle Samuel were the last to straggle in and found their way to the crystal decanters on a sideboard where they filled up their almost empty glasses.

When Uncle Samuel spotted Jane, he bee-lined to her, interrupting her reverie.

"You are not in a social mood this evening, Miss Reynolds?"

"Quite the opposite. I've been enjoying the ladies' company."

One lady cheered at her win, pulling Jane's attention. When she turned back, she found Uncle Samuel perked his ears to the two men still lingering at the door. She took the opportunity to excuse herself.

"I am keeping you. It's late. I think I might retire for the evening."

Uncle Samuel smirked, and his gaze lowered to her cleavage the dress generously allowed. "If I was not such a gentleman, my dear, I would have noted that as an invitation."

Jane lowered her eyes and grit her teeth.

He moved aside for her dismissal, but not before he leaned in and inhaled her neck. She heard him moan, prompting her to make her way upstairs without bidding the rest of the room a good night. She shut the door and locked it behind her. Until then, she had not feared for her safety. But something visceral alerted her of dangers arising.

WATCHING

A competitive card game kept up those who played and those who drank past two in the morning, causing most of the guests to sleep in. The breakfast room was empty, prompting Jane to fix herself a plate from the buffet filled with enough food to feed all of London, and make her way to the terrace outside. There, under the shade of the trees, and views of the gardens, she hoped to continue her solitude. Unfortunately, Uncle Samuel had found the spot beforehand and beckoned her to join him.

"Come, come, Miss Reynolds," he waved her over. "Let us not lose the opportunity to enjoy each other's company."

She sat across from him with no obvious excuse to decline his invitation.

"It is good to see you up early. I fear the others are not so fortunate."

"They were having too much fun last night. I see no harm enjoying themselves," Jane said, with the need to defend her newfound friends' tardiness.

Uncle Samuel eyed his breakfast companion, then leaned

across the table. His eyes narrowed, as if interrogating her. "And you, Miss Reynolds…are you enjoying yourself?"

"Very much," Jane said, ignoring his innuendo.

"Hmmm." Uncle Samuel leaned back in his chair, delighted with Jane's temperament. She didn't fluster, nor did she retreat. "I have always found the summer especially entertaining. It seems the weather allows for people to shed their inhibitions and become more open to pleasure."

"I am the last person to pass judgment on how others entertain themselves." She feigned a smile, but thoughts of Uncle Samuel in a threesome turned her stomach. She pushed away her plate and opted for a sip of tea.

"Really? How diplomatic of you." He lifted his head at the woman sitting in front of him. "It would seem the summer air has enticed both you and Mr. Eaton…" His lips spread slowly across his face; his eyes danced. He no longer was being spirited, but downright wicked.

Jane was positive he noticed the flush to her face. "I assure you, Mr. Milton, I am not one to be so easily enticed," she replied in her defense.

"That is a shame. For it can bring such a feeling of euphoria," he concluded on the subject, and popped a strawberry in his mouth, savoring the macerations as it plunked from one cheek to the other.

"There you are," Lillian said, breezing her way onto the terrace.

Uncle Samuel stood. "My dear Mrs. Levongood, you are lovely this morning. May we be honored with your presence for breakfast?"

She declined his offer, but asked, "How is our dearest Anne? I hope she got rest and is recovering."

"I am afraid her efforts took a toll on her last evening. But with the dear girl you sent to tend to her, she will be refreshed to join us this evening," he assured her.

"Splendid! Now, if you don't mind, I have so many details to prepare and was in search of Jane to assist me. Will you excuse us?"

Uncle Samuel tilted his head forward with his approval, but not before his eyes met Jane's. "My loss, but there will be plenty of time in the future, I am almost sure of it."

Jane rose with the request, leaving her uneaten plate on the table, and put her arms through Lillian's, praying to be taken away as quickly as possible.

"I dislike that man!" Jane growled when they left.

"Unfortunately, he will be family soon enough. A consequence of my brother's actions, and not one I approve of," she smirked. "I was not dishonest when I pulled you away, but I had selfish reasons. Maggie and Isabelle are eager to spend the day with you. They have requested your presence and hoped you would join them for a ride. I have set riding clothes out for you hoping you will agree."

Jane squeezed Lillian's arm, confirming her approval, before heading off to join the girls for the afternoon.

It was a long day in the summer heat but being with the girls lifted Jane's mood after a distasteful morning. The encounter with Uncle Samuel faded as she rode through the countryside with her two young companions, along with the Cromwell's daughter, Tatiana. Mr. Cromwell and Mr. Quinby joined the small riding group, as chaperones behind them. Isabelle was unusually talkative, sharing her thoughts about books, her love of music, and hinted about a young man with whom she was smitten. Tatiana, the oldest of the girls, was sweet in temperament, and joined in conversation when she had something to add, otherwise, she skillfully listened. Being the only child of older parents, her upbringing taught her to be seen, not heard. Maggie, full of energy, was entertained by the older girls, and spoke as often as she could insert herself into the conversation. Her youth allowed the others to enjoy her spiritedness, even if it did not meet Lillian's standards of a proper young lady's behavior. Mr. Cromwell, who, when not with his wife, was pleasant to speak with, letting the aristocracy fade, entertaining Jane with stories of his boyhood. She struggled to imagine him any younger than his fifty years with the mischievous boy he described. Mr. Quimby was the same– tolerable and self-absorbed, if not merely pleasurable to look at. The company of an attractive but boorish man suited Jane just fine over the lecherous behaviors of Uncle Samuel. Jane easily assimilated into the afternoon with her nineteenth-century companions, almost forgetting this was not her normal life.

But if you stay too long, your energy will forever remain, and there is no return.

Peyton's words blew in her ear. The line of belonging was becoming seamless, the people too familiar, and she worried she was crossing the line, jeopardizing her energy with the loss of boundaries.

When she finally emerged from the stables, hot, dusty, and needing refreshments, she heard a much-needed voice in the corridor.

"My dearest, Miss Reynolds," Dr. Cummings called to her.

Jane ran to greet him, unable to stop herself from hugging him. His arms surrounded her, and they embraced.

Her face beamed with his. "I did not know you were expected."

"Well, my dear, you were told to stay put and get some rest." His brow darted up. "Upon my return home, eager to tell you of a recent visit to the city and my revelations, I learned you were taken away." He gestured toward his arriving companion. "We came as soon as I could pack my bags."

Henry, who took off his hat and handed it to one of the

attending servants, walked towards them. "Jane…" he cleared his throat, "…Miss Reynolds, it is good to see you again."

Jane recoiled from her previous enthusiasm. "Mr. Eaton. I didn't know you were joining us in London."

"You did not give me the opportunity to discuss my plans," Henry countered.

"But of course," she scowled, "it's not my concern what you choose to do, is it?"

Dr. Cummings didn't miss her eyes piercing Henry's, or Henry's tightening jaw.

Dr. Cummings cleared his throat, breaking their stare. "You've been riding, I see. Lady Levongood is keeping you entertained. She is notorious for the care of her guests."

"Yes," Jane agreed. "Someone we all can learn to be more like." She let the meaning hit its target.

Henry pulled at the cuffs of his sleeves and tugged at the collar of his coat but had no comeback.

Jane brushed her dusty skirt, and removed her riding hat, pushing aside loose hairs behind her ear. She continued, "I have just returned from an afternoon with the girls, along with Mr. Cromwell." Adding, "And the charming, Mr. Quimby."

"Ah yes, a good man. Well, I cannot disapprove of the obvious joy it brings you. Maybe it was a good decision to leave the Eaton Estate, after all."

"Absolutely. Had it been *my* decision, I may not have come. So, I'm grateful for Mr. Eaton's fortuitousness to decide what is best for me after all." She smiled, making sure her dimples were on full display. She might have even batted her eyes, but that was an unintentional added drama.

"Well, bravo to our dear friend for taking good care of you." Dr. Cummings patted Henry's shoulder where it stiffened against his hand.

Jane saw Henry's face, his stoic expressions masking whatever he was thinking; his eyes glassed. A calm sea? Or dead waters? Whatever the darkness hid, she was not privy. No one was. Anything between them forever left unsaid. Unexplored. Unknown.

She couldn't predict her reaction upon seeing him again. She tried to keep the thoughts of him at bay, reminding herself Anne, his soon-to-be wife, was never far from her. But when he stepped in front of her, flushed by the heat of the sun, his brow wetted with sweat, she couldn't ignore the pull towards him… the invisible string from his heart to hers, connecting them, like a tuning fork, their energy tuned to a proper pitch. But that same string is finely twisted with anger, and it is unrecognizable which one is breakable. Her anger or her passion? Maybe neither. Or probably both. Their bonds were never consummated; love never declared. What they shared was merely a moment in time. A slip in the universe not meant to be. If anyone understood, it was Jane. She would soon be gone, and a mere memory to him. Except not to her. She had to bear the memory through his lifetime and hers. Her heart ached, and she hated him for that. For it all.

Time.

She needed time to heal. She needed to stay away from him. She needed to go home.

"Dr. Cummings…Henry! I thought I heard your voices." Lillian broke up the threesome, refreshed and vibrant as if she had just risen from a nap. Her ability to manage a household of guests, and their entertainment, did not change her temperament, or her charm. "I was not expecting you so early. But of course, we have rooms ready. Why don't you head upstairs to freshen up? The men will wait in the study for drinks when you are ready."

Without instruction, a servant came to retrieve the two men. Dr. Cummings took Jane's hand and bid her farewell; Henry lowered his lids, bowed his head, and turned away to follow Dr.

Cummings ascending the stairs. He turned back, but Jane did not, and he continued.

"Isn't it lovely to have all of us together again?" Lillian said.

Jane didn't answer but eyed an escape. *Up the stairs? Down the corridor? Through the main entrance?* But before she could retreat, Lillian tugged at her arm, stopping her.

"Jane, is something wrong?"

Jane placed her hands against her cheeks, the heat singeing with the touch. Her face was always an open book. She shook her head, for fear of crying, and chose the stairs, her shoes clapping against the wood in quick repetition as she retreated.

"Jane!" Lillian called after her.

Jane dared not stop until she was at her door, safely away from anyone who would see the tears falling down her cheeks. But when she opened the door, her maid waited to help her bathe and dress. The young girl didn't pry but offered her a glass of sherry and a wetted towel for her eyes, promising her the cooling effect would have her '*as if nothing ever happened.*' Jane thanked the girl for her discreet care, hoping the episode would not make it to downstair to the gossip mill, where in turn, it would assuredly make its way back to Lillian.

Coiffed and dressed, the girl delivered on her promise. Jane's face showed no signs of distress. Her cheeks were rosy, her eyes bright, and her lips the color of a pink peony.

A knock came at her door.

Jane held her breath, fearing it might be Henry. It would be like a man to explain himself–free himself of his guilt. She didn't want his excuses. What was done was done! Although she couldn't avoid him, she would do her best to stay away from him.

If it was Lillian, it was because she wanted an explanation for her earlier behavior. The situation was complicated, especially because it involved her brother, and was better left unexplained.

When the knock came again, she had no other choice but to instruct her maid to answer it.

To her relief, it was Anne who stood at the threshold. "May I interrupt you?"

Jane shewed her in as the maid excused herself, allowing the two ladies their privacy.

Anne looked lovely in a soft powder-blue dress, highlighting her eyes. Her lips were tinted pink, accentuating their youthful fullness, giving her the splash of color she needed after so many days of a pallor complexion. Sapphires hung from her ears, and pearls decorated her neck. Jealousy was natural, but when Jane saw Anne struggling with something, her maternal instincts took over.

"Anne, is everything okay?"

She nodded and sat on the bed. "Jane, may I ask a favor?"

"Of course," she replied, sitting herself next to her.

"Henry has arrived."

Jane already knew.

"And…I am nervous to see him." She cupped her hands over her mouth.

Jane's eyes widened. "What are you talking about, you're engaged to the man? You shouldn't be afraid of him."

"Please, Jane, do not be harsh with me," she begged.

Anne was so frail and delicate, her thin frame wispy. Jane feared she'd break her in two if she pushed with more questions. So, she waited for her to continue.

"Henry," she said the name cautiously, "and I parted with some tension between us. I fear our relationship is very fragile due to it."

Jane cringed. She didn't want to get involved. But she had no other choice.

"I'm sorry, Anne, but how can I help?"

"Be my chaperone for the evening?"

Jane stood and walked across the room. She didn't want to agree to her favor. She needed to avoid Henry.

"Please Jane!" Anne pleaded, seeing Jane's hesitancy. "I do not want to be alone with him. Not tonight. Not yet. And as a guest of Henry's, he would not question your presence by my side. It seems rather childish, but I would not ask such a favor if it wasn't terribly important." She stammered, "...My mother...my uncle, they don't understand. I have no one else to ask, and if I am not mistaken, I think we have grown rather close." Her lashes fluttered. "I...I cannot do this alone." Her voice cracked, and her eyes watered.

Jane couldn't watch the girl's struggle. "Please don't get upset, Anne. If it will help you, I'll do it."

A tear slipped down Anne's cheek, and she wiped it away. She opened her mouth, wanting to say more, but hesitated. "You see, I...Uncle Samuel asked Henry something exceedingly difficult of him. I knew he would act honorably. But I am concerned he has agreed to marry me out of a great hardship to himself. He did not express those concerns, but I fear things are not the way they should be."

Jane cursed herself. She was the reason things were not the way they should be. It was apparent she was interfering with fate and needed to find her way home before she did more damage. Until then, she had to make things right.

"Maybe they are strained. Haven't you and Henry been apart from each other?"

Anne nodded

"If Henry is as honorable as you say, he wouldn't have agreed to move forward with your engagement."

"It is different this time." Anne sighed deeply. "Last winter, when Henry proposed, it was extremely exciting. I was honored when he asked for my hand in marriage. He could have chosen any of a dozen women, yet he chose me. To find a man of his standing was all my mother hoped for me. But I fear the excitement is but a memory. I believe he is burdened with the renewal of our engagement."

"I'm sure he is just as excited as he was before. You're a lovely young woman. What's not to love?" She made Anne smile. "I think you just need time with each other. Time to discover the reasons you fell in love the first time."

Another tear fell on Anne's cheek. Jane reached for a handkerchief–one of a monogrammed collection found in a drawer by her bed that she had used herself not more than an hour ago with her own tears–and handed it to her.

"Now, don't worry. It will all work out," She put her arm around her. "Let's freshen your face, then we'll go downstairs, together."

With a little help from powder, and some color on the cheeks, the two women, arm in arm, headed to the parlor.

Most of the men had gathered, filling the room with conversation, awaiting the ladies to arrive. Mrs. Parsons arrived first, Mrs. Cromwell followed, both cordially greeted by the attending men, where they convened on the sofa to swap gossip of the day, each having called upon several friends that afternoon who supplied them with new, if not titillating, stories. When Anne and Jane entered, conversation lulled. All eyes turned to them. Mrs. Parsons and Mrs. Cromwell smiled towards the two younger women but did not attempt to greet them. The men around the room nodded their greetings upon eye contact, taking in the two beauties from afar, not daring to approach them too quickly in scrutiny of their wives. Henry, who was in conversation with Uncle Samuel, was the first to cross the room, but it was not Anne he targeted. Much to her discomfort, it was Jane his dark eyes locked onto. For a moment she was transported back to the pond, Henry holding her, never wanting to let go, as if she was, and always would be, his, forever. Anne grabbed her arm as he approached, bringing her back to reality that it was Anne's betrothed coming towards her.

He bowed to Anne and took the hand she offered. "Good evening, dearest Anne."

"Henry," she batted her long lashes in feminine blandishment.

He bowed to Jane. "Good evening, Miss Reynolds."

"Mr. Eaton," she reciprocated his greeting but did not offer her hand. Had she not promised Anne to be her chaperone, she would have fled the room.

Mr. Davenport, with no attending wife to condemn his admiration of two young ladies, sauntered up to the threesome. "Charming, just charming, ladies. A lucky, lucky man, indeed, Mr. Eaton, I say, to have two beautiful women in your company."

Mr. Eaton cleared his throat, and stepped aside, closer to Jane, to allow Mr. Davenport to join their small circle. He knew she would recoil from his presence…to escape him. Her repudiation expected. She was angry, which only meant he hurt her. He was the source of her pain and deserved her rebuff. He never imagined she would return his feelings. Now he felt ashamed he gave his love to her so unguarded. He knew better, and she had to pay the price for his misstep. He paid the price of losing her. But he indulged in the moment, granted by Mr. Davenport, to stand next to her, but not *with* her.

He would never be with her…

Jane was caged. Anne held onto her for dear life, on one side, while Henry, a fortress wall on the other. She had nowhere to go. She surveyed the room for Dr. Cummings–a lifeline to be rescued–but did not see him. Instead, Mr. Quimby caught her frantic gaze surveying the room. He lifted his glass towards her, trapped himself in a conversation with Mr. Cromwell, unable to accept what he thought was an invitation. Jane sighed in desperation.

Mr. Davenport continued in conversation an education to the soon-to-be couple of the many advantages of married life that he and his 'dear wife had the blessing of knowing.' His voice droned on, but Jane stopped listening. She was only aware of Henry, his presence looming; the weight of his shadow pressing against her. When Mr. Parsons joined the conversation, adding his version of marital bliss, Jane sank in dread.

Anne further intertwined her arm into Jane's, only securing her confinement.

It was Sir Levongood's laugh which came into the room that sparked Jane's hope for escape. He and Lillian joined the guest from the gardens, with Dr. Cummings following the couple, holding a crystal glass filled with amber liquid. Jane eyed the glass from afar, wishing for a swig, only to find Dr. Cummings meeting her gaze when she looked up. He smiled from across the room at her with a knowing. Her whole body giddied prompting a smile right back at him.

Henry spotted his friend's zealous expression and followed his gaze, where it landed, bullseye, directly on Jane. He watched helplessly as he beelined to her, greeted the small group, and with the invitation for her hand, pulled Jane out from under them, taking her away.

Jane couldn't hide her pleasure of being plucked from Parson's and Davenport's gibber, from Anne's captivity, and from Henry's side, but guilt overcame her. "You shouldn't have done that. Anne was relying on me. I have left her to fend for herself with those men" she reprimanded but dared not look back to see Anne's reproach.

"Miss Benning will never have to fend for herself. She has Henry by her side. And what will you really miss? I assure you; nothing will be said that hasn't been said before. Mr. Parson's will soon bore them about the woeful tale about his brother, who wasted his inheritance on poorly advised investments. The poor Parsons are not a bit poor, but not as wealthy as they could be. It is a case of pride more than anything." He pointed to Mr. Quimby, Mr. Cromwell, and Uncle Samuel. "They argue the merits of investments, whether speculation is a noble venture or superfluous actions of the wealthy. It is an ongoing debate." He then pointed to the two ladies sitting on the sofa. "Mrs. Cromwell complains about her husband's snoring, while Mrs. Parson claims she cannot sleep without a little sip of sherry to calm her nerves. It is all quite dull," he revealed. "All the mundane details of their everyday lives, repeated dance after dance, party after party, night after night, year after year."

"Then you didn't save me from my captivity to be a gentleman, but only to be rescued from boredom?"

"You are a dear woman to think me so noble," he laughed. "But I fear our reprieve is to be interrupted." Dr. Cummings touched Jane's arm to acknowledge Uncle Samuel's approach.

Jane scowled.

"Miss Reynolds, our intriguing conversation was interrupted this morning. Maybe we can make up for lost time?"

"If Dr. Cummings doesn't hoard my company," Jane replied in the most charming way she could summon despite the distaste for the man.

"It is difficult not to monopolize my dear cousin," Dr. Cummings moved closer to Jane as a signal for retreat. "We have had so little time together."

It did not deter Uncle Samuel. "Ah yes, Miss Reynolds told us she is a relative of your late wife. I did not realize your family extended as far as the colonies."

"It is surprising to us all." Dr. Cummings gave Jane a look.

"You are a fortunate man to have such handsome women, all in one family. I can see the resemblance of loveliness in Miss Reynolds and your dear wife," Uncle Samuel said.

"You are kind to remember my wife so fondly."

Jane slipped her hand behind Dr. Cummings' elbow. "I hate to interrupt, but you wanted to discuss my plans to return home?"

"You are leaving us soon?" Uncle Samuel asked.

"Soon enough, unfortunately," Dr. Cummings replied. "If you will excuse us?"

With an approving nod by Uncle Samuel, he, as well as Henry, followed their retreat to the terrace. Henry was not a suspicious man, but it was becoming a habit for Dr. Cummings to escort Jane in private conversations.

Away from further interruption, Jane pounced with questions, awaiting the news since his arrival.

"Did you find her? Can I get home? What do I have to do?"

"Calm your nerves and let us sit," Dr. Cummings gestured to two chairs. "Yes, I have found the woman. It was difficult, but I eventually found her at the south end of town. They call her *The Black Raven*. She claims she has sight of things to come. She is a healer and reads the stars. She is a curious woman, but I did not find her threatening on any terms. She goes by the name Agnes Ramsey. She is adamant about meeting you in person."

"She knows of me?"

"That was most unusual. She was expecting me!" He rubbed his chin. "She calls you the woman of the black moon. And most interesting, she said you and I are born of the same stillness."

"What does that mean?"

"I asked the same question. She said she would explain when I bring you to her. She would like to meet you. She says it must be soon since you have interrupted your line of connection. Thus, you are threatening your return."

"Is there a problem? Have I done something wrong?"

Had she not sensed it?

A chill ran through her.

"Wrong? That is not what she meant. She said it was a matter of the heart. That is all she explained," he replied.

"So, it will be possible for me to return?"

"She did not say exactly. But she left me with the possibility."

Jane wanted to finish her conversation with Dr. Cummings, but saw Anne looking for her, her fragile eyes darting between shoulders of the men who surrounded her. Jane asked Dr. Cummings to escort her back inside only after they agreed to meet in the morning.

"Dinner is being served. If you all would join us, please," Lillian called to the group.

Mr. Quimby, who had found his way to Anne' side, escorted her. Mr. Parson's found his wife, as did Mr. Cromwell. Lillian laid her hand upon Mr. Davenport's sleeve, who declared he was the luckiest man on earth, and Sir Levongood and Uncle Samuel followed. The two remaining men, Henry and Dr. Cummings, looked at each other. Henry bid a stern nod, and Dr. Cummings stepped back. Henry outstretched his arm to Jane. With reluctance, she accepted, hoping he didn't notice her legs wobble as he escorted her to dinner.

THE BLACK RAVEN

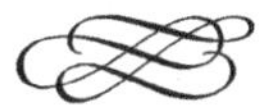

The rain arrived, as the humidity promised. It poured all morning, causing slick streets and fresh stench. Dr. Cummings wrapped his arm around Jane, protecting her from slipping on the uneven, water-logged, muddy streets. Her wool cape smelled of wet dog, and her shoes sloshed. She leaned into him, his warm embrace authoritative and assuring. Together, they pushed forward, in a search for answers to the unknown–time travel, which even for a modern girl like Jane was mystifying and uncertain. The course of her future was in the knowledge of the woman mere steps away, and nothing, not even the dreadful weather, would stop her.

"Just a little ahead," he yelled under the patter of the rain against the pavement and rooftops.

They slipped into a side alley, where they came upon a black door. Dr. Cummings knocked three times, heavy fisted, to be heard over the downpour.

They listened to approaching footsteps.

Jane held her breath.

An old woman in black, with gold eyes and jagged teeth, haunted her dreams the night before. Much to her surprise, when the door opened, a young woman closer to Jane's age greeted them. Her complexion was clear, flawless, and pale, her lips naturally rouged. She had a delicate frame, petite and bony, her face childlike. Her hair parted in the middle, pulled tightly into a braid down her back and tied at the end with a red ribbon, the crimson stark against the black velvet strands. She was delicate; her voice soft and melodic, but her piercing emerald eyes dispelled any misconception she was weak or timid.

"Miss Agnes Ramsey," Dr. Cummings greeted, taking off his hat. "May I present, Miss Jane Reynolds…"

"Aye," her headed shook up and down, "I know you from my dreams." She rushed them into the small, darkened quarters. She took their coats and hung them by the door. Water pooled on the floor. "It's a nasty afternoon to be out. You must be terribly cold. Come sit nearer to the heat." She gestured to two chairs by the fire.

A small cat meowed at Jane's feet, reminding her of Mr. Bingley, but Agnes shooed the creature away as he tried to jump on her lap. "He's been waiting for you, but the birds keep his attention," she said matter of fact.

Jane didn't know if she was talking about the cat who found a spot on a pillow near the fire, or Mr. Bingley, whose pastime was watching the birds. A chill ran up her back and she shuddered.

Agnes pulled a spindly chair from the corner of the room and sat next to Jane. "Now, let's take a good look at you." She held Jane's face and tilted it towards the light of the fire. Her eyes became big, and the firelight made them sparkle golden as they met Jane's.

"Did you have a rough journey of it?"

"I don't remember. I was unconscious when they found me." Jane answered, looking to Dr. Cummings for confirmation.

"It is an amazement. I cannot believe I am sitting here myself even discussing it," Dr. Cummings interjected.

"Others have done it," she said. "You were meant to come. Your birth gave you the power, but your purpose was guided. Destiny is not in *your* hands."

Agnes's words were enigmatic, but her delivery was unequivocal. The meanings were purposeful. Jane became frightful of the outcome. "Miss Ramsey, will I be able to go home?"

"Aye, my dear, but your destiny is not sealed yet. Everything has a cycle. One can return upon one's connection. Your energy still connects you, and thus it remains open. But it must be pure of heart, or you shall remain in two planes, with time dividing your soul."

"When?" Dr. Cummings' deep baritone voice commanded attention.

Agnes turned her green eyes to him. "That has not been shown to me."

Agnes rose, took Jane's hands into hers, and suddenly it was silent. Jane did not hear the rush of water on the rooftops, the crackle of the fire, or even the beating of her heart. Dr. Cummings disappeared from her periphery; the room became a blur. The walls melted away, and she was in a fog, the golden centers of Agnes' eyes entrancing her.

"Your energy force is the link. If you choose to stay, it remains here forever. You have allowed your energy a connection that may alter your life and those around you. Be careful." She ended with an ominous warning, "Choices have consequences."

Agnes let go, and Jane was back in the darkened space, sitting in her chair, the glow of the fire highlighting Dr. Cummings' face.

"Miss Reynolds?" He leaned forward. "Did you hear what she said? You're going home."

Did he hear what she heard?

Agnes continued, "Time will stop, and it is then you will fall back." She placed her hand on her cheek. "I will come when it is time."

It was only then, the firelight flashed across her hand, did Jane see it, the outline of an iris on her lower thumb. Instinctively, she grabbed Agnes's hand and turned the birthmark upward to reveal it to Dr. Cummings.

"You're marked." Jane rubbed the spot with her finger. "I saw this before–on Peyton. She told me to find you."

"Yes, this is the curse of my bloodline. My kin have been brutally killed because of it. We cannot hide who we are."

"And who are you?" Dr. Cummings asked.

"If you choose to believe, I can only tell you what I know to be true. I am a messenger and a link between heaven and earth. I come from the light, not the dark. Many have mistaken the difference."

Jane took Agnes's hand into hers and squeezed. "I know the difference."

The two women hugged.

"Thank you, thank you, thank you..." Jane whispered. "I would be truly lost without you."

"My dear, you were never lost. You just needed to be found."

The rain subsided, and Agnes encouraged them to escape before the downpour started again. Dr. Cummings paid the woman for her help and advanced her for any future inconvenience she might incur to expeditiously find Jane with future information.

As they walked through the door, Agnes grabbed Dr. Cummings and pulled him inside.

She lived in the back alley; hidden. In her little corner, she was sought after for many things and brought comfort to the downtrodden community in which she resided. The people used her gift with fearful adoration. But she did her work with the cautious tale from her ancestors and avoided the horrid fates they suffered for their gift. Dr. Cummings thought he was cunning to have found her. But it was not his will. He was only granted access to her with guidance from her dreams.

"You were born as she, and thus, linked to her forever. Her decisions will affect your fate. She does not know of your power, but you must be willing to give in completely, or you, too, will fall in between time. A soul has nowhere to go if it is divided. Make your decision pure of heart, as she must. You'll come to me when the time is right."

Dr. Cummings crushed his brow. Her green eyes were intense as he peered into the depths, trying to see beyond her words. His inner soul shivered at her warning. He knew not what she saw in store for him *and* was not willing to delve into the possibilities. As did the townspeople, he respected her gift, but feared of the power it held.

THE DANCE

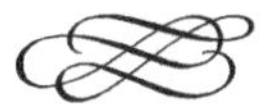

Jane lingered in her room, not rushing to the party below, with thoughts of the day's excursion after her visit with The Black Raven. Her eagerness to meet the mysterious woman was fulfilled, but her visit only heightened the anxiety about going home. Agnes was confident about her return.

It was the news Jane wanted to hear, but it did not bring her the happiness she thought it would.

When she first arrived in nineteenth-century England, fear gripped her with the possibility she may be stuck in time. As the weeks progressed in moments of solitude, Jane's feelings transformed from fear to a fondness. It wasn't logical or even prudent, living in a world rampant with disease, future war, social strife, and human injustices, but she grew comfortable with the situation, and the people, almost forgetting she had a twenty-first century life waiting for her. Agnes's news was the realization she was leaving. For Anne's sake alone, she should have been gleeful about the psychic's revelations. But as much as she wanted to deny it, her feelings were complicated, because it meant leaving Henry as well.

Excitement brewed downstairs. The Levongood house was abuzz with guests arriving every few minutes, with grand displays of gowns and fine suits. The house twinkled in a sea of white candles, lighting the way to the grand ballroom, filled with food, drink and merriment.

The evening promised young women, with large and small bosoms alike on display, a gallant search for future husbands, while allowing the men, with overlooked approval, the opportunity to intermingle freely among them. The mothers sat on the sidelines and pushed their daughters toward acceptable prospects, hoping for future proposals, while the fathers gathered in small groups, drinks in constant fulfillment, to stay out of the business of pimping their daughters for matrimonial pursuits.

Lillian knocked on Jane's door, and upon permission, entered, followed by a maid with a pink silk-chiffon gown in hand. "I wanted to give this to you earlier, but you've been gone. I see I caught you in time." She eyed the yellow gown hanging from the armoire. "Lovely, but I had this altered for you." She splayed the dress on the bed and insisted Jane try it on.

"It's beautiful beyond words." Jane ran her fingers over the crystal beaded skirt.

With Lillian's insistence, Jane stepped into the dress, and the maid buttoned up the back.

She ran to the mirror. Jane gasped, but Lillian just rolled her eyes.

The competition was fierce in the ballroom below, and she wanted Jane to equally compete against the others, many of them offering more youth than beauty, but still an advantage in the game of coupling.

It was stunning, if not daring. The exposed cleavage and the synched waist were purposeful, allowing onlookers to appreciate the full shape of the woman who adorned it. Modesty was left on the seamstress's floor. The glory of the dress was the collection of crystal beads scattered from the bodice to skirt, collecting at the hem in a pattern of puddling flowers. The dress sparkled in the dim light of her room.

Jane could only imagine what it would do when it swooshed across a room full of candelabras.

Lillian was pleased with the effects of the dress on Jane. "I knew you would like it. You have quite an eye and appreciation for such intricate beadwork. Mr. Levongood brought it back from Paris as a surprise. It was upon his return he learned I was pregnant, and it was put away, the opportunity never to be worn. My figure completely transformed under duress of the second pregnancy."

Jane knew only of Isabel. "You had another child?"

"Oh my, you wouldn't know." Lillian turned away, finding it still difficult to discuss.

"Oh, Lillian," Jane placed her hand on her friend. "I'm so sorry."

"It was a boy. We named him little Henry, in honor of my brother. After losing his own son, I had hoped it would bring him comfort–to have a namesake. Of course, I did not know how fate was to play out. Another loss only adding to his two." She paused in reflection. "Henry never faltered with his support when little Henry died. With his heart already so wounded, the additional sorrow just melted into the heartache he already endured, making him steadfast." She shook her head. "I could not find the strength he did. It was more than I could bear. Sir Levongood was but a shadow of a man with grief, unable to support himself, and yet there he was by my side, morning until night, seeing me through..." Lillian's words drifted. A melancholy dimmed the sparkle in her eyes, the loss still raw.

Jane put her arms around Lillian. She stilled in the embrace.

Lillian pulled away and patted Jane's hand, "That time is

now gone but held in my heart forever." She wiped away her tears. "So, I have this lovely dress, and a beautiful woman to breathe life back into it."

"Lillian, I just can't. It brings back too many memories for you." Jane instructed the maid to get her out of it.

"No! I won't hear it. It was a joyous gift, and you need to honor me by wearing it." She stood behind her and pointed to the woman in the mirror. "You will be the most stunning woman in the room."

Seeing Lillian's determination, she had no other choice. "Then, I am honored."

Lillian's arms wrapped around Jane. "Life has a strange way of finding people for each other, Jane. We are very blessed to have you in our lives."

Jane smiled, but her heart tugged. She would be gone soon and lose them forever.

Dr. Cummings waited at the bottom of the stairs and smiled like a schoolboy when Jane appeared at the landing. He was dressed in an onyx black suit and a crisp white shirt with a cravat of grey surrounding his collar, the solemn shades handsomely highlighting his white hair, neatly brushed back into wavy curls spilling over his collar. Jane giddied looking down at the handsome man who would escort her into the party.

"You are a vision of loveliness, if I may be so forward," Dr. Cummings said when she took her last step to stand before him.

"You may be so forward, Dr. Cummings," Jane twirled for him, letting him see the dress in its full beauty. She had to admit, she looked lovely in the gown. The pink of the dress was a great complement to her dark hair, pulled into a ponytail of cascading curls. She had the luxury of powder, rouge, and lip color Anne generously provided. And the doctor graciously adorned her neckline for the evening. Early that morning, he sent a note of invitation to escort her to the party along with a wish for her to wear a small token, a ruby centered necklace, in memory of his late wife.

"Stunning..." He cooed.

"You can thank Lillian. It is her dress."

"You do yourself a disservice, my dear. It is you who compliments the dress." He extended his arm. "Shall we?"

As they walked to the ballroom, Jane rubbed the sparkling pendant, feeling like a princess. It had the promise of a magical evening.

When they entered the room, heads turned. Some asking who the woman on Dr. Cummings arm was. Others whispered rumors of Dr. Cummings' interest in his wife's distant cousin. And many, handsomely clad, single prospects admired the young woman they did not know, calculating their introductions.

Henry was among the many observing how the two dramatically complemented one another, between Jane's sparkling beauty in an aura of pink, and Dr. Cummings' distinguished refinement in striking black and grey. Much to Henry's dismay, his friend was still a man of handsome qualities. As the doctor paraded Jane around the room, Henry noted the young women in attendance, as well as Jane, whose smile revealed her pleasure to be by his side, believed Dr. Cummings not a man to be overlooked. It was Anne who caused Henry to break his stare.

"Does she not look like a goddess?" Anne remarked, awed by Jane's appearance.

Henry did not answer.

Mr. Davenport, standing with the couple, agreed whole heartedly, eagerly adding, "She is a quite...quite charming, young lady. It is a shame Mrs. Davenport will not meet her this visit. I do hope Miss Reynolds does not return soon to America. Maybe we can entrust Dr. Cummings to convince her otherwise. They seem to get along splendidly…quite splendidly."

"They do make a fine couple," Anne said. "I am not privy to Miss Reynolds' feelings, but she seems to enjoy his companionship."

Henry grimaced.

"Ah, the music has started again," Mr. Davenport noted. "Miss Benning, would you do me the great honor of a dance?"

She accepted, and he took her hand.

Henry watched his fiancée as she floated on the dance floor. The men glanced her way as she glided about. She was a beautiful woman. It was her power over him when they were first introduced at a dinner party. Their union was methodically planned by his sister, who conspired for his wellbeing. Upon their first introduction, he was captivated. Anne's demure sweetness was entrancing. No man would dare question his motivation to pursue her admiration. Her companionship brought the comfort of a woman he had not experienced since his wife passed away. Although much younger, she did not withdraw from his advances. He thought he could bring her happiness, and she would be good for Maggie, who longed for the comfort of a mother. As he watched her intoxicated admirers, he questioned his motives then, and more so now. When he first proposed to Anne, it was for the purposes of fulfilling the roles of wife and mother that were vacant. He wondered now if that was enough for either of them.

Lillian sauntered over to her brother. "You may not have the opportunity to dance with your betrothed. She seems to be the most popular woman in the room. That is, besides Jane. Look at those men hovering about her." She waved towards the three men jockeying to engage Jane in conversation.

"Well, my dear sister, you provided the opportunity for those scoundrels to prowl so flagrantly," Henry snarled.

"You used to be one of those scoundrels, my dear brother. Give them the opportunity you have been so blessed with," she countered. "It would be nice to play a part in finding Jane a partner. She is far too charming to be so unattached." She scanned the room for candidates.

"There is no one in the room suitable for a woman of such quality. Look at those fools," he nodded, indicating to the men swarming Jane. "Which of them is worthy to care for her?"

Lillian noted her brother's unusual concern. "If you find none of them worthy, save her from the perils of love and ask her to dance. Go," she ordered, and pushed him towards her.

Henry was apprehensive. Jane avoided him all morning. He tried to approach her before breakfast, when he spotted her in the library, perusing through the shelves. One look at him and she darted past him. She barely took a sip of her tea at the table when he showed up. When he sat across from her, she shot up and dashed out the door, making her excuses she had somewhere to go. When he called after her, down the hall, to his dismay, she turned away. He had no words that would bring comfort; his explanations were meaningless to her. He acted dishonorably, and no apology could rectify that. But he wanted to make amends, and she was making it difficult to fulfill his intentions.

Jane tried to dismiss the pounding in her chest as he approached the group. She placed her hand over her heart, willing it to stop beating. It didn't obey. When his eyes met hers, she looked away, hoping to dispel any notion of addressing her.

He defied her dismissal. "May I have the pleasure of a dance, Miss Reynolds?"

"I embarrassingly admit I don't know how to dance. These gentlemen have been trying to persuade me as well. I had to decline their insistence to teach me. It's only my gift of conversation they have had to settle with. I must decline your offer, Mr. Eaton."

She heard herself–the Elizabeth Bennet rejection. *Who was she becoming?*

Henry persisted. "Then, may I have the pleasure of escorting you for refreshments?"

The three men eyed Jane, waiting to see if she would refuse him twice, his pride in danger.

His presence was firm. He was not going away until he got what he wanted.

"Gentlemen," she bowed to her three prospecting suitors, begrudgingly accepting Henry's extended arm, "If you'll excuse me…"

All three bowed their permission and allowed her to retreat, congratulatory of Henry's win to his honor.

Jane fell to Henry's side as they walked the outer corner of the room. "And what do I owe this pleasure of your company, Mr. Eaton?"

"It is I who holds the honor."

"Mr. Eaton," she stopped in earnest. "Let's not play games. Although probably a gallant requirement, it's not necessary with me."

"I have no other obligation other than my sincerest regard." She was being blunt and honest. He countered equally candidly, "You are angry with me."

"No. Yes…if I must admit." She flustered, letting her irritation get the best of her. "I was having a perfectly good time with three charming men, and you chose to take me away?"

"I…" He cleared his throat. "Lillian was concerned you needed rescuing."

"I need rescuing? You have a sense of humor indeed, Mr. Eaton," she scoffed.

Henry huffed, his chest expanding and releasing in three successions, and then stridently ignored her indifference. "I was hoping we could have a friendly conversation. It is becoming clear you are not willing to be so generous."

"I'm not willing?" Her gloved hands curled into a fist, neatly hidden in the folds of her dress. "Mr. Eaton," she paused and feigned a smile at two women walking past them, curious about their conversation. Eyes were on them. Jane, not wanting to give them something to talk about, leaned into Henry with a lowered voice. "It is admirable that you feel the need to protect me. And I realize you have been burdened with the responsibility to care for me since you found me. But as you're well aware, I'm a grown woman who is not easily swayed by the overt flirtations of a man. I can take care of myself."

His jawed hardened; his eyes grew cold. "Jane!"

"No!" She pointed at him. "You have no right to be so personal." Her cheeks grew hot. Red blotches splattered her chest. "You have no right to ask anything of me other than my debt to be paid for your hospitality. I wish I had the means to throw it at your feet so I could be free of the burden. I can only grant you this: I'll be gone soon, no longer beholden to you. Now, if you will excuse me…" She bowed, allowing a smile to cross her face for the onlookers, and retreated.

Lillian watched her brother from where she stood. She knew him well and displayed before her was a man in anguish. His brow was firm, his jaw was clenched, and his eyes were sullen and dark. He suddenly straightened and tensed as he watched Jane bolt away from him.

Jane sought a reprieve on the terrace. The cool air breezed against her hot cheeks, the rain having stopped just in time for the guests to arrive, dropping the temperature and leaving everything layered in raindrops. She leaned over the balustrade wall, the dampness penetrating her gloves as she gripped the edge, and inhaled, filling her lungs with the heady petrichor. Suddenly, the heat of a man's breath was upon her neck, sending an icy chill down her spine.

"Passion suits you, my dear. It brings color to your cheeks," the slithering voice whispered in her ear.

Uncle Samuel pressed against her, firmly trapping her between the railing and himself. Jane tried to push away, but he only pressed with more determination, tightening his grip around her wrists. He tucked his hips, and his hardness slapped against her. The more she persisted, the firmer it became.

"If it is passion you seek, I am available to fulfill your desires," he offered. He rubbed his lips behind her ear, and his wet tongue slurped against her flesh.

Jane gagged, struggling for freedom.

Uncle Samuel growled, "Mmm, you are feisty!" He pushed down her defense, crushing her fingers into the cement ledge, causing her to wince. His whisky breath panted against her cheek. "Henry will no longer be available. My niece will be enough for him. But I am more than capable of satisfying the fury that resides within you. With your passion and my desire, we will have more than enough to satisfy us."

"Take yourself off her, or I will remove you myself!"

Uncle Samuel released Jane slowly. He stepped away from her and turned to face the commanding voice. Jane gasped from relief and rubbed her hands to clear the numbness. She looked back to find Henry and Uncle Samuel glaring at each other.

"Ah, my dear man, have you come to finish what you started?" he taunted. "Tell me, who will protect her when you are no longer there? You of all people must know, a woman is defenseless against the desires of man."

"She is not to be bothered by you or your advances again," Henry ordered through gritted teeth, ignoring Uncle Samuel's pointed comment.

"Nor from you! I think she made that evidently clear." He smirked.

Uncle Samuel was not easily threatened. He had his wits

and used them where it suited him. He pulled at the cuffs of his coat and bowed to Jane as if only pleasantries transpired between them.

Henry clenched his fists, wanting to use them. Instead, he cleared the way for Uncle Samuel to leave.

Jane's wide eyes watched as Uncle Samuel passed through the doors. When he was gone, an uncontrollable shivering took over her body.

Henry wanted desperately to wrap himself around her and take away the fear swallowing her. But he didn't have to ask. She fled into his arms, seeking the protection his unspoken words offered. His arms surrounded her, and she tucked her head under his chin. They stood in the warmth of each other, the shadows allowed by the drifting clouds covering the little light the crescent moon provided, hiding their sin.

"Henry?" Anne walked onto the terrace after seeing Henry escape there and her uncle re-entering the ballroom with a notable scowl on his face. "Is everything all right out here?"

Henry didn't move, nor did he answer, wanting to keep Jane in his arms. But the clouds moved, and Jane pulled away.

"Yes, everything is fine," Jane said, revealing herself. "I got dizzy and thought I was going to faint. I wanted some fresh air," she explained, hoping it was enough for Anne. "Let's get some refreshments, shall we?"

She took Anne's arm and walked her away, leaving Henry standing alone, the clouds shadowing him once more.

DEMONS OF MAN

The rain started again during the night. Jane opened her windows to listen to the music of the raindrops as they fell on the rooftop. She inhaled the musky smells of dampened dirt and wet trees.

It was a cleansing.

A release.

She hoped it would lull her to sleep, but rest didn't come. It only toyed with her as shadows from the flickering flames danced across the ceiling. Her mind wouldn't shut off. Thoughts of Uncle Samuel replayed, over and over, no matter how many times she tried to shut them out. The slimy sensation of his tongue lingered on her skin, as did his wretched voice warning Henry, "Tell me, who will protect her when you are no longer there?"

When the flames dwindled to a sprinkling of red embers, she pushed out of the warm covers and threw on two more logs. She then grabbed her cloak and headed to the library to find something, anything, to distract the hauntings of Uncle Samuel.

The house was quiet as she slid across the floors in her bare feet. The drunken and ruckus crowd, who lingered to all hours of the night, had finally retreated, or more like fallen into slumber. She was relieved to find the library empty, the fire gasping for air, the embers all but grey and ashy. She browsed through the bookcases with her lighted candles, squinting to find something of interest. She compiled a few choices and headed back to her room, hoping no one else was foolish enough to roam the halls in the middle of the night. She let out a sigh of relief when she reached her bedroom door, closed it, and locked it behind her. She released the satiny cloak from her shoulders, letting it fall to the floor, and laid the books on the bed. But a shuffle on the wooden floor caused her to freeze. Her heart thudded against her chest cavity as she slowly turned around.

Her eyes froze on his.

"What are you doing here?"

"May I sit?" He gestured to a nearby chair.

Jane nodded in approval, afraid of what he might do if she did not consent. The pungent smell of whiskey wafted from his breath. As he fell into the seat, he placed a glass on the table. The glow of the fire illuminated his face and she could see his eyes were bloodshot, his lids droopy. Sleep eluded him as well.

She asked again, "Henry, why are you here?"

"I need to make amends with you. I can see it in your eyes what I have caused," he replied. "I never wanted to hurt you."

"You cannot undo that, Henry. The deed is done."

"Are you truly that indifferent to my love?"

"Me?" Her head dizzied. She rubbed her temples. "One moment you're passionately kissing me, claiming your love, and the next you're dismissing me, for your fiancée, no less!" Jane flailed her arms in the air, her anger aroused. "I don't understand you!"

"How can I make you understand?" He rose to move towards her, but she stepped back, and he halted.

"What's to understand?" She glared at him. "I obviously misinterpreted your intentions."

"Is that what you think?" He shouted, dragging his hands through his hair. "Jane, my love for you grows stronger with each moment I breathe!"

"Don't!" she shouted back, gritting her teeth at the same time halting the tears just below the surface. "Don't you dare use my heart as your weapon."

Henry pounded his hand against his chest, as if to keep his heart from stopping. "It is with the greatest of will I hold myself back from you, for I fear if I bend, just an inch, I will fall into the depths of hell and be no good…to you, to Anne–not to anyone."

The urge to slap him was overwhelming. "You bastard! Is choosing me so reprehensible?"

"Damn it, Jane," he put his face to hers, "Didn't you hear what I said? I love you." He pulled her towards him, entrapping her in his arms. "I love you," he said again, looking straight into the darkened storm that stared back at him.

Henry came down on her lips, kissing her urgently.

Jane moaned as his passion overwhelmed her. She could not pull away, even if she wanted to.

His mouth wrapped around hers, as if he wanted to swallow her whole being, and drag her down into the depths of his soul. He was not gentle as he thrust his tongue inside, tasting her, breathing her in. His lips were strong muscles exercising their right to overpower her, his body putting no constraints on his desire.

Running her fingers through the waves of his hair, she bit his lower lip to anger the passionate beast, forcing his tongue deeper inside the mouth, devouring her. She slid her hands down his body, guiding his hips towards her.

"Make love to me, Henry," she panted, clawing at his pants.

As if a gale-forced wind blew in, cold air sliced their bodies apart. Henry abruptly pulled away.

Jane stood dumbfounded; her chest heaved as she tried to catch her breath.

Henry turned away, diverting her bewilderment.

When no words uttered from his mouth, she ordered, "Get out!"

Henry looked at her. His eyes notably pained. Still, he uttered no words.

"Get out, and never come near me again," Jane demanded, stretching her arm in the door's direction.

"It's not what you think, Jane."

"Does it matter? You don't want me, Henry. You have chosen the woman you want. And it isn't me."

"Do you think I do this to hurt you?" His voice wavered in the room's quiet.

Jane had no sympathy for his torment. Her arm lingered, pointing towards the door.

Henry moved to exit but stopped.

"Jane, it is because of my heart I stand before you, a man able to love you with every inch of my being but must push you away because of my obligations. This uncontrollable piece of anatomy..." he pounded at his chest, "It is what makes me human. I would have lain down and died the moment my wife and son took their last breath if it were not for the love of my daughter. This heart, a curse of life because of the pain it endures, is also a savior because of the strength it is capable of. It has offered me sanctuary in my darkest hours. When it is being ripped through my chest, it is its way of jolting my memory, reminding me I am alive. It is a double-edge sword that yields its own power despite my mind. I curse God's name, but underneath my breath, I thank Him for every beat that keeps it going. This dichotomy to know love *and* feel pain at the same time is its power. It is the love I have for you that forces me to do what I must do."

Jane met his eyes.

Was it fear, empathy, or anguish he saw in her black depths?

He continued, his words mere whispers of a man.

"It is not that I chose someone else. It is because I love you most, I cannot have you."

He left, as ghostly as he came.

ANNE'S SECRET

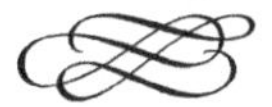

Jane sat at the window most of the night, listening to the last of the rain. It was only when the pitter patter stopped did her eyes give way to exhaustion. She pulled her nightgown over her knees, curled into the window seat, and fell asleep. That is, until the morning light came over the trees, glaring through the glass onto her face. She opened one eye, saw the burnt-yellow orb clearing the sky, and slammed it shut!

Two more hours…maybe three, she begged the omnipresent god of time.

She rolled over, hugged her body, and squeezed her lids shut. They burned, but she ignored the swollen lids and pressed them tighter. She heard dogs bark in the distance, and someone call after them, then fell back to sleep.

Knocks muffled in her ear. Three more knocks came, dragging Jane out of slumber. She blinked, and the blue sky came into view. She sat up, rubbed her eyes with the back of her hand, and stretched to clear the kink from her neck.

"Jane, are you awake?" A voice came from the other side of the door.

Jane froze. She didn't want to see anyone, nor did she want anyone to see her.

"Jane, darling, it's me, Lillian."

She took a deep breath and sighed, "Come in."

Lillian, dressed in layers of white linen, looking as refreshed as a day after rain–dewy and bright. She bustled in with a tray of tea and toast, setting it down next to the bed. Two maids followed, one with an additional tray of food, and the other with a carafe of water and a stack of towels.

"Good afternoon sleepy. I didn't wake you, did I? It's nearly afternoon. You are the last to rise. Albeit no one has made it downstairs. I've been delivering trays all morning. I waited to deliver yours."

Jane didn't move, nor attempt to speak.

"That will be all for now," Lillian excused the two maids and shut the door behind them. She poured a cup of tea and handed it to Jane. "Here, this might help."

Jane accepted the hot tea, coddling the cup in between her hands. She searched the steaming water, wondering what her tea leaves would reveal.

Lillian searched around the room and collected a robe and slippers. Placing the satin shoes on Jane's cold feet, and the robe around her shoulders, she brushed her hair out of her face, and lifted her chin to the light, to reveal the drama she was harboring. "You look a dreadful mess."

"I didn't sleep very well."

"I can see that." Lillian nudged Jane and sat down on the window seat next to her. She didn't speak but allowed Jane to take a few sips of tea before she questioned the distraught creature beside her. Placing her hand on Jane's arm, she asked, "Would you like to talk about it?"

The tears had fallen so heavily the night before, Jane didn't think she had anything left to cry. But she cried again, unable to stop herself.

When the tears slowed, Lillian rose to find a handkerchief. Opening the small drawer next to the bed, she stiffened, and a shiver darted up her neck with the possible causes for Jane's tears. She had no attachments that she was aware, nor did she suspect Dr. Cummings capable of such strife. The only option left her with terror.

"Jane, did someone harm you?"

"What? No!" she insisted with a shake of her head. After Uncle Samuel's unsolicited advancement, Jane wasn't sure how much more he was capable of. But she didn't want Lillian to worry on her account. "It's really nothing. I'm just homesick, brought on by a long night. It's all silly, really. Haven't you ever missed something so much it made you cry?"

"Well, my dear, you have every right to be forlorn. Have a bite to eat and join us when you are better suited." She bent over and kissed her on the head. "I need to check on Anne next. She has fallen ill again. Poor thing. She cannot get herself better but refuses a doctor."

"Oh my, again?" Jane stood. "I will check on her as soon as I'm dressed."

"She will appreciate that. I cannot rely on my brother to show her any sympathy today. I came from Henry's room where he is in worse condition than the both of you. Although I do not feel sorry for the man. I found an empty decanter of Sir Levongood's finest whisky by his side. Serves him right."

Before Lillian left, she spotted a crystal glass with remnants of a golden liquid sitting on a table next to a chair. Bringing the crystal to her nose, she smelled the smokey scent and whispered, "*Whisky!*" She looked back at Jane, weary against the window, eyes swollen and red, the light dimmed from them, and recognized what ailed her. There was no denying a heart stricken with forlorn.

~

Jane didn't know whether to nurse Anne or scold her about her slow recovery. She was relapsing. *The flu needed rest, not dinners and dancing*! When she knocked on Anne's door, she did not wait for an answer, and let herself in, finding Anne stretched on the bed with her hands covering her eyes.

"Anne," she ran over to her, "I beg you, let me call Dr. Cummings? Why must you brave it out?"

Anne's piercing blue eyes peeked out from under her arms. She groaned, "I don't need a doctor."

She rolled away from Jane.

"You are paler than ever. You can't go on like this forever. Enough with parties and gatherings. I insist you stay in bed, drink lots of tea, and rest! You're getting married in a few weeks where you'll need your strength."

"I will soon be better, I promise. I should only be ill a little longer." She moaned again. "I must keep up appearances until then–for Henry."

"Appearances!" Jane rolled her eyes. "You are sicker than a dog and everyone expects you to perform." Not wanting to put more pressure on her, Jane walked away to let her rest, irritated by the archaic expectations of women.

But before she reached the door, Jane looked back at her friend. And then it all made sense. It was like looking at a Georges Seurat painting–if too close, thousands of tiny dots cover the canvas, but if you step back an image appears. Jane had been looking at Anne too closely. When she stepped back, the image suddenly revealed itself.

"Anne? Are you pregnant?"

Anne bolted up. "Please Jane, do not say such a thing so loudly. The walls have ears," she pleaded, revealing her secret.

Jane's heart sank for her friend. "Does Henry know?"

Anne nodded as tears fell onto her cheeks.

Jane now understood everything. She wasn't sure if she was

angry with Henry for being a scoundrel, or proud of him for taking care of Anne.

"What you must think of me," Anne cried out. "I am so ashamed."

Jane opened her arms, allowing Anne to fall into them. She rocked her, stroked her hair, and let Anne's tears fall on her shoulders, until her cries became just whispers of angst.

She pulled out of Jane's arms, sniffled, and wiped her eyes. "Why are you not shocked by my admission and horrified by my circumstance?"

"There's no shame in having a baby."

"I succumbed to my passions…before marriage!" Anne lowered her eyes. "I am to have a bastard child!"

Jane pictured her with Henry, wrapped in his arms, weakened by his touch…his kisses.

Had she not experienced it herself the night before?

"There is no blame, Anne. These things happen."

Anne covered her face with her hands. "It all went so terribly wrong."

Jane treaded carefully. "Do you love him?"

Tears fell again; her shoulders rose and fell as she gasped for air in between sobs. "Oh, Jane! I love him so very much."

The words slammed against Jane's heart, but she dared not expose her agony. She inhaled, exhaled, and then gave Anne the best advice she had. "Well, you hold your head up. Cherish the knowledge that you and Henry created a child out of love."

Anne suddenly stopped crying. Her eyes widened.

"Jane, it's not Henry's baby!"

Jane's mouth fell agape. "Are you sure?"

Anne giggled through her wetted eyes. "Of course, I am sure. Henry has always been a gentleman. Why, the only time he kissed me is after I accepted his proposal."

Jane did not want to seem indelicate, but an uncontrollable smile spread across her face.

She didn't betray Anne!

Or did she?

Her brow knitted. "Then why are you marrying Henry?"

"Oh!" Anne shot up from the bed, her hands twisting together.

Jane held her breath as Anne paced the room, the swishing of her skirt notable in the room's silence, the pounding of her heart like drums in her ears.

After a series of circling hands, she stopped and turned to Jane, creases pushed between her brows. "It's Mother and Uncle Samuel. They did not think Patrick was an appropriate husband. He is the youngest son of the clothier, Mr. Wansey. You met his two sisters," she reminded her. "I broke off my engagement with Henry when I fell in love with Patrick. But mother was strongly against our union. Patrick did not want to defy my mother and take me away from my family. So, he left to travel overseas, thinking it would be best. He did not know I was going to have his child. I have not seen him since. He thought I would forget him. But I haven't." Her lips quivered.

"And you thought you could fool Henry into marrying you?"

"Oh no, I would never do that to him. It was Uncle Samuel's idea," she explained. "Henry is an honorable man. I told him the truth that day on the terrace. I could not disrespect the memory of Patrick with such manipulation. I asked Henry to reconsider his proposal for the sake of the child. He knew not only my reputation would be ruined, but the child would forever be haunted as a bastard. It's not without fondness we became engaged. He had promised me his hand in marriage, and I hoped he would honor that if it meant my safety. He was more than honorable. But it was my uncle who forced the issue. He made it clear to Henry he would ruin his reputation if he refused. Uncle Samuel was very adamant he could prove it was Henry's child if he had decided other than to honor his proposal. He also reminded him he had Margaret Elizabeth's reputation to consider."

"Why would you allow your uncle to treat him in that way?"

"Jane, I was not happy with my uncle's behavior. But it was Henry who insisted we follow through with the wedding. He told me not to worry. He said he would take care of me and the baby."

Jane winced at the truth.

"Oh, Jane, what am I to do?"

"Anne, look at me." She took Anne by the shoulders. "Breathe! It will be alright." She made Anne inhale and exhale…three times. "You're to say nothing and continue with the charade. Henry will take good care of you. As you and I both know, he is a good man. You have nothing to fear from him. I have no doubt he will treat you kindly. You will grow to love him, and he you." She smiled, tears surfacing from her own eyes. "Henry made the right decision. A child is a beautiful gift–cherish it together."

Anne may have been young, but she knew love when she saw it. "You are very fond of Henry, aren't you?"

Jane's face could not hide her feelings, nor did she want to disrespect Anne by lying to her. "The only thing I ask of you is to love him with all your heart. Care for him with tenderness and be patient with him. He can love with passion and need. You will find a love with him, I'm sure of it."

A knock came to the door and the two women jolted.

"Come in," Anne said.

"I have an urgent message for Miss Reynolds. Very urgent, indeed!" A young girl said, not meeting their eyes.

Jane moved closer to the young woman. "What is it?"

"Well Miss, it was *that* woman–the woman who has the sight. Said I was to go directly to you. But you were sleeping, and I had been instructed not to disturb you." The girl dropped her head.

Jane nudged, "Well, what did she say?"

"I am to say it as this: '*The new moon makes a full circle in twenty-nine days. The door is still open only during the exchange of the black moon. Upon interception, the energy force will turn, opening the tunnel. You will fall back at that moment. When the morning awakens at a quarter past eight, it will be too late. Not a minute before, nor a minute after. You are to return to the point you came in order to return to the point you went.*' She made me repeat it several times before I got it right."

She made the sign of the cross.

"Was there anything else?"

The young girl nodded. "She said, '*you must go there with no more interruption, or you may lose the energy you are carrying for a safe return. You have another's energy encircling you that could disrupt your path. Choose wisely, for once connected, you are tied to this time forever. It's your desire that will make it permanent if you so choose.*'"

INTERFERENCE

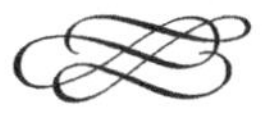

"What do you mean, leaving?" Lillian asked, dumbfounded by the urgency.

"I cannot explain, but it's important I return immediately," Jane said, frantic to explain to her friend the necessity for which she needed to get back to the field where she was found. "Oh Lillian, I wish I could explain. If Dr. Cummings hadn't been called back early this morning, I would have asked him to take me. But as it is, you're the only one I can depend."

"What about Henry? I will have him escort you back."

"No!" Jane threw her hands up. A little too forceful, and a little too quickly. "I wouldn't think of taking him away from Anne, especially with his duties for the upcoming wedding." She swallowed hard, pushing down the tears caught in her throat.

"Jane, you are worrying me." But against her better judgment, Lillian requested her staff to prepare immediately for Jane's return to the Eaton Estate, and with no haste.

Henry walked in while Lillian took the orders to task. Seeing concern on her sister's face, he turned to Jane.

"What is going on?"

"Jane is leaving us unexpectedly," Lillian declared.

"Leaving?"

Jane turned away. With the revelations about him, misjudging his honor, her shame was too great. News for a hurried departure arrived at a most needed time.

"Yes," Lillian snapped at her brother, "Leaving! She must return home–to America! We shall never see her again."

Henry neared Jane but did not touch her. "Must you leave?" With a nod of her head, the realization sent a dagger through his heart. She was inches from him, her eyes refusing to meet his. He wanted to reach for her twisting hands and bring them to his lips; breathe the scent of her skin, wet her lips. "Jane…"

Jane pulled away. Away from the force pulling her to him, his voice hypnotizing her to obey his command: *stay.* She was not his for him to ask anything of her. He had made his choice. The only honorable choice. But the truth about Anne still did not make it easier to be near him or not to want him.

Lillian's voice roared, jolting them both. "How can you stand there and allow her to leave? You realize this is all your doing?"

"My doing? Dear sister, beware the waters in which you tread."

Lillian was not swayed by his warning. "No, dear brother, someone must call you out." She narrowed her eyes and pointed at Jane. "Are you not in love with this woman?"

Jane gulped. She looked at the door, but it was closed. Her escape was a few steps away but didn't move. She wanted to hear his answer.

Henry glared at his sister, not daring to give himself away to Jane's watchful eyes. "The matters of my personal affairs and decisions are not yours to question."

Lillian smirked. "My concern is not for you, but for Jane. I will not stand by and watch you break this woman's heart. Of all hearts to shatter…" She shook her head. "Do you not see the gift that has been granted to you? Look at her and tell me you are willing to let her go."

Both Lillian and Henry turned to the woman, who was the topic of discussion.

Jane eyed the door again. She silently said a prayer to whoever was listening, that she be given the strength to do what she must.

Lillian took her hand, halting her escape. "Jane, if there is a reason as to your hurried departure beyond fleeing my brother, I will let you go without a fight. But I must ask before it is too late. Are you in love with my brother?"

If eyes burned, she would singe from Henry's stare. She could almost hear his heart pound against his chest. *Or was that hers?* She looked away, not knowing how to answer. If she confirmed her love for Henry, he would never marry Anne, and her life would be forever altered. Shame would follow not only for Anne and her child, but for Henry and Maggie alike. Jane was not going to carry that burden. She had no right to ruin all those she had grown to love.

"Lillian, you're a dear and sweet friend. You're a romantic as well, which inspires me, but cannot dissuade me to do what I must. You told me once to love with passion, but with guarded honor. I wasn't sure I understood what that meant until I met all of you. Sometimes love isn't enough. I have learned that lesson all too well. Life gets in the way and love gets complicated." She glanced at Henry. "Henry's personal affairs, as he said, are none of our business. All I know is my time is up, and I need to get home."

She hugged Lillian before she could refute and left the room.

Henry stayed firmly planted, not sure he could do the honorable thing, binding him to his commitment.

Lillian threw her arms in the air. "You are a bigger fool than I originally assumed."

"There are things beyond your control, Lillian. You mean well, but this is one situation that love cannot fix. There are practical issues at stake, and romantic notions will not wash them away. I have to be a sensible man."

"Damn your sensibility!" Lillian argued. "Henry, you are my brother, and there is nothing I would not do to see you content. But you are a man first! Do you not see the reality of that? If not in the way you look at her, admit your attraction to her. Are you the only one who does not realise that?"

Henry allowed Lillian's words to fill his head…anything to distract him, erase the way Jane looked at him; muddle the sound of her voice lingering in his ears. She didn't scowl at him. Her lips were soft across her face. There was no bitterness in her words, no direct line of attack, her eyes gentle, taking him in. Something changed, but she left with no explanation. Had it been any other circumstance, he would have stopped her from leaving and declared his love in front of his sister–to everyone. But he was steadfast in his decision. *Yes, he was a man! An honorable one.* He proceeded in the only honorable way he knew to be. If he were any less, he would have followed Jane.

"Henry?" Lillian called.

Henry stopped mid-paced. His brow furrowed. "What?" he demanded.

A smile crossed her face. "Jane did not answer my question."

Henry dragged his hand through his hair and walked out of the room with no more to say.

THE GIFT

Jane didn't waste time before she boarded the carriage. She prepared to leave with little more than she arrived–barely the clothes on her back. The beautiful dresses Lillian graciously allowed her to borrow were left on the bed with a note of gratitude tucked underneath the layers of fabric artistry.

She found Uncle Samuel outside Anne's room, just notified of Jane's soon departure. He wished Jane a safe journey home, no longer a threat to his plans for his niece. But living up to his reputation, he took Jane's hand without permission and smothered his wet lips against it–leaving his mark. He might as well have marked her. But Jane gave him no effect, dragging the wetted surface across her skirt to rid herself of his marked scent, grateful to leave him behind.

Anne sat at the window when she entered.

"I wanted to say goodbye." Jane said.

Anne's head turned, her tearful blue eyes targeting Jane. "You are leaving because of me." She took Jane's hands in hers. "You are a good woman, Jane Reynolds. I don't deserve your friendship." And kissed her on the cheek.

Jane insisted it was nothing of the sorts, but Anne shewed her out with no more argument, owning not wanting to cry.

Jane found Maggie outside, playing with a basket of kittens. The gardener found them in the stables and cursed the devil at the mother cat, so Maggie said. She was too preoccupied, cuddling their furry bodies, swooping them into the basket as they tried to escape, to realize the finality of Jane's goodbye. Jane was grateful for the little girl's distraction, and hugged her one last time, hoping it would last a lifetime—at least for her.

Isabelle, upon hearing the news from her mother, sought Jane out before she reached the entrance hall. She said little, but the compression hug, and fleeing with tears, told Jane everything she couldn't express.

Lillian remained stoic as she walked her to the carriage. She didn't push for more and gave her instruction about her return. Jane was to stop at a friend's house by the evening, making the second day's drive a long and arduous one. But she was promised the driver would push, without delay, only stopping to refresh the horses, and Jane would arrive at the Eaton Estate by late evening the following day. She promised she would write often, and hugged her goodbye, holding onto her longer than intended, and spilling tears onto Jane's shoulder before she pulled away.

Henry was nowhere to be found. Lillian apologized before sending her off in a flurry of waves.

Jane was grateful for the privacy of her return trip to the Eaton Estate. It gave her the opportunity to sort her emotions without scrutiny. If she wanted to cry, she did. If she wanted to feel sorry for herself, she did. When she wanted to forget it all and sleep, she did. The carriage pushed forward, stopping, per Lillian's instructions. Her first, and only overnight stop, was a small house of a widow, a friend of Sir Levongood's mother. She was well into her eighties, friendly and hospitable–Jane's every comfort taken care of, from hot water for a sponge bath, a delicious dinner of lamb, potatoes and carrots, and an abundance of port, *"To ease the aches and pains of her long ride,"* the old woman insisted. But Jane was most thankful when she asked to retire early, allowing Jane to do the same. By sunrise, breakfast was brought to her room, and she was back in the carriage to finish her journey home.

When the carriage finally arrived at the Eaton Estate, the night's sky had turned dark, the waxing crescent moon promising a new moon cycle–the black moon hours away. Mrs. Bishop greeted Jane at the door and asked questions about her trip, unaware of the drama left behind. Jane willingly answered her inquiries to satiate her curiosity, then requested tea to be delivered to the study, where she composed a note to Dr. Cummings. By the time Mrs. Bishop returned with a tray, cook sending along a plate of biscuits, her note was signed and sealed, and she asked Mrs. Bishop to have the note delivered, 'swiftly and with great urgency.' Time was running out, and she needed his help to leave.

Jane had little time left, until early morning, as Agnes described, '*When the black moon passed the sun, stopped, and gave her homage.*'

Or, as she understood it, when the full moon ended its cycle, and the new moon began. Jane needed to return to the same spot where she was found. It was there the passageway would open for her return, where the energy she brought with her from the future would send her back. But if she stayed much longer, her energy would blend into the present energy field.

'*Choose wisely, for once connected, you are tied to this time forever.*'

It was impossible for her to stay. Too many lives would be interrupted, and she had no right to change their destiny.

Hadn't she interfered enough?

Tired from her journey, she asked Mrs. Bishop not to

disturb her for the rest of the evening, and to wake her before dawn.

"Are you sure you don't want a hot meal before you bed?" she asked

"Mrs. Bishop, I cherish meeting you. You served me without question and have been there when I needed someone to care for me." Jane threw her arms around Mrs. Bishop's round body and gave her a tight squeeze. "Thank you, forever."

Mrs. Bishop brushed away Jane's gratitude, but her face reddened, and her retort caught in her throat, leaving her speechless. She left Jane at the bottom of the stairs, wiping a tear from her eyes with her apron as she walked away.

When she reached her room, Jane closed the door behind her, kicked off her shoes, lit the candles by her bed, and sighed heavily, finally reaching the day's end. It had been a long day of travel–a long few days, a long month, a whole lifetime–and she was ready to go home and make it all stop. She stripped down to her chemise, noting the little details of fabric puckered at the breast, the thin satin ribbon edging the collar, and the cap sleeves trimmed in lace, as was the hemline. She would be sure to note the beautiful intricacies of even the most insignificant of clothing in her exhibit when she returned. *She wanted to remember every detail of her experience!* She unpinned her hair and let it fall to her shoulders before she laid down in exhaustion. She stared at the ceiling and watched the shadows caused by the dancing flames of the candles, wondering if time travel was possible, and if she was crazy enough to believe The Black Raven had the answers to get her home.

Was she crazy?

But before she contemplated the what ifs–what if Agnes's prediction didn't work, what if she was stuck in time, what if Henry answered Lillian's question? A knock came at the door. Too exhausted to move, she called for Mrs. Bishop to '*come in.*'

The door creaked open, and the candles flickered as the air rushed through the door. A deep voiced startled her.

"You never answered the question."

Jane jolted up to find Henry at the door. She didn't move, but watched as he entered, closing the door behind him, unbutton his coat and place it on a chair near the fire.

He looked around the room, then at her, unwrapping his cravat and laid it over his coat. Still, he said nothing. He bent over the fire, threw on more logs, and stood, arching his back in a stretch.

The flames grew, exposing his emotions concealed in the dark.

Lines contoured his face, heavy around his brow, and deeper around his mouth. Dark circles hung below his eyes, with two days of growth shadowing his jawline. He looked tired…worn.

Jane reached out for his hands, and he accepted the invitation, placing them in hers. She drew him near, inviting him to sit next to her. Still no words. She cupped his face, holding his stubbled cheeks in the palm of her hands, and ran her thumbs around the deepened lines.

"I have caused these," she said.

Henry closed his eyes, allowing her touch to transcend his body. When he finally spoke, his voice was deep and craggy. "It would be a small sacrifice for a woman I love."

"Henry," she nudged him, making him look at her, "I'm not yours to love. You cannot dishonor your dignity, nor can I betray a friend. It's not who we are."

He took her hand in his, turned it over, and pressed his lips against her lifelines. His finger followed the long grooves to her wrist, where he planted another kiss. And another.

Shivers lifted the hairs on Jane's neck, and she withdrew her hands. "Henry, please don't make this difficult," she pleaded. "I'm not that strong."

"Jane, I am an honorable man. I do not commit my heart and walk away. It is mine to give, and I give it to you."

"There's a fine line between committing your heart and committing your life. There are many mistresses who understand the difference."

"And I commit both to you," he declared.

"No! You can't." She pushed away.

He reached for her and tugged her back. His eyes met hers.

"Jane, please don't run away from me."

"Henry…" she whispered, allowing herself to fall into them. She had no intention of resisting him. She couldn't.

He neared her, so close his lips hovered over hers, but he didn't indulge in his wanting. He caressed her neck, sliding his fingers against her skin as if it was the finest silk between his fingers. When his touch reached her chemise, he pushed down the sleeve and brushed his lips against her shoulder, along her collarbone, to her neck, lingering just below her ear. His breath blew against her cheek, waiting for her response.

Jane gulped. If she let go–put her lips to his–her body would explode from passion.

Henry did not pursue. He pulled away, releasing her from his bondage. He would not shame her again. Never, if she would have him.

"I will not force myself on you. I offer my love if you will have me."

"I cannot do this Henry, as much as I…" Jane sighed, "Anne. You have Anne," she reminded him of his betrothed.

"Jane." He paused; not sure she would believe him. "Anne sent me…back to you."

Jane blinked, then shook her head.

What did Anne do?

He took her hand. "She told me to tell you, *breathe.*"

Jane touched his face, looking for the truth. His eyes were

but a calm sea of blue, open to her, and wanting. As if he willed it, her lips moved to his. Her hands brushed through his hair and she pressed him for more…

More! More! More!

Henry had no willpower with Jane. It was a force beyond his controlled temperament. Jane's mere presence stripped him of his body; freed his soul from its confinement. He was not gentle when her mouth craved more of him. He pushed her lips open to taste the bittersweet sensation of her. His rapture was uncontrollable–his tongue tasting the salt of her skin.

Jane could see he wanted to devour her; seize her, make her writhe under him.

Pulling the thin veil of her chemise over her head she revealed her nakedness. His hands slithered around the shape of her slender hips, the curve of her waist, and the small rounds of her breasts. Her nipples hardened to his touch, enticing his tongue to explore their ripeness.

Jane moaned with delight.

Her hunger urged her. She pulled off his shirt, caressing the sinewy lines of his wide shoulders, his strong arms, down to his solid forearms. As they wrapped around her, she gripped his muscular back, pulling him against her, absorbing the heat radiating from his own. His kisses wetted her neck, sending shivers along her spine. She found his lips again, but this time, he lingered in languid kisses, driving her need for him. Without apology, she undid his pants and slid her hands between his legs to feel his need for her. He moaned and pulled his head back as if she were torturing him. Her hands moved around his body, and the heat of her touch brought him into spasms. With a nudge, she slid her hips against his, allowing him inside. Their bodies pulsated in slow, rhythmic motion, each sensation bringing a new sound as she pulled him deeper within.

Her body's reaction to Henry was intuitive, if not kinetic.

His actions were intimate and passionate, and she equally responded to his touch, his movements…his love. Henry held her with a need to have her close to his heart. Their lips met, and their breathing became as one. Moving in rhythm, they swayed until he released the hot pleasure of their union. Jane held her breath, jerked her hips, and stopped moving to allow the warmth to spread between her legs, up her spine, to the tips of her fingers.

As their breathing quieted, Henry kissed her, and a smile spread across his face.

"I'll always love your smile," Jane promised.

"Because of you, I will always smile."

Jane placed a kiss on each of his dimpled cheeks, pulled the quilt up, and laid it over their tired and naked bodies. Henry's arms embraced her and they both drifted to sleep, each in a different dream-state.

Jane slept so deep, the first knocks at her door came into her dream. The subsequent knocks stirred her awake. She looked at Henry, who lay still, undisturbed, and slipped out of his arms, careful not to wake him. She threw on her chemise, tiptoed to the door, and cracked it open to find Mrs. Bishop before her.

"Dawn is almost here. You gave me instruction to awaken you at this hour," she reminded her.

"That I did, and I'm extremely grateful. Thank you."

Mrs. Bishop turned to leave but halted. "Miss, are you in need of anything?"

Jane glanced over her shoulder to see Henry's body across the bed, entangled in a quilt. "No, nothing. I have everything I need."

Jane peered behind the drapes to find the morning grey and cold. She wondered if it was a sign. She nudged the embers, adding logs to keep the room warm. She curled into the chair next to the heat and stared into the darkened room, watching Henry's body rise and fall with his breathing. She wanted desperately to get back into bed, snuggle against his warm body, enwrap in his arms. But she knew better. Henry's love was sincere, but he had honor as well. If he would not guard it, she had to do it for him.

She dressed quietly and headed downstairs. She had a few things to do before she disappeared.

GUARDING HONOR

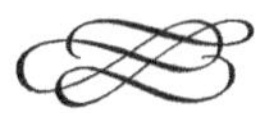

Henry awoke to the sounds of the crackling fire. He slept soundly, his body succumbing to the pleasures of making love to Jane. His soul was invigorated, and his body yearned for more of her, but she was not next to him, or, as he scanned through the greyed darkness, in the room. He dragged himself from the bed, and splashed some water on his face, twice lifting the towel to dry. Once to wipe, the second to inhale the lingering scent of Jane, dragging a smile across his face. He pulled on his breeches, shirt, and boots, leaving behind the formality of his cravat and coat. As he opened the door, he bumped into Regina, holding a pitcher of water and fresh towels.

"Sir," she said, stepping aside to let him retreat.

As he cleared the door, she peered inside for Jane, but found her room empty. She eyed the messy sheets at the end of the bed, and the remnants of Mr. Eaton's clothing on the chair by the fire but said nothing when he re-entered the room.

"Has Miss Reynolds been down for breakfast?" he asked.

"No, sir."

He rubbed his chin. "Thank you…" he said with a nod.

Stepping beyond the threshold, he looked down the hall towards his room, contemplating a shave and a change of clothes, when Mrs. Bishop came up the stairs.

"Good morning, sir…" she said, stopping at Jane's door. She glanced in the room, giving Regina a nod of dismissal. The young girl set down her things and left without haste.

"Mrs. Bishop…" He cleared his throat; aware his lack of discretion was not overlooked by his long-time caretaker.

She eyed her master, unkempt, hastily dressed, but ignored the implications she was sure would be rumored about in the servant's quarters below. Although happy for her master to discover Jane as a suitable companion, an obvious conclusion by all who had eyes, she was damning her job of mitigating the scandalous behavior under the roof.

"May I bring fresh water and a tray of tea to your room, sir?"

"Please," he said, and turned to retreat to his rooms. "And if you will, inform Miss Reynolds I will be down shortly to join her for breakfast."

"But Sir," the words stopped him, "Miss Reynolds is gone."

"What do you mean she's gone?" Without knowing why, his gut wrenched.

"She's left with Dr. Cummings, after the youngest Baker boy and he came for her."

"She left?"

"Aye. There's a note for you…left on your desk, shall I bring it to you?"

Henry didn't answer but ran past her, down the stairs and went directly to his study.

It didn't take him long to find it. It sat upright on the book of *Shakespeare's Sonnets*. Henry slouched in his chair and grabbed the letter. He breathed in deeply, trying to steady his hand as he opened it.

Dearest Henry,

If you find this letter, I will have returned home. I sat at your desk for a long time, wondering if I had the courage to leave. You make being honorable look easy. It's not.

I don't pretend, nor am I ashamed to say my heart, body and soul are forever connected with you. I learned there are no boundaries for the depth at which love is capable. You taught me how to love purely. You make me want to crawl deep inside your soul and live there till our deaths can free us to reside in eternity together. But because of this deep love, I'm driven to do what is right. You may never understand the circumstances under which I arrived, or how I must leave. Nothing I could explain would make sense to you. I was never meant to be in this place and time. If I selfishly stayed, I fear it would be at the expense of all those who touched my life and who illustrated true commitment, sacrifice, and love that make one's life meaningful. The lives of those you love would be dramatically altered, especially your dear Maggie, who would suffer a lifetime of shame because of our love. There's no honor in that.

If it weren't for such love I experienced with you, I would selfishly spend the rest of my life with you. Henry, you have shown me the true meaning of love, and forever will it be with me!

"Then happy I, that love and am beloved, Where I may not remove nor be removed." ~William Shakespeare

I love you forever and always,

~Jane~

Henry read the letter again. The second time hurt more than the first time. Without wasting another moment, he had to stop her. He didn't want her to leave—not again. Not ever!

He questioned Mrs. Bishop again about Jane's whereabouts, but she was not informed of Jane's plans, nor were the staff. Jane asked for nothing upon leaving, had no bag with her to indicate a trip, and was dressed only as usual for a typical day. Her only request was for Landry to prepare a horse with a proper saddle for her. Mrs. Bishop thought nothing unusual for the doctor to call on her, nor Egon Baker to accompany them.

"Did I do something wrong?" Mrs. Bishop clasped her

cheeks. "Is Miss Reynolds in danger? The poor girl, after having been through so much already."

"No…yes." Henry shook his head. "I don't know."

"Well, if she is with Dr. Cummings, I'm sure he'll…"

"Wait," he cut her off. Had Jane planned to return to America, she should never have come back to the Eaton Estates…it was the wrong direction. They were taking her back… back to the field. "That's where she is headed…"

"Where, sir?" Mrs. Bishop asked but ignored. Henry had already bolted out the door looking for the earliest riser of the stablemen.

Landry heard the master's cries before he reached the stable and had the mare saddled before he reached him. Pulling the stirrup with a tug, the master grabbed the reins and jumped on the saddled horse. With a click of his boot, the horse obeyed, jolting his force with every slap of the master's reins.

Morning had begun, but the skies were darkened with storm clouds, a mist lingered in the air. Henry shivered, not from the cold but from his rising fear. He raced forward, knowing he was losing time with every stride.

"Damn that woman!" he cursed as he pushed his horse.

Her touch was too fresh on his skin; his desire too strong to subdue. The thought of spending the rest of his life without her was unimaginable.

He didn't want fear getting the best of him, but his stomach sank as he cleared the tree lines and saw no one in the fields below. The corn stalks were restored to their upright positions, hiding any signs of life in between them.

"Why? Why are you running from me?" he shouted to the winds, to God as a prayer to stop her. As if the heavens heard him, a breeze swept across the valley below, swaying the green stalks in rhythmic motion, revealing their scrambling bodies.

"Jane!" Henry called out.

Dr. Cummings stopped and turned. "It's Henry," he informed Jane.

"Please, let's continue. There's not much time," Jane pleaded. "If I don't go now, I won't have the courage to ever go back."

"Is this what you want?" the doctor asked.

Jane nodded.

"Then go, my dear. I will detain him," he said. "Egon," he called out to him, "find the original spot, and take Miss Reynolds there. Swiftly."

"Thank you," Jane squeezed the hand that held hers. "I will never forget your kindness, support, and most of all, your dear friendship."

The doctor smiled. "As are my own sentiments. Now go…"

"Dr. Cummings," she called after him. "Please tell him… about me. Why I had to leave. Make him understand."

"That I'll try, my dear." He signaled to Egon to hurry ahead. "She must stand on the spot at fifteen past eight. No later, not sooner."

The Black Raven's words now became clear, *It is between time, when time stops.*

Pulling Jane through rows of giant leaves, he came upon a flattened area and paced his steps. "Here," Egon stood confidently.

"Are you absolutely sure?" Jane looked at him with hesitation.

"I am a part of this land as if I was formed out of it. I have no doubt, Miss. The Doctor and I planned it precisely. Trust me." He extended his hand towards Jane. She grabbed it, and he led her to the spot.

She let go, and Egon took ten paces back, per Dr. Cummings' instructions, and waited. For what, neither Jane nor he knew. The moment of truth would soon reveal itself. Either she would still be standing there or be transported home.

She looked out into the distance. Dr. Cummings intercepted Henry. Angry voices floated through the wind when they both looked at her. Henry pushed past Dr. Cummings and raced towards her.

"Jane!" he shouted.

His voice echoed across the valley.

Jane's heart pounded. With one step, she would be out of the circle and in his arms. She looked down at her position in the corn. One step, one movement, and it would change her life forever. It would change his life forever. The wind picked up, and a rush of air surrounded her. The last thing she saw was Henry's anguished face, his arms reaching for her, calling her name.

STARK REALITY

"Jane, are you awake?"

Jane opened her eyes. A cement ceiling greeted her. She scanned the room. No wallpaper, no silk drapes, no beautiful wood furniture, Nothing. Just bare, gray-white walls.

She blinked.

She blinked three more times.

Her body lay still, entombed beneath a thin layer of sheets. Then, as if a switch flipped, sounds flooded her ears. She freed her arms from the side of her body and clasped her hands around her head. The noises persisted. Lots of noises!

A clock ticked...*click, click, click.*

Mechanical beeps came every few seconds. An elevator slid open, stopped, and slid back; slamming shut. It dinged and slid open again. Rubber soles squeaked across linoleum floors. It reminded her of gym class when she was in junior high. Voices, pitched high and low, no words discernible, merged into a cacophony of deafening sound. Pulsating pumps of blood pushed through the tiny veins in her head and a pain streaked across her brain.

Jane screamed, "Make it stop! Make it stop!"

Amy jumped from a chair, threw her arms around Jane. "Shh, it's ok," she cooed.

"Please," Jane pleaded, "…it's so loud." Her eyes slammed shut, and she curled into a ball.

The nurse came, poked Jane's IV bag with a sedative, and she was soon out of her misery.

"What was that about?" Amy asked.

"She's been unconscious for a couple of days," answered the nurse. "When someone comes out of that, they're disoriented. She'll be okay. Give her some time."

Jane awoke later into the night. The sounds quieted. The voices hushed. But the clock, a metal framed circle, with a white background and black numbers, still clicked with every second. An elderly coupled passed by her open door and the older woman smiled at her, giving Jane gumption to sit up. It took a few minutes to adjust through the darkness, but it was apparent she was back to the present.

Sterile walls surrounded her, decorated with the ticking clock, an outdated television popular in the nineties, perched on a shelf across from her bed, and two whiteboards hung near the door. Jane's name was on one of them, and the other notified which nurse was on duty and her hours of service. Nurse Camden, according to the clock, was off in ten minutes. Plastic veneer strips dangled in lifeless streaks across a window. The blinds were closed, shutting out the lights from the parking lots two floors below.

Jane found a cord lying next to her, with buttons labeled, TV and light. She pushed the light button and a fluorescent bulb flickered above her, casting a shade of green onto her skin. A blue printed gown covered her body, with two ties in the back, one around her neck. She shifted, untucking the sheets at her feet. A movement in the darkened corner of the room startled her. She leaned forward and squinted at the human form slumped in the chair. Eyes opened, and immediately she recognized the luminous hue of gold.

"Amy!"

"Jane!" Her friend lurched forward, engulfing her in an embrace. "Sweetie, you're awake," she cried. "Dear God, Jane! You scared the life out of me. Ryan, too!" She pulled her tighter. "But it's lovely to have you back."

"That's enough." Jane pulled out of her octopus embrace, embarrassed about the fuss over her. "I'm here, and alive. What more can you ask for?"

"Just that, sweetie! Returned to us."

Jane lowered her eyes. "I'm so sorry, Amy. This must have been hard for you. Please forgive me."

"What's there to forgive? You're safe now. That's all that matters."

Jane felt like a fraud. She was never in danger. Not really.

"Jane?" Amy treaded lightly. "What happened to you?"

Jane covered her face. Memories flooded her head. A lifetime of lovely memories she wanted to hold on to if time would allow it. But her gut wrenched at the loss.

Henry!

"Sweetie, you don't have to tell me anything if it's too hard. I don't want you to have to relive your agony." She poured a glass of water into a pink cup and handed it to Jane.

Her first reaction was to spit out the water. Chemicals and plastic swirled in her mouth. Her second reaction was confusion.

What did Amy believe happened to her?

Her brow furrowed.

Now it was Amy's turn to be confused. "The doctor said..." She paused, scooted Jane over to make room for her on the bed and took Jane's hands in hers. "Sweetie, I know this may be hard, but I'm here for you. The hospital did a test. It confirmed evidence of a sexual assault." Her arms wrapped around Jane. "Oh darling, it's just too horrible to imagine."

Jane stared at the wall, allowing Amy to console her. She understood her reaction, the test's conclusion. But she couldn't let her friend think the worse happened to her. She had told enough lies to last a lifetime. She didn't want to be a fraud to Amy.

Jane wriggled out of Amy's arms and looked her straight in the eyes.

"What is it?" Amy said.

"I have something to tell you. Something you won't believe."

Amy wanted to hear what her friend had to say. Curiosity was an understatement. A guttural fear gripped her after Jane's disappearance. When she left her phone charging, work unfinished, sprawled on the attic floor, and didn't show up after her walk, panic set in. It was unlike Jane to go off and disappear. She was too prudent. The police searched with dogs and a team of volunteers but didn't find her. She disappeared with no trace. Much speculation was given to Ryan Eaton because Jane went missing on his property. Although a respectable member of the community, and a beloved professor, interrogators put him through the rigors of questioning. The lead investigator, who was more than thorough with him, conceded Ryan was not the perpetrator.

Jane's case grew cold and placed in the hands of the Bureau of Missing Persons. Rarely does an adult go missing if not by his or her own will. With further investigation, they discovered Jane's break up with her longtime boyfriend, and assumed she chose to disappear, or worse, take her own life. They did not consider her case a high-risk profile. The files transferred to a small group of officers who continued the investigation, predicting she would show up, one way or another. The longer she was gone, the more likely she was dead. They never imagined she'd be found, breathing. A rape kit was assigned, and evidence concluded a sexual assault occurred. Because she went missing for a month, they suspected she may have been drugged and held captive. But when they tested for foreign substances, nothing showed up in her blood work. And incongruous to the findings–discovered naked, dropped off in the middle of a field, and a positive sexual assault test, no other 'usual' signs appeared, like cuts and bruises, broken nails, scars, malnutrition, poor hygiene, etc., to indicate a violent crime. In fact, the doctors declared her in 'unusually good health.' She vanished and appeared as if by magic. Until Jane explained what happened, the investigators were stumped.

Amy put her cheek against Jane's. "Darling, if it's too hard, let it be. I'll understand."

Jane took a few sips of water, the taste still bitter in her mouth, not sure where to start. "I wasn't kidnapped, taken, or anything like that," she blurted.

"Okaaaay." Amy crossed her arms and leaned back. "Then you ran away? Took a break? Had a mental breakdown? Got lost? Had a mad affair and locked yourself away for a month?" She eyed Jane. "Which is it? Because I spent a good month worried out of my mind, and it bloody well have been for some great sex!"

"No…well, yes," Jane stumbled. Straight forward seemed the only way out. Her words were quick, "I walked into some kind of energy field and transported back in time." She closed her eyes, held her breath, and waited for a reaction. When none came, she opened one eye to find Amy staring at her. "I can't fully explain, but…"

"I hate hospitals…there are no bars when someone needs a drink!" Amy jumped off the bed and rambled through her purse. She found what she was looking for, pulled a chair closer to the bed, sat down, and put her lips around a small bottle of vodka. "You never know when you might need a drink. I think now is a time." She took another swig. "Now Jane, please continue."

Jane pressed her back against a pillow, pulled her hair behind her ears, and swallowed hard. "What I am about to tell you will sound impossible. And I don't have all the answers as to how, or why, but I fell through a time hole. A psychic explained I had a magical energy–a higher vibration when I was born." Her hand flicked through the air, brushing off the fantastical statement. "Anyway, it's not important. The point is, I was perfectly safe, living at the Eaton Estate, and taken care of by relatives of Ryan Eaton," she explained, purposely vague. She couldn't bring herself to say *his* name out loud. "Just in a different year..."

"What year?" Amy asked, but she didn't really want the answer. It all sounded... *Crazy!*

"I transported to eighteen thirty-three."

Amy said nothing. She crossed her legs and began tapping her fingers on her knee. A cold stare passed through Jane.

"Amy? Did you hear what I said?" It sounded ludicrous, even to Jane's ears. How could she explain all she experienced, the people she grew to care about, the man she fell in love with, and the decision to return despite it all? "I never vanished. I was never gone. I existed in a different space and time."

"I'm listening, Jane. But do you hear yourself? You said you traveled through time. Those are dangerous words coming from a woman who is recovering from a traumatic event," Amy cautioned.

"I'm not making this up!"

"Sweetie, you know I love you. But you have to be careful about the things you say. This isn't America. Talk like that can only bring you under suspicion, possibly psychiatric observation. We can't have that. The most important thing right now is to get you out of this hospital."

Jane slumped underneath her covers. If Amy didn't believe her, who would?

"I'm sure you believe what you're saying. But the reality is, time travel doesn't exist. You understand that, right?"

Jane nodded her head in shame. When Amy said the words back to her, '*time travel*,' it sounded ridiculous.

"There's always a logical explanation to the bizarre or unknown experiences. Just give it time. It will reveal itself."

A thumping began in her head.

"You're awake," a nurse interrupted, her Scottish accent thick, rolling off her tongue. "How are ya feel'in?"

"I'm..." She pressed her temples. "Disoriented."

"Well, my dear, you've been out for a while," she said. "Had us a wee bit worried, I'd say."

"How long have I been here?"

"Three days since they brought ya."

"Three days?" she whispered. "It seems like a lifetime."

"Aye, well, no need to worry yourself. You've got a whole life ahead of you to make up for the lost time. If you're better in the morning, I'd say you'll be released to go home."

Home.

Jane had no idea what that meant anymore.

The nurse took Jane's vitals, pleased with the stats. "Get a good night's sleep. You'll feel better in the morning." She walked to the whiteboard by the door and wrote her name. Black dry erase sprawled, *Nurse Bishop, 8pm-8am.*

Jane gasped. "Mrs. Bishop?"

"Aye," she said. "But they call me Big Maggie. No formality for me. If ya need anything, just push the little red button next to the bed. I'll tell the doctor you're quite spry."

"Nurse Maggie?" Jane closed her eyes in a panic. "Please don't tell me his name is Henry."

"Dr. Hank? Aye, but no one calls him that but his wife. One

of the finest, if not the most handsome doctors here." She winked. "You're a lucky girl to be under his care."

Amy's words lingered in the air, "*There's always a logical explanation.*"

Jane's gut knotted. The corresponding names couldn't be a coincidence. And trauma explained away time loss, dreams, alternate worlds, even imaginary people.

So, what happened to her?

She gripped her chest. The truth may be more than she could handle. She never questioned her sanity before, but as she lay there, a mental breakdown made more sense, and most likely the explanation, than time travel.

"Nurse Bishop," Jane called before she left the room. "May I have another sedative?"

DETECTIVES

When Nurse Bishop spotted the detectives outside Jane's room, she kept them waiting in no hurry to let them in. Her concern for her patient far outweighed the business they needed to conduct. Although Jane's vitals were good, dark circles under her eyes indicated a sleepless night. Her instinct told her something tormented the young woman.

"You didn't sleep?"

"Not very well," Jane confirmed, with no explanation.

"The detectives want to speak to ya. They've been waiting since the crack of dawn, sitting impatiently with their coffees. They kept ask'n permission to see ya. I told them to just sit tight," she grimaced. "Who do they think they are, with their badges, pacing up and down the halls?"

"I have to talk to them at some point. It might as well be now." She had a pit in her stomach. Lying to strangers was one thing, lying to the police was a crime, but one more step to getting home. The sooner she spoke with the detectives, the sooner the hospital signed off on her release.

"Well, if you're up to it," Nurse Bishop patted her arm. "Keep in mind, many things come your way. Some good, some bad…some difficult, but it's how you handle them that defines who ya are. You'll get through this. Isn't that why you're still here?" She left Jane to rest, forcing the antsy men to wait another half hour before she let them talk to Jane.

One man stood by Jane's bed, eyeing her. He never spoke. The other man interrogated her. Too many of the same questions just reworded. Jane gave them the same answer–*she couldn't remember.*

"So, your memory is failing you at the moment?" The lead investigator rephrased the question for the third time. He paced the room, reviewed the cards sent to her, reading the personal notes in them. He moved towards the flowers, doing the same.

Jane found it rude, making her more defiant. "As I said before, I fell while on a walk and hit my head. Everything went blank after that."

"And you don't remember meeting anyone or going anywhere?" he persisted.

It might be cliche, but the investigator sensed if someone was telling the truth just by looking at them. Unfortunately, his instincts were off. Jane distracted him. It didn't go unnoticed that she was pretty. Chocolate brown eyes, clear skin, color in her cheeks, the young woman before him looked the vision of health–pretty. Nor did it help her nightgown slipped from her shoulder, revealing the curve of her breast. He looked away, allowing her to adjust the tie at the back of her neck. When he turned back, he had to remind himself she was lying. He didn't like liars, no matter what shape or sex they came in. But when he looked into her eyes, they hid no malice. He saw torment, driving his urgency to find the person/s who caused her agony. Why did she conceal information? He only wanted to help her, and she blocked him in every way.

"Your disappearance caused an uproar to friends, law enforcement, and to this small community." When he didn't get a response, he added, “You are aware it’s a felony to cause a false investigation?”

Jane sighed, frustrated. She had nothing to offer him. The memories in the recesses of her mind had no credence and needed to return from where they came–where dreams are made. “Detective Moore, I haven’t schemed anything. I got lost in those fields. Why I went missing for a month, and what happened to me, I can’t explain. If I could, I would.”

She had no urgency to solve the mystery of her disappearance for fear of what she might discover.

“Miss Reynolds, I don’t wish more problems than what you have already been through. But you must understand, the circumstances of your disappearance and reappearance are all precarious. We are just trying to do our job.”

“I understand. But we’ve been through this many times. I’m exhausted.” She rubbed her forehead with theatrics. “I promise, you will be the first person I contact if I remember anything significant.”

Detective Moore hated defeat, but what more could he do? No one wanted to claim the victim as a fraud. Not the doctors, not the papers…not even him. His gut told him she experienced something. What? He may never find out. If she had demons, who was he to force her to face them? He bid her a good day, frustrated the case may never be resolved.

Amy hovered in the hallway, concerned with what Jane would say. She frightened Amy about stories of time travel and living in the past. Whether Jane actually experienced it was irrelevant. Something imbalanced her friend. Faced with the memories of being taken against her will, raped, and possibly worse, could easily drive her to create an alternate world. The mind would do anything to heal itself. If Jane needed a little fantasy to help her forget, then she would allow it.

When the detectives left the room, Amy rushed in. “You alright?”

"I don't know anymore."

Amy crawled into the bed and put her arms around her. "You don't have to figure it out today. Or tomorrow. Give it some time. When you get home, we'll find you a good therapist."

"I'm not crazy," Jane insisted.

"No, you aren't. Just confused."

Jane shook her head, rattling the memories around her head. "It seemed so real. But whatever is in my head, it's fading quickly." She was now embarrassed about what she told to Amy. "What do I do now?"

"I have no idea. But we have each other," Amy assured. She brushed Jane's hair out of her eyes and kissed her gently on the forehead. "You are a strong woman, and nothing and nobody will break you. But whatever you experienced, maybe it's best to stay in the past…lost forever. Your life isn't what happened to you, it is what you make happen despite it."

"I need to move forward, don't I?" She exhaled, allowing the stress in her shoulders to release. "No more living in the past. No more Stephen. No more fantasies…"

No more Henry.

Jane laughed to herself. "When I came to England. I had hoped to find myself; to get my life together and move on, but instead, I got lost."

"And now you're found." Amy said.

"Yes, I'm found."

HEALING

Ryan insisted Jane stay at the Eaton Estate until fully recovered. Refusal was unacceptable. "I have a lovely housekeeper to tend to your every need. Just until you're as good as new," he insisted.

Amy was even more unyielding.

"I've already had your luggage delivered and made arrangements with your office. You'll work on the exhibit from Ryan's home office, and I will be right beside you to help."

"I'm fine, really," Jane insisted. "I'm not a fragile child."

Ryan's eyebrow arched, as did Amy's.

In all reality, she *was* fragile. Her mental stability questionable. She could neither confirm nor deny the experiences in the past. She lived in limbo, afraid to move forward for fear of what she might discover if she faced the truth. She had no explanation for the missing month of her life, or for the shards of pain streaked across her heart when she thought of Henry. As the days passed, time travel seemed less likely, and something more sinister a possibility.

When they neared the Eaton Estate, Jane shivered. She didn't know what to expect when she entered the house again…

if the memories would rush back or seem silly in the reality of the space. She half-expected Mrs. Bishop to open the door and help her off with her coat. To her chagrin, Mrs. Bishop didn't. Grateful for his arm to hold on to, Ryan assisted her up the walkway, like an invalid, and opened the door.

"Here you are, again."

Jane eyed the entry, as she did the first time, amazed at the aged beauty, but bewildered at the same time. A bouquet, now filled with pink peonies, in the Longwy vase, greeted her, as did the Charles II winged armchair. The room filled with sweet and rosy ripeness.

Jane closed her eyes and inhaled. For a moment, while her lids shut out reality, her ears perked to listen for the familiar sounds common to her over the last month; the hushed sounds of a working household scurrying around from one room to the next, Mrs. Bishop humming a Scottish ballad, Maggie's little footsteps coming down the stairs, the crackling of a fire coming from the front drawing room. Yet, as she strained to listen, she heard nothing but the buzz of the gardener's blower at the back of the house. The echoing of footsteps belonged to Amy's stilettos clacking against the wooden floor, her arms full of flowers from friends in Los Angeles, sent while in the hospital.

Jane could only think about how empty it sounded.

"Is something the matter?" Ryan asked.

Jane opened her eyes. "No, no…I had a déjà vu, that's all."

Amy had warned Ryan about Jane's *fragile sense of reality*. "How about a tour of the house? You never got the chance before."

Jane smiled. She wanted very much to see the house…*again*.

"Very good then," Ryan rubbed his chin. "Where shall we start? The gardens, the drawing rooms?"

Jane wanted to run through the house, look for any sign she wasn't going mad. Go where she last saw Henry, or where it all began…when she found his eyes looking into hers.

"Can we start with the library?"

"Of course, of course..." He led the way.

When Ryan opened the door to the library, a deep part of Jane hoped to see the room as she last remembered, or thought she remembered. But nothing was recognizable. Shelves covered the walls from floor to ceiling, stuffed with books of old and new, but they had been painted white, along with the ceilings, covering up the warm hues of the reddish-brown wood that used to surround the room. The marble fireplace still centered the room, but the portraiture of Henry's and Lillian's mother no longer adorned it. A somber twentieth century Dutch landscape now hung over the mantle. *Jane didn't approve.* A French Louis XVI desk gilded with bronze originally cornered the north end of the room, but the space lay empty, a plant stand it's only decor. Intricate patterned Persian rugs once covered the wood-planked floors, but they were now left bare and unsealed. *She approved of that.* Georgian, mohair-covered chairs, along with a leather topped, mahogany drum table, were gone. And the red damasked sofa, where Henry found her reading late one night–their feelings awakened in the light of a fire, was replaced with a linen sectional, with two lamps on the ends, and a round coffee table with a tray of assorted, liquor-filled, crystal decanters on top. The *bones* of the room hadn't changed, but nothing indicated a nineteenth-century gathering room for reading and conversation, but replaced by a contemporary, sparsely furnished sitting room to house books. Deflated it wasn't the same, or maybe grateful for the reality check, she circled the room, eyeing the titles of the vast collection of rare books. She stopped and pulled out one. Her fingertips studied the lines of the engraved lettering, and for a moment she imagined Henry's fingers turning the pages.

"May I borrow this?"

Ryan peered at the title. "John Locke? You may keep it if you like. It belonged to a bigger assortment, but in his dementia state of mind, my father gave an entire collection of great works to a random bookstore in London. Fortunately, I have so many books here, the loss is but a blessing to someone."

Jane smiled. Ryan couldn't know Peyton benefited from his father. Nor the six degrees of separation, their lives entwined.

"Come, let me show you my study. I have a whole other collection of Byron, Burns, Frost, Emerson…you would not believe what this house holds in literature!"

Somehow, she knew it did.

Ryan's study was the opposite of the library. Dark and masculine, it wreaked of leather, wood, and whiskey. He did not paint over the original paneled walls, opting for the luster of oil-rubbed wood. Bookcases filled one wall, while the other walls showcased artwork from centuries past. An oversized leather couch fronted the bookcase, and two chairs in the same leather were against the other wall, monogrammed pillows resting against the backs. Strangely out of place, an art deco Macassar coffee table filled the space between the couch and chairs, stacked with books of art and theology strewn on top. A half-filled decanter of Scotch, an empty glass, and an open laptop computer exposed a man working through the night. The other side of the room housed Ryan's desk, two scrolled cement-base pillars topped with a thick sheet of glass, covered with more books, mainly English history, and a computer monitor with piles of papers scattered over the keyboard.

Jane wanted to ask about the mahogany desk where Henry stood behind when she admonished him for loving her. The chair she sat in when she wrote her letter of goodbye. But she held back the ridiculous notion.

"Are you working on research?" She pointed to strewn papers on his desk.

"I am, thanks to Amy. When she inquired about donations for the museum, it forced me to rummage through the vast collection in the attic." He walked behind his desk and lifted a pile of letters in his hands. "I found historical archives! Writings, journals, and letters offering great insight into everyday life here at the estate from long ago. In fact, I was just sorting through old business papers from one of my late relatives, Master Henry Eaton."

Jane hadn't planned to gasp, but the sound usurped itself from her throat. Her knees gave way.

Ryan quickly grabbed her arm.

"Oh my, maybe you shouldn't be exerting yourself," he said, and seated her in a nearby chair. "I'll get you some water…"

"No," she called after him, bringing him back from fleeing. "I'm fine."

She wasn't fine. But she insisted he continue, half eager to hear more, the other half, she felt a twist in the gut.

Ryan eyed her. "Are you sure?" When she nodded, he continued, "Although a man of wealth, it seems my dear relative was rather a rebel in his time. He was quite the egalitarian master. He kept detailed diaries about his lands and the people who worked for him. He noted little things like their children's names, when they married, if a building burned down, or if a death occurred. He must have been quite a watchful man. I'm not sure if he did this out of interest, boredom, or for control. I also noticed much of his books were kept by his sister, Lady Levongood. She was a masterful accountant indeed. She was quite savvy about bookkeeping and management."

Jane's head clouded with memories.

"I haven't explored the family tree yet–the who's who, and how everyone is connected. I am sure to find illegitimate relatives hanging about, or of great scandals of the day. Aren't we English known for that?" He laughed. "As with most lineage, lots of marriages and deaths to track." He looked up from behind his desk. "Think you're up for the rest of the tour?"

Regaining her footing, she followed after him.

Jane continued the tour in a quiet state of mind, allowing Ryan to ramble about the historical elements. She viewed the beautiful surroundings as if seeing it for the first time, although there was a sense of familiarity she couldn't shake. She examined the tapestries on the walls, viewed the paintings hung in each room, sat in the chair that was placed in a lonely corner of the hallway, and tugged at the drawers of a Regency desk cornering a small alcove. But she couldn't help seeing Lillian write a note at that same desk or thinking a chair in the drawing room really belonged in the study. *Why did she know this?* She hoped by touching the items they would jog her memory, give her credibility. But her memories were distant…as if a boat sailing away in fog. She just couldn't grasp reality. Interacting with the house and listening to its history meshed with her memories, confusing her more. Did she live in the past? Or did the sense of history of the old house and the present get convoluted, creating a world to escape while she was unconscious?

After the tour, Ryan walked her to the room she would settle into over the next couple of days. She froze at the door. It was the room she awoke after she was found in the fields. The room where Maggie crawled into bed with her and told her stories. The room where she made love to Henry…and left him sleeping.

She closed her eyes and held her breath.

"This is my favorite room in the house now that the remodel is completed." Ryan opened the door. "I hope you like it…"

She sighed.

Patterns of blue and textural fabrics in shades of white dominated the decor, with the walls covered in wainscoting from floor to ceiling, painted in glossy white. No dainty wallpaper, floral prints, heavy drapes, or wood furniture remained. The only wooded antique was an eighteenth-century writing desk near the window, updated with a linen covered

Parson's chair, her laptop and notebooks placed on top, awaiting her return to work. Jane did not miss the light switch by the door that powered the chandelier in the middle of the ceiling and two light fixtures on each side of the bed. She played with the switch, turning the lights on and off several times, adding her astonishment at the television over the fireplace mantle. A settee, with room for two, and a blanket over its arm, sat in front of the fireplace, along with a basket full of books beside it. A mixed bouquet of wildflowers decorated the bedside table, and her bags were already unpacked, clothes hanging in a newly constructed closet, the empty suitcase tucked at the top.

"Is this acceptable?"

"Ryan, you're amazing. It's like a five-star hotel. Only better!" She kissed him on the cheek. "And thank you for the flowers…they're beautiful."

"You are very welcome, my dear," he grinned. "I want you to be comfortable; to heal." He reached for her hand and gave it a squeeze. "Come, let me show you the toilet. I had a door installed to the adjoining room and made this a suite, with the goal to create a private sanctuary." He pointed to the newly added threshold that opened to what would have been Maggie's room on the other side of the wall. "These old houses had no indoor plumbing to speak of and I had to take the square footage from somewhere. But adding plumbing wasn't the biggest hurdle. Tearing the old wallpaper from the walls nearly destroyed them. That's when I decided to wainscot the walls. Love the results, but it took me well over budget. My designer, the clever woman, framed pieces of the wallpaper, not only as remnants of the history of the house, but to remind me of the disastrous attempts to strip the walls of the two-hundred-year-old paper." Ryan pointed to the framed art. Two shadow boxes, one atop the other, cleverly displayed pieces of the wallpaper that once decorated the original two rooms. One showcased a red child's toile pattern, the other a yellow scrolled damask.

Jane's face went white.

"Jane, are you alright?"

She didn't hesitate to answer. "I think I'd like to lie down."

When Ryan left, she took two sedatives the doctor prescribed, and laid down on the settee, pulling the blanket over her. She wondered what was worse. Finding herself living in the past, or being left to live in the present, both inextricably tied to her sanity, or lack thereof.

SURRENDER TO THE TRUTH

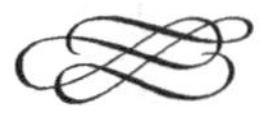

Is there healing in solitude?

For Jane, the difficulty lay in her memory. Was she healing from memories of time travel, or from repressed memories of something worse? None of the options encouraged her. She was crazy, damaged, or depressed. She wanted herself back.

The Eaton Estate offered her the time to reset the course of her life and get it back on track. Walks in the gardens, reading a book in cozy quarters of her room, breakfasts on the terrace as the sun rose, didn't give her the answers she sought, but it allowed her to replace old memories with new ones. New sounds to replace the old echoes haunting her. Fresh smells and new sensations, printing over the old ones. Substituting old memories with new ones seemed like the best strategy to move on. For that reason, she asked Ryan to take her back into the field where it all began.

"Are you sure about this?" Ryan questioned. "It's quite a distance, and I'm not sure you're up to it, yet."

Jane nodded. "The long hike will do me good. It'll refresh my mind… possibly renew my soul a little."

Ryan conceded, admitting, "There is a spark returned in your eyes. It's nice to see."

They walked in silence. Ryan, because he wanted Jane to have the experience she was seeking. Jane, because she wanted to listen to the trees, the wind, the echoes...she didn't exactly know.

Clearing the trees at the top of the hill, they spotted flags–remnants of the police investigation. Much of the grass, where a passerby found her body naked and vulnerable, still laid flat against the dirt. Was it some kind of crop circle? Or caused by a wind tunnel? The officials didn't want to delve into the supernatural. The possibilities too extraordinary to consider.

Ryan said some people at the university studied the flattened pattern, considering Jane's disappearance. But they struggled for answers. Alien abduction circulated throughout the locals, but with no memory from Jane, the rumors ceased, as did the interests in the spot.

Jane laid down among the fresh growth of grass, closed her eyes, and spread her arms toward the sun. The warm rays penetrated her. Her memories of Henry returned, and her heart filled with longing. As much as she tried to suppress it, she could not transcend the genuine pain that gripped her.

Ryan looked down, shadowing the sun from her face. "Jane? Are you sure you're okay? Are the memories coming back?"

She opened her eyes to find ocean blue orbs staring at her. They were so much like Henry's, only not stormy or somber, but temperate and tranquil. "I'm fine, why do you ask?"

"You're crying."

She touched the droplets falling down her face.

"I shouldn't have brought you here. It can't be of any good to bring back those memories."

Jane wiped away the mess on her face with the back of her hand. "It's nothing bad. Truly."

Jane stood, brushing blades of grass clinging to her clothes.

"Come on Ryan. There's nothing here for me anymore. Whatever happened is in the past and gone."

It was one step closer to healing.

Ryan played an important role in her recovery. His teaching duties for summer involved an online computer course, freeing his time to take Jane on tours of historical sites, exploring towns, and eating. Lots of eating! One of Ryan's favorite pastimes.

Nights turned quiet, and Jane would retreat to the library and read, or curl on the couch and watch old movies–another of Ryan's pastimes. But only when she tucked in bed did the still of the house, the creak of the floors, the tatting of the rain on the window did her memories return from the recesses of her mind. Did ghosts of the past truly haunt inside the walls of the Eaton Estate? If Jane were asked, she would definitely answer, *yes!*

Amy had to return to London for work–the museum's exhibit pressing for completion, especially with Jane's absence. She volunteered to act on Jane's behalf while missing, and again, during her recovery. But by week's end, exhausted and overworked, she joined them at the Estate, with a bottle of gin and stories of her past erotic interludes, her language getting cruder as the bottle of gin emptied.

"God, he was a good lay," she said, referencing an older gentleman she had met on a trip to the Bahamas. "He didn't hurry to enter me, opting to fondle me, erotically touching me between my legs."

"Amy!" Jane shrieked. She feigned covering her ears but was curious to learn more.

"Ah, the fine art of patience that younger men just don't possess," Ryan added, equally intrigued by Amy's prurient stories.

Amy took another sip from her glass. A growl escaped her throat as the liquid poured down. "His fingers were as skillful as his..."

"Amy!" Jane shrieked again, before Amy's crassness got the best of her.

Amy rolled her eyes but laughed at her ability to shock Jane. She continued, "The anticipation nearly killed me. But he did not disappoint! The way he grabbed my hips and pulled me back and forth in slow, rhythmic strides was calculating. Just when I thought I would burst with pleasure, he stopped, and pulled me in to suckle on my tits. Euphoria spread through my whole body. Probably the best sex I ever had!"

Ryan sighed, reminiscent of his youthful, carefree days of sex. "Those days have long passed me by. I used to be a player, but I'm no longer attractive to 'the crowd,'" he said, referring to the gay scene. "I'm not looking for a quick fix anymore. I want true love. Stupid, forever kind of love. Or maybe, I just don't want to grow old alone."

Jane touched his arm. "You'll never be truly alone...we'll always be here for you."

He smiled. "And what's your true heart's desire?"

"Me? I don't have one. Not anymore."

Amy snorted. "Sweetie, who are you fooling? If Stephen proved anything, your heart was made for romance, no matter how many times it's broken. You are my inspiration, even if my own heart has grown cold. With you there's hope, and people like me need that in the world."

At that moment, Jane wanted to tell them about Henry. Maybe they would laugh at her, call her silly, or most likely think her insane. Both hovered like protective parents. One false move, or crazy notion, and they would postpone her going home. And it was time to return to Los Angeles. Her strength renewed, her mind cleared, there were no more excuses to stay.

Time healed her, giving her the confidence to face life again. She told them so.

Two days later, a ticket in one hand, and her handbag in the other, Jane took one last look at the estate before she got into Amy's awaiting car.

"Ready to leave and get back to real life?" Amy asked.

She sighed. "Being here, with you guys was amazing."

"Even with all that happened?" Amy said, opening the door to the car.

"Well, because of it, I guess."

"Now, you are a funny sort. Come on crazy girl, I don't want you to be late for your plane."

"Jane! Jane!" Ryan ran towards them, arms flailing. Out of breath, he handed Jane a letter, folded and wax sealed. "I almost forgot to give this to you."

"What's this?"

"I don't know. I happened upon it, sorting through the papers and letters on my desk. I thought it unusual, but as plain as day, your name was written on it. I assumed it fell out of one of your folders."

Sure enough, scrolled in black ink, *Miss Jane Reynolds*.

Jane thanked Ryan and placed it in her purse before hugging him.

"Have a safe flight," he said, and closed the door of the car. "Call me when you arrive home."

Amy pulled out of the drive and away from the Eaton Estate. Jane watched from the side mirror, the house grew smaller and smaller, until it disappeared from view. Neither she nor Amy spoke until they cleared the two-lane road and turned onto the main motorway to London. It was an end to an adventure, and the beginning of a new chapter on the horizon.

"What did Ryan give to you as we left?" Amy asked, breaking the silence.

"Oh my gosh, I almost forgot." Grabbing her purse, she reached for the letter and unfolded the weighted paper, revealing an ink-stained letter. Before she could decipher the words, she screamed for Amy to stop.

Amy slammed on the brakes, stopping the car in the middle of the road, "Dear God in heaven! What's the matter?"

Jane's fingers slid across the paper and caressed the name that appeared at the bottom:

My Dearest Jane,

Words cannot express the sentiments tugging at my heart. You entered my life in the most unusual time, and with no question, in an unusual way. I cannot explain the circumstance, nor the purpose. But your absence is felt with great depths of despair. I am a man with little expression, a man of humble feelings, but fervent and pure. But more importantly, I am true to my word. I committed to you all my heart and with the deepest expression of love.

Love! My dearest Jane, of an incredible understanding of the word, you have shown me the overwhelming power of the sentiment. I am not ashamed to admit that I am truly a broken man without you. My love for you stays with me in every moment of the day, only to indulge in them in the darkened hours of the night where you reside in my dreams.

I write this letter with the intent it finds you, however that may be possible. I am not sure of anything anymore, and my efforts may be futile at best. But the impulse to share the love I endure is too great for me to be cautious.

I miss you, Jane. Forever and always I will miss you! I take with me your love and will cherish it to my dying day.

Henry

Amy pulled the car to the side of the road. When she looked over, Jane was shaking, her face in a pool of tears. Thinking it was about time, Amy watched her friend finally breakdown.

"I didn't imagine any of it," Jane exclaimed. "It was all real!"

"I don't understand..."

Jane grabbed Amy's shoulders. "I'm not crazy! Don't you see? Henry was as real as you are!"

SHATTERED

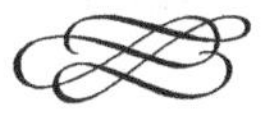

The winds swirled with rage, sweeping leaves and dried grass into a funnel. As the whirlwind settled to a subtle rustling of leaves, they stared at emptiness.

Henry didn't move. His mind conflicted with what he saw.

Dr. Cummings walked behind him and put a firm hand on his shoulder.

Henry jerked, rejecting his friend's sympathy. He stepped inside the flattened area, swinging his arms through the air, feeling for something, anything, that would explain why Jane was not standing there.

His eyes narrowed on the doctor. "Where did she go?"

"Home," he said, offering no other explanation.

"Where to? How does one disappear from the middle of a field?" He paced the space where Jane once stood. His anger swelled with each step.

"What was she, a witch, a demon? What in God's name happened to her?"

As much as he wanted to stay calm and reasonable, Dr. Cummings equally questioned what occurred. One moment Jane stood in front of him, a strong silhouette of a woman, and in a split second, she was gone. Nothing prepared him for such a fantastical occurrence. With his own inability to comprehend, he could not calm his friend's hysteria, let alone his own.

Henry pushed him, wanting to fight. Jane would not have disappeared without his help. He struck his friend again.

Dr. Cummings, not a young man, but certainly still a man to contend with, pushed Henry back with equal force. "Henry, get a hold of yourself!"

Egon, who stood on the sidelines, was in no position to fight against his master. But it was the doctor who called upon him to help with Jane's return. With his allegiance to Dr. Cummings, he jumped in front of Master Eaton, arms raised. The doctor tapped him on the shoulder, stopping the young man from intervening, and waited for Henry's next move.

Henry brushed his hair out of his face and went after Dr. Cummings again but halted. He looked at him in disbelief. "God, man, what have you done? Why did you let her go?"

"If I had the power, Henry, I would have prevented it. She wanted to go." Dr. Cummings stepped towards him and put a hand on him. This time, Henry did not pull away. "She did not belong here. She needed to go home."

"She belonged with me!" Henry yelled to the wind…to Jane if she could hear him.

Dr. Cummings shook his head, "No Henry. She understood. She was not yours to have. She was an outsider, always. You are obligated to another. Jane would never have allowed you to make any other decision."

"Did she think me so dishonorable?" As he lay with Jane the night before, he had bared his soul, but he did not express it thoroughly. He never told her of his intentions. She left before he got the chance to tell her. He cringed at the damage it caused. Her decision was going to haunt him forever.

"At whose expense? She would not ask that of you."

Henry stood frozen, unable to respond. His shirt tattering in the wind, the cold, damp air penetrating him.

A storm was brewing.

"Henry, no one could have stopped her. Not me, not you. She never meant to affect our lives in the way she did." He added, quietly, "She did not intend to fall in love with you."

Henry looked at him.

Dr. Cummings saw him search, desperate for reasoning. Had he not seen Henry's eyes filled with loss before? "She told me to tell you…forever and always."

Henry fell to the ground, his body succumbing to his grief.

Jane was gone.

Egon watched his master bring his hands to his face. He was just a young man of sixteen, but he knew the sight of a broken man.

"Egon, get Master Eaton's horse," Dr Cummings called to the boy, deterring his stare. The boy grabbed the reins and led it to Dr. Cummings. "This is among us, do you understand? You are not to discuss what happened here to anyone!"

He handed the reins to Dr. Cummings, who then instructed him to go home.

The rains began. Dr. Cummings adjusted his hat, but stood stoic in the field, a respectful distance from his friend, allowing him to grieve. Unfortunately, he had watched Henry endure too many losses for a man still young. He did not know all that had transpired between Jane and Henry. It was none of his business. But the loss was apparent. He, too, had known a love so enduring and losing it. It can raise a man to the highest of euphoria. But the loss can bring you to the depths of despair. This was his friend's anguish. So, he waited in the distance until Henry was ready to go home. Dr. Cummings would then share his tale of time, travel, and finding Jane.

LEGACY

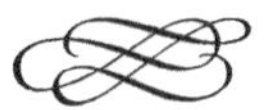

Henry lay in bed, his nightly duty as caretaker completed. He locked the house, extinguished candles, and put out the fires. No one lingered in the drawing room, no slammed doors, no creaking footsteps along the hall. He was alone, the house empty.

Maggie stayed with his sister, safely removed from the melancholy that lingered in the halls of the Eaton Estate.

Henry would soon depart to join her–join everyone waiting for him, but he sulked in his solitude, if only to have privacy to mourn Jane's loss.

Mrs. Bishop kept to herself. Jane's arrival had been unexpected, but her departure more so. Her spiritedness revived the house, brought life back to it. A stranger's affect or a lady in the house, she didn't distinguish. But Jane infused joy into the Eaton Estate, and her departure left her and the household forlorn. She was not unaware of the relationship growing between the master and Jane. Her prayers at night wished for it. But the anguish on his face, as well as his disagreeable disposition after she left, only solidified her intuition as he mourned her absence as well.

Henry tossed in bed from one empty side to the other. The lack of sounds in the house was deafening. He prayed to fall asleep quickly and end the agony of his day without Jane. But when he shut his eyes, her face came into view. He no longer could hear her voice, losing a piece of her in his memory.

He shot up and walked to her room. As he turned the handle, the memories flooded him. The room was cold. The fire unlit in days. Mrs. Bishop aired out the last remnants of Jane, the windows opened to let the summer breeze through. Henry inhaled the sweet tanginess of orange blossoms wafting in the night air. The scent reminded him of Jane from the first day he held her in his arms. Had he known she would become so important to him, he would have held her tighter, never letting her go. He sat on the bed and smoothed his hand against the fresh quilt covering where he had laid with Jane, his body drowning in the gift of her love. He never encountered a woman who gave with so much abandon. His body ached for her. He needed her there, to talk to her again, to touch her again…to explain to him. Just one more moment in time to be with her. She was lost in time, never to be seen again.

He missed Jane–denial would be useless. But after Dr. Cummings explained the truth about her, betrayal rolled in like fog over the ocean–the swelling sea shrouded by a veil of white.

She should have trusted him!

He breathed her very essence into his soul, but that did not excuse the secrets she kept from him. She behaved fraudulently and with intent, despite what they shared. The dagger still stabbed at his heart. And with her gone, he could not resolve the two issues–loving her and feeling betrayed.

He left her room, angrier than when he walked in. With the loss so heavy on him, he sought what would alleviate the pain. He poured himself a glass of whisky and let the numbing sensation spread through his body. But even that reminded him of Jane.

Mrs. Bishop scurried around the house to prepare for Master Eaton's departure, although the preparation for his return was more worrisome. The sooner he left, the sooner she started with the transformation of the household for a woman's arrival.

"Good morning to you, Master Eaton," she greeted as he passed her in the hallway.

He nodded, but he showed no pleasantry on his face–dark eyes, stern brow, gripped jaw.

Henry rubbed his head. Too much whisky. His body also ached from his restless night on the sofa, never making it to bed. With travel ahead, he was now regretful of his choices from the following evening. He went straight to his study to complete last-minute business before he headed to his sister's. Cook kindly sent in a tray, but he balked at the assortment of breads, sausage, and eggs, sending it away no sooner than it arrived.

"Excuse me, Sir?" Mrs. Bishop interrupted him. "Dr. Cummings has arrived. He wishes to speak to you. I've shown him onto the terrace. I thought you might enjoy the fresh air."

"Thank you. I will be with him shortly," he grumbled, sending Mrs. Bishop off with a fling of his wrist.

Henry did not rush to greet his guest, avoiding all communication with his friend since Jane left.

It wasn't until evening, when she disappeared, that Dr. Cummings returned to explain the story behind finding Jane. Although not angry with him–Henry understood the predicament by which his friend made his decisions. Unfortunately, his company only reminded him of the fateful morning, and for that reason, Henry avoided him. But he would have to resolve the rift between them, and the morning of his departure to London allowed him the opportunity.

Stepping onto the terrace, Henry extended his hand. "John, it is good to see you."

"Yes, the same here," Dr. Cummings reciprocated.

"Were you not to leave early morning yesterday? You discussed you had business along the way before you arrived at my sister's."

"Mrs. Kileroy's baby arrived the evening before last, delaying my plans. Hence my visit this morning. I was hoping I could join you on your journey."

He eyed his friend. "You do realize you do not have to look after me? Or did my sister instruct you to assure my arrival?"

Dr. Cummings laughed. It would be exactly like Lillian to manage Henry. But he came out of his own concern for his friend. Henry suffered a blow. A note from Mrs. Bishop confirmed his concerns: Henry escaped into quiet resolve, isolating himself and drinking too much. It was hard for Henry to show vulnerability, and Dr. Cummings was one of the few who witnessed his suffering. Henry trusted him with that knowledge, and he wanted to fortify his commitment to that trust.

"No, no," Dr. Cummings confirmed. "My visit is more personal."

Henry's brow lifted.

"Henry, I am not so old to not remember what it is like to feel love, or loss. Nor am I worried you do not intend to act honorably." He lifted his chin. "But it is with concern for your well-being, and much also for Miss Benning, that I question your motives. Are you moving forward with this marriage without regret?"

How honest did Henry want to be with his friend? When he first asked for Anne's hand in marriage, it never occurred to him love was a variable. Desire for companionship, attraction of a beautiful woman, and having a mother for his daughter, as well as producing future heirs, all factored in his decision to marry. He had experienced love as a younger man. Olivia brought him much happiness and all he desired in a marriage. With her loss, and the loss of their son, his heart seemed depleted of the capability to love in the same way ever again. So, he chose Anne out of obligation and hoped it would be enough.

Not until he met Jane did his heart open to love again. There was no denying his reaction to her, but something unexpected happened. Feelings of love renewed and pushed to a different level of fulfillment. He had not known the heart could be so bountiful.

The heart's capacity was unlimited. But it was a double-edged sword. Unlimited for love; unlimited to agony. Jane's departure slashed the very essence of Henry's being–the price paid for loving her. The caution to the wind his sister would have been proud. However, he lost…lost Jane, and he needed to move on. He needed to heal. But his commitments did not allow for him to indulge in the process. He was to marry Anne in a few days. With her pregnancy soon to reveal itself, he felt he could not postpone the ceremony another day. He had committed his name and protection to Anne, and he would not falter. More importantly, Jane asked him to honor his commitment. She sacrificed her love for his honor. He was not sure if it stirred anger or pride, but either way, he would not let her down.

"Henry?"

Henry shuffled, clearing his throat, "Yes…yes, of course, without any other reason than to secure the happiness of Miss Benning, that I am committing to her," he assured his friend.

"Henry," the doctor eyed him, "I am not treading lightly. What about your endearment to Jane? What have you done with the torment I personally witnessed?"

Henry stiffened. "Please do not treat me like one of your patients. Miss Benning and I are under no false pretense. She has committed to me and I to her."

Henry never gave Dr. Cummings cause to question his motives or actions. He was, without a doubt, most fond of Jane.

But having witnessed her disappear into nothing and nowhere, Henry understood her return as unlikely, if not impossible. Miss Benning was Henry's destiny. Both Dr. Cummings and Jane understood disrupting the course of history was against the laws of nature. Jane was from the future, and therefore, her presence was an interruption of what had already been predisposed. They both agreed she could not affect the past, or the people in it. She had to leave. Henry and Miss Benning were to marry and continue with their lives as written in time.

"Good man," Dr. Cummings slapped Henry on the back. "It is best for all involved."

Henry clutched his jaw.

It was not best for him!

He wanted to prove to Jane it was not best for her. But she did not give him the chance. She made a different decision all together. Passion rushed through his veins once again, but for other reasons. Resentment and anger now pulsated through his blood. His love turning so bitter he tasted the bile in his mouth.

His heart was scabbing over. He was on the mend.

COMFORTS OF HOME

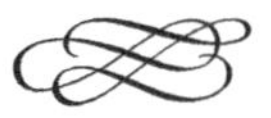

Jane stood in front of her door searching for the keys, exhausted from her long trip, eager to step inside. By comparison to the airport, the quiet of the long, carpeted corridor of her condo was deafening. She wished to be back in the airport, lost amongst the crowds, not facing the reality she was home. But before she had the chance to use her key, the door swung open, much to her surprise.

"Stephen?"

He threw his arms around her and held tight. "Jane! God, I thought we lost you for sure."

She had the instinct to pull away, but as his voice cooed her name, her body sank into the familiar comforts of his arms, like muscle memory. With her head in the crook of his neck, his arms surrounding her back, and firm hands sliding up and down her spine, he offered a safe harbor. She exhaled and succumbed to his loving embrace.

The cat meowed at her feet, and his arms released her.

"Mr. Bingley," she swooped him up, "did you miss me?"

"We both missed you." Stephen flashed his smile–white teeth against a sun-drenched tan, his face freshly shaved.

God, he looked good!

Jane hated that he still affected her. "What are you doing here?"

"I've been taking care of Mr. Bingley. The damn cat and I have actually bonded." He reached over and rubbed the cat under the chin.

Mr. Bingley lifted his head and allowed the show of affection.

"I thought old Mrs. Miller next door was taking care of him?"

He needn't explain. She knew why he was there.

Jane put the cat down and he scurried off, leaving nothing between her and Stephen. She turned and opened the refrigerator, seizing a bottle of water. Anything to distract his dark brown eyes…the depths she fell into for so many years. "You shopped for me?" she questioned the full refrigerator.

"Who isn't tired after an overseas trip? I bought a few things to hold you over."

How she had forgotten the little niceties between them. He'd put toothpaste on her toothbrush before he left for work in the morning, and she would leave two bananas and a protein bar on the counter, near his keys, Saturday mornings when he'd leave early to go surfing.

"Thank you, Stephen, for doing that." She took a swig of water and looked around her place, avoiding eye contact at all costs.

Nothing had changed. The condo remained exactly as she left it. The magazines piled on her coffee table with the television remote control crowning the stack. The shades drawn, except for one window, cracked open to allow fresh air in. The chairs at the table tucked, perfectly aligned, across from each other. The kitchen clean, except for a pile of mail spread across the counter.

"Why don't you shower and get cozy. I'll fix you my famous scrambled eggs, and we can relax. Maybe talk?"

Jane shook her head. "Stephen, I've been through a lot. We've been through a lot, and now is not the time."

"Babe, I'm not asking anything from you. I just want to be here for you." He took her hand. "When I heard you went missing, my entire world exploded. I never imagined my life without you in it. I just assumed you'd always be there. And when it seemed I might have lost you forever, it nearly destroyed me." His dark eyes caught hers. "I hurt you. You bore the brunt of my mistakes. I'm sorry, Jane. I'm sorry for all the pain I caused you. I'm sorry for the man I wasn't. Can you ever forgive me?"

What about Patti? The Baby?

Stephen didn't explain. He didn't need to. Something happened or he wouldn't be there. She wasn't sure what exactly he wanted from her, but whatever he was offering, it was strangely comforting.

"Let me get unpacked and settle for a few days. Maybe we can talk then?" Her hand was still in his. "I promise to think about what you said."

Stephen kissed her on the top of her head. The way he usually said goodbye. A protective, father-like sentiment that always made her feel safe. Her arms enveloped him. She wasn't sure why. She wanted Henry. But Stephen was tangible. There. Henry would never be. Stephen pulled away, saying he would call her in the morning. As Jane closed the door behind him, his scent lingered. He had been to the beach because the salty ocean fragrance saturated his blonde curls and sun-tan lotion permeated his skin. If the beach could be bottled, it would be the essence of Stephen, surf, sand, and sun. It was one of the many things she missed when he left.

She grabbed the arm of her luggage and rolled it into the bedroom. Her bed was neatly tucked, pillows fluffed, and the down comforter folded at the end. The shades were drawn, and the windows closed…her little world untouched and in order awaiting her return.

Alone.

She ripped off her dress, bra, and panties, and threw them on the floor, the ease of undressing not lost on her before she turned on the shower. She wanted to erase all the smells lingering on her body–airplanes, taxicabs, sweat…Stephen.

She dried off, wrapped the towels around her body, and wiped down the fogged mirror. A reflection of a woman stared back. But who? She should have found comfort to get back to her modern life–cars, planes, showers, and kitchens with instant coffee pots. But something deep inside her wriggled, like she was covered in plastic and needed to get out. Jane, the face staring back at her, looked the same, her modern body belonging in the right time and place, but someone underneath her skin screamed to escape. Something was missing.

Where was her soul?

She knew. It was back with Henry.

She poured herself a glass of wine, grateful for the bottle Stephen brought, a French chardonnay he knew she liked. Looking at the stack of mail, she decided tomorrow would be a better day to start her life again and pushed it aside, taking the bottle to bed.

As she lay in the darkened room, the wine gone, and her glass dry, she allowed herself to imagine she was back in the Eaton Estate. She tried to listen for the clanking of Mrs. Bishop's shoes dragging across the wooden floor, Maggie's giggles carrying through the house, the crackle of the fire coming from the library.

The sounds didn't come.

She curled herself into a ball, covered her head with a pillow, and squeezed her lids closed to stop the world outside her windows.

Only then did she hear Henry's breathing.

I take with me your love and will cherish it to my dying day.

Henry's words streamed through her head before she fell asleep. Where she allowed herself to dream about the life she once lived but could never go back to.

COMMITMENT

The social season was coming to an end. Social gatherings and events played out, and the summer bore down its wretched heat and stagnant air on its inhabitants. Party dwellers planned to retreat to the country for reprieve, where for the most part, the entertaining continued with equal fury, or where they headed to cooler more temperate destinations. The last and final invitation anticipated before their departures was the wedding of the beautiful Miss Anne Benning to the distinguished Mr. Henry Eaton.

Anne's mother timed the event so it would be the last party on people's minds as they left the summer fun, carrying their memories back to the country where it would be talked about until the end of the season. Albeit the heat would hinder the perfection of the event, but the price was worth the admiration and notoriety.

Mrs. Benning, draped in layers of purple silk, and bobbled in diamonds, circled her daughter to admire her work of art. After all, it was her design that the dress was tailored, careful to conceal any signs of Anne's *condition*.

"Dearest daughter, you are a painting of beauty. If only

your father, may he rest in peace, could have had the honor to see you wed so handsomely."

"Oh mother, how can you be so joyful. It is dreadfully hot."

Mrs. Benning eyed a maid, who rushed to the side table, dampened a towel, and wiped away any signs of water droplets around Anne's hairline, careful not to disturb her powdered face.

A knock at the door opened to Lillian.

"Good morning Mrs. Benning," Lillian cheeked the older woman, careful not to disturb her coiffing. "Anne, darling," she eyed the bride standing in front of the mirror. "You truly are a vision of beauty. My brother is a lucky man."

"Henry? Has he safely arrived?"

Lillian nodded but said nothing more.

Henry had not arrived until late evening the previous night. When he came into the foyer the guests' laughter was evident that the party still progressed into the late hours. But he had no desire to join them. The ride was long and tiring, only making him more ill-tempered as he neared his sister's house. He did not want to be with people or celebrate. Rumors surfaced he would not show up at all, with bets placed among the men, but Lillian laughed off the idea. She had no intention of allowing her guests privy to her own fears.

Anne feigned smiles when asked about Henry's arrival. She never doubted he would show, but his delayed return before the nuptials concerned her, and she went to bed questioning the amount of honor he had to offer. She had put him to the test, and he came through despite her demands. When she received his note that the wedding would continue as planned, she fell to her knees humbled, once again, at his strength of character and his commitment to his honor.

Because it was she who sent Henry after Jane.

The morning Jane came to her door to say goodbye, her

instinct told her something, or someone, caused her quick departure. She questioned her motives, but Jane refused to give a reason. When she boldly asked, "Does this concern Henry?" Jane's body language told her everything Anne needed to know. Her shoulders stiffened, her eyes closed, and she turned away. Jane whispered her goodbye, and left Anne to wonder about the intrigue laid at her feet. Knowing time was of the essence, she sought the one person who could help clarify the situation at hand.

"Henry?" Anne pushed open the bedroom door when she did not get a response from knocking. A languid creature lay on the couch. A pillow covered his face, and he did not react to her footsteps across the floor. "Henry!"

Henry bolted up, realizing it was not his sister who called his name. "Anne!" He rose and reached for his coat, tucked in his shirt, and fumbled with his cravat before addressing her.

Watching Henry dress was an intimate sight, and Anne stirred with desire. Henry's handsomeness brought envy to the many women who failed to capture his attention. Anne was not oblivious to his ability to arouse desire. She had watched him from afar with temptation. But in the presence of his bedchamber, she became all too aware she would soon be more accustomed to his dressing and undressing. Her eyes did not dart away, but she watched with surprised delight.

When he was presentable, he gave Anne his attention. "Did you want something of urgency?"

"Yes, Henry." She clasped her hands. "I have been searching for you all day. It is only by chance I overheard your valet reveal your whereabout."

"Shall I meet you downstairs, in the salon?" he offered, hoping to take her out of the confines of his bedroom. His sanctuary. His very private space.

"No. I would like to speak to you now, in privacy. I do not wish to make this a public affair." She looked around the room for a proper place to sit. When she spotted two chairs, nose to nose, by the window, Henry seated her.

Henry leaned forward. "What is it you wish to discuss?"

Anne squirmed in her chair. In her despair to find Henry, she did not untangle the thoughts in her head before she entered Henry's room. "I…" her voice cracked. She put her hand to her chest and cleared her throat before she started again. "I ask this of you not because I have personally witnessed a misstep in your behavior, nor of your dedication to me. You have been nothing but kind and attentive." She looked at the statuesque man across from her. Did he ever conceive Jane had feelings for him? He was so guarded with his own feelings; she struggled to imagine him allowing such a circumstance to happen. She now felt silly and questioned if she should continue.

"Anne." He reached for her hand and placed it in his. "Please, if we are to be man and wife, then we cannot be so apprehensive to share of ourselves."

Anne pulled away, and he wondered if she was afraid of him.

"Anne, my dear if I seem unapproachable, I apologize. You, of all people, need to know I am open to your address." He looked at her with his blue eyes, offering sincerity. How deeply would he allow her to fall into them?

Anne did not love Henry. He offered her a status and protection she was seeking. Her feelings were not without a deep sentiment of fondness, and she now admitted, as she studied him, there was a physical attraction. She was willing to continue with the charade they agreed to if he was.

She lowered her eyes. "You must know how grateful I am you agreed to follow through with your commitment. I am forever humbled by your actions. It is my intention to make you proud that I am your wife."

"Anne, you will be more than my wife in name. I commit myself to you as well."

She saw him look away, giving her the courage to ask, "Do you want to give yourself to me?"

His brow furrowed. "Anne, what are you asking?"

She put her hands up. "I did not come to you as a virginal maiden. We are not fooling each other by admitting that. I have no misconceptions about your ability to charm other women. But if there is one who has stolen your heart, I do not want to stand in your way. Especially if that someone is as special as Jane."

Henry's jaw hardened; his eyes darkened. He turned away; sure she saw the truth in his eyes.

Did not his whole body radiate love for Jane?

Anne did not need him to confirm or deny. Henry rose and paced the room while she sat on the edge of her seat, waiting for whatever came next.

He stopped, leaned against the mantle, and turned to the petite woman waiting for him to answer. Waiting for him to confirm his love that he could not give to her. "If you are questioning my loyalty to you, Anne, I gave that to you the day you came to me on the terrace," he reminded her.

"And before then?" Anne asked, keenly aware he was not answering her question. "Henry, are you in love with Jane?" she repeated.

He could not conjure his voice. He cleared his throat in defense.

She rose, walked towards him, and put her hand on his sleeve. "Because I believe she is in love with you."

Those words sank to the bottom of his heart. "Did she express those sentiments?"

"Henry, I am a woman. Love is something we do not discuss lightly. If she had not the same reaction you had, I would not be telling you that she loves you deeply. More deeply than you possibly can know." Their eyes met. "So, I ask you again, Henry. Are you in love with Jane?"

He dropped his chin to his chest, ashamed of his answer to his wife to be.

"Henry?"

"With the deepest parts of my soul," he uttered.

Anne's lips twitched upward, relieved to hear the truth. "Henry, I do not want you this way. Had I known your heart was not mine to take, I would not have asked what I did. You deserve love. And if you have found it with Jane, I will give you the freedom to go after it."

"Anne, you are in no condition to ask that of me. I will not abandon you."

"Oh, dearest Henry," she pressed her cheek next to his and whispered in his ear, "Always so noble." She pulled away and smiled. "Jane is as dear to me as a sister. She could not have shown me more compassion in her care for me. Now I see how much she truly did love me by leaving you behind."

"I wish I could be so sure of her love as you are," he sighed in resign.

"Then go to her and ask her directly. Do not allow her silence to haunt you forever."

Henry looked at Anne. Her eyes were calm, loving, giving. If love was possible between them, it sparked in that moment.

"Go now, Henry. If she loves you, then take her in your arms and cherish her until your dying day."

"And if she doesn't?" he asked.

"I will be here waiting for you," she offered. "I am honored to be your wife, Henry. I am no fool of what you can offer. I see a man I can grow to love from the mere fact you have the capacity to love so dearly. I would be a fool not to have that for myself."

"I cannot allow the shame that would come to you," he reminded her.

She pointed to the door. "Go Henry. Find Jane!"

Those were the orders she sent him off with. She did not expect to hear from him so quickly. But it was only a few days later when she received a note from Henry.

Dearest Anne,

It is with intention that I return in good faith to be your husband. Continue with preparations without haste.

With Regard,

Henry

He gave no more indication of what transpired. Anne continued the wedding preparation with earnest, leading to her standing before the mirror, not having the chance to see him or discuss all that had happened between him and Jane. She knew the intensity of Henry's feeling but did not fully consider Jane and how she would accept his declaration of love. Jane's feelings were very apparent, but that did not always translate into marriage. Anne knew this more than anyone.

Henry stood stoic at the altar, more handsome than usual as Anne walked towards him.

She blushed with great pride at the well-dressed man, who would soon be her husband.

He did not turn away when she appeared before him and took his side.

Anne dared not look at him, thankful the veil concealed her fears. She did not want to see the truth hidden in the depths of his eyes; he was there for no other reason than to honor his commitment. He did not love her. But he was there, standing firmly beside her petite frame dressed in a sea of creamy white silk and lace. He answered the minister with no hesitation, acting the role of an eager husband, accepting his bride's hand in marriage. A soft touch of his lips to hers sealed the commitment, and they walked side by side as husband and wife.

LILLIAN'S SCOLDING

Lillian found Henry in Sir Levongood's study, lying on the sofa with his eyes closed and a drink in his hand. The lingering warm weather did not warrant a fire, leaving the room unusually dark without one.

"What are you doing, Henry?" she asked, as any concerned sister would.

"I am relaxing, now go away."

"Henry!" She nudged him. "You have been here for over two weeks. You need to go home."

Henry swung his legs to the floor, slumped against the back cushion–not budging from the sofa, and ignored his sister's chiding.

Lillian pulled open the drapes, allowing the afternoon light to fill the room. Henry covered his eyes and moaned.

"With the news of a baby, and so soon, you should be overjoyed! You have a wife at home waiting for you. She needs you now more than ever." She walked to her lump of a brother and put her hands on her hips. "Why did you come here, Henry?"

Henry never planned on staying so long at his sister's home. But he didn't have the willpower to face Anne. Nor the dignity. When Anne and he walked side by side, congratulated by the many guests attending the wedding, he could not have been more conscious of the fraud he helped to perpetuate. The Cromwell's gleeful admiration of him and Anne, or Mr. Davenport's incessant apologies for his wife who was unable to witness their '*blissful union*' were more than he deserved. He crumbled under his deceit.

Likewise, Anne humbled herself in their adoration. She demanded nothing of Henry and compensated for his lack of demonstrative gratitude with class and grace. As well as beauty and feminine charm, Anne had good breeding. A benefit many congratulated him on. She accepted the well-wishes with a generous smile and joyous heart, hiding the anxiety that lay below the surface. Grateful for her *performance*, no one was the wiser of their charade. He knew he would find it in his heart to care for her the way she deserved. He just was not ready on their wedding day, or after.

Lillian offered her home for their first night as husband and wife. Special quarters were prepared, and Anne retreated to hers, while Henry retreated to Sir Levongood's study to find his brother-in-law equally willing to indulge in a drink.

Sir Levongood smirked as he offered Henry a cigar, "Not so eager to end the evening?"

Henry declined the smoke but lifted his glass to indicate more.

"If I didn't know better, I would say you are nervous," he teased, refilling the empty crystal.

"I am more than acquainted with my duties as a husband, Edward."

Sir Levongood laughed. "I cannot say I am not envious. New love and a beautiful woman would make any man take pause in reflection." He puffed a cloud of smoke and sipped his drink. "Henry, my dear man, if there is one thing I have learned, never keep a woman waiting." He looked at him directly, and added, "Especially if she is your wife!"

Henry accepted his advice. He took another swig of his drink, emptying the glass, and headed out the door.

Anne waited in her cotton gown of white, loosely falling around her form. Her breasts gathered fullness as the days of morning sickness ended and her curving hips took shape, her tummy showing little signs of pregnancy on her petite frame. She stood before the mirror, wanting to see what Henry would look upon as he entered the room. Blonde waves fell over her shoulders, and her nipples peeked through her gown as the candle illuminated the body underneath the veil of white. *Was she enough?* She could not deny her desire to be with Henry. Making love to a man was not new to her, and she anticipated the union with eagerness.

The door slammed in the room next to hers, and she quickly retreated to the bed to await his arrival. She listened to his footsteps, the shuffling movement of a chair, and the clunking of his shoes as they landed on the floor. Her ears perked, thinking of his every move before he entered. Was he undressing? Washing his face? Was he anticipating walking through the door that separated them?

She did not remember when she fell asleep. The candles melted, and she was left alone in the dark. He never came to her.

Henry took Anne to the shore for their honeymoon. To all, they seemed like a happy couple as they strolled in the afternoon and dined in the evening. He was pleasant and conversational, attentive to her needs. If she was tired, he found a place to sit. If she admired something in a shop, he bought it. But they spent most of their time in the company of strangers, and not with each other. Gatherings of guests in the hotel's salon, invitations to a play or music ensemble, an exhibit opening or a museum visit. Their honeymoon time turned into a whirlwind of social affairs, as most of whom they encountered were eager to entertain the newlyweds.

Anne did not push Henry for more. Nor was she concerned about his lack of intimacy. They had a lifetime to learn to love each other.

When he brought Anne home, he made sure she was settled at the Eaton Estate. He gave her the biggest room, ensuring it had a woman's charm, his personal items moved into a room down the hall, allowing Anne all the privacy she may desire.

Mrs. Bishop hired a highly respected maid for the new Mrs. Eaton's benefit, and the regular staff were trained as to the special attention to be given to their new mistress. Henry wanted to ensure Anne her place as his wife, and head of the house, before he announced his departure for a business trip that would take him away.

He had not returned since.

"Henry, are you listening to me?" Lillian nagged, jolting Henry.

"Leave me be, Lillian. This is none of your concern," he barked, hating to be ordered around by his older sibling.

"You are hiding away in my house from your wife. Of course, this is my concern. People are beginning to chatter."

"People need to stay out of what is not their business." He jolted from the sofa and paced the room, avoiding eye contact with Lillian.

"Dearest little brother, I am not the one you should be so angry with."

"Then please do not hound me as to my obligations. I am a grown man, and fully aware of my responsibilities."

"A grown man indeed. She is your wife and needs you home, for God's sake," Lillian shouted.

"In name only!" He shouted back.

Lillian's brow shot up. "What have you done, Henry? Please tell me you have sanctified your marriage."

Henry's jaw clenched, searing a look she could only interpret as a "no."

"Oh my." She fell to the sofa. "Please do not deny…is the child yours?" She suspected the baby's early conception, but assumed it was Henry's, and the spontaneous decision to honor his previous engagement to Anne. It now shed light on Jane's quick disappearance, and lack of communication since. "Henry, give me the truth!"

"If you want the truth, then I cannot tell you what you want to hear."

Lillian clutched at her chest and whispered, "God help you, Henry."

Silence befell the room, the truth now out. Henry continued to pace; Lillian calculated the situation.

"What do you want from her, Henry? She is your wife now, and you must act honorably."

"My honor is not tarnished. I did what I was asked."

"By whom? Who would have asked such a sacrifice of you?"

Henry did not answer. He had not said her name since she left. Only in his head did her name scream at him, waking him from his sleep in the wee hours of the morning.

"Oh," Lillian sighed. She could only assume to whom he did not speak. Henry never explained what transpired between him and Jane. He only asked that her name not be mentioned while in his presence.

Henry swallowed the last of his drink and poured himself another.

"You cannot drown out your life. You need to go home and face what you are hiding from."

"Why, damn it?" His eyes dimmed. "I am perfectly aware of what I must face. But I cannot do it just yet. It hurts too much,

Lillian." He dragged his fingers through his hair. His voice weakened, "My heart is raw."

In that moment, Lillian saw her little brother–the boy who ran to the fields, and endlessly cried, his tear-stained cheeks hidden to only her when she found him curled into a ball, mourning his greatest loss, his mother. She wrapped her arms around him and cradled his head then, but he was a man now. A grown, prideful, belligerent…and hurting man. Her only choice was to prop him up and push him forward.

"Because Anne needs you," she said. "Her child is yours to care for. You made your choice."

"I did not make that choice. *She* did!" He seethed, remembering the morning she left him–the warmth of her touches still lingering on his skin when he awakened to find her gone. He could not escape her words imprinted in his memory after reading her letter, over and over again. Her face is forever in front of him.

"She is gone, Henry. She left for whatever the reasons." Lillian hated to say the words. But it was the truth, and he needed to accept the facts. "She is never coming back to you. It is time to move on."

"Do you not realize I know that? I have never hated in my heart, but she has brought forth feelings I cannot deny. She has damaged my ability to feel happiness or sadness, both equal torments. I have never known the power of such a love but with her, and yet I am left without the one who inspires such capacity. Half of my soul is entwined with hers and she has taken it away for it never to be united. The other severed half is tattering in the wind. I walk with no life. I breathe with no air. I try to forget, but if not for life, my heart must ache." He put his head into his hands, "I am afraid I have nothing left to give to Anne."

Lillian allowed him to mourn. He needed to purge if he was to make a new life for himself and Anne. If he did not, the ghost of Jane would take his soul. But he had to move forward…he had no other choice.

Lillian gave him orders, "Go home, Henry, and make Anne your wife in body as she is in name." She sat next to him, wrapped her hands around his, and whispered, "You will never have more than that to give her, for I fear your soul will always be forever with Jane."

MRS. EATON

Anne sat at her mirror, combing her hair, while her maid laid out a dress for the morning. She hummed a sweet melody as she brushed long, determined strokes through her blonde waves, which fell over her shoulders and down to her chest. As the pregnancy progressed, her curls loosened, the effects creating soft golden waves framing her fair skin and delicate features.

"You are a very beautiful woman," a deep voice startled Anne from behind her.

"Henry!" She faced him. "I wasn't expecting you."

"I have come home to be with you, Anne."

He said nothing more. He didn't have to. She understood.

She stood, placed her brush down on the table, and excused the maid, "Please make sure we are not disturbed."

The maid curtsied and closed the door behind her.

Their eyes met. Anne held her breath. Henry didn't move towards her, instead sat on a chair, and took off his boots.

She watched as he untied his cravat and unbuttoned his shirt. She still didn't move and waited.

Breathe…

Henry didn't rush. He rose and moved towards her, never taking his gaze away from her. As he came close, she could feel his breath against her face. He brushed his hands through her hair, absorbing the golden strands through his fingers.

"You are so young and innocent..." He touched the pink of her lips with his thumb, separating them, tempted by the fullness. But his lips never touched hers. He pulled away and studied her face.

He recalled the first time he realized the young girl he overlooked at gatherings had grown into a woman. It was winter, and she had worn a dress of sapphire-blue velvet trimmed in black lace. The bodice curved around her breast, and her skin was pale white, contrasting with the rich, sumptuous fabric. The gem color drew him to her blue eyes, with their long lashes protecting any admirer from looking into them. She was stunning, and every man in the room was mesmerized. She had many requests to dance, but she chose him for the first dance. He also got the last one.

Anne closed her eyes. She wanted his lips on hers, but he taunted her. His lips hovered over hers, hesitant to indulge. "I am not as innocent as you claim," she reminded him, pressing her hand against the small bump that separated them.

A surge of jealousy pierced him, knowing another man shared the pleasure of her body. But the fact that she was not naïve to a man's desire made him pulsate. He was in no mind set to be delicate. He had a hunger to fill.

Anne stood still, not afraid of Henry or what he wanted. She patiently waited for him to come to her. How many times did she imagine what it would be like to lie with him? She pictured his broad shoulders and thick legs wrapped around her as their bodies intertwined. He now stood in front of her and no longer needed her imagination. She could see his appetite in the depths of his eyes. She shivered with desire.

He was ready to take her.

He glided his hand from her cheek, along her delicate neck, stroking her flesh against his fingertips, his burning desire creating shivers down her spine. His palm slid along her shoulder, draping his touch across her chest, until he found her ripe breast in the palm of his hand. It was hard to miss the plumpness; the hard nipples poking through the sheer fabric. They were dark and large, and on full display for his taking. He pushed aside her nightgown, exposing the curves of her shoulder, the possibilities of her nakedness to come–his willpower lost to the glistening skin. He brushed his lips along the curvature and tasted the saltiness of her flesh, his tongue feasting on the bounty of her chest until his mouth rested on the protrusion that made him go hard at the sight of it.

Anne gasped, but that did not stop him from his need. He grabbed at her waist and pulled her body to him, pushing the pleasure of suckling further into his mouth. His hands slid down her body, caressing the delicate curves of the feminine form. Anne's breath quickened, her chest heaving against him, and his desire accelerated. Only when he came for her lips, plunging his tongue into her eager mouth, did she lead him to the bed.

He stood before her, ravenous for the woman who lay before him. She had a fire in her eyes, making him lose control of his need. He pulled off his shirt but fumbled with loosening his pants. She stopped his hands with hers and completed the undressing. As she slid the fabric down his legs, she caressed the roundness of his backside, sending rockets of energy through him. The stimulation was evident, and she took him between her hands. He closed his eyes to relish a woman's touch. She pulled the edge of her gown to her thighs, inviting Henry to her body.

He had no control or the desire to stop. He needed her body, and she was a willing participant. He draped himself over her and moved inside.

Her breath blew in his ear, driving him to push harder with

his rising need. With her hand on his back, she guided his movement, and he followed, adjusting his fit to hers, causing their bodies to move together. She groaned with a long sigh; her body consumed with pleasure. With her release, his own body surged.

He lay aside her, too depleted to move. With rhythmic strokes along his back, brushing his skin against her fingertips, he fell asleep.

Henry succumbed to his sleepy lids; his dream-state faded into oblivion.

The curtains were drawn and the room was dark when he finally awoke. Rolling over, he found Anne face to face with him. She smiled and he could not help but lazily return the gesture.

"You slept rather well," she teased.

He closed his eyes, recalling what caused the tiredness. His heart sank.

Anne watched his expression go from a sleepy contentment to heaviness on his brow. He did not lift his head from the pillow but sank further into it, hiding his shame. She sat up and her gown fell off her shoulder, exposing her breast. Henry's eyes didn't miss the mishap before she adjusted the sleeve. She may have seen guilt permeate his face, but his body moved with new readiness. She used it to her advantage.

"Henry, please sit up," she ordered.

He obliged, fluffing his pillow against the back of the bed.

"You are thinking about her, aren't you?" She did not need him to answer. His lowered eyes told her what she wanted to know. "I am not jealous, Henry. She is in my thoughts as well."

Henry sat a little taller. She had his attention.

Anne was not daunted to explain, "I am not as naïve as you make me out to be. You love her. You will always love her, as I will always love Patrick. When I look at you, I see her. The two of you forever linked. It is your fate, as well as mine."

Henry turned away; the truth uncomfortable to hear. He laid next to his wife–a beautiful, passionate woman. He had every right to make love to her. Didn't he? But Anne was not wrong. It was Jane whom he dreamed of; wished he was next to when he awoke.

"Henry," she grabbed his chin and turned his face to hers. "Your soul is not mine to have. I would never take that from her. She sacrificed her love for me, and I will always be indebted to her. You are mine to cherish and honor because she gave that to me." She caressed his face, his stubbled cheeks scratching her fingers. "She declared you a good man, Henry, and you are. You did not force yourself on me. I wanted you to have me, for her sake. You can come to me anytime and it will always be a gift of love we both share with her. Don't you see?"

Henry's heart lurched, shocking his languid body. He leaned in and kissed Anne's lips. It sent a shiver through him, and he brushed them again, wanting to repeat the sensation.

Anne's capacity to love warmed his heart, and he began to understand a new dimension to love he could not have imagined existed. Loving Anne was not an erasing of Jane, just a different space in his heart. He wrapped his arms around her and pulled her to him, kissing the top of her head.

She snuggled up to him and rested her head on his chest, finding *her* spot with him.

"I promised to love, honor, and cherish you on our wedding day. I promise from this point to uphold those vows," he whispered in her ear.

"Jane said you would." She smiled at him, enticing him to kiss her again. She brushed her hand down his chest and ran her fingers through the hairline that swirled downward in between his legs. He took the bait. His lips pressed harder against hers. She did not miss the intention.

"Again Mr. Eaton?" she invited him.

"Again, Mrs. Eaton."

LONDON MUSEUM

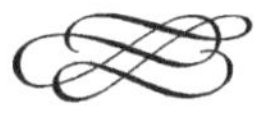

Jane stood outside the concrete monolith of the Museum of London. It didn't have an impressive exterior, but to create a successful exhibit inside thrilled her. The front desk attendant congratulated her upon her introduction and gave her the guest employee museum pass Amy left for her.

She put the lanyard around her neck that announced:

Jane Reynolds, Exhibit Creator: Dressing Through Time.

She was only four steps into the exhibit when she heard her name being shrieked across the corridor. Amy ran up to her with open arms.

"Sweetie, Wow! You have transformed into, well…" She pushed her out at arm's length. "Bright. Fully charming, indeed! A longer hairstyle, a sassy, short dress, and are those high-heeled pumps? If I didn't know better, I would say you're getting shagged. Maybe last night? I didn't hear a word from you after you landed."

Jane ran her fingers through her long strands, pushing it away from her face. "Amy, you know perfectly well, I was alone last night, the pumps are a practical three inches, and I've had no replacement since Stephen." Jane rolled her eyes. "I am single and happily alone…exactly where I am supposed to be in life."

"Hmm, well a girl has needs," Amy quipped. "But you're in a good place, Sweetie and that is what matters." She gave her a cheeky kiss before walking her towards the exhibit.

Ever since Jane read the letter in the car, Amy worried her friend would pine away for a man who no longer existed. Something extraordinary happened to her. The letter proved it. She didn't question Jane after that but accepted the experience as fantastical–one of life's mystery. Was it possible? She would never truly know. If Jane believed, then she believed, too. When all explanations were exhausted, Jane was still left with a great love affair; an experience of a lifetime deeply affecting her. Changing her. Who was she to deny that? But there was no going back. She had to move forward with her life in the present. When Jane told her Stephen was back in her life, she worried. Unfinished business or a rebound to heal? Thankfully, he didn't last long, opening possibilities for another man to come along and, dare she say it, replace Henry and create new memories.

Jane appreciated there was no more indictment about her life, dating, or her relationship with Stephen. The loss of the baby after their encounter at the Farmer's Market instigated a breakup with Patti. Their beginning built on deception and obligation; their ending based on sadness and regret. None on the foundation of love and honor. They had no chance. Reflection and the almost loss of Jane forever, prompted Stephen to realize he wasn't through with Jane.

Nor was Jane through with Stephen.

Love is pure, but relationships are complicated. Didn't Henry and Anne prove that? Jane gave him a second chance. Maybe because she needed to place her love somewhere, anywhere, other than allow her heart to anguish. But her thoughts were never far from Henry. It took her three weeks, one late-night phone call, and a text to finally let go.

Stephen got the forgiveness he requested, and Jane got the closure she needed, mending the bonds between them, allowing them to mutually untether from each other. Because love is not breakable, but people are. Her time in the past gave her time to heal in the future. When she returned, her heart no longer hollowed, allowed the love for Stephen to be healed and harbored, making room for more–the *heart's capabilities* to love again, and give without abandon.

Henry showed her that.

She threw herself into work, ten hours a day, to launch the exhibit in September. After its debut, the museum kept the exhibit open for nine months to the delight of management and museum patrons. Afterwards, the whole showcase was shipped to London where Amy assumed the role of exhibit manager. Jane flew to London to congratulate Amy on a successful launch, which is what brought her back a year later.

"Come," Amy grabbed Jane's arm. "I want to show you something special."

She guided Jane to a display halfway through the exhibit. On a platform before them, Amy replicated the room at the Eaton Estate, pulling hundreds of details from Jane's description. It had all the elements she remembered: yellow damask wallpaper as the backdrop, silk cream drapes outlining a faux window, a Queen Anne chair in front of a painted fireplace, and a round mahogany table with a silver candelabra. In the center of the display, a mannequin wore a chemise made of white linen with a hem trimmed in lace and satin ribbon. Jane leaned in, eyed the chemise, and blinked, questioning her sanity. She pulled the rope aside and entered the display.

Amy followed her behind the ropes. "Do you like it? Did I do it justice?"

A flush of memories surfaced; emotion flooded. "It's

perfect, Amy…just perfect." Tears fell on her cheeks. She swiped them away, but more came.

"Oh my, I was afraid of that." Amy pulled her away from the gawking visitors and out of the exhibit.

Through her tears, Jane asked, "But how…I don't understand."

"Ryan offered his estate's antiques to add to the exhibit. I rummaged through the vast collection, when behold, I found the furniture that once decorated *your* room–the dresser, armoire, even the bed, albeit in pieces against the wall. I couldn't use every item, but it was all there as if waiting for this moment."

"And the chemise? How did you ever find that?"

Her eyes widened. "You won't believe it, Jane! Someone took the time to preserve it, because I found it wrapped with care tucked in a drawer of the armoire. It needed repair, for sure. Time is not kind to delicate fabrics, no matter how well preserved. If you look closely, the pleats tore, and the yellowing of the fabric couldn't be renewed," she explained. "I swear, the moment I held it in my hands, I saw you standing in it, with *him* staring at you…" She smirked, bumping Jane with her elbow, "All hot and bothered, of course."

"Stop it," Jane laughed through her tears.

"That's better," Amy said, encouraged by the curling of her lips, although quavering. "I didn't mean to make you cry. I wanted to bring you joy."

"You did. It brings back many happy memories."

"Now come on, let's get some coffee and catch up." Amy tugged her hand and guided her through hidden corridors leading outside.

A cloudy morning provided thick, cool air across Jane's face, drying the residual tears lingering at the corner of her eyes. She inhaled a few times, taking in the English air, albeit city air… but it was refreshing all the same. A far cry from the triple digit temperatures she left back in Los Angeles. All that mattered, it helped clear her head and ground her.

The past was gone…gone…gone.

Jane rarely thought about her *experiences* in the light of day, suppressing emotions attached to her memories of Henry and the Eaton Estate. During the last moments, before she descended into sleep, did she relinquish control of her mind and surrender to her heart. She saw his face, his dark blue eyes searching into the depths of hers, his mouth breathing her in, allowing their souls to touch. Only then, in the far reaches of her consciousness, did she allow him to come to her.

Amy saw Jane struggling. "You're not over him, are you?"

"I'm fine," Jane assured. But Amy gave her *a look*. The look that said, *spill it!*

"It's just…being back here, a year later, I'll admit, is overwhelming. And I did something stupid last night." She touched her cheek. Amy's brow arched, but Jane already confirmed nothing provocative happened…at least on Amy's terms. "I visited Peyton's book shop …"

"And?"

"She remembered me! I entered, only two steps in, when Peyton ran up to me and said, 'You're back!' I didn't understand if she meant back in London, or back to the future. But before I could ask, she added, 'but you left a part of you behind.'"

"Then what did you say?" Amy crossed her arms and leaned in.

"I said, 'I know.' Then she hugged me and whispered in my ear, 'Don't worry, you will be reunited…a soul is never separated from its destiny. Choose.'"

Amy looked perplexed. "What does that mean?"

Jane shook her head. "I wanted to ask but before I could, she disappeared to assist a customer. I left, scared; excited. Unsure if I really wanted her to explain. Do I want a psychic to predict what my life is fated? I have control over whatever comes my way. Don't I?" She tilted her head, not needing Amy to answer. "When I awoke this morning, I shook off all those questions, and found my footing–grounded in the present. But obviously," she pointed to her wetted eyes, "I'm not. Peyton sparked hope. But hope for what? It's silly when you think about it. I had a strange experience. A month of my life…a tiny millisecond, really, for a lifetime…with Henry. Although real, nothing about it was logical. Or practical. I mean, come on, Stephen and I shared years together, and we didn't end up working out. What fate did Henry and I have?"

"But you didn't love Stephen the way you love Henry," Amy reminded her.

"You mean, *loved*, in the past tense."

"No sweetie, I got it right the first time." Her phone vibrated, and she read the text. "Hmm, my assistant says that Ryan Eaton is at the exhibit and asking if you arrived." She pulled out a lipstick and handed it to Jane. Amy's instant weapon to beautify. She went nowhere without a shade in one of her pockets. "Come on, put on a little color, and pinch those cheeks. Ryan is eager to see you."

Jane did as she instructed, dabbing her lips, before they headed back to the exhibit, and to the awaiting Ryan.

The exhibit room filled with the lunch crowd, tourist, and locals alike, moving from one exhibit to the next. Amy scanned the room, looking for Ryan's bald head.

She pointed. "There he is, over there."

Jane followed her gaze to two men standing side by side in front of the chemise display. Ryan in a Burberry shirt made him easy to identify, the other, distinguishable for his height, lean, and erect in stature, overdressed in a suit. Jane pushed through the crowd, but as she moved closer to the two men, her stomach twisted. There was something too familiar about the man next to Ryan. If she was correct, her two worlds, the one she was living in and the one she had lived, were about to collide. The man turned, and he was face to face with Jane.

"My dear, Miss Reynolds," the man greeted, wrapping his hand around hers.

Jane's head wobbled and her knees buckled.

The man grabbed her by the waist and swooped her up.

INTERFERENCE

The winds whipped through his coat as he braved the elements. The snow lightly dusted the grounds, but much of it had melted away from the warmer days that prevailed. That was coming to an end. Henry felt the temperature drop, the icy wind freezing his face. He reached his destination and stopped where he had marked with a pile of stones. The sun was disappearing below the horizon, the night sneaking in. He should not have ventured to the field with the darkness soon to cover him, but he needed to talk.

"Sorry for my absence." He squatted closer to the stones. "I brought Maggie to Lillian's. I also had business affairs to attend in the city."

He paused to collect his thoughts. He looked out at the desolate landscape. Everything was brown, dormant, or dead.

"I thought it best for Maggie to stay with her aunt. Anne is growing more frail as the baby gets bigger. I fear it is consuming everything she eats, leaving nothing for her. She has not grown large as most women do at this stage." Henry paused to put his collar up around his neck. "I'm getting concerned."

The wind whipped up around him. He brought his hands to

his face and blew on them. "Dr. Cummings has tended to her with great care. That man is truly a saint." He smirked and shook his head. "You were right to be so good to him. I did not see it then. I could not see anything past you."

He recalled the night at the dance when his jealousy raged over Dr. Cummings parading Jane around the room. She looked so beautiful in the pink dress, the golden beads dancing on the silken skin of her arms. Her lips were as pink as her dress, and all he thought about was pressing his own against them.

"Anne tries to assure me all will be fine. She reminds me women have babies all the time. Anne is under such scrutiny by Dr. Cummings, she has no fear for herself. But I fear," he admitted. He had seen death come too often, losing Anne a real possibility.

"Anne is good to me. I truly am a blessed man. Blessed? Is that what you planned when you left her with me? You have me a more noble man than I pretend to be. If you must know, her mere presence keeps me connected to you. She loves you as I do, and thus, what bonds us so dearly. Please do not judge me harshly for admitting as much." Guilt churned his gut. "She is not without knowing. She has more understanding than any one person should. Maybe it is because her heart is elsewhere as well. Or because her capacity to love is so great. I have done all you asked. She is safe and well cared for. She does not go without tenderness from my own heart. You know my heart, for you hold it in your hands."

Henry could no longer see in front of him, but a few yards. The moon was casting little light, and his eyes found it hard to adjust to the descending darkness.

"I must go. I hope you are safe, my love."

He tugged his coat tight around his chest, hung his head low, and pushed through the wind as he made the long walk back to the house. His hands were numb and his legs ached from the bitter cold sweeping around him, but nothing was more miserable than not being with Jane.

Mrs. Bishop greeted him at the door. "Master Eaton, what on earth are you doing in that freezing weather? You might have never come back alive, barely with a coat."

"I will not deny the weather is turning. I promise not to go out in it again unless properly suited," he assured her.

"Henry, is that you?" Anne called from the drawing room.

He entered, thankful for the heat blaring from the fireplace.

"Ah, Dr. Cummings, you braved the cold weather as well, I see." Henry shook hands with the doctor. He gave Anne a kiss and stroked her cheek. She leaned into his touch and smiled before he pulled away.

The doctor noted the relationship growing before him. He was privy to the secret circumstance of their union. He also was aware of their sacrifices they both made for the child soon to arrive. It was his hope Henry and Anne learned to love each other along the way. But he had not expected the progression of their affection so quickly.

He smiled at the two of them.

"Pray tell, Dr. Cummings, what is so amusing?" Anne did not miss the upward twist of his lips.

"It is nothing, my dear. I am enjoying the blessing of the company of my dear friends, in a warm room, on such a night."

"The night is certainly dreadful, but how grateful we are to equally enjoy your visits." Anne didn't like the doctor living alone. He was too charming, still handsome, and spared no vigor to grow old untethered. It would be her sole purpose of finding him a suitable companion after the baby. Until then, it pleased her he chose to spend time with them and encouraged him to do so often. Although he never confided the reason, his visits were not for his benefit, only. She was not carrying the baby well, and he was keeping a close watch on her as the birth neared.

"Will you sit and join Dr Cummings with a drink before dinner, Henry?"

He cleared his throat. "I must change out of my travel clothes. If you excuse me, I will meet you in the dining room."

Anne nodded, allowing his retreat.

Dr. Cummings waited for Henry to leave. "You should congratulate yourself, my dear. Henry seems happy."

Anne looked at the door from which he just parted.

Happy?

Henry's brow remained firm, but his kindness to her was endless, not sparing his attention. His disappearing acts grew less as the baby's arrival neared, choosing to linger in the evenings with her. Most nights she retreated early, and how he engaged his time after that was of no concern to her. Rarely did he come to her. Only when he had a need to be with a woman did he accompany her to bed. He was always gentle, but there was a sense of guilt that lingered, and he never stayed long afterwards, retreating to his own rooms. She did not question his need. She was his wife and promised him to be a good one. But she knew it was Jane that kept him away, not why he came. She could gladly accept the latter. And as her body changed, fragility apparent, he kept away all together.

"Anne?" Dr. Cummings interrupted her thoughts. "I am complimenting you… Henry is adjusting to married life."

"Yes," Anne agreed. "'*Adjusting*'."

"Anne," he touched her arm, "Henry is fond of you. You have nothing to worry about."

"I am not concerned, John. I have more than I could possibly have asked for. From this marriage, and from Henry. But…"

"Her ghost lingers," he finished her thoughts.

Anne bowed her head to confirm.

"How often does he walk to the field?"

The doctor was aware Henry often visited the place where

Jane disappeared. At first, he saw no harm with his walks, an opportunity to release his hidden emotions… away from Anne's purview. But after so many months, he grew concerned his friend was neglecting the woman who was tangible, and not a ghost.

"Not every day," she sighed. "But I do not fret. He always returns a renewed man. Call it guilt or a release. Either way, it is not she who is the beneficiary."

His grey-blue eyes met hers. "You are a wise woman to understand that."

"I have no other choice," Anne said, resigned to the circumstance.

A maid interrupted, "Dinner is ready."

He gave her his arm. "Come, let me escort you to dinner."

SURPRISED

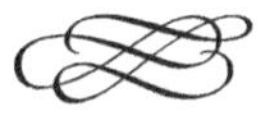

"Jane, can you hear me?"

Jane opened her eyes. Three faces stared at her. Amy knitted her brow. Ryan widened his eyes. And Dr. Cummings' lips curled upward when she blinked at him.

"I have frightened you?"

Jane jumped into his arms. "Yes, terribly," she scolded, and pulled him tighter.

"There, there, my dear, it is really me."

Jane pushed him to arm's length. "It's so wonderful…I mean truly wonderful to see you!"

She hugged him again.

Ryan cleared his throat, reminding the two huggers Amy and he were in the room.

Jane reached for her friend and drew her closer. "Amy, this is the wonderfully kind Dr. Cummings."

"Yes, Sweetie. When you fainted, we had a lovely introduction."

Jane eyed Ryan, smiling from the sidelines, terribly pleased with the reunion. "I really don't understand. How did Dr. Cummings and you find each other?"

"Well, I must admit it is an unusual story." Ryan motioned for everyone to sit. "When Amy uncovered the items in the attic, she frightened me with the most highly pitched scream. Imagining the worst–ghosts came to take her to Hell with them, I ran up to find her in a frenzy of excitement. It's there she explained the reason for the outburst. I listened with curiosity but did not really believe it possible. Time travel–ha! You know Amy, always one for a good story!" He looked apologetically at Amy. She laughed, disregarding his admonishment. He continued, "Not until a few days ago, when a man appeared at my doorstep, completely naked, and ready to fall upon my feet, did it all click."

Jane peered over at Dr. Cummings, recovered and eager to continue the story.

"I am afraid traveling through time caused delirium, as well as joint pain and dehydration." His clinical mind assessed. "But the kind, Mr. Eaton, offered me his home, where I refreshed and collected myself, before I told him of *our* journey," Dr. Cummings said, explaining he too had been through the vortex. "I feared he would either think me insane, or a danger, neither of which occurred. Instead, he listened. When I finished, he laughed. Loud and heartily. Curiously, it was I who presumed *him* insane!"

Ryan laughed, "It amused me to discover Amy told the truth about you."

Amy kicked him with her pointed pump. Ryan feigned pain, accepting his punishment for doubting her.

"What happened then?" Jane pushed for more.

"I was eager to discover if I had journeyed to the place and time of one, Miss Jane Reynolds. Mr. Eaton grabbed me by the shoulders and shouted…"

Ryan jumped from his chair, too eager to tell the end of the story. "Yes, my dear man. And she'll soon be here. She is coming to London!"

Everyone laughed.

"But how did you actually get *here*?" Amy asked what everyone else was thinking.

Dr. Cummings leaned in, and the rest followed, creating a bubble of secrecy. "It is the energy field. It opened up for me during the black moon," Dr. Cummings explained. "'*When the moon moves past the sun, stopping to greet her beauty, she accepts his homage. As she rises in her glory, she takes her time to be admired. As darkness descends, she lifts him up to be praised in full glory, only to slowly descend into the depths of darkness again.*'"

"Agnes helped you then?"

Dr. Cummings nodded.

"She said it was rare," Jane recalled. "So how…"

"She told me, the afternoon we visited her, that we were connected. Later she explained, I, too, was born under the black moon. I have a magnetic energy, she said." Dr. Cummings met Jane's stare. "This energy we both possess. It stirs during a super moon, and if we step into that moment of emptiness during a super moon, we can fall through time."

"It's a portal," Ryan jumped in to explain, offering knowledge from overindulgent years of studies, and too many drunken nights with his fellow professors debating the merits of under-used information. "The moon, when it cycles, creates vibrational pulls around it. When it is nearer the earth, as in a super moon, it becomes stronger. During the black moon cycle–when the light extinguishes, but right before it resurfaces, an emptiness remains. A nothingness. A black zone. A portal. The vibrational frequencies must quicken or pulsate faster as the moon changes. Like static, it draws higher frequencies to it, creating vortexes of energy. A wind tunnel of electricity if one is to understand it. Your energy syncs with it. Like being zapped by electricity, but instead of igniting your molecules, as most experience, you sync into the frequency and travel along the vibration. You two fall into the emptiness, like falling into a slide. When the vibration slows again, as the first phase of the moon appears, your frequencies stop syncing and you get kicked out of the vibration…and land on the other side of time."

"Is that even possible?" Amy questioned.

Ryan pointed to Jane and Dr. Cummings. "How do you explain them?"

Jane knew time travel was possible. She experienced it. But for Dr. Cummings to connect at a precise time and place seemed nearly unattainable.

"But that still doesn't explain how Dr. Cummings ended up here, at this place and time?"

Dr. Cummings cut in. *"One could only follow on one's own energy,"* Dr. Cummings quoted the mysterious words from the Black Raven, adding, "You did not completely leave. You know you are still connected."

Jane gave a part of her soul to Henry. It was forever attached to him. The moment she fell forward, she wanted to step back and run into his arms. A part of her stayed in the past.

"Did Henry understand?" Those thoughts haunted her. "How I came into his world…and why I had to leave?"

"Not exactly," he replied. "After you left, he was broken. He implored me to explain. I treaded lightly as I broached the conversation about who you really were and where you came from. The man could either think I was mad, had done something with you for myself, or believe my story."

Ryan asked in anticipation, "Well, did he believe you?"

"He had seen her disappear himself. So, he could not deny the voracity. He grew angry many times with you, and with me. But his love for you was always in the forefront."

Jane leaned back, allowing the pictures in her head to play out. "And Anne, what became of her?"

"Are you talking about Anne Eaton? I read about her in my

papers. She was the second wife of Henry Eaton," Ryan interjected.

"So, they were married?" Although happy for her dear friend, pain streaked across her heart. She did not interfere with destiny, after all.

Dr. Cummings leaned into Jane and put a hand on her arm. "He did as you asked of him. He married Anne." Seeing her eyes lower, he requested she hold her judgment until he explained the purpose of his return. "They lived a quiet life sharing a tender relationship from what I observed. He was not unkind to her, but his heart was not for her to have. She accepted the marriage on those terms. But they did not have long together, and she passed soon after giving birth to her baby boy."

Jane brought her hand to her mouth. Tears swelled in her eyes, as well as Amy's and Ryan's, the story keeping them on the edge of their seats.

"Upon her death, Henry was in a tailspin of sadness that left him distant. He had lost too much in life to ask of one man. Lillian tried to reason with him, with little acceptance."

"Did she even get to hold her baby in her arms?" Jane asked.

Dr. Cummings was silent.

Ryan jumped in. "But Henry Eaton had only one son by Olivia. And if I remember, he died in infancy. His one heir was to a daughter, Margaret…" He thumped his fingers against the arm of the chair.

"Margaret Elizabeth," Jane interjected.

Maggie.

"You are correct, Mr. Eaton. Henry had only the two children. Anne's son, whose father was Patrick Wansey, was named Sorley Eaton Wansey. It is an old Gaelic name, meaning summer traveler." He pointed to Jane. "He was named in honor of you."

Nothing should have surprised Jane anymore. The 'summer traveler' was the guide Peyton spoke about. The information still caused her to pale at the realization.

"Are you alright, my dear?" Dr. Cummings asked, noticing the rash of goosebumps cover her skin.

No! But she nodded, wanting him to continue.

"As soon as the baby was old enough for safe travels, Henry left for America to find his rightful father. He found Patrick Wanney, manager of his own shop in Massachusetts, just outside of Boston, a town called Quincy. Maybe you have heard of it?"

"That is where I was born!" Jane shrieked.

"How amazing," Amy interjected.

Another coincidence Jane had to piece together. The circle of fate seemed uncanny.

"To relinquish a son to his rightful father is very noble. The scandal alone would have caused him hardship," Ryan said, already mentally adding the tidbit of knowledge to his book.

"To your point, Mr. Eaton, the rumor mills produced much gossip. When Henry returned, he shut himself from everyone. He allows no one to visit but me." He looked at Jane. "I believe it is because I am the closest connection to you."

They all fell silent, exhausted from the emotional rollercoaster. Sadness the common thread for all listening.

Jane suddenly grabbed the doctor. "Something's happened! Why do you come to me now? Has anything happened to him?" She braced herself for the answer.

"No," he sighed. "I wished it was more definitive; something I can solve with medicine. It is not that Henry is harmed–he is a broken man. Lillian came to me for help. She wants to find you. That is when I had to tell her the truth." He looked at Jane to assure her it was the best thing for him to do. "It was she who encouraged me to seek Agnes Ramsey. Lillian sent me to bring you back!"

"I still don't understand," Amy asked, grappling with the details. "Why are *you* here? Why didn't Henry come himself?"

"Ah, that is the trick here." Dr. Cummings explained, "Only one can enter the vortex, and only one can return on that same energy."

Jane saw Amy's confusion and added, "It's because our energy fields vibrate at the same frequency, only we can travel through time," she pointed to Dr. Cummings and herself. "And because part of me remains on the other side, it connected our timelines. Dr. Cummings followed my energy–a roadmap to me." She paused, with the truth hitting her. "Henry couldn't come because he isn't of the same frequency. But more important," she realized, "he is not the one asking me to come back."

She looked at Dr. Cummings to confirm. She was correct.

"I have come here to plead a case of love. With the utmost sacrifice of yourself, Lillian knows she is not asking lightly for you to return. Henry needs you. And from what I can see on your face, you need him."

Jane stood. Three faces stared at her, awaiting her response.

"If I go back, I will take all of me, mind, body, and soul. You know what that means. My energy may no longer stay connected to the present. It may mean you never return. That is too much to ask of you. We have no idea of what is possible."

"Possible," he laughed. "I have seen more than a lifetime one deserves. But yet, God grants me more." He stood and took Jane's hands in his. "I would give a thousand lives to see you happy, my dear. You inspired me, and I am ready to '*start my second half.*'"

Jane smiled. She could only imagine the possibilities Dr. Cummings had ahead of him satisfying his childlike appetite for knowledge. "You realize, with all the good you will discover, there is so much more not good about the modern world. It seems unfair to burden you with that."

"To know it is there, and not to experience it, would be the harder of the two choices."

Dare she return to Henry?

Her heart didn't quite jump but felt heavy and burdened. "Okay, let's just pretend I wanted to return..."

Amy squealed with anticipation. Ryan fluttered his hands together.

Jane narrowed her eyes, squelching any further sounds from Amy, and silencing Ryan's claps. She needed to think about the thoughts screaming through her head.

Her eyes met Dr. Cummings.' "Who am I to disrupt Henry's life once again?" She cringed with shame at what she put him through. "And how do you know it will all work out in the end? There are no promises to happy endings when it comes to love. Haven't we all learned that lesson?"

"I have bet my life on it," the doctor replied.

Jane froze at the prospect. Dare she dream?

Henry was possible.

Her heart pounded with excitement and fear. Possible wasn't always practical. Traveling back through time was illogical. Leaving her life as she knew it was irrational. No sane person would contemplate such a life altering decision. The pounding in her chest grew harder, clouding her hearing, the *what ifs* running through her mind.

What if Henry…

As if Dr. Cummings read her mind, he whispered, "*I miss you, Jane. Forever and always, I will miss you. I take with me your love and will cherish it to my dying day.*"

Jane's eyes teared.

Dr. Cummings pulled a handkerchief from his pocket, and with a tender touch, dabbed at the droplets pooling at the corner of her eyes. "He went over that letter a thousand times until he got it right. He hoped you would get it one day. I see that you have."

FORGIVENESS

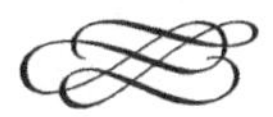

The summer evening was surprisingly cool. It rained all morning, but stopped by mid-day, leaving the air moist, and the night's sky a cetacean blue.

The color reminded Jane of the first night in London, the crescent moon night, the bookshop, and Peyton, who predicted the unusual twists her life would follow.

Was it a sign?

Pockets of clouds rolled by, blocking the little light the moon offered for the four to walk along the path leading through the forest. The darker it got, the more they became ghostly apparitions wandering through the trees, the echoing of crunching branches and twigs under their feet.

With flashlights in hand, they walked in silence, anxious for what was about to happen. They had all but exhausted their goodbyes earlier that evening, where they sat in the comforts of the library–Jane's favorite room, drinking expensive wine. Sending Jane through time seemed like the best of reasons for Ryan to pull the finest from his coveted collection and uncork the priceless bottles. He had food delivered from a local restaurant–to fully appreciate the aged liquid, but no one really had an appetite.

As happy as they were for Jane to return to Henry, they were all acutely aware they were going to say goodbye to Jane, maybe forever. No one was ready for the finality of that moment. Walking late at night, half drunk, and disoriented by the darkness, there seemed little to say among them.

Dr. Cummings led the way. He walked the distance many times prior to that night in preparation, marking the spot with heavy stones, not leaving anything to chance. When they reached the rocky pile, Ryan, in his infinite wisdom, brought blankets, which he splayed out on the wet grass, and passed a bottle of whiskey after taking a swig.

A breeze washed through the valley, sending chills through them. Amy and Ryan, for the unknown about to happen; Dr. Cummings and Jane knowing what was to come.

Amy finally broke the silence, "Why did the crop circles happen…the first time?"

Jane researched crop circles, as well as time travel, hoping to find explanations. Much of the information was speculation or imagination, and a lot was fiction. Some of the information helped her to understand the experience she had, but nothing brought her any closer to explaining *why* it happened.

"It's the opening of the vortex," Ryan explained. "It's magnetic force caused the flattening of the crop, and the patterns seem to have something to do with cylindrical forces of energy. It still is a cosmic mystery, the relationship between vibrational energy and the geometry of the universe. But now established, this vortex opens and closes with little effect. No one knows why these force fields open, how they open, or even by whom. The patterning is a whole other issue, but the cause seems to have something to do with cylindrical forces of energy. Once the vortex opens, it can remain so forever. And by the same token, it may close for no reason."

Jane added, "It's by chance, Dr. Cummings and I entered and returned. Agnes gave us the knowledge to find and manipulate the openings, but the portals' existence is beyond our controls."

"And what are your chances now?" Amy shared her doubt.

Jane didn't know. None of them did. But they all would soon discover, one way or the other, their eyes towards the sky, waiting for the movement of the moon.

"What are we doing here?" Jane asked to no one; to everyone.

The doctor quoted *James* from the Bible, his resonate voice lifting through the nights air as if in sermon, "*Yet you do not know what your life will be like tomorrow. You are just a vapor that appears for a little while and then vanishes away.*"

Jane crinkled her brow. "Is what I am doing all meaningless?"

"No, my dear." Dr. Cummings smirked. "I am saying, accept the span and events of your life as a providence of God. I would not have sacrificed myself if I did not believe in such a fate deemed by a greater source than ourselves. How else am I here before you?"

Jane reached over and touched his face, cradling it in her hand. She needed to touch him, to feel the realness of the man who unselfishly helped her through so much. "Are you sure this is truly what you want? Because having you here, if only for a moment in time, is enough for me. You can go back…let Henry know I got his letter." She paused, searching for the right words he would accept. "Tell him he is still tethered to my heart, the string unbroken, our destinies only interrupted until our fates meet again."

The doctor shook his head. "I have nothing tying me down. My life was blessed with a devoted wife, good friends, and a stellar career. But as I get older, my complacent life brings me loneliness. You breathed life into me and pushed my mind to explore possibilities. I feel alive again. In all your beauty, kindness, and friendship, you inspired me. I did not come here for Henry. No, my dearest Jane, I am here for love."

A wind swirled. It felt familiar, sending a shiver down Jane's neck.

Both Dr. Cummings and she looked at the sky. The crescent moon was almost gone.

Dr. Cummings stood, offering his hand to Jane. "Come my dear, your destiny awaits…"

As his hand touched hers, an energy surged between them, like two magnets drawn towards each other. He opened his arms, and she fell into his embrace, her head cradled under his chin.

"Can you feel it?" she whispered.

He nodded.

"I'm scared."

"Don't be. I've got you." He took her chin and lifted her face to the sky, peering through the darkness, to imprint the details in his memory before she disappeared. He brushed his lips against hers. "If I was a younger man, I would have never let you go the first time."

The warmth of his kiss lingered on her lips, and she smiled, understanding what it meant. The words whispered in the wind, "*One can return upon one's connection.*"

Dr. Cummings grinned as he watched her accept his gift of love that would bring her home. He took a few steps back, letting her go. "We are forever connected."

Jane's hair whipped against her face, and he lost sight of her eyes.

"We truly are," Jane shouted, over the wind.

As the moon went black, she was gone.

~

The sun rose over the hill, filling the horizon with light. Jane laid still, waking to consciousness. She felt the coldness of the damp grass beneath her naked body, but a heavy woolen blanket on top kept her warm. She sat up, opening her eyes slowly to adjust to the morning light. As her vision cleared, she became aware of a tall, broad-shouldered young man standing a few feet away. His white shirt was a beacon amid the lifting darkness, the sleeves billowing in the wind. His hand tucked strands of his wavy hair behind his ears. He pulled a string from his pocket and tied the loose mass to keep it out of his face, revealing a strong, muscular jaw and a long, pointed nose, slightly crooked. When he saw her awake, he smiled and ran to her.

"Miss!" He called.

The young man was no other than a grown version of Egon Baker. Now sixteen years old, he was on his way to becoming a strapping man.

"Egon," Jane's scraggy voice called. She tried to move, but her head only wobbled.

"Miss," Egon bent down and put his hand on her shoulder. "Don't move. Not yet."

Jane brought her hand to her head, obeying his orders. "It seems you found me once again."

Egon had waited hours for Jane to return most of the night, and into the early morning. He had been charged with her safety but was unsure if he could fulfill the expectations Dr. Cummings placed upon him. He could not explain what he saw when she disappeared into the field a year ago and pushed it aside as unbelievable until it happened again with the doctor's disappearance in the same way.

He waited, eager and anxious, not knowing what to expect, or if Miss Reynolds would appear. He only lowered his lids for a few minutes when a wind swooshed across his face, causing him to jolt awake. He didn't notice the lump laying in the field until he blinked through the grey haze. Without sound or commotion, her body appeared under the cover of the new morning, barely breathing. Panic raced through him. He covered her with one blanket and put her head atop another. Her breathing steadied, and he sighed with relief. When her body finally moved, he knew he would safely deliver her to Mr. Eaton exactly as he was instructed.

"I've been expecting you," he explained. "The doctor gave me instruction to wait for your return and tend to your care." He eyed the blanket covering her.

Naked, once again in the presence of Egon Baker, she lowered her eyes. "Yes, I see."

He opened a bag alongside him, pulled out a jug, and told her to drink. She accepted, gulping down the fresh water. "Here." He handed her a portion of bread and cheese. "The doctor said you might be hungry as well."

She smiled, but declined, her stomach not ready for consumption.

"Dr. Cummings planned for everything, didn't he?"

"Almost everything. I brought you some of mother's things," Egon pulled out a skirt, a blouse, a knitted shawl, and a pair of boots. "I remembered how we found you last time."

Embarrassment, worry, and relief all compiled into a burst of uncontrollable laughter out of Jane. It was contagious. Egon joined her, allowing the two to release the stress, fear, and anxieties each was feeling.

When her laughter exhausted, she motioned for Egon to turn around and pulled the blouse over her head. It was large, its sole purpose to cover her nakedness. That it did. The skirt was equally sized for a woman of a fuller shape, and when Jane held the excess fabric at the waist, Egon pulled a ribbon from a satchel pocket and handed it to her. She cinched the fabric and double tied the ribbon to secure the fit, creating a bow at the end. The outfit wasn't fashionable, but practical all the same.

"If you are ready, I will take you to Master Eaton." He extended his hand, but she swayed. "We should take it slow, Miss. The doctor warned me..."

Jane nodded. "Maybe I am not quite ready."

She wasn't. Physically or mentally. She was worried.

Would Henry take her with loving arms?

The possibility of worse loomed. She bet her whole life on Henry. Now she panicked in the face of reality. To face him, with the prospect he might reject her, was frightening.

Egon made her drink again and handed her a piece of bread. "Please, Miss, you need some nourishment."

This time she obeyed and bit off a piece of the crusty bread. To her surprise, her appetite returned and before she knew the loaf was half eaten.

When she looked up, Egon was smiling.

She motioned for him to sit next to her on the blanket.

"Thank you," she said. "You are very kind to look after me."

"It's not me, Miss. It's all the doctor's doing."

"Yes, well, he did make this all happen...made it possible for me to return." Jane sighed, grateful but forlorn about leaving him behind.

"I'm going to miss him," he shared.

She reached over and squeezed his arm. "Me, too."

"Did he tell you he is sending me to school? I'm going to be a doctor someday. Maybe some great man who explains time travel."

"Well, you are witness to the extraordinary. But how much did Dr. Cummings explain, especially about me?"

"Enough as needed." He met Jane's stare. "Your secrets are safe with me."

"That's a lot to ask of a young man."

"I do so with honor. The doctor is good to me. He teaches me, gives me books, and is sending me to school when I am ready. I'm going to make him proud of me some day." Then added, "And you will always have me to protect you, no matter what happens."

No matter what happens.

The words rang in her ears. Her heart pulled towards the Eaton Estate; to find Henry.

"Shall we try again? I'm ready," Jane said.

Egon extended his hand and Jane stood on her own. Her brain wobbled at first, but Egon's strong arms held onto her until her feet were grounded.

The morning sun radiated heat, penetrating her chilled bones, warming her through. Fresh air swept across her face, and she inhaled, filling her lungs, rejuvenating her body to push ahead. Egon pointed to a small stream in the distance and suggested she freshen herself while he collected the horses.

Jane wetted her face, the cold water shocking her. She could only imagine what she looked like, staring into the water, a poor substitute for a mirror. She brushed down her hair with wetted hands and pushed the frayed mess behind her ears, pinching her cheek to encourage color. She gurgled water around her mouth and spit out the rest into the flowing stream, smacking her lips with the satisfaction of freshness.

Egon walked up to her with the horses in tow. "Ready?"

She shook her head. It is not how she wanted to present herself after a year's absence. But if she didn't go straight to Henry, she was sure to never go.

Egon did not let her answer discourage him from his duty. "Come," he said and offered her a lift onto the horse. "It won't take us long to get to the Eaton Estate."

It didn't.

Upon clearing the trees, the red and stone structure appeared amid the verdant green surroundings. It still took her breath away.

Egon stopped and saddled next to Jane, their faces mere

inches from each other. He wanted her to understand what she was facing. "I am witness to my father's love for my mother. He is good to her and shows his adoration. I know myself what love offers, for I have someone special as well. But I will never forget the sight of a man who has lost the one thing that makes him want to breathe. That is your Mr. Eaton. I know that for sure."

Jane leaned to him, touched his face, and gently planted a kiss on his cheek. "You are quite a young man, Mr. Egon Baker. I hope your special someone loves you the way you deserve."

Red blotted his cheeks, and he tugged his horse with the excuse he must get her to her destination.

Jane followed Egon, a slow and steady pace, growing anxious with every step.

When they reached the property, Egon dismounted from his horse and helped Jane down from hers, grabbing her reins.

Jane eyed the house standing tall before her. Emotions flooded her heart. "It hasn't changed."

"Aye, but the people inside have," Egon warned. "Much has happened in a year. Be patient, for the wounds are fresh. But with time, and love, we all heal...the better for it."

A door swung open, jolting their attention.

"If my old eyes do not deceive me!" Mrs. Bishop's robust body engulfed Jane. "You've come back to him?"

Jane nodded, tears choking her. "It's so good to see you, Mrs. Bishop."

"Oh, my dear, may God be so good at answering my prayers." She kissed her on the forehead. "You'll find him," she pointed, "under the oak tree."

Jane looked ahead to where she needed to go. Around the house, across the lawn, and down the path–she knew the way. There she would see the tree looming in the distance. The tree of life, linking the past, present and future. The reason it was planted, and stood through time, a testimony of those who have found sanctuary under its arms. There she would find Henry and come face to face with her fate.

She wanted to move her feet, but she couldn't.

Egon extended his arm. "Come, I will take you."

With a reassuring smile from Mrs. Bishop, Jane took Egon's arm.

When the oak tree came into view, he pointed to the two figures in the distance. "You have come a long way for this," Egon encouraged, gently releasing Jane's grip on his arm.

Maggie spotted her first, and yelled out, the breeze carrying her voice through the air, "Father, look, it's Miss Jane!" She ran as fast as her feet would allow, shouting along the way, "Miss Jane, Miss Jane!" When she reached Jane, she threw her arms around her, almost knocking her over. "Miss Jane, you have returned!"

Jane bent down and wrapped herself around the little girl who had grown taller over the last year. "Yes, my little one, I'm back."

Searching beyond Maggie's shoulder, she saw Henry's figure stood stoic against the trunk of the solid tree. He did not move towards Jane. Instead, he watched from the distance, as his daughter lovingly opened her arms to her.

"Henry," Jane whispered.

"Come on, little Miss Margaret. Let me walk you back to the house." Egon took her hand. "Maybe Cook will give us some of her famous walnut bread coming from the ovens. I smell it from here." He led Maggie away, leaving Jane to face her fears.

When he saw they were alone, he stepped out of the shadows of the tree, the sun highlighting his face. The lines across his forehead and around his eyes bore witness to the hardships endured, the greying near the temples aging him. His brow was still heavy, and his eyes were dark and determined. He stared straight at her, his jaw strong, his lips straight across his face.

Always controlled.

Jane looked over her shoulder for Maggie and Egon, but they already disappeared. She had no one to run to, and nowhere else to go, except forward, toward Henry.

He watched her walk towards him, forcing his feet to hold ground. Had he allowed, he would have already been by her side. As she neared him, he braced for what was to come.

She stopped mere inches from him.

He wondered if time had made her more beautiful, or if he had just forgotten the power, she had over him. It was her eyes he met first. The golden sparkles shimmering within the brown depths.

Were her eyes reflecting his own agony?

He knew her face and all its little expressions. He studied it in detail–remembering. They were the memories that haunted his dreams. Dreams he never imagined would be fulfilled. Yet she was standing in front of him. Her eyes inviting him in, her lips ready to taste, her hair waiting to be touched.

He wanted desperately to thread the dark silken strands between his fingers and place his lips upon the white, tender skin that was hidden just below her ear. But time had lessened the urge to be so spontaneous. The cost was too high to indulge in such overt emotions.

"Hello, Henry…"

His jaw tightened.

Did she expect him to run towards her and take her in his arms?

He didn't.

"Henry, say something," she begged.

He turned away from her to break the spell she had over him. Time had not healed him, it only allowed for him to be preoccupied. The moment he heard Maggie call out her name, the dagger left in his heart ripped open the scar tissue to reveal the bleeding wound. When he saw her ethereal presence standing in the distance, he did not know how to control his buckling legs. To look away was his only defense from falling over in crippled torment.

She took one step closer, wanting to touch the strong jaw, no matter how clenched, and bring her lips to his. Instead, she reached for his hand. "Please allow me in, Henry. I have so much I want to say…so much to explain."

Her touch startled him. He did not expect the uncontrollable surge of heat through his body. But he pulled his hand away. Away from her touch; her power over him.

Jane stepped back.

His eyes roared with fury. Dr. Cummings and Lillian were wrong. Her return only fueled his pain and anger. She turned, defeated. But before she could walk away, his voice–deep, controlled–stopped her.

"If I have shown anyone the power within me, it is you who was the recipient." He moved towards her, eliminating any distance between them. "You, who inspired the possibilities. Many, I lost, not for want, but because it was beyond my power. It was the hand of God. But you, Jane! I wept at your loss in a way a man should never be driven. For that, I curse you. I gave you my soul, and with you, it was taken. I wandered amongst the living as a walking dead man, trying to find the reason for loving someone so deeply, only to have you ripped away from me. There is no consolation for that," he admonished. He closed his eyes to push away the desire to touch the woman who stood before him. "I would have given up my whole life for you. But instead, you took it."

His words cut her heart bitterly. She looked away in shame. Henry was an honorable man, and she had not trusted him to act on his honor. Love can only exist in true conviction. She left, thinking she was doing right by him. But it wasn't her decision to make. The realization she hurt him to his core devastated her. She closed her eyes to stop the tears. If he was rejecting her, she wanted to leave with dignity.

"Henry, can words of regret heal the divide between us? If you want me to leave, I will go, but not before I say what I came here for. I left in body, but my heart and soul remained. You were the person I was destined to love. I just didn't figure it out in time to understand you are my future."

"Jane!" He slid his hands through his hair and sighed. "I am not unhappy about your return. I am overjoyed! I want you with every shred of my being. But I cannot, will not, lose you again. You had no right to my heart if you were not going to stay. For that was the hardest to accept. You left me stranded in heartache. Your choice was not mine. I had a plan, Jane. I was a foolish man, but not dishonorable. You should have trusted me. Did you think it would be so easy to let you go?"

The words stung.

Agony throbbed through every inch of her being. She was fumbling. Her words were not conveying her sentiments. She needed to tell him how she felt, lest she lose him forever.

"I was arrogant and selfish with your love. I took it and hoarded it. Now I want it back," she confessed. "But it isn't for me to ask, is it? Henry, I want nothing, will take nothing, from you. I came to give back to you what was always yours…my love. It is yours always. It will remain with you forever. I will never take it away again."

He moved towards her. Slow. Careful. If he allowed, his body would lunge toward her, embrace her, devour her. He took her hand in his. "You have every right to ask for my love, for I gave it to you as a mirrored reflection of what you gave to me. If I did not express this to you the night I made love to you, I say it now with fervor. Stay. Marry me, Jane, and be mine until death do us part. Share with me your heart, and I will give you my soul. As long as I have breath, I will love you."

He placed his lips upon hers and indulged in the familiar

taste of her mouth. He wanted to linger with the warm sensation spreading through his body, but pulled away, awaiting her answer.

She had no other choice. Her future was in the past, with Henry.

"Yes, Henry, forever and always, I love you, until the end of time."

The End

ACKNOWLEDGMENTS

Jane Austen: For inspiring me through your wonderful stories.

Lee Ann Schertz: For reading every, single rendition of this story and still loving it in its final draft. This has been years in the making and you were by my side every step of the way.

Therese Conte: For your annoying, but loving push to move forward and finish "my art." You will always be the true artist in my mind, and whom I aspire to be when I grow up.

Mike Conte: Your belief in me put wind in my sails, and your support took away some of the stress which allowed me to focus on publication.

Beta Readers: You know who you are. An author doesn't always like to get feedback, but it is a process not to be missed. Thank you for all the catches and insights. I may not have been able to accommodate for all the feedback, but I know my book is better because of your help.

Vicki Jaeger: the first editor to set eyes on a the first manuscript–words bastardized on paper. You didn't hate it, (unlike my third novel, but that is a story for another day), and that was enough to keep me going.

Mary O'Brien, Shayla Cantrell, Lisa Peters, and Angela Grant: With friends like you, who needs more readers? Well, I do, but you get my point.

Authors Janet Simcic, Billie Kelpin, Tammy Pasterick, Barb De Long, Cee Cee Wakefield: It is always scary to share your work with other writers, but your experience and knowledge went a long way to making this book happen.

Michelle Morrow: Editor extraordinaire! I didn't know what was in me until you brought it out. You made me a better writer, reminded me of my superpowers, and always led me in the direction I needed to go in. This book is all I want it to be because you believed in my vision, and in me.

Elizabeth Rose Conte: I miss you and wish you were still alive to see the final copy. Thank you for letting me read to you and share precious time together. A mother's love and support is never lost.

Louis Conte: I did this for you, because of you. Not only my wise father, you were my teacher and mentor of words. We finally have our name in print!

ABOUT THE AUTHOR

Elizabeth Conte is a writer of novels, poetry, and short stories. She is a native Californian where she lives with her husband and her almost out-of-the-house college kids. When she isn't writing, you will find her in her garden, walking her dog, Winston--the only one who will sit and listen to her reading out loud, or mixing up a cocktail. She prefers whiskey above all else. Her love for writing is only equal to her love of gardening.

Join her mailing list at ElizabethConte.com

CPSIA information can be obtained
at www.ICGtesting.com
Printed in the USA
LVHW111646290822
727098LV00022B/553/J